THE PRINCESS AND THE GOBLIN
THE PRINCESS AND CURDIE

GEORGE MACDONALD was born in 1824 in Huntly, Aberdeenshire. His father operated a farm at Upper Pirriesmill and was a member of the Missionar Kirk. From an early age, MacDonald fell under the influence of both the affairs of this world and of the other world. His Calvinist background was an important element in his imaginative life, although he later joined the Church of England under prompting from F. D. Maurice. His mother died when he was eight, and his relationship with his father was close and formative. In 1840, he left Huntly to study at King's College, Aberdeen, and from then to the end of his life he wandered like the hero of his first prose fantasy, *Phantastes* (1858), with little direction but with a clear growth in the life of the spirit. After leaving King's College in 1845 and trying his hand as a tutor, MacDonald studied at Highbury College for the Congregational ministry and he received a call to the Congregational pulpit in Arundel, Sussex, in 1850. In 1853 he left Arundel under the cloud of heresy, for it seems his congregation disapproved of his German influenced thought, and of his belief that animals and heathens would be saved. He had married Louisa Powell in 1851 and he now had the responsibility of providing for a growing family, which would eventually include eleven children. MacDonald's life in the mid-1850s was filled with anxiety, hardship, and ill health, but by the end of the decade he had moved to London, begun his career as a writer, made friends with influential people such as Lady Byron, widow of the famous poet, Henry Crabb Robinson, the famous diarist, Lewis Carroll, and John Ruskin. By the 1860s he had secured a place among the popular novelists of his day, and he worked as a professor of English Literature at Bedford College. His fame grew and in the 1870s he travelled to the United States for a long lecture tour. By the 1880s he lived in Bordighera, Italy, in winter and travelled in England performing in his family's theatrical productions in summer. Although he wrote novels, fairy tales, poems, essays, sermons, and critical works, he is best known today as perhaps the greatest of the Victorian fantasists and writers for children. He died in 1905.

RODERICK MCGILLIS is Associate Professor of English at the University of Calgary, and editor of the *Children's Literature Association Quarterly*. He has published articles on several facets of children's literature and on such Romantic writers as William Blake and William Wordsworth. He is editor of a forthcoming volume of essays on the children's books of George MacDonald.

THE WORLD'S CLASSICS

GEORGE MACDONALD

The Princess and the Goblin

and

The Princess and Curdie

Edited with an Introduction by
RODERICK McGILLIS

Prof. Knoepflmacher

Best wishes

Rod

Oxford New York
OXFORD UNIVERSITY PRESS
1990

Oxford University Press, Walton Street, Oxford OX2 6DP

Oxford New York Toronto
Delhi Bombay Calcutta Madras Karachi
Petaling Jaya Singapore Hong Kong Tokyo
Nairobi Dar es Salaam Cape Town
Melbourne Auckland

and associated companies in
Berlin Ibadan

Oxford is a trade mark of Oxford University Press

First issued as a World's Classics paperback 1990

British Library Cataloguing in Publication Data
Macdonald, George, 1824–1905
The princess and the goblin, and,
The princess and Curdie
I. Title   II. McGillis, Roderick
823.8 [J]
ISBN 0–19–282579–8

Library of Congress Cataloging in Publication Data
Data available

Typeset by Selectmove Ltd.
Printed in Great Britain by
BPCC Hazell Books
Aylesbury, Bucks.

CONTENTS

INTRODUCTION

I for one can really testify to a book that has made a
difference to my whole existence, which helped me to see
things in a certain way from the start; a vision of things
which even so real a revelation as a change of religious
allegiance has substantially only crowned and confirmed.
Of all the stories I have read, including even all the novels
of the same novelist, it remains the most real, the most
like life. It is called *The Princess and the Goblin*, and is by
George MacDonald.

(G. K. Chesterton)

I BEGIN with Chesterton not only because his praise is high,
but also because it well represents the powerful spiritual
effect George MacDonald can have on his readers. For
Chesterton, MacDonald's *The Princess and the Goblin* was
'from the start' as profound an experience as MacDonald's
Phantastes was for C. S. Lewis who claims, in *Surprised
by Joy*, that MacDonald's book 'baptized' his imagination.
Chesterton's 'from the start' is sufficiently vague to keep us
from knowing at what age he first read the book, but one
thing is certain: *The Princess and the Goblin* is not a book
Chesterton put aside with his childish things either once
he became an adult or because he was an adult when he
encountered it. This book, and its sequel *The Princess and
Curdie*, conform to C. S. Lewis's 'canon': 'a children's story
which is enjoyed only by children is a bad children's story'.[1]
These books offer exciting reading to the young, and yet they
are rich enough to remain rewarding for the adult reader. As
MacDonald himself says: 'I do not write for children, but for
the childlike, whether of five, or fifty, or seventy-five'.[2]

As a writer, MacDonald pursued his nonconformist and

[1] Lewis, 'On Three Ways of Writing for Children', in Sheila Egoff *et al.*,
Only Connect (Toronto, Oxford University Press, 1980), 210.
[2] *A Dish of Orts* (London, Sampson Low, Marston, 1895), 317.

evangelical calling which had taken him from his home in the north-east of Scotland—Huntly in Aberdeenshire, where he was born in 1824—to London's Highbury College in 1848, and to a pastorate in Arundel, Sussex, in 1850. He left Arundel and the ministry for good in 1853 because of the suspicion among the parishioners that he was tainted with 'German' theology and that he believed in the salvation of animals as well as humans. MacDonald did hold unorthodox theological opinions: in addition to those mentioned above, he, like Origen, believed in the ultimate salvation of the Devil. After leaving Arundel, MacDonald tried for a while to set up an independent ministry in Manchester, but as the 1850s progressed, as his family grew (he had married Louisa Powell in 1851), and as his need for money increased, he turned more and more to writing, publishing his first important work, the poetical drama *Within and Without*, in 1855. By 1860, MacDonald had taken up a Professorship at Bedford College, a women's college, in London, and had found his calling as an author.

MacDonald's talent for writing in the faerie vein was clear from the beginning, but his early work *Phantastes* (1858) did not make a great deal of money. Mid-Victorian readers wanted fiction that combined a realistic portrayal of modern life with the *frisson* of romance, and MacDonald's creative genius for the fantastic found an outlet in writings for children. His first children's story, created like so many children's books in an author's moment of storytelling with his children, appeared as an interpolated story in the novel *Adela Cathcart* (1864). This is *The Light Princess*. MacDonald's success in writing for children prompted several other stories for the young which appeared in magazines throughout the 1860s and which were collected in *Dealings with the Fairies* in 1867. The book was illustrated by Arthur Hughes. MacDonald's importance as a children's writer was acknowledged when in 1870 Alexander Strahan offered him the editorship of *Good Words for the Young*. Over the next seven years, MacDonald's major work for children appeared in this magazine (or its successors—*Good Things for the Young of All Ages* (1872–3), *Good Things: A Picturesque Magazine for the Young of All Ages* (1874–7), and *Good Things: A Picturesque Magazine for Boys and Girls* (1877)): *At the Back of the North Wind, The Princess and the Goblin, The Wise Woman: A Parable* (also known as *The Lost Princess: A Double Story,* and *Princess Rosamund*), and *The Princess and Curdie*.

 The Princess and the Goblin, which MacDonald calls a 'goblin story'—a term he says in the serial version of *The Princess and the Goblin* is more accurate than 'fairy story'—is a revisionary fairy-tale, a tale which he assures the young readers of *Good Words for the Young* (it appeared between November 1870 and June 1871), 'is quite a new one'. This book is new in at least two ways: first, it is not a transcription of traditional tales such as Diana Mulock's *The Fairy Book* (1863)[3] or the anonymous *The Fairy Repertory* (*c*.1830),[4] or the many other versions of Perrault, D'Aulnoy, and Grimm which appeared in the mid-century; and second, unlike the many original fairy-tale books such as *Fairy Favours* (1825)[5] or *Seven Fairy Tales* (1848),[6] both anonymous, MacDonald's sense of audience issues a challenge. The reader finds no challenge in a story like 'The Fairy Devoirgilla',[7] the opening sentence of which sets the tone of the whole: 'There was once a fairy named Duty, which name in fairyland talk sounds like Devoirgilla.' Other characters in this book include: Conscienza, Contento, Industria, and Soigneuse. The reader enters fairyland to find a lesson out of school. MacDonald too has his didactic moments, but these, moments of slippage in which the author turns away from his invented world are relatively rare and certainly they do not overpower the symbolic resonance and instructive ambiguity of the books.

[3] *The Fairy Book: The Best Popular Fairy Stories Selected and Rendered Anew* (London, Golden Treasury Series).
 [4] (Edinburgh, Oliver & Boyd).
 [5] E[lizabeth] F. D[agley], *Fairy Favours, with Other Tales* (London, printed for Wiliam Cole).
 [6] (London, John Henry Parker).
 [7] Ibid. 1–17.

Meaning is not self-evident in MacDonald's works which partake of the questioning spirit of the *Alice* books. The reader of *The Princess and the Goblin* and *The Princess and Curdie*, young or old, must learn to live with doubts and uncertainty.

That MacDonald's children's books challenge young readers has been evident to adult readers since they first appeared. The *Athenæum*, which noticed nearly all of MacDonald's fiction, speaks of the 'mystery' and 'subtle charm'[8] of *The Princess and the Goblin* and 'the strange parables and mystic moralities'[9] of *The Princess and Curdie*. Interesting, but oblique, reviews of both books appear in the *Saturday Review*; both reviews reflect an unease with the frightening aspects of the books (the review of the first book concentrates almost exclusively on the Arthur Hughes illustrations), or what the reviewer of *The Princess and Curdie* calls 'a dreary melancholy mood'.[10] The *Westminster Review* notes that *The Princess and the Goblin* has 'charms for others besides children',[11] and Sidney Colvin in the *Academy* praises the book as a children's book while pointing out that adult readers will observe 'that there is allegory in all this' and will 'guess what the beneficent grandmother is meant more or less explicitly to stand for'.[12] The imprecision of Colvin's 'more or less explicitly' indicates that this is not an easy book. Edward Salmon, in *Juvenile Literature As It Is* (1888), praises MacDonald's imaginative fertility, but points out that he 'soars above the intelligence of children of tender years'.[13] In 1937, Elva Smith remarked of MacDonald's children's books: 'They are difficult for the average child of today'.[14] Recently, William Raeper has generously and wisely complimented the two 'Princess'

[8] 23 Dec. 1871, p. 835.
[9] 25 Nov. 1882, p. 697.
[10] 23 Dec. 1871, p. 823; 25 Nov. 1882, p. 711.
[11] 41 (1872), p. 581.
[12] 15 Jan. 1872, p. 24.
[13] (London, Henry J. Drane), 173.
[14] Smith, *The History of Children's Literature: A Syllabus with Selected Bibliographies*, rev. and enlarged by Margaret Hodges and Susan Steinfirst (Chicago, American Library Assoc., 1980), 165.

books because 'they take children seriously and do not underestimate their ability to cope with difficult existential, moral and metaphysical problems. At the same time they allow children some free rein to participate imaginatively in the stories.'[15] Some adult readers might not accept that children are able to cope with such weighty problems.

Noticing the difficulty MacDonald's books present to the child reader, David Robb has asked, 'Who, then, is MacDonald writing for?'[16] Robb cites a passage from Chapter 20 of *Ranald Bannerman's Boyhood* (which first appeared in the second volume of *Good Words for the Young* (1871)) in which MacDonald's narrator interrupts the narrative to remark that he has forgotten 'that those for whom I write are young—too young to understand this'. Robb suggests: 'Such moments occur sufficiently frequently for one to doubt whether his writing is being completely and securely controlled by a sense of the tender years of his audience'.[17] Both Edward Salmon and Robb refer to a readership of 'tender years' and it is perhaps worth noting that the female hero of *The Princess and the Goblin* is eight years old. She is only a year older in the sequel, *The Princess and Curdie*. Also worth noting is my reference to MacDonald's 'consciously' presenting his young reader with complex material. Robb takes MacDonald's narrator at his word when he refers to 'forgetting' his young readers' abilities and he goes on to argue: 'In an important sense, [MacDonald] is writing for himself.'[18] This is no doubt true, as it is no doubt true that in the children's books MacDonald focuses on 'insights and topics particularly liable to trouble the mind'.[19] These topics include: death, the nature of perception, the nature of evil, language as power,

[15] Raeper, *George MacDonald* (Icknield Way, Tring, Lion, 1987), 332.

[16] Robb, *George MacDonald* (Edinburgh, Scottish Academic Press, 1987), 113.

[17] Ibid. 112–13.

[18] Ibid. 113.

[19] Robb, *George MacDonald* (Edinburgh, Scottish Academic Press, 1987), 114.

class differences, economic disparity, impermanence, political corruption.

Yet I return to MacDonald. He, unlike his narrator in *Ranald Bannerman's Boyhood*, is impressively in control of his work. He wrote to his wife, Louisa, in February 1871, just a week prior to the fourth instalment of *The Princess and the Goblin* appearing in *Good Words for the Young* and after twelve chapters had already appeared, to say: 'I know [*The Princess and the Goblin*] is as good work of the kind as I can do, and I think it will be the most complete thing I have done'.[20] And it probably is. What is noticeable here, however, is MacDonald's self-consciousness regarding his own work. He knows what he is about. We ought, I think, to set aside C. S. Lewis's famous assessment of MacDonald as a mythopoeic writer whose prose is 'undistinguished, at times fumbling'.[21] Mythopoeic he undoubtedly is, but his writing is much more distinguished than Lewis allows for. It has a density which demands thought from the reader, and which the young reader will grasp only on repeated readings. For example, here is the description of Irene in her great-great-grandmother's bath:

When she opened her eyes, she saw nothing but a strange lovely blue over and beneath and all about her. The lady and the beautiful room had vanished from her sight, and she seemed utterly alone. But instead of being afraid, she felt more than happy—perfectly blissful. And from somewhere came the voice of the lady, singing a strange sweet song, of which she could distinguish every word; but of the sense she had only a feeling—no understanding. Nor could she remember a single line after it was gone. It vanished, like the poetry in a dream, as fast as it came. In after years, however, she would sometimes fancy that snatches of melody suddenly rising in her brain, must be little phrases and fragments of the air of that song; and the very fancy would make her happier, and abler to do her duty.

Few children, if any, will catch the allusion to Novalis here.

[20] Greville MacDonald, *George MacDonald and his Wife* (London, George Allen & Unwin, 1924), 412.
[21] 'Preface', *George MacDonald: An Anthology* (London, Geoffrey Bles, 1946), 14.

Few will realize the connection between this passage and MacDonald's conception of the fairy-tale as a feeling, a musical experience. Few will make the comparison with moments of epiphany in other works of literature. Few will consciously notice the careful rhythm of the prose with its alliteration and modulation of syntax and sentence length. Co-ordinating conjunctions here connect separate grammatical units with the aid of the comma or semicolon and despite the impediment of the period. The paradox of discontinuity amid continuity is carried by the prose. In short, MacDonald here provides the young reader with an experience to grow into.

Another way of puting this is to note that MacDonald treats his reader in a manner similar to the manner in which the great-great-grandmother in the book treats Irene. She protects, nourishes, and comforts Irene in the way a mother cares for a child, yet she also speaks to her as she would speak to an adult. She does not hesitate to present the child with difficult ideas. She tells Irene that she is her 'father's mother's father's mother', and Irene responds: 'Oh, dear! I can't understand that.' The grandmother then remarks: 'I didn't expect you would. But that's no reason why I shouldn't say it.' She speaks in paradox: 'no one ever gives anything to another properly and really without keeping it.' When Irene asks how her great-great-grandmother's lamp could hang outside the tower room in which it is lodged especially when the tower has no window, the grandmother tells Irene she cannot yet understand, implying that in time she will grow to understand. For now, she simply sees and believes and continues to question.

Irene will take from her strange and demanding conversations with her grandmother what she can; later she will take more than she is now capable of taking. She will grow into, not out of her grandmother's words. Nowhere did MacDonald write explicitly and at length about children's books, but he here offers us a lesson in what a good children's book should be: at once, sensitive to a child's nature and a child's interests, and sensitive to the difference between imaginative growth and accumulation of facts. Like Dickens, MacDonald views the best education as an enlivening, inspiriting, and teasing encouragement to thought, rather than the choking and stultifying accumulation of facts which parades as maturity and wisdom, but which puts a quiescence to thought. A didactic impulse does exist in MacDonald's books; he inherits the tradition of Bunyan. But in MacDonald's hands this tradition reflects the change that came over children's books with the publication in 1865 of Lewis Carroll's *Alice's Adventures in Wonderland*. In fact, this change is evident in *The Light Princess* which appeared a year before the first *Alice* book.

It is worth reminding ourselves that MacDonald and Lewis Carroll were friends, and Greville MacDonald is proud to assert that the MacDonald family, and he especially, were the catalysts that encouraged Carroll to publish *Alice*.[22] R. B. Shaberman has written at length on the relationship between Carroll and MacDonald, and the influences which exist between MacDonald's books and Carroll's.[23] He does not, however, note the similarities between *The Princess and the Goblin* and *Alice*. At the beginning of MacDonald's story a young girl (one year older than Alice) is bored with her toys, and although she does not fall down a rabbit hole, she does find herself in a long hallway lined with doors and in frustration she cries. Irene, like Alice, is a curious child and her curiosity leads her into strange adventures. Her adventures are, in effect, an educative sort of play.

For MacDonald, as well as for Carroll, the spirit of play is important, and both men understand that education is 'a process of growth and development' from within.[24] Also present in the work of MacDonald and Carroll is an element

[22] Greville MacDonald, *Reminiscences of a Specialist* (London, George Allen & Unwin, 1932), 15.
[23] 'Lewis Carroll and George MacDonald', *Jabberwocky*, 5 (1976), 67–87.
[24] Juliet Dusinberre, *Alice to the Lighthouse* (London, Macmillan, 1987), 7, 8.

of subversion. In this they follow Frances Browne's *Granny's Wonderful Chair* (1856), which questions such Victorian values as the sacredness of work and the appropriateness of charity. (MacDonald's wise woman character may have her source in Browne's Lady Greensleeves and the hardness of the goblins' feet in *The Princess and the Goblin* may derive from the large-footed people of Stumpinghame in Browne's book.) MacDonald's work, especially *The Princess and Curdie*, recognizes the need to examine and question the myths with which Victorian society orders itself. The separation of rich and poor and the Victorian view of female dependence and fragility are two social myths with which MacDonald is concerned. He does not provide his young readers with an easy escape into fantasy; rather, he encourages them to think about social and spiritual matters. MacDonald's children's books are as much about growing up in this world as they are about preparing ourselves for heaven.

MacDonald's books are not for the idle of mind; like poetry, they rouse the faculties to act. And like poetry, they must be heard. He asserts: 'A poem is a thing not for the understanding or heart only, but likewise for the ear; or, rather, for the understanding and heart through the ear.'[25] In his well-known essay, 'The Fantastic Imagination', MacDonald compares the ideal fairy-tale to a sonata which, like Nature, is and ought to be 'mood-engendering, thought-provoking'.[26] As to the question of meaning, MacDonald points out that children are seldom troubled about it: 'They find what they are capable of finding, and more would be too much'.[27] The dialogue between Irene and her great-great-grandmother or the implied dialogue between the narrator and the reader ('Guess what she was spinning.') are metonymic of the effect MacDonald is after. Not only this mysterious, open-ended dialogue, but also the very rhythms of the prose, rich in image, simile, alliteration, repetition, and

[25] *A Dish of Orts*, 216.
[26] Ibid. 320.
[27] *A Dish of Orts*, 317.

running participles convey the energy of constant inquiry. MacDonald's world, as Denis Donoghue eloquently notices, finds exhilaration in change: 'Metaphor, metamorphosis, inventions, Nature as the Aeolian lyre: the imaginative unity of MacDonald's work relies upon these fictions.'[28] The most sought-after change is change in people: the change in Irene from a childish little girl easily bored with her toys (her material possessions), quickly given to tears, and eagerly in need of parental love, to a confident and mature child grown wise beyond her years; or the change in Curdie from a cheerful but rather unthinking young boy to a serious and dutiful young man. MacDonald's Romantic commitment to change is, however, complete. Without contraries we would not be human, and change may be degeneration as the goblins or the people of Gwyntystorm evidence.

MacDonald's sense of change leads him to approach and yet avoid eschatology. We cannot rest easy with notions of last things. Meaning, we can now see, is always an approximation of meaning, never an end. This explains MacDonald's reluctance to offer stories with clear-cut endings; with a prescience for what we think of as the postmodern spirit, MacDonald avoids closure in his books. At the close of *The Lost Princess* (1875) he counters his reader's objection that the story is 'not finished' by stating: 'I never knew a story that was',[29] and for Cosmo Warlock in MacDonald's *Castle Warlock* (1882), 'the end of things never came'.[30] *The Princess and the Goblin* ends with the promise of a sequel: 'The rest of the history of *The Princess and Curdie* must be kept for another volume.' Readers had to wait five years before this second book appeared in the magazine *Good Things: A Picturesque Magazine for Boys and Girls*,[31] and eleven years before it appeared in book form. In it MacDonald

[28] Donoghue, 'The Other Country', *New York Review of Books*, 21 Dec. 1967, pp. 34–7.

[29] (London, J. M. Dent, 1967 edn.), 142.

[30] (London, Kegan Paul, Trench, Trubner, n.d.), 327.

[31] (Jan.–June 1877).

appears aggressively and pessimistically eschatological. He isn't.

Many readers have found the ending of *The Princess and Curdie* bleak and disturbing. Robert Lee Wolff asserts that MacDonald is 'convinced that evil triumphs in the end' and that the joy of the first book has become 'a choking pessimistic gloom'.[32] For Stephen Prickett 'the ending is startlingly bleak'.[33] Humphrey Carpenter notes the eschatological resonance of the book's ending: 'this is the Last Judgement. But it is a very strange Last Judgement: no one is saved.'[34] And he too speaks of MacDonald's pessimism. If indeed the book is as dark as these comments indicate, then MacDonald was ahead of his time in writing a book for children that confronted directly the ironies of human life. Not until the 1970s and 1980s would children's books offer young readers visions of life's defeats, of contingency and uncertainty, of the weakness of the human enterprise.

But we need not read the book as tragedy or irony. Jack Zipes has spoken of it as reflecting MacDonald's 'sober optimism'. He asks: 'was this a warning to children? Was this MacDonald's way to keep the utopian impulse alive in his readers by pointing to the dangers of slumbering?'[35] But the end of *The Princess and Curdie* is more than a warning; it is MacDonald's most uncompromising vision of what he calls in *Lilith* (1895) 'the endless ending' (this is the title of the last chapter). MacDonald's visionary integrity in *The Princess and Curdie* is exhilarating. He has the Christian's belief in a centred universe, in a time no longer when all dualities are reconciled. Yet he senses the impossibility of either a secular utopia or a sacred paradise regained, which

[32] Wolff, *The Golden Key: A Study of the Fiction of George MacDonald* (New Haven, Conn., Yale University Press, 1961), 178–9.

[33] Prickett, *Victorian Fantasy* (Bloomington, Ind., Indiana University Press, 1979), 187.

[34] Carpenter, *Secret Gardens* (Boston, Mass., Houghton Mifflin, 1985), 84.

[35] Zipes, *Fairy Tales and the Art of Subversion* (New York, Wildman Press, 1983), 110.

can only mean dullness and stagnation, an end to creative energy. We must move our tents close to groves Elysian, Fortunate Fields, but to pitch them in those fields is to cease to believe in growth and progression. On the final page of *The Princess and Curdie* MacDonald writes, 'The End', but the reader catches the irony: the end is a beginning. Just as the book begins with a lyric expression of the world's geological beginnings (indebted undoubtedly to Sir Charles Lyell), it comes full circle to an expression of yet another beginning. The wilderness of wild deer and the raving river of the book's final paragraph are, in the age of Darwin, a sign of renewal, of new beginnings. Creation begins anew in an unpeopled world. The possibilities of hope fill this as yet untainted wild. MacDonald's imagination is apocalyptic; the conclusion of *The Princess and Curdie* is what MacDonald calls in his sermon, 'The Consuming Fire', a 'partial' revelation. In a universe of infinite meaning, created by an infinite God, all revelations must be partial, encouragements to keep us on the look-out for further revelations.[36]

This explains why MacDonald's books are intensely symbolic, and why allegoric explanations of burning roses, white pigeons, a globe of light, a cosmic bath, gems, spatial metaphors, flowers, wastelands, cities, sun, moon, eucharistic meals, and such inevitably leave us with the feeling that not all has been explained. These books cannot be read; they can only be reread. This is what makes them so rewarding and so challenging as children's books. Most readers are like Curdie who must learn through experience before he can see the great-great-grandmother; we must fall from the innocence of reading for the adventure before we are either ready for the impassioned satire of *The Princess and Curdie* or to see the formal and thematic complexities of *The Princess and the Goblin*. In other words, MacDonald provides in these two books a lesson in reading. The first book is clearly a child's book; its source is the fairy-tale and romance traditions with which most young readers are

[36] See *Unspoken Sermons: First Series* (Alexander Strahan, 1867), 35.

familiar. The second book elaborates this simple beginning by extending the sources for plot and convention to the epic and comedic traditions. Where the first book invokes romance, the second book invokes comedy. Another way of putting this is to say the first book is pastoral, the second social. The first book is about individual reparation, the second is about social integration and responsibility. But a reading of the second book must send us back to the first one prepared to see more than we did in our first experience of it. The destruction of the goblins has its social and sombre implications; these funny misshapen creatures have lost their chance for betterment this side of the grave. The loss of his wife prepares the king for his weakness and loss of control in the second book. The feminine power so effective in *The Princess and the Goblin* gives way to the aggressiveness of masculine power in *The Princess and Curdie*. Despite the obvious differences in tone and action, these two books do speak to each other. Like Blake's innocence and experience, they satirize each other.

True to its fairy-tale tradition, *The Princess and the Goblin* is pastoral. Here nature serves largely as a reassuring presence, a playmate for Irene. The underground caverns and their goblin inhabitants are not so much sinister as they are comic. The goblins are duffers; they pose no real threat. A stamp on the feet is all it takes to send them scurrying away, or a good rhyme rousingly delivered. *The Princess and Curdie*, however, takes us to an urban setting in which humanity is poisoned with selfishness and greed; the threat to the king and his house is real. We move from a world in which poetry survives and serves humanity (interpolated poems are a feature of *The Princess and the Goblin*), to one which is darkly prosaic. Only one poem appears in *The Princess and Curdie* and this appears early in the book before Curdie sets out for Gwyntystorm. The goblins pervert language but remain underground; the king's minions pervert language and spread their perversions through the city. The control of events by the feminine spirit secures us in the first book, but she and her power are less evident in the second. This explains why the myths of

Persephone and the Virgin Mary inform *The Princess and the Goblin*, and the myths of Odysseus and Christ inform *The Princess and Curdie*.

In both books, however, MacDonald's sense of two worlds interconnecting and inter-influencing is apparent. His child protagonists experience imaginative participation in a spiritual realm presided over by a mysterious maternal figure. In *The Princess and Curdie*, this figure is the 'Mother of Light'. Both Irene and Curdie encounter this 'divinely "other" presence, and then return to the ordinary world, where they may enact visionary truth in a social and ethical context.'[37] In other words, their imaginations receive evidence of spiritual truth which enables them to survive and succeed in the world of mundane reality. Their success depends upon their seeing the two worlds as one. Seeing, in this sense, is revelatory.

For MacDonald, the imagination reveals; it does not create. Only God is capable of creation. And the imagination reveals by what Greville MacDonald calls, in describing his father's writing of *Lilith*, 'unconscious cerebration'.[38] As MacDonald himself puts it in his essay. 'The Imagination: Its Function and its Culture': 'a man is rather being thought than thinking, when a new thought arises in his mind. He knew it not till he found it there, therefore he could not even have sent for it.'[39] MacDonald's characters often must lose themselves (pass from states of consciousness to unconsciousness) to find themselves. Thus Colin, in 'The Carasoyn', must lose himself to find the old fairy woman who spins and who holds the secrets of the Carasoyn which is necessary to the rescue of the little girl stolen away by the fairies seven years ago. The unconscious, then, is the source of our thinking, of our imagination; it is that in us closest to the influences of the divine, provided we are pure. The purest person, according

[37] Anita Moss, 'Sacred and Secular Visions of Imagination and Reality in Nineteenth Century British Fantasy for Children', in Joseph O'Beirne Milner and Lucy Floyd Morcock Milner (eds.), *Webs and Wardrobes* (Lanham, Md., University Press of America, 1987), 67.

[38] *Reminiscences*, 320.

[39] *A Dish of Orts*, 4.

to MacDonald's Romantic sensibility, is the child. This may explain why so often his child heroes are paragons, Christ figures such as Diamond in *At the Back of the North Wind* (1871) or Gibbie Galbraith in *Sir Gibbie* (1879). In the latter novel, MacDonald defends his habit of using unbelievably good characters instead of realistically flawed characters as his heroes: 'But whatever the demand of the age, I insist that which *ought* to be presented to its beholding, is the common good uncommonly developed, and that not because of its rarity, but because it is truer to humanity.'[40] Before the story gets under way in *The Princess and the Goblin*, MacDonald makes it clear, in his description of Irene's eyes, that she is a type of common good uncommonly developed.

In Chapter 2 of *The Princess and the Goblin*, Irene loses herself to find herself, her namesake the great-great-grandmother who reveals the truths of a divinely ordered universe. Similarly, at the beginning of the *The Princess and Curdie*, Curdie loses himself by thoughtlessly shooting a pigeon, only to find his true self in seeking for the same grandmother. He seeks and he finds. For those who have not found the grandmother or what she represents, imagination dulls and they cease to believe in what cannot be seen or touched. Lootie in the first book and the miners who speak disparagingly of Old Mother Wotherwop in the second book are examples of those whose imaginations have become dull. Since we are not born with our imaginations fully formed, our imaginative capacity may grow stronger or weaker. When it grows weak to the limits of opacity, the result is the intellectual hard-headedness and selfishness of the goblins or of the conspirators in the king's house.

Since for MacDonald a strong imagination is the foundation of moral and spiritual health, he writes fantasy that appeals to this faculty by setting feeling, and so thinking, to work.[41] His advice to his adult readers regarding

[40] *Sir Gibbie* (London, J.M. Dent, 1924), 48.
[41] *A Dish of Orts*, 320.

their children is that they cultivate their children's visions and dreams: 'Seek not that your sons and your daughters should not see visions, should not dream dreams; seek that they should see true visions, that they should dream noble dreams.'[42] MacDonald's use of the words 'vision' and 'dream' is noteworthy. He is at pains in his fantasy and other fiction to indicate the reality of vision and dream. Irene repeatedly wonders whether her visits to grandmother are only a beautiful dream, and the grandmother visits Curdie when he is feverish and dreaming. Yet the evidence of Irene's cured finger and Curdie's cured leg suggests the reality of the experiences. In *The Princess and Curdie*, Curdie tells his mother that he may have dreamed his duty, that his trip to the grandmother's tower room may have been a dream. His mother replies: 'Then dream often, my son: for there must be more truth in your dreams than in your waking thoughts.' MacDonald is fond of quoting Novalis's epigram, 'Our life is no dream but it should and perhaps will become one', and in these two books life has become dream and dream has become life.

This blending of dream and reality is what gives MacDonald's books their mystery and compelling power. True, as several commentators have noted, he sometimes allows his Calvinist background to control his vision, and his words carry the timbre of the sermon. He cannot escape his Victorian environment, and he emphasizes, at times with patriarchal earnestness, duty, obedience, and work. However, when he is at his best, dialectic is his mode of thought, not assertion. This is why these two books delight in paradox. In *The Princess and the Goblin* and *The Princess and Curdie* opposites are reconciled: male and female, dream and reality, age and youth, work and rest, day and night, the natural and the supernatural, good and evil, fire and water, heights and depths, inside and outside. To accomplish this visionary end, MacDonald must speak the unspeakable, and it is this that makes his books so

[42] Ibid. 30.

challenging and rewarding. We may measure his success by his influence.

MacDonald's influence in the nineteenth century is apparent in such later works as Dinah Mulock's *The Little Lame Prince* (1874), Mary Molesworth's *The Cuckoo Clock* (1877), and some of Mary DeMorgan's stories. In the twentieth century, MacDonald has influenced such important writers for children as Frances Hodgson Burnett, J. R. R. Tolkien, C. S. Lewis, Phillipa Pearce, and Maurice Sendak. What captures each of these writers is MacDonald's fierce belief in the power of our imaginations to find reality other than the one perpetrated on us by social mythology. In MacDonald's books true authority comes from an understanding of the independence of the other; the drawing together into cabals, institutions, governments, sects is the drawing down of darkness. In both *The Princess and the Goblin* and *The Princess and Curdie*, patriarchal authority, rule by law, is vanity; the feminine grace of the great-great-grandmother proves effective in its distance, its mystery, its encouragement rather than coercion, perhaps even in its *jouissance*. Sylvia Plath understood something of this when she wrote her version of MacDonald's 'Princess' story.[43] For Plath the hard voice of reason, of masculine appropriation, can only destroy the possibility of redemption held out by the 'cryptic whir' of the grandmother's spindle. But we need not judge MacDonald by the failures of our culture to match his vision; we need rather to return to those visions in a ceaseless attempt to hope for and reach for that which they embrace. If we seek for our daughters and sons to dream noble dreams and see true visions, then we will do well to pass these books on to them.

[43] 'The Princess and the Goblins', *Collected Poems* (London, Faber & Faber, 1981), 333–5.

NOTE ON THE TEXT

THE manuscript of *The Princess and the Goblin* (with thirteen pages missing) is in The George MacDonald Collection, Brander Library, Huntly, Aberdeenshire. The story first appeared in *Good Words for the Young*, which MacDonald edited, between November 1870 and June 1871 (vol. 3, pp. 1–5, 65–72, 129–36, 185–91, 279–86, 301–5, 353–63, 409–20). The first publication in book form was in London by Strahan & Co. in 1872. The magazine version contains a frame in which a child reader speaks with the 'Editor'. This frame appeared in two early American editions, but it has not appeared with the rest of the book since 1924. Relevant passages are included in the Explanatory Notes.

The Princess and Curdie first appeared in *Good Things: A Picturesque Magazine for Boys and Girls* between January and June 1877 (vol. 6, pp. 1–5, 65–8, 177–80, 193–200, 257–63, 321–52; pp. 345–6 are wrongly numbered). The first publication in book form, the text of which does not depart from the magazine version, was in London by Chatto & Windus, in 1883.

The editions of both books used here are those published by Blackie & Son in 1888. These appear to have been printed from the first edition plates; they depart from the first editions only in the odd shift of punctuation. Modern paperback reprints of the books invariably alter MacDonald's paragraphing, and often drop words or even change words altogether. I have tried to present the books as MacDonald wrote them.

SELECT BIBLIOGRAPHY

EDITIONS

The Princess and the Goblin, with illustrations by Arthur Hughes (London, Strahan & Co., 1872). Reprinted, apparently from the Strahan plates (London, Blackie & Son, 1888). Modern editions include: with illustrations by Charles Folkard (London, J. M. Dent, 1949); with illustrations by Nora S. Unwin (New York, Macmillan, 1951).

The Princess and Curdie, with illustrations by James Allen (London, Chatto & Windus 1883). Reprinted, apparently from the Chatto & Windus plates, (London, Blackie & Son, 1888). Modern editions include: with illustrations by Charles Folkard (London, J. M. Dent, 1949); with illustrations by Nora S. Unwin (New York, Macmillan, 1954).

BIBLIOGRAPHICAL

Bulloch, John Malcolm 'A Bibliography of George Mac-Donald', *Aberdeen University Library Bulletin*, 5 (1925), 679–745.

Hutton, Muriel, 'Sour Grapeshot: Fault-finding in *A Centennial Bibliography of George MacDonald*', *Aberdeen University Review*, 41 (1965), 85–8.

—— 'The George MacDonald Collection, Brander Library, Huntly', *The Book Collector*, 17 (1968), 13–25.

—— 'The George MacDonald Collection', *Yale University Library Gazette*, 51 (1976), 74–85.

Shaberman, R. B., *George MacDonald's Books for Children: A Bibliography of First Editions* (London, Cityprint Business Centres, 1979).

BIOGRAPHICAL

MacDonald, Greville, *George MacDonald and his Wife* (London, George Allen & Unwin, 1924).

Phillips, Michael R., *George MacDonald: Scotland's Beloved Storyteller* (Minneapolis, Minn., Bethany House, 1987).

Raeper, William, *George MacDonald* (Icknield Way, Tring, Lion, 1987).

Saintsbury, Elizabeth, *George MacDonald: A Short Life* (Edinburgh, Canongate, 1987).

Triggs, Kathy, *The Stars and the Stillness: A Portrait of George MacDonald* (Cambridge, Lutterworth Press, 1986).

CRITICAL STUDIES

General

Auden, W. H., 'George MacDonald', *Forewords and Afterwords* (New York, Vintage, 1974), 268–73.

Bergmann, Frank, 'The Roots of Tolkien's Tree: The Influence of George MacDonald and German Romanticism Upon Tolkien's Essay "On Fairy Stories"', *Mosaic*, 10 (1977), 5–14.

Carpenter, Humphrey, 'George MacDonald and the Tender Grandmother', in id., *Secret Gardens* (Boston, Mass., Houghton Mifflin, 1985), 70–85.

Donoghue, Denis, 'The Other Country', *New York Review of Books*, 21 Dec. 1967, pp. 34–7.

Douglas, Alison, 'The Scottish Contribution to Children's Literature', *Library Review*, 20 (1965), 241–6.

Douglass, Jane, 'Dealings with the Fairies', *Horn Book Magazine*, 37 (1961), 327–35.

Hein, Roland, *The Harmony Within: The Spiritual Vision of George MacDonald* (Grand Rapids, Mich., W. B. Eerdmans, 1982).

Lewis, C. S., 'Preface', *George MacDonald: An Anthology* (London, Geoffrey Bles, 1946), 10–22.

Lewis, F. W., 'The Pedagogics of George MacDonald', *Education*, 19 (1899), 357–67.

Lochhead, Marion, 'George MacDonald and the World of Faerie', *Seven*, 3 (1982), 63–71.

McGillis, Roderick, 'Fantasy as Adventure: Nineteenth Century Children's Fiction', *Children's Literature Association Quarterly*, 8 (1983), 18–22.

MacNeice, Louis, 'The Victorians', in id., *Varieties of Parable* (Cambridge, Cambridge University Press, 1965), 76–101.

Manlove, Colin, 'George MacDonald (1824–1905)', in id., *Modern Fantasy* (Cambridge, Cambridge University Press, 1975), 55–98.

—— 'Circularity in Fantasy: George MacDonald', in id., *The Impulse of Fantasy Literature* (Kent, Ohio, Kent State University Press, 1983), 70–92.

Moss, Anita, 'Sacred and Secular Visions of Imagination and Reality in Nineteenth Century British Fantasy for Children', in Joseph O'Beirne Milner and Lucy Floyd Morcock Milner (eds.), *Webs and Wardrobes* (Lanham, Md., University Press of America, 1987), 67–78.

Prickett, Stephen, 'Demythologising and Myth-making: Arnold versus MacDonald', in id., *Romanticism and Religion* (Cambridge, Cambridge University Press, 1976), 223–47.

—— 'Adults in Allegory Land: Kingsley and MacDonald', in id., *Victorian Fantasy* (Bloomington, Ind., Indiana University Press, 1979), 151–97.

Reis, Richard, *George MacDonald* (New York, Twayne, 1972).

Robb, David, *George MacDonald* (Edinburgh, Scottish Academic Press, 1987).

Shaberman, R. B., 'Lewis Carroll and George MacDonald', *Jabberwocky*, 5 (1976), 67–87.

Wolff, Robert Lee, *The Golden Key: A Study of the Fiction of George MacDonald* (New Haven, Conn., Yale University Press, 1961).

Zipes, Jack, 'Inverting and Subverting the World with Hope: The Fairy Tales of George MacDonald, Oscar Wilde and L. Frank Baum', in id., *Fairy Tales and the Art of Subversion* (New York, Wildman Press, 1983), 97–111.

The 'Princess Books'

Kirkpatrick, Mary, 'An Introduction to the *Curdie* Books of George MacDonald', *Bulletin of the New York C. S. Lewis Society*, 5 (1974), 2–4.

McGillis, Roderick, 'George MacDonald's *Princess* Books: High Seriousness', in Perry Nodelman (ed.), *Touchstones: Reflections on the Best in Children's Literature* (West Lafayette, Ind., Children's Literature Association, 1985), 146–62.

Tanner, Tony, 'Mountains and Depths—An Approach to Nineteenth Century Dualism', *Review of English Literature*, 3 (1962), 51–61.

Willis, Lesley, '"Born Again": The Metamorphosis of Irene in George MacDonald's *The Princess and the Goblin*', *Scottish Literary Journal*, 12 (1985), 24–39.

A CHRONOLOGY OF
GEORGE MACDONALD

1824 Born 10 December at Huntly, Aberdeenshire.

1826 MacDonald family moves to The Farm, Huntly.

1832 Death of MacDonald's mother, Helen MacKay MacDonald.

1840 Enters King's College, Aberdeen. MacDonald recalls his college days in the poem, *A Hidden Life* (1864).

1842 Spends time away from college, possibly at Thurso Castle in the north of Scotland.

1845 MA from King's College.

1846 Publishers his first poem, 'David', in the *Congregational Magazine*.

1848 Attends Highbury Theological College, London; engaged to Louisa Powell.

1850 Assumes the pastorate at Arundel, Sussex.

1851 Marries Louisa Powell; private publication of his translation of Novalis, *Twelve of the Spiritual Songs of Novalis*.

1852 Lilia Scott MacDonald born.

1853 Resigns pastorate over heresy charge; death of his brother Alexander; birth of the MacDonalds' second child, Mary Josephine MacDonald.

1854 Caroline Grace MacDonald born. MacDonald living in Manchester.

1855 MacDonald's first book, the poetic drama *Within and Without* published; death of MacDonald's sister Bella.

1856 Spends winter in Algiers (with financial assistance from Lady Byron); birth of Greville MacDonald.

1857 *Poems*; birth of Irene MacDonald. MacDonalds live in Hastings.

1858 *Phantastes*; deaths of MacDonald's father, George MacDonald, Senr., and of his brother, John Hill; birth of Winifred Louisa MacDonald.

1859 Move to Tudor Lodge, Regent's Park; MacDonald assumes Professorship at Bedford College.

1860 Death of Lady Byron; birth of Ronald MacDonald.

1862 Meets Lewis Carroll (probably); birth of Robert Falconer MacDonald.

1863 *David Elginbrod*; meets Mrs LaTouche and John Ruskin.

1864 *Adela Cathcart*; *The Portent*; birth of Maurice MacDonald.

1865 Spends summer in Switzerland; *Alex Forbes*; lectureship at King's College, London; birth of Bernard Powell MacDonald.

1867 *Dealings with the Fairies*; *Annals of a Quiet Neighbourhood*; *Unspoken Sermons* (First Series); *The Disciple and Other Poems*; move to the Retreat, Hammersmith; birth of George MacKay MacDonald.

1868 *Guild Court*; *Robert Falconer*; *The Seaboard Parish*; MacDonald reveives LL D from Aberdeen University.

1869 Sea voyage on The Blue Bell (cut short because of a painfully swollen knee); friendship with F. D. Maurice.

1870 MacDonald becomes editor of *Good Words for the Young*; *The Miracles of Our Lord*; Louisa MacDonald publishes *Chamber Dramas for Children*.

1871 *Works of Fancy and Imagination* (10 volumes); *At the Back of the North Wind*; *Ranald Bannerman's Boyhood*.

1872 Lecture tour in the United States and Canada; *The Princess and the Goblin*; *The Vicar's Daughter*; *Wilfrid Cumbermede*.

1873 *Gutta Percha Willie.*

1875 *Malcolm; The Wise Woman.*

1876 *Thomas Wingfold, Curate; Exotics* (translations); *St. George and St. Michael.*

1877 First public performance of *The Pilgrim's Progress*; *The Marquis of Lossie*; MacDonald receives Civil List Pension.

1878 The MacDonalds winter at Porto Fino, Italy; death of Mary Josephine MacDonald.

1879 *Paul Faber, Surgeon*; *Sir Gibbie*; Death of Maurice MacDonald.

1880 *A Book of Stife: The Diary of an Old Soul.*

1881 *Mary Marston*; MacDonalds adopt two children, Honey and Joan; move to Casa Corraggio, Bordighera, Italy.

1882 *Castle Warlock*; *Weighed and Wanting*; *The Gifts of the Christ Child*; *Orts*.

1883 *Donal Grant*; *A Threefold Cord*; *The Princess and Curdie*.

1885 *The Tragedie of Hamlet*; *Unspoken Sermons* (Second Series).

1886 *What's Mine's Mine*.

1887 *Home Again*; an earthquake damages Bordighera (MacDonald mentions this in his novel *A Rough Shaking*, 1890).

1888 *The Elect Lady*.

1889 *Unspoken Sermons* (Third Series).

1890 *A Rough Shaking* (MacDonald's last work for children).

1891 *There and Back*; *The Flight of the Shadow*; *A Cabinet of Gems* (selections from the work of Sir Philip Sidney); death of Lilia Scott MacDonald.

1982 *The Hope of the Gospel*.

1893 *Poetical Works* (2 volumes); *Heather and Snow*; *Scotch Songs and Ballads*; *A Dish of Orts*.

1895 *Lilth*.

1897 *Rampolli, Growths from a Long Planted Root* (translations); *Salted with Fire*.

1898 'Far Above Rubies' in *The Sketch*, MacDonald's last published work.

1900 MacDonald retires to Haslemere, England.

1901 MacDonalds celebrate Golden Wedding Anniversary.

1902 Death of Louisa MacDonald; buried at Bordighera, Italy.

1905 Death of George MacDonald at Ashtead, Surrey; buried at Bordighera, Italy.

THE PRINCESS AND
THE GOBLIN

CONTENTS

Contents

I

Why the Princess Has a Story About Her

There was once a little princess whose* father was king over a great country full of mountains and valleys. His palace was built upon one of the mountains, and was very grand and beautiful. The princess, whose name was Irene,* was born there, but she was sent soon after her birth, because her mother was not very strong, to be brought up by country people in a large house, half castle, half farmhouse, on the side of another mountain, about half-way between its base and its peak.

The princess was a sweet little creature, and at the time my story begins, was about eight years old, I think, but she got older very fast. Her face was fair and pretty, with eyes like two bits of night sky, each with a star dissolved in the blue. Those eyes you would have thought must have known they came from there, so often were they turned up in that direction. The ceiling of her nursery was blue,* with stars in it, as like the sky as they could make it. But I doubt if ever she saw the real sky with the stars in it, for a reason which I had better mention at once.

These mountains were full of hollow places underneath;* huge caverns, and winding ways, some with water running through them, and some shining with all colours of the rainbow when a light was taken in. There would not have been much known about them, had there not been mines there, great deep pits, with long galleries and passages running off from them, which had been dug to get at the ore of which the mountains were full. In the course of digging, the miners came upon many of these natural caverns. A few of them had far-off openings out on the side of a mountain, or into a ravine.

Now in these subterranean caverns lived a strange race of beings, called by some gnomes, by some kobolds, by some goblins.* There was a legend current in the country, that at one time they lived above ground, and were very like other people. But for some reason or other, concerning which there were different legendary theories, the king had laid what they thought too severe taxes upon them, or had required observances of them they did not like, or had begun to treat them with more severity, in some way or other, and impose stricter laws; and the consequence was that they had all disappeared from the face of the country. According to the legend, however, instead of going to some other country, they had all taken refuge in the subterranean caverns, whence they never came out but at night, and then seldom showed themselves in any numbers, and never to many people at once. It was only in the least frequented and most difficult parts of the mountains that they were said to gather even at night in the open air. Those who had caught sight of any of them said that they had greatly altered in the course of generations;* and no wonder, seeing they lived away from the sun, in cold and wet and dark places. They were now, not ordinarily ugly, but either absolutely hideous, or ludicrously grotesque both in face and form. There was no invention, they said, of the most lawless imagination expressed by pen or pencil, that could surpass the extravagance of their appearance. But I suspect those who said so, had mistaken some of their animal companions for the goblins themselves—of which more by and by. The goblins themselves were not so far removed from the human as such a description would imply. And as they grew misshapen in body, they had grown in knowledge and cleverness, and now were able to do things no mortal could see the possibility of. But as they grew in cunning, they grew in mischief, and their great delight was in every way they could think of to annoy the people who lived in the open-air storey above them. They had enough of affection left for each other, to preserve them from being absolutely cruel for cruelty's sake to those that came in their way; but still they so heartily cherished the ancestral grudge against those who occupied their former possessions, and especially against the descendants of the king who had caused their expulsion,* that they sought every opportunity of tormenting them in ways that were as odd as their inventors; and although dwarfed and misshapen, they had strength equal to their cunning. In the process of time they had got a king and a government of their own, whose chief business, beyond their own simple affairs, was to devise trouble for their neighbours. It will now be pretty evident why the little princess had never seen the sky at night. They were much too afraid of the goblins to let her out of the house then, even in company with ever so many attendants; and they had good reason, as we shall see by and by.

II

The Princess Loses Herself

I have said the Princess Irene was about eight years old when
my story begins. And this is how it begins.*

One very wet day, when the mountain was covered with
mist which was constantly gathering itself together into
raindrops, and pouring down on the roofs of the great
old house, whence it fell in a fringe of water from the
eaves all round about it, the princess could not of course
go out. She got very tired, so tired that even her toys could
no longer amuse her. You would wonder at that if I had time
to describe to you one half of the toys she had. But then you
wouldn't have the toys themselves, and that makes all the
difference: you can't get tired of a thing before you have it.*
It was a picture, though, worth seeing—the princess sitting
in the nursery with the sky-ceiling over her head, at a great
table covered with her toys. If the artist would like to draw
this, I should advise him not to meddle with the toys.* I am
afraid of attempting to describe them, and I think he had
better not try to draw them. He had better not. He can do
a thousand things I can't, but I don't think he could draw
those toys. No man could better make the princess herself
than he could, though—leaning with her back bowed into
the back of the chair, her head hanging down, and her hands
in her lap, very miserable as she would say herself, not even
knowing what she would like, except it were to go out and
get thoroughly wet, and catch a particularly nice cold, and
have to go to bed and take gruel. The next moment after you
see her sitting there, her nurse goes out of the room.*

Even that is a change, and the princess wakes up a little,
and looks about her. Then she tumbles off her chair, and
runs out of the door, not the same door the nurse went out

of, but one which opened at the foot of a curious old stair of worm-eaten oak,* which looked as if never any one had set foot upon it. She had once before been up six steps, and that was sufficient reason, in such a day, for trying to find out what was at the top of it.

Up and up she ran—such a long way it seemed to her! until she came to the top of the third flight. There she found the landing was the end of a long passage. Into this she ran. It was full of doors on each side. There were so many that she did not care to open any, but ran on to the end, where she turned into another passage, also full of doors. When she had turned twice more, and still saw doors and only doors about her, she began to get frightened. It was so silent! And all those doors must hide rooms with nobody in them! That was dreadful. Also the rain made a great trampling noise on the roof. She turned and started at full speed, her little footsteps echoing through the sounds of the rain—back for the stairs and her safe nursery. So she thought, but she had lost herself long ago. It doesn't follow that she *was* lost, because she had lost herself, though.*

She ran for some distance, turned several times, and then began to be afraid. Very soon she was sure that she had lost the way back. Rooms everywhere, and no stair! Her little heart beat as fast as her little feet ran, and a lump of tears was growing in her throat. But she was too eager and perhaps too frightened to cry for some time. At last her hope failed her. Nothing but passages and doors everywhere! She threw herself on the floor, and burst into a wailing cry broken by sobs.

She did not cry long, however, for she was as brave as could be expected of a princess of her age. After a good cry, she got up, and brushed the dust from her frock. Oh what old dust it was! Then she wiped her eyes with her hands, for princesses don't always have their handkerchiefs in their pockets, any more than some other little girls I know of. Next, like a true princess,* she resolved on going wisely to work to find her way back: she would walk through the

passages, and look in every direction for the stair. This she
did, but without success. She went over the same ground
again and again without knowing it, for the passages and
doors were all alike. At last, in a corner, through a half
open door, she did see a stair. But alas! it went the wrong
way: instead of going down, it went up. Frightened as she
was, however, she could not help wishing to see where yet
further the stair could lead. It was very narrow,* and so
steep that she went up like a four-legged creature on her
hands and feet.

III

The Princess and—We Shall See Who

When she came to the top, she found herself in a little square place, with three doors, two opposite each other, and one opposite the top of the stair. She stood for a moment, without an idea in her little head what to do next. But as she stood, she began to hear a curious humming sound. Could it be the rain? No. It was much more gentle and even monotonous than the sound of the rain, which now she scarcely heard. The low sweet humming sound went on, sometimes stopping for a little while and then beginning again. It was more like the hum of a very happy bee that had found a rich well of honey in some globular flower, than anything else I can think of at this moment. Where could it come from? She laid her ear first to one of the doors to hearken if it was there—then to another. When she laid her ear against the third door, there could be no doubt where it came from: it must be from something in that room. What could it be? She was rather afraid, but her curiosity* was stronger than her fear, and she opened the door very gently and peeped in. What do you think she saw? A very old lady who sat spinning.*

Perhaps you will wonder how the princess could tell that the old lady was an old lady, when I inform you that not only was she beautiful, but her skin was smooth and white.* I will tell you more. Her hair was combed back from her forehead and face, and hung loose far down and all over her back. That is not much like an old lady—is it? Ah! but it was white almost as snow. And although her face was so smooth, her eyes looked so wise that you could not have helped seeing she must be old. The princess, though she could not have told you why, did think her very old indeed—quite fifty—she said to herself. But she was rather older than that, as you shall hear.

While the princess stared bewildered, with her head just inside the door, the old lady lifted hers, and said, in a sweet, but old and rather shaky voice, which mingled very pleasantly with the continued hum of her wheel: 'Come in, my dear; come in. I am glad to see you.'

That the princess was a real princess, you might see now quite plainly; for she didn't hang on to the handle of the door, and stare without moving, as I have known some do who ought to have been princesses but were only rather vulgar* little girls. She did as she was told, stepped inside the door at once, and shut it gently behind her.

'Come to me, my dear,' said the old lady.

And again the princess did as she was told. She approached the old lady—rather slowly, I confess, but did not stop until she stood by her side, and looked up in her face with her blue eyes and the two melted stars in them.

'Why, what have you been doing with your eyes, child?' asked the old lady.

'Crying,' answered the princess.

'Why, child?'

'Because I couldn't find my way down again.'

'But you could find your way up.'

'Not at first—not for a long time.'

'But your face is streaked like the back of a zebra. Hadn't you a handkerchief to wipe your eyes with?'

'No.'

'Then why didn't you come to me to wipe them for you?'

'Please, I didn't know you were here. I will next time.'

'There's a good child!' said the old lady.

Then she stopped her wheel, and rose, and, going out of the room, returned with a little silver basin and a soft white towel, with which she washed and wiped the bright little face.* And the princess thought her hands were so smooth and nice!

When she carried away the basin and towel, the little princess wondered to see how straight and tall she was, for, although she was so old, she didn't stoop a bit. She was dressed in black velvet with thick white heavy-looking lace about it; and on the black dress, her hair shone like silver.* There was hardly any more furniture in the room than there might have been in that of the poorest old woman who made her bread by her spinning. There was no carpet on the floor—no table anywhere—nothing but the spinning-wheel and the chair beside it. When she came back, she sat down again, and without a word began her spinning once more, while Irene, who had never seen a spinning-wheel, stood by her side and looked on. When the old lady had got her thread fairly going again, she said to the princess, but without looking at her:

'Do you know my name, child?'

'No, I don't know it,' answered the princess.

'My name is Irene.'

'That's *my* name!' cried the princess.

'I know that. I let you have mine. I haven't got your name. You've got mine.'

'How can that be?' asked the princess, bewildered. 'I've always had my name.'

'Your papa, the king, asked me if I had any objection to your having it; and of course I hadn't. I let you have it with pleasure.'

'It was very kind of you to give me your name—and such a pretty one,' said the princess.

'Oh, not so *very* kind!' said the old lady. 'A name is one of those things one can give away and keep all the same. I have a good many such things. Wouldn't you like to know who I am child?'

'Yes, that I should—very much.'

'I'm your great-great-grandmother,'* said the lady.

'What's that?' asked the princess.

'I'm your father's mother's father's mother.'

'Oh dear! I can't understand that,' said the princess.

'I daresay not. I didn't expect you would. But that's no reason why I shouldn't say it.'

'Oh, no!' answered the princess.

'I will explain it all to you when you are older,' the lady went on. 'But you will be able to understand this much now: I came here to take care of you.'

'Is it long since you came? Was it yesterday? Or was it today, because it was so wet that I couldn't get out?'

'I've been here ever since you came yourself.'

'What a long time!' said the princess. 'I don't remember it at all.'

'No. I suppose not.'

'But I never saw you before.'

'No. But you shall see me again.'

'Do you live in this room always?'

'I don't sleep in it. I sleep on the opposite side of the landing. I sit here most of the day.'

'I shouldn't like it. My nursery is much prettier. You must be a queen too, if you are my great big grandmother.'

'Yes, I am a queen.'

'Where is your crown then?'

'In my bedroom.'

'I *should* like to see it.'

'You shall some day—not today.'

'I wonder why nursie never told me.'

'Nursie doesn't know. She never saw me.'

'But somebody knows that you are in the house?'

'No; nobody.'

'How do you get your dinner then?'

'I keep poultry—of a sort.'

'Where do you keep them?'

'I will show you.'

'And who makes the chicken broth for you?'

'I never kill any of my chickens.'

'Then I can't understand.'

'What did you have for breakfast this morning?' asked the lady.

'Oh! I had bread and milk, and an egg.—I dare say you eat their eggs.'

'Yes, that's it. I eat their eggs.'

'Is that what makes your hair so white?'

'No, my dear. It's old age. I am very old.'

'I thought so. Are you fifty?'

'Yes—more than that.'

'Are you a hundred?'

'Yes—more than that. I am too old for you to guess. Come and see my chickens.'

Again she stopped her spinning. She rose, took the princess by the hand, led her out of the room, and opened the door opposite the stair. The princess expected to see a lot of hens and chickens, but instead of that, she saw the blue sky first, and then the roofs of the house, with a multitude of the loveliest pigeons, mostly white, but all colours, walking about, making bows to each other, and talking a language she could not understand. She clapped her hands with delight, and up rose such a flapping of wings, that she in her turn was startled.

'You've frightened my poultry,' said the old lady, smiling.

'And they've frightened me,' said the princess, smiling too. 'But what very nice poultry! Are the eggs nice?'

'Yes, very nice.'

'What a small egg-spoon you must have! Wouldn't it be better to keep hens, and get bigger eggs?'

'How should I feed them, though?'

'I see,' said the princess. 'The pigeons feed themselves. They've got wings.'

'Just so. If they couldn't fly, I couldn't eat their eggs.'

'But how do you get at the eggs? Where are their nests?'

The lady took hold of a little loop of string in the wall at the side of the door, and lifting a shutter, showed a great many pigeon-holes with nests, some with young ones and some with eggs in them. The birds came in at the other side, and she took out the eggs on this side. She closed it again quickly, lest the young ones should be frightened.

'Oh what a nice way!' cried the princess. 'Will you give me an egg to eat, I'm rather hungry.'

'I will some day, but now you must go back, or nursie will be miserable about you. I daresay she's looking for you everywhere.'

'Except here,' answered the princess. 'Oh how surprised she *will* be when I tell her about my great big grand-grandmother!'

'Yes, that she will!' said the old lady with a curious smile. 'Mind you tell her all about it exactly.'

'That I will. Please will you take me back to her?'

'I can't go all the way, but I will take you to the top of the stair, and then you must run down quite fast into your own room.'

The little princess put her hand in the old lady's, who, looking this way and that, brought her to the top of the first stair, and thence to the bottom of the second, and did not leave her till she saw her half way down the third. When she heard the cry of her nurse's pleasure at finding her, she turned and walked up the stairs again, very fast indeed for such a very great grandmother, and sat down to her spinning with another strange smile on her sweet old face.

About this spinning of hers I will tell you more another time.

Guess what she was spinning.

IV

What the Nurse Thought of It

'Why, where can you have been, princess?' asked the nurse, taking her in her arms. 'It's very unkind of you to hide away so long. I began to be afraid— '

Here she checked herself.

'What were you afraid of, nursie?' asked the princess.

'Never mind,' she answered. 'Perhaps I will tell you another day. Now tell me where you have been?'

'I've been up a long way to see my very great, huge, old grandmother,' said the princess.

'What do you mean by that?' asked the nurse, who thought she was making fun.

'I mean that I've been a long way up and up to see my GREAT grandmother. Ah, nursie, you don't know what a beautiful mother of grandmothers I've got upstairs. She is *such* an old lady! with such lovely white hair!—as white as my silver cup. Now, when I think of it, I think her hair must be silver.'

'What nonsense you are talking, princess!' said the nurse.

'I'm not talking nonsense,' returned Irene, rather offended. 'I will tell you all about her. She's much taller than you, and much prettier.'

'Oh, I dare say!' remarked the nurse.

'And she lives upon pigeons' eggs.'

'Most likely,' said the nurse.

'And she sits in an empty room, spin-spinning all day long.'

'Not a doubt of it,' said the nurse.

'And she keeps her crown in her bedroom.'

'Of course—quite the proper place to keep her crown in. She wears it in bed, I'll be bound.'

'She didn't say that. And I don't think she does. That wouldn't be comfortable—would it? I don't think my papa wears his crown for a nightcap. Does he, nursie?'

'I never asked him. I dare say he does.'

'And she's been there ever since I came here—ever so many years.'

'Anybody could have told you that,' said the nurse, who did not believe a word Irene was saying.

'Why didn't you tell me then?'

'There was no necessity. You could make it all up for yourself.'

'You don't believe me then!' exclaimed the princess, astonished and angry, as she well might be.

'Did you expect me to believe you, princess?' asked the nurse coldly. 'I know princesses are in the habit of telling make-believes, but you are the first I ever heard of who expected to have them believed,' she added, seeing that the child was strangely in earnest.

The princess burst into tears.

'Well, I must say,' remarked the nurse, now thoroughly vexed with her for crying, 'it is not at all becoming in a princess to tell stories *and* expect to be believed just because she is a princess.'

'But it's quite true, I tell you.'

'You've dreamt it, then, child.'

'No, I didn't dream it.* I went upstairs, and I lost myself, and if I hadn't found the beautiful lady, I should never have found myself.'

'Oh, I dare say!'

'Well, you just come up with me, and see if I'm not telling the truth.'

'Indeed I have other work to do. It's your dinner-time, and I won't have any more such nonsense.'

The princess wiped her eyes, and her face grew so hot that they were soon quite dry. She sat down to her dinner, but ate next to nothing. Not to be believed does not at all agree with princesses; for a real princess cannot tell a lie. So all the afternoon she did not speak a word. Only when the nurse spoke to her, she answered her, for a real princess is never rude—even when she does well to be offended.

Of course the nurse was not comfortable in her mind—not that she suspected the least truth in Irene's story, but that she loved her dearly, and was vexed with herself for having been cross to her. She thought her crossness was the cause of the princess's unhappiness, and had no idea that she was really and deeply hurt at not being believed. But, as it became more and more plain during the evening in her every motion and look, that, although she tried to amuse herself with her toys, her heart was too vexed and troubled to enjoy them, her nurse's discomfort grew and grew. When bedtime came, she undressed and laid her down, but the child, instead of holding up her little mouth to be kissed, turned away from her and lay still: Then nursie's heart gave way altogether, and she began to cry. At the sound of her first sob, the princess turned again, and held her face to kiss her as usual. But the nurse had her handkerchief to her eyes, and did not see the movement.

'Nursie,' said the princess, 'why won't you believe me?'

'Because I can't believe you,' said the nurse, getting angry again.

'Ah! then, you can't help it,' said Irene, 'and I will not be vexed with you any more. I will give you a kiss and go to sleep.'

'You little angel!' cried the nurse, and caught her out of bed, and walked about the room with her in her arms, kissing and hugging her.

'You *will* let me take you to see my dear old great big grandmother? won't you?' said the princess, as she laid her down again.

'And *you* won't say I'm ugly, any more—will you, princess?'

'Nursie! I never said you were ugly. What can you mean?'

'Well, if you didn't say it, you meant it.'

'Indeed, I never did.'

'You said I wasn't so pretty as that——'

'As my beautiful grandmother—yes, I did say that; and I say it again, for it's quite true.'

'Then I *do* think you *are* unkind!' said the nurse, and put her handkerchief to her eyes again.

'Nursie, dear, everybody can't be as beautiful as every other body, you know. You are *very* nice looking, but if you had been as beautiful as my grandmother——'

'Bother your grandmother!' said the nurse.

'Nurse, that's very rude.* You are not fit to be spoken to—till you can behave better.'

The princess turned away once more, and again the nurse was ashamed of herself.

'I'm sure I beg your pardon, princess,' she said, though still in an offended tone. But the princess let the tone pass, and heeded only the words.

'You won't say it again, I am sure,' she answered, once more turning towards her nurse. I was only going to say that if you had been twice as nice looking as you are, some king or other would have married you, and then what would have become of me?'

'You are an angel!' repeated the nurse, again embracing her.

'Now,' insisted Irene, 'you *will* come and see my grand-mother—won't you?'

'I will go with you anywhere you like, my cherub,' she answered; and in two minutes the weary little princess was fast asleep.

V

The Princess Lets Well Alone

When she woke the next morning, the first thing she heard was the rain still falling. Indeed, this day was so like the last, that it would have been difficult to tell where was the use of it. The first thing she thought of, however, was not the rain, but the lady in the tower; and the first question that occupied her thoughts was whether she should not ask the nurse to fulfil her promise this very morning, and go with her to find her grandmother as soon as she had had her breakfast. But she came to the conclusion that perhaps the lady would not be pleased if she took anyone to see her without first asking leave; especially as it was pretty evident, seeing she lived on pigeons' eggs, and cooked them herself, that she did not want the household to know she was there. So the princess resolved to take the first opportunity of running up alone and asking whether she might bring her nurse. She believed the fact that she could not otherwise convince her she was telling the truth, would have much weight with her grandmother.

The princess and her nurse were the best of friends all dressing time, and the princess in consequence ate an enormous little breakfast.

'I wonder, Lootie'—that was her pet-name for her nurse—'What pigeons' eggs taste like?' she said, as she was eating her egg—not quite a common one, for they always picked out the pinky ones for her.

'We'll get you a pigeon's egg, and you shall judge for yourself,' said the nurse.

'Oh, no, no!' returned Irene, suddenly reflecting they might disturb the old lady in getting it, and that even if they did not, she would have one less in consequence.

'What a strange creature you are,' said the nurse— 'first to want a thing and then to refuse it!'

But she did not say it crossly, and the princess never minded any remarks that were not unfriendly.

'Well, you see, Lootie, there are reasons,' she returned, and said no more, for she did not want to bring up the subject of their former strife, lest her nurse should offer to go before she had had her grandmother's permission to bring her. Of course she could refuse to take her, but then she would believe her less than ever.

Now the nurse, as she said herself afterwards, could not be every moment in the room, and as never before yesterday had the princess given her the smallest reason for anxiety, it had not yet come into her head to watch her more closely. So she soon gave her a chance, and, the very first that offered, Irene was off and up the stairs again.

This day's adventure, however, did not turn out like yesterday's, although it began like it; and indeed today is very seldom like yesterday, if people would note the differences—even when it rains. The princess ran through passage after passage, and could not find the stair of the tower. My own suspicion is that she had not gone up high enough, and was searching on the second instead of the third floor. When she turned to go back, she failed equally in her search after the stair. She was lost once more.

Something made it even worse to bear this time, and it was no wonder that she cried again. Suddenly it occurred to her that it was after having cried before that she had found her grandmother's stair. She got up at once, wiped her eyes, and started upon a fresh quest. This time, although she did not find what she hoped, she found what was next best: she did not come on a stair that went up, but she came upon one that went down. It was evidently not the stair she had come up, yet it was a good deal better than none; so down she went, and was singing merrily before she reached the bottom. There, to her surprise, she found herself in the kitchen. Although she was not allowed to go there alone, her nurse had often taken her, and she was a great favourite with the servants. So there was a general rush at her the moment she appeared, for every one wanted to have her; and the report of where she was soon reached the nurse's ears. She came at once to fetch her; but she never suspected how she had got there, and the princess kept her own counsel.

Her failure to find the old lady not only disappointed her, but made her very thoughtful. Sometimes she came almost to the nurse's opinion that she had dreamed all about her; but that fancy* never lasted very long. She wondered much whether she should ever see her again, and thought it very sad not to have been able to find her when she particularly wanted her. She resolved to say nothing more to her nurse on the subject, seeing it was so little in her power to prove her words.

VI

The Little Miner

The next day the great cloud still hung over the mountain, and the rain poured like water from a full sponge. The princess was very fond of being out of doors, and she nearly cried when she saw that the weather was no better. But the mist was not of such a dark dingy grey; there was light in it; and as the hours went on, it grew brighter and brighter, until it was almost too brilliant to look at; and late in the afternoon, the sun broke out so gloriously that Irene clapped her hands, crying,

'See, see, Lootie! The sun has had his face washed. Look how bright he is! Do get my hat, and let us go out for a walk. Oh dear! oh dear! how happy I am!'

Lootie was very glad to please the princess. She got her hat and cloak, and they set out together for a walk up the mountain; for the road was so hard and steep that the water could not rest upon it, and it was always dry enough for walking a few minutes after the rain ceased. The clouds were rolling away in broken pieces, like great, over-woolly sheep, whose wool the sun had bleached till it was almost too white for the eyes to bear. Between them the sky shone with a deeper and purer blue, because of the rain. The trees on the roadside were hung all over with drops, which sparkled in the sun like jewels. The only things that were no brighter for the rain, were the brooks that ran down the mountain; they had changed from the clearness of crystal to a muddy brown; but what they lost in colour they gained in sound—or at least in noise, for a brook when it is swollen is not so musical as before. But Irene was in raptures with the great brown streams tumbling down everywhere; and Lootie shared in her delight, for she too had been confined to the house for three days. At length she observed that the sun was getting low, and said it was time to be going back. She made the remark again and again, but, every time, the princess begged her to go on just a little farther and a little farther; reminding her that it was much easier to go downhill, and saying that when they did turn, they would be at home in a moment. So on and on they did go, now to look at a group of ferns over whose tops a stream was pouring in a watery arch, now to pick a shining stone from a rock by the wayside, now to watch the flight of some bird. Suddenly the shadow of a great mountain peak came up from behind, and shot in front of them.* When the nurse saw it, she started and shook, and catching hold of the princess's hand turned and began to run down the hill.

'What's all the haste, nursie?' asked Irene, running along-side of her.

'We must not be out a moment longer.'

'But we can't help being out a good many moments longer.'

It was too true. The nurse almost cried. They were much too far from home. It was against express orders to be out with the princess one moment after the sun was down; and they were nearly a mile up the mountain! If his majesty, Irene's papa, were to hear of it, Lootie would certainly be dismissed; and to leave the princess would break her heart. It was no wonder she ran. But Irene was not in the least frightened, not knowing anything to be frightened at. She kept on chattering as well as she could, but it was not easy.

'Lootie! Lootie! why do you run so fast? It shakes my teeth when I talk.'

'Then don't talk,' said Lootie.

But the princess went on talking. She was always saying, 'Look, look, Lootie!' but Lootie paid no more heed to any-thing she said, only ran on.

'Look, look, Lootie! Don't you see that funny man peeping over the rock?'

Lootie only ran the faster. They had to pass the rock, and when they came nearer, the princess saw it was only a lump of the rock itself that she had taken for a man.

'Look, look, Lootie! There's *such* a curious creature at the foot of that old tree. Look at it, Lootie! It's making faces at us, I do think.'

Lootie gave a stifled cry, and ran faster still—so fast, that Irene's little legs could not keep up with her, and she fell with a clash. It was a hard downhill road, and she had been running very fast—so it was no wonder she began to cry. This put the nurse nearly beside herself; but all she could do was to run on, the moment she got the princess on her feet again.

'Who's that laughing at me?' said the princess, trying to keep in her sobs, and running too fast for her grazed knees.

'Nobody, child,' said the nurse, almost angrily.

But that instant there came a burst of coarse tittering from somewhere near, and a hoarse indistinct voice that seemed to say, 'Lies! lies! lies!'

'Oh!' cried the nurse with a sigh that was almost a scream, and ran on faster than ever.

'Nursie! Lootie! I can't run any more. Do let us walk a bit.'

'What *am* I to do?' said the nurse. 'Here, I will carry you.'

She caught her up; but found her much too heavy to run with, and had to set her down again. Then she looked wildly about her, gave a great cry, and said—

'We've taken the wrong turning somewhere, and I don't know where we are. We are lost, lost!'

The terror she was in had quite bewildered her. It was true enough they had lost the way. They had been running down into a little valley in which there was no house to be seen.

Now Irene did not know what good reason there was for her nurse's terror, for the servants had all strict orders never to mention the goblins to her, but it was very discomposing to see her nurse in such a fright. Before, however, she had time

to grow thoroughly alarmed like her, she heard the sound
of whistling, and that revived her. Presently she saw a boy
coming up the road from the valley to meet them. He was
the whistler; but before they met, his whistling changed to
singing. And this is something like what he sang.*

> 'Ring! dod! bang!
> Go the hammers' clang!
> Hit and turn and bore!
> Whizz and puff and roar!
> Thus we rive the rocks,
> Force the goblin locks.
> See the shining ore!
> One, two, three—
> Bright as gold can be!
> Four, five, six—
> Shovels, mattocks, picks!
> Seven, eight, nine—
> Light your lamp at mine.
> Ten, eleven, twelve—
> Loosely hold the helve.
> We're the merry miner-boys,
> Make the goblins hold their noise.'

'I wish you would hold *your* noise,' said the nurse rudely,
for the very word goblin at such a time and in such a place
made her tremble. It would bring the goblins upon them to a
certainty, she thought, to defy them in that way. But whether
the boy heard her or not, he did not stop his singing.

> 'Thirteen, fourteen, fifteen—
> This is worth the siftin';
> Sixteen, seventeen, eighteen—
> There's the match, and lay't in.
> Nineteen, twenty—
> Goblins in a plenty.'

'Do be quiet,' cried the nurse, in a whispered shriek.* But
the boy, who was now close at hand, still went on.

> 'Hush! scush! scurry!
> There you go in a hurry!

> Gobble! gobble! goblin!
> 'There you go a wobblin';
> Hobble, hobble, hobblin'!
> Cobble! cobble! cobblin!
> Hob-hob-goblin!—Huuuuuh!'

'There!' said the boy, as he stood still opposite them. 'There! that'll do for them. They can't bear singing, and they can't stand that song. They can't sing themselves, for they have no more voice than a crow; and they don't like other people to sing.'

The boy was dressed in a miner's dress, with a curious cap on his head. He was a very nice-looking boy, with eyes as dark as the mines* in which he worked, and as sparkling as the crystals in their rocks. He was about twelve years old. His face was almost too pale for beauty, which came of his being so little in the open air and the sunlight—for even vegetables grown in the dark are white; but he looked happy, merry indeed—perhaps at the thought of having routed the goblins; and his bearing as he stood before them had nothing clownish or rude about it.

'I saw them,' he went on, 'as I came up; and I'm very glad I did. I knew they were after somebody, but I couldn't see who it was. They won't touch you so long as I'm with you.'

'Why, who are you?' asked the nurse, offended at the freedom with which he spoke to them.

'I'm Peter's son.'*

'Who's Peter?'

'Peter the miner.'

'I don't know him.'

'I'm his son though.'

'And why should the goblins mind *you*, pray?'

'Because I don't mind* them. I'm used to them.'

'What difference does that make?'

'If you're not afraid of them, they're afraid of you. I'm not afraid of them. That's all. But it's all that's wanted—up here, that is. It's a different thing down there. They won't always mind that song even, down there. And if any one sings it, they stand grinning at him awfully; and if he gets frightened, and misses a word, or says a wrong one,* they—oh! don't they give it him!'

'What do they do to him?' asked Irene, with a trembling voice.

'Don't go frightening the princess,' said the nurse.

'The princess!' repeated the little miner, taking off his curious cap. 'I beg your pardon; but you oughtn't to be out so late. Everybody knows that's against the law.'

'Yes, indeed it is!' said the nurse, beginning to cry again. 'And I shall have to suffer for it.'

'What does that matter?' said the boy. 'It must be your fault. It is the princess who will suffer for it. I hope they didn't hear you call her the princess. If they did, they're sure to know her again: they're awfully sharp.'

'Lootie! Lootie!' cried the princess. 'Take me home.'

'Don't go on like that,' said the nurse to the boy, almost fiercely. 'How could I help it? I lost my way.'

'You shouldn't have been out so late. You wouldn't have lost your way if you hadn't been frightened,' said the boy. 'Come along. I'll soon set you right again. Shall I carry your little highness?'

'Impertinence!' murmured the nurse, but she did not say it aloud, for she thought if she made him angry, he might take his revenge by telling some one belonging to the house, and then it would be sure to come to the king's ears.

'No, thank you,' said Irene. 'I can walk very well, though I can't run so fast as nursie. If you will give me one hand, Lootie will give me another, and then I shall get on famously.'

They soon had her between them, holding a hand of each.

'Now let's run,' said the nurse.

'No, no,' said the little miner. 'That's the worst thing you can do. If you hadn't run before, you would not have lost your way. And if you run now, they will be after you in a moment.'

'I don't want to run,' said Irene.

'You don't think of *me*,' said the nurse.

'Yes, I do, Lootie. The boy says they won't touch us if we don't run.'

'Yes, but if they know at the house that I've kept you out so late, I shall be turned away, and that would break my heart.'

'Turned away, Lootie! Who would turn you away?'

'Your papa, child.'

'But I'll tell him it was all my fault. And you know it was, Lootie.'

'He won't mind that. I'm sure he won't.'

'Then I'll cry, and go down on my knees to him, and beg him not to take away my own dear Lootie.'

The nurse was comforted at hearing this, and said no more. They went on, walking pretty fast, but taking care not to run a step.

'I want to talk to you,' said Irene to the little miner; 'but it's so awkward! I don't know your name.'

'My name's Curdie, little princess.'

'What a funny name! Curdie! What more?'

'Curdie Peterson. What's your name, please?'

'Irene.'

'What more?'

'I don't know what more.—What more is my name, Lootie?'

'Princesses haven't got more than one name. They don't want it.'

'Oh then, Curdie, you must call me just Irene and no more.'

'No, indeed,' said the nurse indignantly. 'He shall do no such thing.'

'What shall he call me, then, Lootie?'

'Your royal Highness.'

'My royal Highness! What's that? No, no, Lootie. I won't be called names. I don't like them. You told me once yourself it's only rude children that call names; and I'm sure Curdie wouldn't be rude.—Curdie, my name's Irene.'

'Well, Irene,' said Curdie, with a glance at the nurse which showed he enjoyed teasing her, 'it is very kind of you to let me call you anything. I like your name very much.'

He expected the nurse to interfere again; but he soon saw that she was too frightened to speak. She was staring at something a few yards before them, in the middle of the path, where it narrowed between rocks so that only one could pass at a time.

'It is very much kinder of you to go out of your way to take us home,' said Irene.

'I'm not going out of my way yet,' said Curdie. 'It's on the other side those rocks the path turns off to my father's.'

'You wouldn't think of leaving us till we're safe home, I'm sure,' gasped the nurse.

'Of course not,' said Curdie.

'You dear, good, kind Curdie! I'll give you a kiss when we get home,' said the princess.

The nurse gave her a great pull by the hand she held. But at that instant the something in the middle of the way, which had looked like a great lump of earth brought down by the rain, began to move. One after another it shot out four long things, like two arms and two legs, but it was now too dark to tell what they were. The nurse began to tremble from head to foot. Irene clasped Curdie's hand yet faster, and Curdie began to sing again.

> 'One, two—
> Hit and hew!
> Three, four—
> Blast and bore!

> Five, six—
> There's a fix!
> Seven, eight—
> Hold it straight.
> Nine, ten—
> Hit again!
> Hurry! scurry!
> Bother! smother!
> There's a toad
> In the road!
> Smash it!
> Squash it!
> Fry it!
> Dry it!
> You're another!
> Up and off!
> There's enough!—Huuuuh!'

As he uttered the last words, Curdie let go his hold of his companion, and rushed at the thing in the road, as if he would trample it under his feet. It gave a great spring, and ran straight up one of the rocks like a huge spider. Curdie turned back laughing, and took Irene's hand again. She grasped his very tight, but said nothing till they had passed the rocks. A few yards more and she found herself on a part of the road she knew, and was able to speak again.

'Do you know, Curdie, I don't quite like your song: it sounds to me rather rude,' she said.

'Well, perhaps it is,' answered Curdie. 'I never thought of that; it's a way we have. We do it because they don't like it.'

'Who don't like it?'

'The cobs,* as we call them.'

'Don't!' said the nurse.

'Why not?' said Curdie.

'I beg you won't. Please don't.'

'Oh! if you ask me that way, of course I won't; though I don't a bit know why.—Look! there are the lights of your great house down below. You'll be at home in five minutes now.'

Nothing more happened. They reached home in safety. Nobody had missed them, or even known they had gone out; and they arrived at the door belonging to their part of the house without any one seeing them. The nurse was rushing in with a hurried and not over-gracious goodnight to Curdie; but the princess pulled her hand from hers, and was just throwing her arms round Curdie's neck, when she caught her again and dragged her away.

'Lootie! Lootie! I promised Curdie a kiss,' cried Irene.

'A princess mustn't give kisses. It's not at all proper,' said Lootie.

'But I promised,' said the princess.

'There's no occasion; he's only a miner-boy.'

'He's a good boy, and a brave boy, and he has been very kind to us. Lootie! Lootie! I *promised*.'

'Then you shouldn't have promised.'

'Lootie, I promised him a kiss.'

'Your royal Highness,' said Lootie, suddenly grown very respectful, 'must come in directly.'

'Nurse, a princess must *not* break her word,' said Irene, drawing herself up and standing stock-still.

Lootie did not know which the king might count the worst—to let the princess be out after sunset, or to let her kiss a miner-boy. She did not know that, being a gentleman, as many kings have been, he would have counted neither of them the worse. However much he might have disliked his daughter to kiss the miner-boy, he would not have had her break her word for all the goblins in creation. But, as I say, the nurse was not lady enough to understand this, and so she was in a great difficulty, for, if she insisted, some one might hear the princess cry and run to see, and then all would come out. But here Curdie came again to the rescue.

'Never mind, Princess Irene,' he said. 'You mustn't kiss me tonight. But you sha'n't break your word. I will come another time. You may be sure I will.'

'Oh, thank you, Curdie!' said the princess, and stopped crying.

'Good night, Irene; good night, Lootie,' said Curdie, and turned and was out of sight in a moment.

'I should like to see him!' muttered the nurse, as she carried the princess to the nursery.

'You *will* see him,' said Irene. 'You may be sure Curdie will keep his word. He's *sure* to come again.'

'I should like to see him!' repeated the nurse, and said no more. She did not want to open a new cause of strife with the princess by saying more plainly what she meant. Glad enough that she had succeeded both in getting home unseen, and in keeping the princess from kissing the miner's boy, she resolved to watch her far better in future. Her carelessness had already doubled the danger she was in. Formerly the goblins were her only fear: now she had to protect her charge from Curdie as well.

VII

The Mines

Curdie went home whistling. He resolved to say nothing about the princess for fear of getting the nurse into trouble, for while he enjoyed teasing her because of her absurdity, he was careful not to do her any harm. He saw no more of the goblins, and was soon fast asleep in his bed.

He woke in the middle of the night, and thought he heard curious noises outside. He sat up and listened; then got up, and, opening the door very quietly, went out. When he peeped round the corner, he saw, under his own window, a group of stumpy creatures, whom he at once recognized by their shape. Hardly, however, had he begun his 'One, two, three!' when they broke asunder, scurried away, and were out of sight. He returned laughing, got into bed again, and was fast asleep in a moment.

Reflecting a little over the matter in the morning, he came to the conclusion that, as nothing of the kind had ever happened before, they must be annoyed with him for interfering to protect the princess. By the time he was dressed, however, he was thinking of something quite different, for he did not value the enmity of the goblins in the least.

As soon as they had had breakfast, he set off with his father for the mine.

They entered the hill by a natural opening under a huge rock, where a little stream rushed out. They followed its course for a few yards, when the passage took a turn, and sloped steeply into the heart of the hill. With many angles and windings and branchings off, and sometimes with steps where it came upon a natural gulf, it led them deep into the hill before they arrived at the place where they were at present digging out the precious ore. This was of various kinds, for the mountain was very rich in the better sorts of metals. With flint and steel, and tinder-box, they lighted their lamps, then fixed them on their heads, and were soon hard at work with their pickaxes and shovels and hammers. Father and son were at work near each other, but not in the same *gang*—the passages out of which the ore was dug, they called *gangs*—for when the *lode*, or vein of ore, was small, one miner would have to dig away alone in a passage no bigger than gave him just room to work—sometimes in uncomfortable cramped positions. If they stopped for a moment they could hear everywhere around them, some nearer, some farther off, the sounds of their companions burrowing away in all directions in the inside of the great mountain—some boring holes in the rock in order to blow it up with gunpowder, others shovelling the broken ore into baskets to be carried to the mouth of the mine, others hitting away with their pickaxes. Sometimes, if the miner was in a very lonely part, he would hear only a tap-tapping, no louder than that of a woodpecker, for the sound would come from a great distance off through the solid mountain rock.

The work was hard at best, for it is very warm underground; but it was not particularly unpleasant, and some of the miners, when they wanted to earn a little more money for a particular purpose, would stop behind the rest, and work all night. But you could not tell night from day down there, except from feeling tired and sleepy; for no light of the sun ever came into those gloomy regions. Some who had thus remained behind during the night, although certain there were none of their companions at work, would declare the next morning that they heard, every time they halted for a moment to take breath, a tap-tapping all about them, as if the mountain were then more full of miners than ever it was during the day; and some in consequence would never stay over night, for all knew those were the sounds of the goblins. They worked only at night, for the miners' night was the goblins' day.* Indeed, the greater number of the miners were afraid of the goblins; for there were strange stories well known amongst them of the treatment some had received whom the goblins had surprised at their work during the night. The more courageous of them, however, amongst them Peter Peterson and Curdie, who in this took after his father, had stayed in the mine all night again and again, and although they had several times encountered a few stray goblins, had never yet failed in driving them away. As I have indicated already, the chief defence against them was verse, for they hated verse of every kind, and some kinds they could not endure at all. I suspect they could not make any themselves, and that was why they disliked it so much. At all events, those who were most afraid of them were those who could neither make verses themselves, nor remember the verses that other people made for them; while those who were never afraid were those who could make verses for themselves; for although there were certain old rhymes which were very effectual, yet it was well known that a new rhyme, if of the right sort, was even more distasteful to them, and therefore more effectual in putting them to flight.

Perhaps my readers may be wondering what the goblins could be about, working all night long, seeing they never carried up the ore and sold it; but when I have informed them concerning what Curdie learned the very next night, they will be able to understand.

For Curdie had determined, if his father would permit him, to remain there alone this night—and that for two reasons: first, he wanted to get extra wages that he might buy a very warm red petticoat for his mother, who had begun to complain of the cold of the mountain air sooner than usual this autumn; and second, he had just a faint hope of finding out what the goblins were about under his window the night before.

When he told his father, he made no objection, for he had great confidence in his boy's courage and resources.

'I'm sorry I can't stay with you,' said Peter; 'but I want to go and pay the parson a visit this evening, and besides I've had a bit of a headache all day.'

'I'm sorry for that, father,' said Curdie.

'Oh! it's not much. You'll be sure to take care of yourself, won't you?'

'Yes, father; I will. I'll keep a sharp look out, I promise you.'

Curdie was the only one who remained in the mine. About six o'clock the rest went away, every one bidding him good night, and telling him to take care of himself; for he was a great favourite with them all.

'Don't forget your rhymes,' said one.

'No, no,' answered Curdie.

'It's no matter if he does,' said another, 'for he'll only have to make a new one.'

'Yes; but he mightn't be able to make it fast enough,' said another; 'and while it was cooking in his head, they might take a mean advantage and set upon him.'

'I'll do my best,' said Curdie. 'I'm not afraid.'

'We all know that,' they returned, and left him.

VIII
The Goblins

For some time Curdie worked away briskly, throwing all the ore he had disengaged on one side behind him, to be ready for carrying out in the morning. He heard a good deal of goblin-tapping, but it all sounded far away in the hill, and he paid it little heed. Towards midnight he began to feel rather hungry; so he dropped his pickaxe, got out a lump of bread which in the morning he had laid in a damp hole in the rock, sat down on a heap of ore, and ate his supper. Then he leaned back for five minutes' rest before beginning his work again, and laid his head against the rock. He had not kept the position for one minute before he heard something which made him sharpen his ears. It sounded like a voice inside the rock. After a while he heard it again. It was a goblin-voice—there could be no doubt about that—and this time he could make out the words.

'Hadn't we better be moving?' it said.

A rougher and deeper voice replied—

'There's no hurry. That wretched little mole won't be through tonight, if he work ever so hard. He's not by any means at the thinnest place.'

'But you still think the lode does come through into our house?' said the first voice.

'Yes, but a good bit farther on than he has got to yet. If he had struck a stroke more to the side just here,' said the goblin, tapping the very stone, as it seemed to Curdie, against which his head lay, 'he would have been through; but he's a couple of yards past it now, and if he follows the lode it will be a week before it leads him in. You see it back there—a long way. Still, perhaps, in case of accident, it would be as well to be getting out of this.

Helfer, you'll take the great chest. That's your business, you know.'

'Yes, dad,' said a third voice. 'But you must help me to get it on my back. It's awfully heavy, you know.'

'Well, it isn't just a bag of smoke, I admit. But you're as strong as a mountain, Helfer.'

'You say so, dad. I think myself I'm all right. But I could carry ten times as much if it wasn't for my feet.'

'That *is* your weak point, I confess, my boy.'

'Ain't it yours too, father?'

'Well, to be honest, it is a goblin-weakness. Why *they* come so soft,* I declare I haven't an idea.'

'Specially when your head's so hard, you know, father.'

'Yes, my boy. The goblin's glory is his head. To think how the fellows up above there have to put on helmets and things when they go fighting! Ha! ha!'

'But why don't we wear shoes like them, father? I should like it—specially when I've got a chest like that on my head.'

'Well, you see, it's not the fashion. The king never wears shoes.'

'The queen does.'

'Yes; but that's for distinction. The first queen, you see—I mean the king's first wife—wore shoes of course, because she came from upstairs; and so, when she died, the next queen would not be inferior to her as she called it, and would wear shoes too. It was all pride. She is the hardest in forbidding them to the rest of the women.'

'I'm sure I wouldn't wear them—no, not for—that I wouldn't!' said the first voice, which was evidently that of the mother of the family. 'I can't think why either of them should.'

'Didn't I tell you the first was from upstairs?' said the other. 'That was the only silly* thing I ever knew his majesty guilty of. Why should he marry an outlandish* woman like that—one of our natural enemies too?'

'I suppose he fell in love with her.'

'Pooh! pooh! He's just as happy now with one of his own people.'

'Did she die *very* soon? They didn't tease her to death, did they?'

'Oh dear no! The king worshipped her very footmarks.'

'What made her die, then? Didn't the air agree with her?'

'She died when the young prince was born.'

'How silly of her! *We* never do that. It must have been because she wore shoes.'

'I don't know that.'

'Why do they wear shoes up there?'

'Ah! now that's a sensible question, and I will answer it. But in order to do so, I must first tell you a secret. I once saw the queen's feet.'

'Without her shoes?'

'Yes—without her shoes.'

'No! Did you? How was it?'

'Never you mind how it was. *She* didn't know I saw them. And what do you think!—they had *toes*!'

'Toes! What's that?'

'You may well ask! I should never have known if I had not seen the queen's feet. Just imagine! the ends of her feet were split up into five or six thin pieces!'

'Oh, horrid! How *could* the king have fallen in love with her?'

'You forget that she wore shoes. That is just why she wore them. That is why all the men, and women too, upstairs wear shoes. They can't bear the sight of their own feet without them.'

'Ah! now I understand. If ever you wish for shoes again, Helfer, I'll hit your feet—I will.'

'No, no, mother; pray don't.'

'Then don't you.'

'But with such a big box on my head—'

A horrid scream followed, which Curdie interpreted as in reply to a blow from his mother upon the feet of her eldest goblin.

'Well, I never knew so much before!' remarked a fourth voice.

'Your knowledge is not universal quite yet,' said the father. 'You were only fifty last month. Mind you see to the bed and bedding. As soon as we've finished our supper, we'll be up and going. Ha! ha! ha!'

'What are you laughing at, husband?'

'I'm laughing to think what a mess the miners will find themselves in—somewhere before this day ten years.'

'Why, what do you mean?'

'Oh, nothing.'

'Oh yes, you do mean something. You always do mean something.'

'It's more than you do, then, wife.'

'That may be; but it's not more than I find out, you know.'

'Ha! ha! You're a sharp one. What a mother you've got, Helfer!'

'Yes, father.'

'Well, I suppose I must tell you. They're all at the palace consulting about it tonight; and as soon as we've got away from this thin place, I'm going there to hear what night they fix upon. I should like to see that young ruffian there on the other side, struggling in the agonies of—'

He dropped his voice so low that Curdie could hear only a growl. The growl went on in the low bass for a good while, as inarticulate as if the goblin's tongue had been a sausage; and it was not until his wife spoke again that it rose to its former pitch.

'But what shall we do when you are at the palace?' she asked.

'I will see you safe in the new house I've been digging for you for the last two months. Podge, you mind the table and chairs. I commit them to your care. The table has seven legs—each chair three. I shall require them all at your hands.'

After this arose a confused conversation about the various household goods and their transport; and Curdie heard nothing more that was of any importance.

He now knew at least one of the reasons for the constant sound of the goblin hammers and pickaxes at night. They were making new houses for themselves, to which they might retreat when the miners should threaten to break into their dwellings. But he had learned two things of far greater importance. The first was, that some grievous calamity was preparing, and almost ready to fall upon the heads of the miners; the second was—the one weak point of a goblin's body: he had not known that their feet were so tender as he had now reason to suspect. He had heard it said that they had no toes: he had never had opportunity of inspecting them closely enough in the dusk in which they always appeared, to satisfy himself whether it was a correct report. Indeed, he had not been able even to satisfy himself as to whether they had no fingers, although that also was commonly said to be the fact. One of the miners, indeed, who had had more schooling than the rest,* was wont to argue that such must have been the primordial condition of humanity, and that education and handicraft had developed both toes and fingers—with which proposition Curdie had once heard his father sarcastically agree, alleging in support of it the probability that babies' gloves were a traditional remnant of the old state of things; while the stockings of all ages, no regard being paid in them to the toes, pointed in the same direction. But what was of importance was the fact concerning the softness of the goblin-feet, which he foresaw might be useful to all miners. What he had to do in the mean time, however, was to discover, if possible, the special evil design the goblins had now in their heads.

Although he knew all the gangs and all the natural galleries with which they communicated in the mined part of the mountain, he had not the least idea where the palace of the king of the gnomes was; otherwise he would have set out at once on the enterprise of discovering what the said design was. He judged, and rightly, that it must lie in a farther part of the mountain, between which and the mine there was as yet no communication. There must be one nearly completed, however; for it could be but a thin partition which now separated them. If only he could get through in time to follow the goblins as they retreated! A few blows would doubtless be sufficient—just where his ear now lay; but if he attempted to strike there with his pickaxe, he would only hasten the departure of the family, put them on their guard, and perhaps lose their involuntary guidance. He therefore began to feel the wall with his hands, and soon found that some of the stones were loose enough to be drawn out with little noise.

Laying hold of a large one with both his hands, he drew it gently out, and let it down softly.

'What was that noise?' said the goblin-father.

Curdie blew out his light, lest it should shine through.

'It must be that one miner that stayed behind the rest,' said the mother.

'No; he's been gone a good while. I haven't heard a blow for an hour. Besides, it wasn't like that.'

'Then I suppose it must have been a stone carried down the brook inside.'

'Perhaps. It will have more room by and by.'

Curdie kept quite still. After a little while, hearing nothing but the sounds of their preparations for departure, mingled with an occasional word of direction, and anxious to know whether the removal of the stone had made an opening into the goblins' house, he put in his hand to feel. It went in a good way, and then came in contact with something soft. He had but a moment to feel it over, it was so quickly withdrawn: it was one of the toeless goblin-feet. The owner of it gave a cry of fright.

'What's the matter, Helfer?' asked his mother.

'A beast came out of the wall and licked my foot.'

'Nonsense! There are no wild beasts in our country,' said his father.

'But it was, father. I felt it.'

'Nonsense, I say. Will you malign your native realms and reduce them to a level with the country upstairs? That is swarming with wild beasts of every description.'

'But I did feel it, father.'

'I tell you to hold your tongue. You are no patriot.'

Curdie suppressed his laughter, and lay still as a mouse—but no stiller, for every moment he kept nibbling away with his fingers at the edges of the hole. He was slowly making it bigger, for here the rock had been very much shattered with the blasting.

There seemed to be a good many in the family, to judge from the mass of confused talk which now and then came through the hole; but when all were speaking together, and just as if they had bottle-brushes—each at least one—in their throats, it was not easy to make out much that was said. At length he heard once more what the father-goblin was saying.

'Now then,' he said, 'get your bundles on your backs. Here, Helfer, I'll help you up with your chest.'

'I wish it *was* my chest, father.'

'Your turn will come in good time enough! Make haste. I *must* go to the meeting at the palace to-night. When that's over, we can come back and clear out the last of the things before our enemies return in the morning. Now light your torches, and come along. What a distinction it is to provide our own light, instead of being dependent on a thing hung up in the air—a most disagreeable contrivance—intended no doubt to blind us when we venture out under its baleful influence! Quite glaring and vulgar, I call it, though no doubt useful to poor creatures who haven't the wit to make light for themselves!'

Curdie could hardly keep himself from calling through to know whether they made the fire to light their torches by. But a moment's reflection showed him that they would have said they did, inasmuch as they struck two stones together, and the fire came.

IX

The Hall of the Goblin Palace

A sound of many soft feet followed, but soon ceased. Then Curdie flew at the hole like a tiger, and tore and pulled. The sides gave way, and it was soon large enough for him to crawl through. He would not betray himself by rekindling his lamp, but the torches of the retreating company, which he found departing in a straight line up a long avenue from the door of their cave, threw back light enough to afford him a glance round the deserted home of the goblins. To his surprise, he could discover nothing to distinguish it from an ordinary natural cave in the rock, upon many of which he had come with the rest of the miners in the progress of their excavations. The goblins had talked of coming back for the rest of their household gear: he saw nothing that would have made him suspect a family had taken shelter there of a single night. The floor was rough and stony; the walls full of projecting corners; the roof in one place twenty feet high, in another endangering his forehead; while on one side a stream, no thicker than a needle, it is true, but still sufficient to spread a wide dampness over the wall, flowed down the face of the rock. But the troop in front of him was toiling under heavy burthens. He could distinguish Helfer now and then, in the flickering light and shade, with his heavy chest on his bending shoulders; while the second brother was almost buried in what looked like a great feather-bed.

'Where do they get the feathers?' thought Curdie; but in a moment the troop disappeared at a turn of the way, and it was now both safe and necessary for Curdie to follow them, lest they should be round the next turning before he saw them again, for so he might lose them altogether. He darted after them like a greyhound. When he reached the corner and looked cautiously round, he saw them again at some distance down another long passage. None of the galleries he saw that night bore signs of the work of man—or of goblin either. Stalactites far older than the mines, hung from their roofs; and their floors were rough with boulders and large round stones, showing that there water must have once run. He waited again at this corner till they had disappeared round the next, and so followed them a long way through one passage after another. The passages grew more and more lofty, and were more and more covered in the roof with shining stalactites.

It was a strange enough procession which he followed. But the strangest part of it was the household animals which crowded amongst the feet of the goblins. It was true they had no wild animals down there—at least they did not know of any; but they had a wonderful number of tame ones. I must, however, reserve any contributions towards the natural history of these for a later position in my story.

At length, turning a corner too abruptly, he had almost rushed into the middle of the goblin family; for there they had already set down all their burthens on the floor of a cave considerably larger than that which they had left. They were as yet too breathless to speak, else he would have had warning of their arrest. He started back, however, before any one saw him, and retreating a good way, stood watching till the father should come out to go to the palace. Before very long, both he and his son Helfer appeared and kept on in the same direction as before, while Curdie followed them again with renewed precaution. For a long time he heard no sound except something like the rush of a river inside the rock; but at length what seemed the far-off noise of a great shouting reached his ears, which however presently ceased. After advancing a good way farther, he thought he heard a single voice. It sounded clearer and clearer as he went on, until at last he could almost distinguish the words. In a moment or two, keeping after the goblins round another corner, he once more started back—this time in amazement.

He was at the entrance of a magnificent cavern, of an oval shape, once probably a huge natural reservoir of water, now the great palace hall of the goblins. It rose to a tremendous height, but the roof was composed of such shining materials, and the multitude of torches carried by the goblins who crowded the floor lighted up the place so brilliantly, that Curdie could see to the top quite well. But he had no idea how immense the place was, until his eyes had got accustomed to it, which was not for a good many minutes. The rough projections on the walls, and the shadows thrown upwards from them by the torches, made the sides of the chamber look as if they were crowded with statues upon brackets and pedestals, reaching in irregular tiers from floor to roof. The walls themselves were, in many parts, of gloriously shining substances, some of them gorgeously coloured besides, which powerfully contrasted with the shadows. Curdie could not help wondering whether his rhymes would be of any use against such a multitude of goblins as filled the floor of the hall and indeed felt considerably tempted to begin his shout of *One, two, three!* but as there was no reason for routing them, and much for endeavouring to discover their designs, he kept himself perfectly quiet, and peeping round the edge of the doorway, listened with both his sharp ears.

At the other end of the hall, high above the heads of the multitude, was a terrace-like ledge of considerable height, caused by the receding of the upper part of the cavern wall. Upon this sat the king and his court, the king on a throne hollowed out of a huge block of green copper ore, and his court upon lower seats around it. The king had been making them a speech, and the applause which followed it was what Curdie had heard. One of the court was now addressing the multitude. What he heard him say was to the following effect:

'Hence it appears that two plans have been for some time together working in the strong head of his majesty for the deliverance of his people. Regardless of the fact that we were the first possessors of the regions they now inhabit, regardless equally of the fact that we abandoned that region from the loftiest motives; regardless also of the self-evident fact that we excel them as far in mental ability as they excel us in stature, they look upon us as a degraded race, and make a mockery of all our finer feelings. But the time has almost arrived when—thanks to his majesty's inventive genius—it will be in our power to take a thorough revenge upon them once for all, in respect of their unfriendly behaviour.'*

'May it please your majesty—' cried a voice close by the door, which Curdie recognized as that of the goblin he had followed.

'Who is he that interrupts the Chancellor?' cried another from near the throne.

'Glump,' answered several voices.

'He is our trusty subject,' said the king himself, in a slow and stately voice: 'let him come forward and speak.'

A lane was parted through the crowd, and Glump having ascended the platform and bowed to the king, spoke as follows:—

'Sire, I would have held my peace, had I not known that I only knew how near was the moment to which the Chancellor had just referred. In all probability, before another day is past, the enemy will have broken through into my house—the partition between being even now not more than a foot in thickness.'

'Not quite so much,' thought Curdie to himself.

'This very evening I have had to remove my household effects; therefore the sooner we are ready to carry out the plan, for the execution of which his majesty has been making such magnificent preparations, the better. I may just add, that within the last few days I have perceived a small outbreak in my dining-room, which, combined with observations upon the course of the river escaping where the evil men enter, has convinced me that close to the spot must lie a deep gulf in its channel. This discovery will, I trust, add considerably to the otherwise immense forces at his majesty's disposal.'

He ceased, and the king graciously acknowledged his speech with a bend of his head; whereupon Glump, after a bow to his majesty, slid down amongst the rest of the undistinguished multitude. Then the Chancellor rose and resumed.

'The information which the worthy Glump has given us,' he said, 'might have been of considerable import at the present moment, but for that other design already referred to, which naturally takes precedence. His majesty, unwilling to proceed to extremities, and well aware that such measures sooner or later result in violent reactions, has excogitated* a more fundamental and comprehensive measure, of which I need say no more. Should his majesty be successful—as who dares to doubt?—then a peace, all to the advantage of the goblin kingdom, will be established for a generation at least, rendered absolutely secure by the pledge which his royal highness the prince will have and hold for the good behaviour of her relatives. Should his majesty fail—which who shall dare even to imagine in his most secret thoughts?—then will be the time for carrying out with rigour the design to which Glump referred, and for which our preparations are even now all but completed. The failure of the former will render the latter imperative.'

Curdie perceiving that the assembly was drawing to a close, and that there was little chance of either plan being more fully discovered, now thought it prudent to make his escape before the goblins began to disperse, and slipped quietly away.

There was not much danger of meeting any goblins, for all the men at least were left behind him in the palace; but there was considerable danger of his taking a wrong turning, for he had now no light, and had therefore to depend upon his memory and his hands. After he had left behind him the glow that issued from the door of Glump's new abode, he was utterly without guide, so far as his eyes were concerned.

He was most anxious to get back through the hole before the goblins should return to fetch the remains of their furniture. It was not that he was in the least afraid of them, but, as it was of the utmost importance that he should thoroughly discover what the plans they were cherishing were, he must not occasion the slightest suspicion that they were watched by a miner.

He hurried on, feeling his way along the walls of rock. Had he not been very courageous, he must have been very anxious, for he could not but know that if he lost his way it would be the most difficult thing in the world to find it again. Morning would bring no light into these regions; and towards him least of all, who was known as a special rhymster and persecutor, could goblins be expected to exercise courtesy. Well might he wish that he had brought his lamp and tinder-box with him, of which he had not thought when he crept so eagerly after the goblins! He wished it all the more when, after a while, he found his way blocked up, and could get no farther. It was of no use to turn back, for he had not the least idea where he had begun to go wrong. Mechanically, however, he kept feeling about the walls that hemmed him in. His hand came upon a place where a tiny stream of water was running down the face of the rock. 'What a stupid I am!' he said to himself. 'I am actually at the end of my journey!—And there are the goblins coming back to fetch their things!' he added, as the red glimmer of their torches appeared at the end of the long avenue that led up to the cave. In a moment he had thrown himself on the floor, and wriggled backwards through the hole. The floor on the other side was several feet lower, which made it easier to get back. It was all he could do to lift the largest stone he had taken out of the hole, but he did manage to shove it in again. He sat down on the ore-heap and thought.

He was pretty sure that the latter plan of the goblins was to inundate the mine by breaking outlets for the water accumulated in the natural reservoirs of the mountain, as well as running through portions of it. While the part hollowed by the miners remained shut off from that inhabited by the goblins, they had had no opportunity of injuring them thus; but now that a passage was broken through, and the goblin's part proved the higher in the mountain, it was clear to Curdie that the mine could be destroyed in an hour. Water was always the chief danger to which the miners were exposed. They met with a little choke-damp sometimes, but never with the explosive firedamp* so common in coal mines. Hence they were careful as soon as they saw any appearance of water.

As the result of his reflections while the goblins were busy in their old home, it seemed to Curdie that it would be best to build up the whole of this gang, filling it with stone, and clay or lime, so that there should be no smallest channel for the water to get into. There was not, however, any immediate danger, for the execution of the goblins' plan was contingent upon the failure of that unknown design which was to take precedence of it; and he was most anxious to keep the door of communication open, that he might if possible discover what that former plan was. At the same time they could not then resume their intermitted labours for the inundation without his finding it out; when by putting all hands to the work, the one existing outlet might in a single night be rendered impenetrable to any weight of water; for by filling the gang entirely up, their embankment would be buttressed by the sides of the mountain itself.

As soon as he found that the goblins had again retired, he lighted his lamp, and proceeded to fill the hole he had made, with such stones as he could withdraw when he pleased. He then thought it better, as he might have occasion to be up a good many nights after this, to go home and have some sleep.

How pleasant the night air felt upon the outside of the mountain after what he had gone through in the inside of it!

He hurried up the hill, without meeting a single goblin on the way, and called and tapped at the window until he woke his father, who soon rose and let him in. He told him the whole story, and, just as he had expected, his father thought it best to work that lode no farther, but at the same time to pretend occasionally to be at work there still, in order that the goblins might have no suspicions. Both father and son went then to bed, and slept soundly until the morning.

X

The Princess's King-Papa

The weather continued fine for weeks, and the little princess went out every day. So long a period of fine weather had indeed never been known upon that mountain. The only uncomfortable thing was that her nurse was so nervous and particular about being in before the sun was down, that often she would take to her heels when nothing worse than a fleecy cloud crossing the sun threw a shadow on the hillside; and many an evening they were home a full hour before the sunlight had left the weathercock on the stables. If it had not been for such odd behaviour, Irene would by this time have almost forgotten the goblins. She never forgot Curdie, but him she remembered for his own sake, and indeed would have remembered him if only because a princess never forgets her debts until they are paid.

One splendid sunshiny day, about an hour after noon, Irene, who was playing on a lawn in the garden, heard the distant blast of a bugle. She jumped up with a cry of joy, for she knew by that particular blast that her father was on his way to see her. This part of the garden lay on the slope of the hill, and allowed a full view of the country below. So she shaded her eyes with her hand, and looked far away to catch the first glimpse of shining armour. In a few moments a little troop came glittering round the shoulder of a hill. Spears and helmets were sparkling and gleaming, banners were flying, horses prancing, and again came the bugle-blast, which was to her like the voice of her father calling across the distance, 'Irene, I'm coming.' On and on they came, until she could clearly distinguish the king. He rode a white horse, and was taller than any of the men with him. He wore a narrow circle of gold set with jewels around his helmet, and as he came still nearer, Irene could discern the flashing of the stones in the sun. It was a long time since he had been to see her, and her little heart beat faster and faster as the shining troop approached, for she loved her king-papa very dearly, and was nowhere so happy as in his arms. When they reached a certain point, after which she could see them no more from the garden, she ran to the gate, and there stood till up they came clanging and stamping, with one more bright bugle-blast which said 'Irene, I am come.'

By this time the people of the house were all gathered at the gate, but Irene stood alone in front of them. When the horsemen pulled up, she ran to the side of the white horse, and held up her arms. The kind stooped, and took her hands. In an instant she was on the saddle, and clasped in his great strong arms. I wish I could describe the king so that you could see him in your mind. He had gentle blue eyes, but a nose that made him look like an eagle. A long dark beard, streaked with silvery lines, flowed from his mouth almost to his waist, and as Irene sat on the saddle and hid her glad face upon his bosom, it mingled with the golden hair which her mother had given her, and the two together were like a cloud with streaks of the sun woven through it. After he had held her to his heart for a minute, he spoke to his white horse, and the great beautiful creature, which had been prancing so proudly a little while before, walked as gently as a lady—for he knew he had a little lady on his back—through the gate and up to the door of the house. Then the king set her on the ground, and dismounting, took her hand and walked with her into the great hall, which was hardly ever entered except when he came to see his little princess. There he sat down with two of his councillors who had accompanied him, to have some refreshment, and Irene sat on his right hand, and drank her milk out of a wooden bowl, curiously carved.

After the king had eaten and drunk, he turned to the princess and said, stroking her hair—

'Now, my child, what shall we do next?'

This was the question he almost always put to her first after their meal together; and Irene had been waiting for it with some impatience, for now, she thought, she should be able to settle a question which constantly perplexed her.

'I should like you to take me to see my great old grand-mother.'

The king looked grave, and said—

'What does my little daughter mean?'

'I mean the Queen Irene that lives up in the tower—the very old lady, you know, with the long hair of silver.'

The king only gazed at his little princess with a look which she could not understand.

'She's got her crown in her bedroom,' she went on; 'but I've not been in there yet. You know she's here, don't you?'

'No,' said the king, very quietly.

'Then it must be all a dream,' said Irene. 'I half thought it was; but I couldn't be sure. Now I *am* sure of it. Besides, I couldn't fine her the next time I went up.'

At that moment a snow-white pigeon flew in at an open window and settled upon Irene's head. She broke into a merry laugh, cowered a little, and put up her hands to her head, saying—

'Dear dovey, don't peck me. You'll pull out my hair with your long claws if you don't mind.'

The king stretched out his hand to take the pigeon, but it spread its wings and flew again through the open window, when its whiteness made one flash in the sun and vanished. The king laid his hand on his princess's head, held it back a little, gazed in her face, smiled half a smile, and sighed half a sigh.

'Come, my child; we'll have a walk in the garden together,' he said.

'You won't come up and see my huge, great beautiful grandmother, then, king-papa?' said the princess.

'Not this time,' said the king very gently.

'She has not invited me, you know, and great old ladies like her do not choose to be visited without leave asked and given.'

The garden was a very lovely place. Being upon a mountain side there were parts in it where the rocks came through in great masses, and all immediately about them remained quite wild. Tufts of heather grew upon them, and other hardy mountain plants and flowers, while near them would be lovely roses and lilies, and all pleasant garden flowers. This mingling of the wild mountain with the civilized garden was very quaint, and it was impossible for any number of gardeners to make such a garden look formal and stiff.

Against one of these rocks was a garden-seat, shadowed from the afternoon sun by the overhanging of the rock itself. There was a little winding path up to the top of the rock, and on the top another seat; but they sat on the seat at its foot, because the sun was hot; and there they talked together of many things. At length the king said—

'You were out late one evening, Irene.'

'Yes, papa. It was my fault; and Lootie was very sorry.'

'I must talk to Lootie about it,' said the king.

'Don't speak loud to her, please, papa,' said Irene. 'She's been so afraid of being late ever since! Indeed she has not been naughty. It was only a mistake for once.'

'Once might be too often,' murmured the king to himself, as he stroked his child's head.

I cannot tell you how he had come to know. I am sure Curdie had not told him. Some one about the palace must have seen them, after all. He sat for a good while thinking. There was no sound to be heard except that of a little stream which ran merrily out of an opening in the rock by where they sat, and sped away down the hill through the garden. Then he rose, and leaving Irene where she was, went into the house and sent for Lootie, with whom he had a talk that made her cry.

When in the evening he rode away upon his great white horse, he left six of his attendants behind him, with orders that three of them should watch outside the house every night, walking round and round it from sunset to sunrise. It was clear he was not quite comfortable about the princess.

XI

The Old Lady's Bedroom

Nothing more happened worth telling for some time. The autumn came and went by. There were no more flowers in the garden. The winds blew strong; and howled among the rocks. The rain fell, and drenched the few yellow and red leaves that could not get off the bare branches. Again and again there would be a glorious morning followed by a pouring afternoon, and sometimes, for a week together, there would be rain, nothing but rain, all day, and then the most lovely cloudless night, with the sky all out in full-blown stars —not one missing. But the princess could not see much of them, for she went to bed early. The winter drew on, and she found things growing dreary. When it was too stormy to go out, and she had got tired of her toys, Lootie would take her about the house, sometimes to the housekeeper's room, where the housekeeper, who was a good, kind old woman, made much of her—sometimes to the servants' hall or the kitchen, where she was not princess merely, but absolute queen, and ran a great risk of being spoiled. Sometimes she would run of herself to the room where the men-at-arms whom the king had left, sat, and they showed her their arms and accoutrements, and did what they could to amuse her. Still at times she found it very dreary, and often and often wished that her huge great grandmother had not been a dream.

One morning the nurse left her with the housekeeper for a while. To amuse her, she turned out the contents of an old cabinet upon the table. The little princess found her treasures, queer ancient ornaments, and many things the uses of which she could not imagine, far more interesting than her own toys, and sat playing with them for two hours or more. But at length, in handling a curious old-fashioned brooch, she ran the pin of it into her thumb, and gave a little scream with the sharpness of the pain, but would have thought little more of it, had not the pain increased and her thumb begun to swell. This alarmed the housekeeper greatly. The nurse was fetched; the doctor was sent for; her hand was poulticed, and long before her usual time she was put to bed. The pain still continued, and although she fell asleep and dreamed a good many dreams, there was the pain always in every dream. At last it woke her up.

The moon was shining brightly into the room. The poultice had fallen off her hand, and it was burning hot. She fancied if she could hold it into the moonlight, that would cool it. So she got out of bed, without waking the nurse who lay at the other end of the room, and went to the window. When she looked out, she saw one of the men-at-arms walking in the garden, with the moonlight glancing on his armour. She was just going to tap on the window and call him, for she wanted to tell him all about it, when she bethought herself that that might wake Lootie, and she would put her into her bed again. So she resolved to go to the window of another room, and call him from there. It was so much nicer to have somebody to talk to than to lie awake in bed with the burning pain in her hand. She opened the door very gently and went through the nursery, which did not look into the garden, to go to the other window. But when she came to the foot of the old staircase, there was the moon shining down from some window high up, and making the worm-eaten oak look very strange and delicate and lovely. In a moment she was putting her little feet one after the other in the silvery path up the stair, looking behind as she went, to see the shadow they made in the middle of the silver. Some little girls would have been afraid to find themselves thus alone in the middle of the night, but Irene was a princess.

As she went slowly up the stair, not quite sure that she was not dreaming, suddenly a great longing woke up in her heart to try once more whether she could not find the old old lady with the silvery hair.

'If she is a dream,' she said to herself, 'then I am the likelier to find her, if I am dreaming.'

So up and up she went, stair after stair, until she came to the many rooms—all just as she had seen them before. Through passage after passage she softly sped, comforting herself that if she should lose her way it would not matter much, because when she woke she would find herself in her own bed, with Lootie not far off. But as if she had known every step of the way, she walked straight to the door at the foot of the narrow stair that led to the tower.

'What if I should realliality-really find my beautiful old grandmother up there!' she said to herself, as she crept up the steep steps.

When she reached the top, she stood a moment listening in the dark, for there was no moon there. Yes! it was! it was the hum of the spinning-wheel! What a diligent grandmother to work both day and night!

She tapped gently at the door.

'Come in, Irene,' said the sweet voice.

The princess opened the door, and entered. There was the moonlight streaming in at the window, and in the middle of the moonlight sat the old lady in her black dress with the white lace, and her silvery hair mingling with the moonlight, so that you could not have told which was which.

'Come in, Irene,' she said again. 'Can you tell me what I am spinning?'

'She speaks,' thought Irene, 'just as if she had seen me five minutes ago, or yesterday at the farthest.'—'No,' she answered' 'I don't know what you are spinning. Please, I thought you were a dream. Why couldn't I find you before, great-great-grandmother?'

'That you are hardly old enough to understand. But you would have found me sooner if you hadn't come to think I was a dream. I will give you one reason though why you couldn't find me. I didn't want you to find me.'

'Why, please?'

'Because I did not want Lootie to know I was here.'

'But you told me to tell Lootie.'

'Yes. But I knew Lootie would not believe you. If she were to see me sitting spinning here, she wouldn't believe me either.'

'Why?'

'Because she couldn't. She would rub her eyes, and go away and say she felt queer, and forget half of it and more, and then say it had been all a dream.'

'Just like me,' said Irene, feeling very much ashamed of herself.

'Yes, a good deal like you, but not just like you: for you've come again; and Lootie wouldn't have come again. She would have said, No, no—she had had enough of such nonsense.'

'Is it naughty of Lootie then?'

'It would be naughty of you. I've never done anything for Lootie.'

'And you did wash my face and hands for me,' said Irene, beginning to cry.

The old lady smiled a sweet smile and said—

'I'm not vexed with you, my child—nor with Lootie either. But I don't want you to say anything more to Lootie about me. If she should ask you, you must just be silent. But I do not think she will ask you.'

All the time they talked, the old lady kept on spinning.

'You haven't told me yet what I am spinning,' she said.

'Because I don't know. It's very pretty stuff.'

It was indeed very pretty stuff. There was a good bunch of it on the distaff attached to the spinning-wheel, and in the moonlight it shone like—what shall I say it was like? It was not white enough for silver—yes, it was like silver, but shone grey rather than white, and glittered only a little. And the thread the old lady drew out from it was so fine that Irene could hardly see it.

'I am spinning this for you, my child.'

'For me! What am I to do with it, please?'

'I will tell you by-and-by. But first I will tell you what it is. It is spider-webs—of a particular kind. My pigeons bring it me from over the great sea. There is only one forest where the spiders live who make this particular kind—the finest and strongest of any. I have nearly finished my present job. What is on the rock* now will be enough. I have a week's work there yet, though,' she added, looking at the bunch.

'Do you work all day and all night too, great-great-great-great grandmother?' said the princess, thinking to be very polite with so many *greats*.

'I am not quite so great as all that,' she answered, smiling almost merrily. 'If you call me grandmother, that will do.—No, I don't work every night—only moonlit nights, and then no longer than the moon shines upon my wheel. I shan't work much longer tonight.'

'And what will you do next, grandmother?'

'Go to bed. Would you like to see my bedroom?'

'Yes, that I should.'

'Then I think I won't work any longer tonight. I shall be in good time.'

The old lady rose, and left her wheel standing just as it was. You see there was no good in putting it away, for where there was not any furniture, there was no danger of being untidy.

Then she took Irene by the hand, but it was her bad hand, and Irene gave a little cry of pain.

'My child!' said her grandmother, 'what is the matter?'

Irene held her hand into the moonlight, that the old lady might see it, and told her all about it, at which she looked grave. But she only said—'Give me your other hand;' and, having led her out upon the little dark landing, opened the door on the opposite side of it. What was Irene's surprise to see the loveliest room she had ever seen in her life! It was large and lofty, and dome-shaped. From the centre hung a lamp as round as a ball, shining as if with the brightest moonlight, which made everything visible in the room, though not so clearly that the princess could tell what many of the things were. A large oval bed stood in the middle, with a coverlid of rose-colour, and velvet curtains all round it of a lovely pale blue. The walls were also blue*—spangled all over with what looked like stars of silver.

The old lady left her, and going to a strange-looking cabinet, opened it and took out a curious silver casket. Then she sat down on a low chair, and calling Irene, made her kneel before her, while she looked at her hand. Having examined it, she opened the casket, and took from it a little ointment. The sweetest odour filled the room—like that of roses and lilies—as she rubbed the ointment gently all over the hot swollen hand. Her touch was so pleasant and cool, that it seemed to drive away the pain and heat wherever it came.

'Oh, grandmother! it is *so* nice!' said Irene. 'Thank you; thank you.'

Then the old lady went to a chest of drawers, and took out a large handkerchief of gossamer-like cambric,* which she tied round her hand.

'I don't think I can let you go away tonight,' she said. 'Would you like to sleep with me?'

'Oh, yes, yes, dear grandmother!' said Irene, and would have clapped her hands, forgetting that she could not.

'You won't be afraid then to go to bed with such an old woman?'

'No. You are so beautiful, grandmother.'

'But I am *very* old.'

'And I suppose I am very young. You won't mind sleeping with such a *very* young woman, grandmother?'

'You sweet little pertness!' said the old lady, and drew her towards her, and kissed her on the forehead and the cheek and the mouth.

Then she got a large silver basin, and having poured some water into it, made Irene sit on the chair, and washed her feet.* This done, she was ready for bed. And oh, what a delicious bed it was into which her grandmother laid her! She hardly could have told she was lying upon anything: she felt nothing but the softness. The old lady having undressed herself lay down beside her.

'Why don't you put out your moon?' asked the princess.

'That never goes out, night or day,' she answered. 'In the darkest night, if any of my pigeons are out on a message, they always see my moon, and know where to fly to.'

'But if somebody besides the pigeons were to see it—somebody about the house, I mean—they would come to look what it was, and find you.'

'The better for them then,' said the old lady. 'But it does not happen above five times in a hundred years that any one does see it. The greater part of those who do, take it for a meteor, wink their eyes and forget it again. Besides, nobody could find the room except I pleased.* Besides again—I will tell you a secret—if that light were to go out, you would fancy yourself lying in a bare garret, on a heap of old straw, and would not see one of the pleasant things round about you all the time.'

'I hope it will never go out,' said the princess.

'I hope not. But it is time we both went to sleep. Shall I take you in my arms?'

The little princess nestled close up to the old lady, who took her in both her arms, and held her close to her bosom.

'Oh dear! This is so nice!' said the princess. 'I didn't know anything in the whole world could be so comfortable. I should like to lie here for ever.'

'You may if you will,' said the old lady. 'But I must put you to one trial—not a *very* hard one, I hope.—This night week you must come back to me. If you don't, I do not know when you may find me again, and you will soon want me very much.'

'Oh! please, don't let me forget.'

'You shall not forget. The only question is whether you will believe I am anywhere—whether you will believe I am anything but a dream. You may be sure I will do all I can to help you to come. But it will rest with yourself after all. On the night of next Friday, you must come to me. Mind now.'

'I *will* try,' said the princess.

'Then good night,' said the old lady, and kissed the forehead which lay in her bosom.

In a moment more the little princess was dreaming in the midst of the loveliest dreams—of summer seas and moonlight and mossy springs and great murmuring trees, and beds of wild flowers with such odours as she had never smelled before. But after all, no dream could be more lovely than what she had left behind when she fell asleep.

In the morning she found herself in her own bed. There was no handkerchief or anything else on her hand, only a sweet odour lingered about it. The swelling had all gone down; the prick of the brooch had vanished;—in fact her hand was perfectly well.

XII

A Short Chapter About Curdie

Curdie spent many nights in the mine. His father and he had taken Mrs Peterson into the secret, for they knew mother could hold her tongue, which was more than could be said of all the miners' wives. But Curdie did not tell her that every night he spent in the mine, part of it went in earning a new red petticoat for her.

Mrs Peterson was such a nice good mother! All mothers are nice and good more or less, but Mrs Peterson was nice and good all *more* and no *less*. She made and kept a little heaven in that poor cottage on the high hillside*—for her husband and son to go home to out of the low and rather dreary earth in which they worked. I doubt if the princess was very much happier even in the arms of her huge-great-grandmother than Peter and Curdie were in the arms of Mrs Peterson. True, her hands were hard and chapped and large, but it was with work for them; and therefore in the sight of the angels, her hands were so much the more beautiful. And if Curdie worked hard to get her a petticoat, she worked hard every day to get him comforts which he would have missed much more than she would a new petticoat even in winter. Not that she and Curdie ever thought of how much they worked for each other: that would have spoiled everything.

When left alone in the mine, Curdie always worked on for an hour or two first, following the lode which, according to Glump, would lead at last into the deserted habitation. After that, he would set out on a reconnoitring expedition. In order to manage this, or rather the return from it, better than the first time, he had bought a huge ball of fine string, having learned the trick from Hop-o'-my-Thumb,* whose history his mother had often told him. Not that Hop-o'-my-Thumb had ever used a ball of string—I should be sorry to be supposed so far out in my classics—but the principle was the same as that of the pebbles. The end of this string he fastened to his pickaxe, which figured no bad anchor, and then, with the ball in his hand, unrolling it as he went, set out in the dark through the natural gangs of the goblins' territory. The first night or two he came upon nothing worth remembering; saw only a little of the home-life of the *cobs* in the various caves they called houses; failed in coming upon anything to cast light upon the foregoing design which kept the inundation for the present in the background. But at length, I think on the third or fourth night, he found, partly guided by the noise of their implements, a company of evidently the best sappers* and miners amongst them, hard at work. What were they about? It could not well be the inundation, seeing that had in the mean time been postponed to something else. Then what was it? He lurked and watched, every now and then in the greatest risk of being detected, but without success. He had again and again to retreat in haste, a proceeding rendered the more difficult that he had to gather up his string as he returned upon its course. It was not that he was afraid of the goblins, but that he was afraid of their finding out that they were watched, which might have prevented the discovery at which he aimed. Sometimes his haste had to be such that, when he reached home towards morning, his string, for lack of time to wind it up as he 'dodged the cobs,' would be in what seemed the most hopeless entanglement; but after a good sleep though a short one, he always found his mother had got it right again. There it was, wound in a most respectable ball, ready for use the moment he should want it!

'I can't think how you do it, mother,' he would say.

'I follow the thread,' she would answer—just as you do in the mine.'

She never had more to say about it; but the less clever she was with her words, the more clever she was with her hands; and the less his mother said, the more Curdie believed, she had to say.

But still he had made no discovery as to what the goblin miners were about.

XIII

The Cobs' Creatures

About this time, the gentlemen whom the king had left behind him to watch over the princess, had each occasion to doubt the testimony of his own eyes, for more than strange were the objects to which they would bear witness. They were of one sort—creatures—but so grotesque and misshapen as to be more like a child's drawings upon his slate than anything natural. They saw them only at night, while on guard about the house. The testimony of the man who first reported having seen one of them was that, as he was walking slowly round the house, while yet in the shadow, he caught sight of a creature standing on its hind legs in the moonlight, with its fore feet upon a window-ledge, staring in at the window. Its body might have been that of a dog or wolf—he thought, but he declared on his honour that its head was twice the size it ought to have been for the size of its body, and as round as a ball, while the face, which it turned upon him as it fled, was more like one carved by a boy upon the turnip inside which he is going to put a candle, than anything else he could think of. It rushed into the garden. He sent an arrow after it, and thought he must have struck it; for it gave an unearthly howl, and he could not find his arrow any more than the beast, although he searched all about the place where it vanished. They laughed at him until he was driven to hold his tongue; and said he must have taken too long a pull at the ale-jug. But before two nights were over, he had one to side with him; for he too had seen something strange, only quite different from that reported by the other. The description the second man gave of the creature he had seen, was yet more grotesque and unlikely. They were both laughed at by the rest; but night after night another came

over to their side, until at last there was only one left to laugh
at all his companions. Two nights more passed, and he saw
nothing; but on the third, he came rushing from the garden
to the other two before the house, in such an agitation that
they declared—for it was their turn now—that the band of
his helmet was cracking under his chin with the rising of his
hair inside it. Running with him into that part of the garden
which I have already described, they saw a score of creatures,
to not one of which they could give a name, and not one
of which was like another, hideous and ludicrous at once,
gambolling on the lawn in the moonlight. The supernatural
or rather sub-natural ugliness of their faces, the length of legs
and necks in some, and the apparent absence of both or either
in others, made the spectators, although in one consent as to
what they saw, yet doubtful, as I have said, of the evidence
of their own eyes—and ears as well; for the noises they made,
although not loud, were as uncouth and varied as their forms,
and could be described neither as grunts nor squeaks nor
roars nor howls nor barks nor yells nor screams nor croaks
nor hisses nor mews nor shrieks, but only as something like all
of them mingled in one horrible dissonance. Keeping in the
shade, the watchers had a few moments to recover themselves
before the hideous assembly suspected their presence; but all
at once, as if by common consent, they scampered off in the
direction of a great rock, and vanished before the men had
come to themselves sufficiently to think of following them.

My readers will suspect what these were; but I will now
give them full information concerning them. They were of
course household animals belonging to the goblins, whose
ancestors had taken their ancestors many centuries before
from the upper regions of light into the lower regions of
darkness. The original stocks* of these horrible creatures
were very much the same as the animals now seen about
farms and homes in the country, with the exception of a few
of them, which had been wild creatures, such as foxes, and
indeed wolves and small bears, which the goblins, from their
proclivity towards the animal creation, had caught when cubs

and tamed. But in the course of time, all had undergone even greater changes than had passed upon their owners. They had altered—that is, their descendants had altered—into such creatures as I have not attempted to describe except in the vaguest manner—the various parts of their bodies assuming, in an apparently arbitrary and self-willed manner, the most abnormal developments. Indeed, so little did any distinct type predominate in some of the bewildering results, that you could only have guessed at any known animal as the original, and even then, what likeness remained would be more one of general expression than of definable conformation. But what increased the gruesomeness tenfold, was that, from constant domestic, or indeed rather family association with the goblins, their countenances had grown in grotesque resemblance to the human. No one understands animals who does not see that every one of them, even amongst the fishes, it may be with a dimness and vagueness infinitely remote, yet shadows the human: in the case of these the human resemblance had greatly increased: while their owners had sunk towards them, they had risen towards their owners. But the conditions of subterranean life being equally unnatural for both, while the goblins were worse, the creatures had not improved by the approximation, and its result would have appeared far more ludicrous than consoling to the warmest lover of animal nature. I shall now explain how it was that just then these animals began to show themselves about the king's country-house.

The goblins, as Curdie had discovered, were mining on—at work both day and night, in divisions, urging the scheme after which he lay in wait. In the course of their tunnelling, they had broken into the channel of a small stream, but the break being in the top of it, no water had escaped to interfere with their work. Some of the creatures, hovering as they often did about their masters, had found the hole, and had, with the curiosity which had grown to a passion from the restraints of their unnatural circumstances, proceeded to explore the channel. The stream was the same which ran out by the seat on which Irene and her king-papa had sat as I have told, and the goblin-creatures found it jolly fun to get out for a romp on a smooth lawn such as they had never seen in all their poor miserable lives. But although they had partaken enough of the nature of their owners to delight in annoying and alarming any of the people whom they met on the mountain, they were of course incapable of designs of their own, or of intentionally furthering those of their masters.

For several nights after the men-at-arms were at length of one mind as to the fact of the visits of some horrible creatures, whether bodily or spectral they could not yet say, they watched with special attention that part of the garden where they had last seen them. Perhaps indeed they gave in consequence too little attention to the house. But the creatures were too cunning to be easily caught; nor were the watchers quick-eyed enough to descry the head, or the keen eyes in it, which, from the opening whence the stream issued, would watch them in turn, ready, the moment they should leave the lawn, to report the place clear.

XIV

That Night Week

During the whole of the week, Irene had been thinking every other moment of her promise to the old lady, although even now she could not feel quite sure that she had not been dreaming. Could it really be that an old lady lived up in the top of the house, with pigeons and a spinning-wheel, and a lamp that never went out? She was, however, none the less determined, on the coming Friday, to ascend the three stairs, walk through the passages with the many doors, and try to find the tower in which she had either seen or dreamed her grandmother.

Her nurse could not help wondering what had come to the child—she would sit so thoughtfully silent, and even in the midst of a game with her, would so suddenly fall into a dreamy mood. But Irene took care to betray nothing, whatever efforts Lootie might make to get at her thoughts. And Lootie had to say to herself, 'What an odd child she is!' and give it up.

At length the longed-for Friday arrived, and lest Lootie should be moved to watch her, Irene endeavoured to keep herself as quiet as possible. In the afternoon she asked for her doll's-house, and went on arranging and rearranging the various rooms and their inhabitants for a whole hour. Then she gave a sigh and threw herself back in her chair. One of the dolls would not sit, and another would not stand, and they were all very tiresome. Indeed there was one would not even lie down, which was too bad. But it was now getting dark, and the darker it got the more excited Irene became, and the more she felt it necessary to be composed.

'I see you want your tea, princess,' said the nurse: 'I will go and get it. The room feels close: I will open the window a little. The evening is mild: it won't hurt you.'

'There's no fear of that, Lootie,' said Irene, wishing she had put off going for the tea till it was darker, when she might have made her attempt with every advantage.

I fancy Lootie was longer in returning than she had intended; for when Irene, who had been lost in thought, looked up, she saw it was nearly dark, and at the same moment caught sight of a pair of eyes, bright with a green light, glowering at her through the open window. The next instant, something leaped into the room. It was like a cat, with legs as long as a horse's, Irene said, but its body no bigger and its legs no thicker than those of a cat. She was too frightened to cry out, but not too frightened to jump from her chair and run from the room.

It is plain enough to every one of my readers what she ought to have done—and indeed Irene thought of it herself; but when she came to the foot of the old stair, just outside the nursery door, she imagined the creature running up those long ascents after her, and pursuing her through the dark passages—*which, after all, might lead to no tower*. That thought was too much. Her heart failed her, and turning from the stair, she rushed along to the hall, whence, finding the front-door open, she darted into the court, pursued—at least she thought so—by the creature. No one happening to see her, on she ran, unable to think for fear, and ready to run anywhere to elude the awful creature with the stilt-legs. Not daring to look behind her, she rushed straight out of the gate, and up the mountain. It was foolish indeed—thus to run farther and farther from all who could help her, as if she had been seeking a fit spot for the goblin-creature to eat her in at his leisure; but that is the way fear serves us:* it always sides with the thing we are afraid of.

The princess was soon out of breath with running up hill, but she ran on, for she fancied the horrible creature just behind her, forgetting that, had it been after her, such legs as those must have overtaken her long ago. At last she could run no longer, and fell, unable even to scream, by the roadside, where she lay for some time, half dead with terror. But finding nothing lay hold of her, and her breath beginning to come back, she ventured at length to get half up, and peer anxiously about her. It was now so dark that she could see nothing. Not a single star was out. She could not even tell in what direction the house lay, and between her and home she fancied the dreadful creature lying ready to pounce upon her. She saw now that she ought to have run up the stairs at once. It was well she did not scream; for, although very few of the goblins had come out for weeks, a stray idler or two might have heard her. She sat down upon a stone, and nobody but one who had done something wrong could have been more miserable. She had quite forgotten her promise to visit her grandmother. A raindrop fell on her face. She looked up, and for a moment her terror was lost in astonishment.* At first she thought the rising moon had left her place and drawn nigh to see what could be the matter with the little girl, sitting alone, without hat or cloak, on the dark bare mountain; but she soon saw she was mistaken, for there was no light on the ground at her feet, and no shadow anywhere. But a great silvery globe was hanging in the air; and as she gazed at the lovely thing, her courage revived. If she were but in doors again, she would fear nothing, not even the terrible creature with the long legs! But how was she to find her way back? What could that light be? Could it be—? No, it couldn't. But what if it should be—yes—it must be—her great-great-grandmother's lamp, which guided her pigeons home through the darkest night! She jumped up: she had but to keep that light in view, and she must find the house.

Her heart grew strong. Speedily, yet softly, she walked down the hill, hoping to pass the watching creature unseen. Dark as it was, there was little danger now of choosing the wrong road. And—which was most strange—the light that filled her eyes from the lamp, instead of blinding them for a moment to the object upon which they next fell, enabled her for a moment to see it, despite the darkness. By looking at the lamp and then dropping her eyes she could see the road for a yard or two in front of her, and this saved her from several falls, for the road was very rough. But all at once, to her dismay, it vanished, and the terror of the beast, which had left her the moment she began to return, again laid hold of her heart. The same instant, however, she caught the light of the windows, and knew exactly where she was. It was too dark to run, but she made what haste she could, and reached the gate in safety. She found the house-door still open, ran through the hall, and, without even looking into the nursery, bounded straight up the stair, and the next, and the next; then turning to the right, ran through the long avenue of silent rooms, and found her way at once to the door at the foot of the tower stair.

When first the nurse missed her, she fancied she was playing her a trick, and for some time took no trouble about her; but at last, getting frightened, had begun to search; and when the princess entered, the whole household was hither and thither over the house, hunting for her. A few seconds after she reached the stair of the tower, they had even begun to search the neglected rooms, in which they would never have thought of looking had they not already searched every other place they could think of in vain. But by this time she was knocking at the old lady's door.

XV

Woven and Then Spun

'Come in, Irene,' said the silvery voice of her grandmother.

The princess opened the door, and peeped in. But the room was quite dark, and there was no sound of the spinning-wheel. She grew frightened once more, thinking that, although the room was there, the old lady might be a dream after all. Every little girl knows how dreadful it is to find a room empty where she thought somebody was; but Irene had to fancy for a moment that the person she came to find was nowhere at all. She remembered however that at night she spun only in the moonlight, and concluded that must be why there was no sweet, bee-like humming: the old lady might be somewhere in the darkness. Before she had time to think another thought, she heard her voice again, saying as before—

'Come in, Irene.'

From the sound, she understood at once that she was not in the room beside her. Perhaps she was in her bedroom. She turned across the passage, feeling her way to the other door. When her hand fell on the lock, again the old lady spoke—

'Shut the other door behind you, Irene. I always close the door of my workroom when I go to my chamber.'

Irene wondered to hear her voice so plainly through the door: having shut the other, she opened it and went in. Oh, what a lovely haven to reach from the darkness and fear through which she had come! The soft light made her feel as if she were going into the heart of the milkiest pearl; while the blue walls and their silver stars for a moment perplexed her with the fancy that they were in reality the sky which she had left outside a minute ago covered with rainclouds.

'I've lighted a fire for you, Irene: you're cold and wet,' said her grandmother.

Then Irene looked again, and saw that what she had taken for a huge bouquet of red roses on a low stand against the wall, was in fact a fire which burned in the shapes of the loveliest and reddest roses,* glowing gorgeously between the heads and wings of two cherubs of shining silver.* And when she came nearer, she found that the smell of roses with which the room was filled, came from the fire-roses on the hearth. Her grandmother was dressed in the loveliest pale-blue velvet, over which her hair, no longer white, but of a rich golden colour, streamed like a cataract, here falling in dull gathered heaps, there rushing away in smooth shining falls. And ever as she looked, the hair seemed pouring down from her head, and vanishing in a golden mist ere it reached the floor. It flowed from under the edge of a circle of shining silver, set with alternated pearls and opals. On her dress was no ornament whatever, neither was there a ring on her hand, or a necklace or carcanet about her neck. But her slippers glimmered with the light of the milky way, for they were covered with seed-pearls and opals in one mass. Her face was that of a woman of three-and-twenty.

The princess was so bewildered with astonishment and admiration that she could hardly thank her, and drew nigh with timidity, feeling dirty and uncomfortable. The lady was seated on a low chair by the side of the fire, with hands outstretched to take her, but the princess hung back with a troubled smile.

'Why, what's the matter?' asked her grandmother. 'You haven't been doing anything wrong—I know that by your face, though it *is* rather miserable. What's the matter, my dear?'

And she still held out her arms.

'Dear grandmother,' said Irene, 'I'm not so sure that I haven't done something wrong. I ought to have run up to you at once when the long-legged cat came in at the window, instead of running out on the mountain, and making myself such a fright.

'You were taken by surprise, my child, and are not so likely to do it again. It is when people do wrong things wilfully that they are the more likely to do them again. Come.'

And still she held out her arms.

'But, grandmother, you're so beautiful and grand with your crown on! and I am so dirty with mud and rain!—I should quite spoil your beautiful blue dress.'

With a merry little laugh, the lady sprung from her chair, more lightly far than Irene herself could, caught the child to her bosom, and kissing the tear-stained face over and over, sat down with her in her lap.

'Oh, grandmother! you'll make yourself such a mess!' cried Irene, clinging to her.

'You darling! do you think I care more for my dress than for my little girl? Besides—look here.'

As she spoke she set her down, and Irene saw to her dismay that the lovely dress was covered with the mud of her fall on the mountain road. But the lady stooped to the fire, and taking from it, by the stalk in her fingers, one of the burning roses, passed it once and again and a third time over the front of her dress; and when Irene looked, not a single stain was to be discovered.

'There!' said her grandmother, 'you won't mind coming to me now?'

But Irene again hung back, eyeing the flaming rose which the lady held in her hand.

'You're not afraid of the rose—are you?' she said, about to throw it on the hearth again.

'Oh! don't, please!' cried Irene. 'Won't you hold it to my frock and my hands and my face? And I'm afraid my feet and my knees want it too!'

'No,' answered her grandmother, smiling a little sadly, as she threw the rose from her; 'it is too hot for you yet. It would set *your* frock in a flame. Besides, I don't want to make you clean tonight. I want your nurse and the rest of the people to see you as you are, for you will have to tell them how you ran away for fear of the long-legged cat. I should like to wash you, but they would not believe you then. Do you see that bath behind you?'

The princess looked, and saw a large oval tub of silver, shining brilliantly in the light of the wonderful lamp.

'Go and look into it,' said the lady.

Irene went, and came back very silent, with her eyes shining.

'What did you see?' asked her grandmother.

'The sky and the moon and the stars,' she answered. 'It looked as if there was no bottom to it.'

The lady smiled a pleased satisfied smile, and was silent also for a few moments. Then she said—

'Any time you want a bath, come to me. I know you have a bath every morning, but sometimes you want one at night too.'

'Thank you, grandmother; I will—I will indeed,' answered Irene, and was again silent for some moments thinking. Then she said, 'How was it, grandmother, that I saw your beautiful lamp—not the light of it only—but the great round silvery lamp itself, hanging alone in the great open air high up? It was your lamp I saw—wasn't it?'

'Yes, my child; it was my lamp.'

'Then how was it? I don't see a window all round.'

'When I please, I can make the lamp shine through the walls—shine so strong that it melts them away from before the sight, and shows itself as you saw it. But, as I told you, it is not everybody can see it.'

'How is it that I can then? I'm sure I don't know.'

'It is a gift born with you. And one day I hope everybody will have it.'*

'But how do you make it shine through the walls?'

'Ah! that you would not understand if I were to try ever so much to make you—not yet—not yet. But,' added the lady rising, 'you must sit in my chair while I get you the present

I have been preparing for you. I told you my spinning was for you. It is finished now, and I am going to fetch it. I have been keeping it warm under one of my brooding pigeons.'

Irene sat down in the low chair, and her grandmother left her, shutting the door behind her. The child sat gazing, now at the rose-fire, now at the starry walls, now at the silvery light; and a great quietness grew in her heart. If all the long-legged cats in the world had come rushing at her then, she would not have been afraid of them for a moment. How this was she could not tell—she only knew there was no fear in her, and everything was so right and safe that it could not get in.

She had been gazing at the lovely lamp for some minutes fixedly: turning her eyes, she found the wall had vanished, for she was looking out on the dark cloudy night. But though she heard the wind blowing, none of it blew upon her. In a moment more, the clouds themselves parted, or rather vanished like the wall, and she looked straight into the starry herds, flashing gloriously in the dark blue. It was but for a moment. The clouds gathered again and shut out the stars; the wall gathered again and shut out the clouds; and there stood the lady beside her with the loveliest smile on her face, and a shimmering ball in her hand, about the size of a pigeon's egg.

'There, Irene; there is my work for you!' she said, holding out the ball to the princess.

She took it in her hand, and looked at it all over. It sparkled a little, and shone here and shone there, but not much. It was of a sort of grey whiteness, something like spun-glass.

'Is this *all* your spinning, grandmother?' she asked.

'All since you came to the house. There is more there than you think.'

'How pretty it is! What am I to do with it, please?'

'That I will now explain to you,' answered the lady, turning from her, and going to her cabinet.

She came back with a small ring in her hand. Then she took the ball from Irene's, and did something with the two—Irene could not tell what.

'Give me your hand,' she said.

Irene held up her right hand.

'Yes, that is the hand I want,' said the lady, and put the ring on the forefinger of it.

'What a beautiful ring!' said Irene. 'What is the stone called?'

'It is a fire-opal.'

'Please, am I to keep it?'

'Always.'

'Oh, thank you, grandmother! It's prettier than anything I ever saw, except those—of all colours—in your—Please, is that your crown?'

'Yes, it is my crown. The stone in your ring is of the same sort—only not so good. It has only red, but mine have all colours, you see.'

'Yes, grandmother. I will take such care of it!—But—' she added, hesitating.

'But what?' asked her grandmother.

'What am I to say when Lootie asks me where I got it?'

'*You* will ask *her* where you got it,' answered the lady smiling.

'I don't see how I can do that.'

'You will though.'

'Of course I will if you say so. But you know I can't pretend not to know.'

'Of course not. But don't trouble yourself about it. You will see when the time comes.'

So saying, the lady turned, and threw the little ball into the rose-fire.

'Oh, grandmother!' exclaimed Irene; 'I thought you had spun it for me.'

'So I did, my child. And you've got it.'

'No; it's burnt in the fire!'

The lady put her hand in the fire, brought out the ball, glimmering as before, and held it towards her. Irene stretched out her hand to take it, but the lady turned, and going to her cabinet, opened a drawer, and laid the ball in it.

'Have I done anything to vex you, grandmother?' said Irene pitifully.

'No, my darling. But you must understand that no one ever gives anything to another properly and really without keeping it. That ball is yours.'

'Oh! I'm not to take it with me! You are going to keep it for me!'

'You are to take it with you. I've fastened the end of it to the ring on your finger.'

Irene looked at the ring.

'I can't see it there, grandmother,' she said.

'Feel—a little way from the ring—towards the cabinet,' said the lady.

'Oh! I do feel it!' exclaimed the princess.

'But I can't see it,' she added, looking close to her out-stretched hand.

'No. The thread is too fine for you to see it. You can only feel it. Now you can fancy how much spinning that took, although it does seem such a little ball.'

'But what use can I make of it, if it lies in your cabinet?'

'That is what I will explain to you. It would be of no use to you—it wouldn't be yours at all if it did not lie in my cabinet.—Now listen.—If ever you find yourself in any danger—such, for example, as you were in this same evening—you must take off your ring and put it under the pillow of your bed. Then you must lay your forefinger, the same that wore the ring, upon the thread, and follow the thread wherever it leads you.'

'Oh, how delightful! It will lead me to you, grandmother, I know!'

'Yes. But, remember, it may seem to you a very round-about way indeed, and you must not doubt the thread. Of one thing you may be sure, that while you hold it, I hold it too.'

'It is very wonderful!' said Irene thoughtfully. Then suddenly becoming aware, she jumped up, crying—'Oh, grandmother! here have I been sitting all this time in your chair, and you standing! I *beg* your pardon.'

The lady laid her hand on her shoulder, and said—

'Sit down again, Irene. Nothing pleases me better than to see any one sit in my chair. I am only too glad to stand so long as any one will sit in it.'

'How kind of you!' said the princess, and sat down again.

'It makes me happy,' said the lady.

'But,' said Irene, still puzzled, 'won't the thread get in somebody's way and be broken, if the one end is fast to my ring, and the other laid in your cabinet?'

'You will find all that arrange itself.—I am afraid it is time for you to go.'

'Mightn't I stay and sleep with you tonight, grandmother?'

'No, not tonight. If I had meant you to stay tonight, I should have given you a bath; but you know everybody in the house is miserable about you, and it would be cruel to keep them so all night. You must go down stairs.'

'I'm so glad, grandmother, you didn't say—*go home*—for this is my home.* Mayn't I call this my home?'

'You may, my child. And I trust you will always think it your home. Now come. I must take you back without any one seeing you.'

'Please, I want to ask you one question more,' said Irene. 'Is it because you have your crown on that you look so young?'

'No, child,' answered her grandmother; 'it is because I felt so young this evening, that I put my crown on. And I thought you would like to see your old grandmother in her best.'

'Why do you call yourself old? You're not old, grandmother.'

'I am very old indeed. It is so silly of people—I don't mean you, for you are such a tiny, and couldn't know better—but it *is* so silly of people to fancy that old age means crookedness and witheredness and feebleness and sticks and spectacles and rheumatism and forgetfulness! It is so silly! Old age has nothing whatever to do with all that. The right old age means strength and beauty and mirth and courage and clear eyes and strong painless limbs. I am older than you are able to think, and—'

'And look at you, grandmother!' cried Irene, jumping up, and flinging her arms about her neck. 'I won't be so silly again, I promise you. At least—I'm rather afraid to promise—but if I am, I promise to be sorry for it—I do.—I wish I were as old as you, grandmother. I don't think you are ever afraid of anything.'

'Not for long, at least, my child. Perhaps by the time I am two thousand years of age, I shall, indeed, never be afraid of anything. But I confess I have sometimes been afraid about my children—sometimes about you, Irene.'

'Oh, I'm *so* sorry, grandmother!—Tonight, I suppose, you mean.'

'Yes—a little tonight; but a good deal when you had all but made up your mind that I was a dream, and no real great-great-grandmother.—You must not suppose I am blaming you for that. I dare say you could not help it.'

'I don't know, grandmother,' said the princess, beginning to cry. 'I can't always do myself as I should like. And I don't always try.—I'm very sorry anyhow.'

The lady stooped, lifted her in her arms, and sat down with her in her chair, holding her close to her bosom. In a few minutes the princess had sobbed herself to sleep. How long she slept, I do not know. When she came to herself she was sitting in her own high chair at the nursery table, with her doll's-house before her.

XVI
The Ring

The same moment her nurse came into the room, sobbing.
When she saw her sitting there, she started back with a loud
cry of amazement and joy. Then running to her, she caught
her in her arms and covered her with kisses.

'My precious darling princess! where have you been?
What has happened to you? We've all been crying our eyes
out, and searching the house from top to bottom for you.'

'Not quite from the top,' thought Irene to herself; and she
might have added—'not quite to the bottom,' perhaps, if she
had known all. But the one she would not, and the other she
could not say.

'Oh, Lootie! I've had such a dreadful adventure!' she
replied, and told her all about the cat with the long legs, and
how she ran out upon the mountain, and came back again.
But she said nothing of her grandmother or her lamp.

'And there we've been searching for you all over the house
for more than an hour and a half!' exclaimed the nurse. 'But
that's no matter, now we've got you! Only, princess, I must
say,' she added, her mood changing, 'what you ought to have
done was to call for your own Lootie to come and help you,
instead of running out of the house, and up the mountain,
in that wild—I must say, foolish fashion.'

'Well, Lootie,' said Irene quietly, 'perhaps if you had a
big cat, all legs, running at you, you mightn't exactly know
which was the wisest thing to do at the moment.'

'I wouldn't run up the mountain, anyhow,' returned
Lootie.

'Not if you had time to think about it. But when those
creatures came at you that night on the mountain, you were
so frightened yourself that you lost your way home.'

This put a stop to Lootie's reproaches. She had been on the point of saying that the long-legged cat must have been a twilight fancy of the princess's, but the memory of the horrors of that night, and of the talking-to which the king had given her in consequence, prevented her from saying what after all she did not half believe—having a strong suspicion that the cat was a goblin; for she knew nothing of the difference between the goblins and their creatures: she counted them all just goblins.

Without another word she went and got some fresh tea and bread and butter for the princess. Before she returned, the whole household, headed by the housekeeper, burst into the nursery to exult over their darling. The gentlemen-at-arms followed, and were ready enough to believe all she told them about the long-legged cat. Indeed, though wise enough to say nothing about it, they remembered, with no little horror, just such a creature amongst those they had surprised at their gambols upon the princess's lawn. In their own hearts they blamed themselves for not having kept better watch. And their captain gave order that from this night the front door and all the windows on the ground floor, should be locked immediately the sun set, and opened after upon no pretence whatever. The men-at-arms redoubled their vigilance, and for some time there was no further cause of alarm.

When the princess woke the next morning, her nurse was bending over her.

'How your ring does glow this morning, princess!—just like a fiery rose!' she said.

'Does it, Lootie?' returned Irene. 'Who gave me the ring, Lootie? I know I've had it a long time, but where did I get it? I don't remember.'

'I think it must have been your mother gave it you, princess; but really, for as long as you have worn it, I don't remember that ever I heard,' answered her nurse.

'I will ask my king-papa the next time he comes,' said Irene.

XVII

Springtime

The spring so dear to all creatures, young and old, came at last, and before the first few days of it had gone, the king rode through its budding valleys to see his little daughter. He had been in a distant part of his dominions all the winter, for he was not in the habit of stopping in one great city, or of visiting only his favourite country-houses, but he moved from place to place, that all his people might know him. Wherever he journeyed, he kept a constant look-out for the ablest and best men to put into office; and wherever he found himself mistaken, and those he had appointed incapable or unjust, he removed them at once. Hence you see it was his care of the people that kept him from seeing his princess so often as he would have liked. You may wonder why he did not take her about with him; but there were several reasons against his doing so, and I suspect her great-great-grandmother had had a principal hand in preventing it. Once more, Irene heard the bugle-blast, and once more she was at the gate to meet her father as he rode up on his great white horse.

After they had been alone for a little while, she thought of what she had resolved to ask him.

'Please, king-papa,' she said, 'will you tell me where I got this pretty ring? I can't remember.'

The king looked at it. A strange beautiful smile spread like sunshine over his face, and an answering smile, but at the same time a questioning one, spread like moonlight over Irene's.

'It was your queen-mamma's once,' he said.

'And why isn't it hers now?' asked Irene.

'She does not want it now,' said the king, looking grave.

'Why doesn't she want it now?'

'Because she's gone where all those rings are made.'

'And when shall I see her?' asked the princess.

'Not for some time yet,' answered the king and the tears came in his eyes.

Irene did not remember her mother, and did not know why her father looked so, and why the tears came in his eyes; but she put her arms round his neck and kissed him, and asked no more questions.

The king was much disturbed on hearing the report of the gentlemen-at-arms concerning the creatures they had seen; and I presume would have taken Irene with him that very day, but for what the presence of the ring on her finger assured him of. About an hour before he left, Irene saw him go up the old stair; and he did not come down again till they were just ready to start; and she thought with herself that he had been up to see the old lady. When he went away, he left another six gentlemen behind him, that there might be six of them always on guard.

And now, in the lovely spring weather, Irene was out on the mountain the greater part of the day. In the warmer hollows there were lovely primroses, and not so many that she ever got tired of them. As often as she saw a new one opening an eye of light in the blind earth, she would clap her hands with gladness, and, unlike some children I know, instead of pulling it, would touch it as tenderly as if it had been a new baby, and, having made its acquaintance, would leave it as happy as she found it. She treated the plants on which they grew like birds' nests; every fresh flower was like a new little bird to her. She would pay visits to all the flower nests she knew, remembering each by itself. She would go down on her hands and knees beside one and say 'Good morning! Are you all smelling very sweet this morning? Good-bye!' And then she would go to another nest, and say the same. It was a favourite amusement with her. There were many flowers up and down, and she loved them all, but the primroses were her favourites.

'They're not too shy, and they're not a bit forward,' she would say to Lootie.

There were goats too about, over the mountain, and when the little kids came, she was as pleased with them as with the flowers. The goats belonged to the miners mostly—a few of them to Curdie's mother; but there were a good many wild ones that seemed to belong to nobody. These the goblins counted theirs, and it was upon them partly that they lived. They set snares and dug pits for them; and did not scruple to take what tame ones happened to be caught; but they did not try to steal them in any other manner, because they were afraid of the dogs the hill-people kept to watch them, for the knowing dogs always tried to bite their feet. But the goblins had a kind of sheep of their own—very queer creatures, which they drove out to feed at night, and the other goblin-creatures were wise enough to keep good watch over them, for they knew they should have their bones by-and-by.

XVIII

Curdie's Clue*

Curdie was as watchful as ever, but was almost getting tired of his ill-success. Every other night or so, he followed the goblins about, as they went on digging and boring, and getting as near them as he could, watched them from behind stones and rocks; but as yet he seemed no nearer finding out what they had in view. As at first, he always kept hold of the end of his string, while his pickaxe, left just outside the hole by which he entered the goblins' country from the mine, continued to serve as an anchor and hold fast the other end. The goblins hearing no more noise in that quarter, had ceased to apprehend an immediate invasion, and kept no watch.

One night, after dodging about and listening till he was nearly falling asleep with weariness, he began to roll up his ball, for he had resolved to go home to bed. It was not long, however, before he began to feel bewildered. One after another he passed goblin-houses, caves that is, occupied by goblin families, and at length was sure they were many more than he had passed as he came. He had to use great caution to pass unseen—they lay so close together. Could his string have led him wrong? He still followed winding it, and still it led him into more thickly populated quarters, until he became quite uneasy, and indeed apprehensive; for although he was not afraid of the *cobs*, he was afraid of not finding his way out. But what could he do? It was of no use to sit down and wait for the morning—the morning made no difference here. It was all dark, and always dark; and if his string failed him, he was helpless. He might even arrive within a yard of the mine, and never know it. Seeing he could do nothing better he would at least find where the end of his string was, and if possible how it had come to play him such a trick. He knew by the size of the ball, that he was getting pretty near the last of it, when he began to feel a tugging and pulling at it. What could it mean? Turning a sharp corner, he thought he heard strange sounds. These grew, as he went on, to a scuffling and growling and squeaking; and the noise increased, until, turning a second sharp corner, he found himself in the midst of it, and the same moment tumbled over a wallowing mass, which he knew must be a knot of the cob's creatures. Before he could recover his feet, he had caught some great scratches on his face, and several severe bites on his legs and arms. But as he scrambled to get up, his hand fell upon his pickaxe, and before the horrid beasts could do him any serious harm, he was laying about with it right and left in the dark. The hideous cries which followed gave him the satisfaction of knowing that he had punished some of them pretty smartly for their rudeness, and by their scampering and their retreating howls, he perceived that he had routed them. He stood for a little, weighing his battle-axe in his hand as if it had been the most precious lump of metal—but indeed no lump of gold itself could have been so precious at the time as that common tool—then untied the end of the string from it, put the ball in his pocket, and still stood thinking. It was clear that the cob's creatures had found his axe, had between them carried it off, and had so led him he knew not where. But for all his thinking he could not tell what he ought to do, until suddenly he became aware of a glimmer of light in the distance. Without a moment's hesitation he set out for it, as fast as the unknown and rugged way would permit. Yet again turning a corner, led by the dim light, he spied something quite new in his experience of the underground regions—a small irregular shape of something shining. Going up to it, he found it was a piece of mica, or Muscovy glass, called sheep-silver in Scotland,* and the light flickered as if from a fire behind it. After trying in vain for some time to discover an entrance to the place where it was burning, he came at length to a small chamber in which an opening high in the wall, revealed a glow beyond. To this opening he managed to scramble up, and then he saw a strange sight.

Below sat a little group of goblins around a fire, the smoke of which vanished in the darkness far aloft. The sides of the cave were full of shining minerals like those of the palace-hall; and the company was evidently of a superior order, for every one wore stones about head, or arms, or waist, shining dull gorgeous colours in the light of the fire. Nor had Curdie looked long before he recognized the king himself, and found that he had made his way into the inner apartment of the royal family. He had never had such a good chance of hearing something! He crept through the hole as softly as he could, scrambled a good way down the wall towards them without attracting attention, and then sat down and listened. The king, evidently the queen, and probably the crown-prince and the prime minister were talking together. He was sure of the queen by her shoes, for as she warmed her feet at the fire, he saw them quite plainly.

'That *will* be fun!' said the one he took for the crown-prince.

It was the first whole sentence he heard.

'I don't see why you should think it such a grand affair!' said his stepmother, tossing her head backward.

'You must remember, my spouse,' interposed his majesty, as if making excuse for his son, 'he has got the same blood in him. His mother—'

'Don't talk to me of his mother! You positively encourage his unnatural fancies. Whatever belongs to *that* mother, ought to be cut out of him.'

'You forget yourself, my dear!' said the king.

'I don't,' said the queen, 'nor you either. If you expect *me* to approve of such coarse tastes, you will find yourself mistaken. *I* don't wear shoes for nothing.'

'You must acknowledge, however,' the king said, with a little groan, 'that this at least is no whim of Harelip's, but a matter of state-policy. You are well aware that his gratification comes purely from the pleasure of sacrificing himself to the public good. Does it not, Harelip?'

'Yes, father; of course it does. Only it *will* be nice to make her cry. I'll have the skin taken off between her toes, and tie them up till they grow together. Then her feet will be like other people's, and there will be no occasion for her to wear shoes.'

'Do you mean to insinuate *I*'ve got toes, you unnatural wretch?' cried the queen; and she moved angrily towards Harelip. The councillor, however, who was betwixt them, leaned forward so as to prevent her touching him, but only as if to address the prince.

'Your royal highness,' he said, 'possibly requires to be reminded that you have got three toes yourself—one on one foot, two on the other.'

'Ha! ha! ha!' shouted the queen triumphantly.

The councillor, encouraged by this mark of favour, went on.

'It seems to me, your royal highness, it would greatly endear you to your future people, proving to them that you are not the less one of themselves that you had the misfortune to be born of a sun-mother, if you were to command upon yourself the comparatively slight operation which, in a more extended form, you so wisely meditate with regard to your future princess.'

'Ha! ha! ha' laughed the queen, louder than before, and the king and the minister joined in the laugh. Harelip growled, and for a few moments the others continued to express their enjoyment of his discomfiture.

The queen was the only one Curdie could see with any distinctness. She sat sideways to him, and the light of the fire shone full upon her face. He could not consider her handsome. Her nose was certainly broader at the end than its extreme length, and her eyes instead of being horizontal, were set up like two perpendicular eggs, one on the broad, the other on the small end. Her mouth was no bigger than a small buttonhole until she laughed, when it stretched from ear to ear—only to be sure her ears were very nearly in the middle of her cheeks.

Anxious to hear everything they might say, Curdie ventured to slide down a smooth part of the rock just under him, to a projection below, upon which he thought to rest. But whether he was not careful enough, or the projection gave way, down he came with a rush on the floor of the cavern, bringing with him a great rumbling shower of stones.

The goblins jumped from their seats in more anger than consternation, for they had never yet seen anything to be afraid of in the palace. But when they saw Curdie with his pick in his hand, their rage was mingled with fear, for they took him for the first of an invasion of miners. The king notwithstanding drew himself up to his full height of four feet, spread himself to his full breadth of three and a half, for he was the handsomest and squarest of all the goblins, and strutting up to Curdie, planted himself with outspread feet before him, and said with dignity—

'Pray what right have you in my palace?'

'The right of necessity, your majesty,' answered Curdie. 'I lost my way, and did not know where I was wandering to.'

'How did you get in?'

'By a hole in the mountain.'

'But you are a miner! Look at your pickaxe!'

Curdie did look at it, answering,

'I came upon it, lying on the ground, a little way from here. I tumbled over some wild beasts who were playing with it. Look, your majesty.' And Curdie showed him how he was scratched and bitten.

The king was pleased to find him behave more politely than he had expected from what his people had told him concerning the miners, for he attributed it to the power of his own presence; but he did not therefore feel friendly to the intruder.

'You will oblige me by walking out of my dominions at once,' he said, well knowing what a mockery lay in the words.

'With pleasure, if your majesty will give me a guide,' said Curdie.

'I will give you a thousand,' said the king, with a scoffing air of magnificent liberality.

'One will be quite sufficient,' said Curdie.

But the king uttered a strange shout, half halloo, half roar, and in rushed goblins till the cave was swarming. He said something to the first of them which Curdie could not hear, and it was passed from one to another till in a moment the farthest in the crowd had evidently heard and understood it. They began to gather about him in a way he did not relish, and he retreated towards the wall. They pressed upon him.

'Stand back,' said Curdie, grasping his pickaxe tighter by his knee.

They only grinned and pressed closer. Curdie bethought himself, and began to rhyme.

> 'Ten, twenty, thirty—
> You're all so very dirty!
> Twenty, thirty, forty—
> You're all so thick and snorty!
>
> Thirty, forty, fifty—
> You're all so puff-and-snifty!
> Forty, fifty, sixty—
> Beast and man so mixty!
>
> Fifty, sixty, seventy—
> Mixty, maxty, leaventy!
> Sixty, seventy, eighty—
> All your cheeks so slaty!
>
> Seventy, eighty, ninety,
> All your hands so flinty!
> Eighty, ninety, hundred,
> Altogether dundred!'

The goblins fell back a little when he began, and made horrible grimaces all through the rhyme, as if eating something so disagreeable that it set their teeth on edge and gave them the creeps; but whether it was that the rhyming words were most of them no words at all, for, a new rhyme being considered the more efficacious, Curdie had made it on the spur of the moment, or whether it was that the presence of the king and the queen gave them courage, I cannot tell; but the moment the rhyme was over, they crowded on him again, and out shot a hundred long arms, with a multitude of thick nailless fingers at the ends of them, to lay hold upon him. Then Curdie heaved up his axe. But being as gentle as courageous and not wishing to kill any of them, he turned the end which was square and blunt like a hammer, and with that came down a great blow on the head of the goblin nearest him. Hard as the heads of all goblins are, he thought he must feel that. And so he did, no doubt; but he only gave a horrible cry, and sprung at Curdie's throat. Curdie however drew back in time, and just at that critical moment, remembered the vulnerable part of the goblin-body. He made a sudden rush at the king, and stamped with all his might on his majesty's feet. The king gave a most unkingly howl, and almost fell into the fire. Curdie then rushed into the crowd, stamping right and left. The goblins drew back howling on every side as he approached, but they were so crowded that few of those he attacked could escape his tread; and the shrieking and roaring that filled the cave would have appalled Curdie, but for the good hope it gave him. They were tumbling over each other in heaps in their eagerness to rush from the cave, when a new assailant suddenly faced him—the queen, with flaming eyes and expanded nostrils, her hair standing half up from her head, rushed at him. She trusted in her shoes: they were of granite—hollowed like French *sabots*.* Curdie would have endured much rather than hurt a woman, even if she was a goblin; but here was an affair of life and death: forgetting her shoes, he made a great stamp on one of her feet. But she instantly returned it with very different effect, causing him frightful pain, and almost disabling him. His only chance with her would have been to attack the granite shoes with his pickaxe, but before he could think of that, she had caught him up in her arms, and was rushing with him across the cave. She dashed him into a hole in the wall, with a force that almost stunned him. But although he could not move, he was not too far gone to hear her great cry, and the rush of multitudes of soft feet, followed by the sounds of something heaved up against the rock; after which came a multitudinous patter of stones falling near him. The last had not ceased when he grew very faint, for his head had been badly cut, and at last insensible.

When he came to himself, there was perfect silence about him, and utter darkness, but for the merest glimmer in one tiny spot. He crawled to it, and found that they had heaved a slab against the mouth of the hole, past the edge of which a poor little gleam found its way from the fire. He could not move it a hair's breadth, for they had piled a great heap of stones against it. He crawled back to where he had been lying, in the faint hope of finding his pickaxe. But after a vain search, he was at last compelled to acknowledge himself in an evil plight. He sat down and tried to think, but soon fell fast asleep.

XIX

Goblin Counsels

He must have slept a long time, for when he awoke, he felt wonderfully restored—indeed almost well, and very hungry. There were voices in the outer cave.

Once more then, it was night; for the goblins slept during the day, and went about their affairs during the night.

In the universal and constant darkness of their dwelling, they had no reason to prefer the one arrangement to the other; but from aversion to the sun-people, they chose to be busy when there was least chance of their being met either by the miners below, when they were burrowing, or by the people of the mountain above, when they were feeding their sheep or catching their goats. And indeed it was only when the sun was away that the outside of the mountain was sufficiently like their own dismal regions to be endurable to their mole-eyes, so thoroughly had they become disused to any light beyond that of their own fires and torches.

Curdie listened, and soon found that they were talking of himself.

'How long will it take?' asked Harelip.

'Not many days, I should think,' answered the king. 'They are poor feeble creatures, those sun-people, and want to be always eating. *We* can go a week at a time without food, and be all the better for it; but I've been told *they* eat two or three times every day! Can you believe it?—They must be quite hollow inside—not at all like us, nine-tenths of whose bulk is solid flesh and bone. Yes—I judge a week of starvation will do for him.'

'If *I* may be allowed a word,' interposed the queen, '—and I think I ought to have some voice in the matter—'

'The wretch is entirely at your disposal, my spouse,'

interrupted the king. 'He is your property. You caught him yourself. We should never have done it.'

The queen laughed. She seemed in far better humour than the night before.

'I was about to say,' she resumed, 'that it does seem a pity to waste so much fresh meat.'

'What are you thinking of, my love?' said the king. 'The very notion of starving him implies that we are not going to give him any meat, either salt or fresh.'*

'I'm not such a stupid as that comes to,' returned her majesty. 'What I mean is, that by the time he is starved, there will hardly be a picking upon his bones.'

The kind gave a great laugh.

'Well, my spouse, you may have him when you like,' he said. 'I don't fancy him for my part. I am pretty sure he is tough eating.'

'That would be to honour instead of punish his insolence,' returned the queen. 'But why should our poor creatures be deprived of so much nourishment? Our little dogs and cats and pigs and small bears would enjoy him very much.'

'You are the best of housekeepers, my lovely queen!' said her husband. 'Let it be so by all means. Let us have our people in, and get him out and kill him at once. He deserves it. The mischief he might have brought upon us, now that he had penetrated so far as our most retired citadel, is incalculable. Or rather let us tie him hand and foot, and have the pleasure of seeing him torn to pieces by full torchlight in the great hall.'

'Better and better!' cried the queen and the prince together, both of them clapping their hands. And the prince made an ugly noise with his harelip, just as if he had intended to be one at the feast.

'But,' added the queen, bethinking herself, 'he is so troublesome. For as poor creatures as they are, there is something about those sun-people that is *very* troublesome. I cannot imagine how it is that with such superior strength and skill and understanding as ours, we permit them to exist at all. Why do we not destroy them entirely, and use their cattle and grazing lands at our pleasure? Of course, we don't want to live in their horrid country! It is far too glaring for our quieter and more refined tastes. But we might use it for a sort of outhouse, you know. Even our creatures' eyes might get used to it, and if they did grow blind, that would be of no consequence, provided they grew fat as well. But we might even keep their great cows and other creatures, and then we should have a few more luxuries, such as cream and cheese, which at present we only taste occasionally, when our brave men have succeeded in carrying some off from their farms.'

'It is worth thinking of,' said the king; 'and I don't know why *you* should be the first to suggest it, except that you have a positive genius for conquest. But still, as you say, there is something very troublesome about them; and it would be better, as I understand you to suggest, that we should starve him for a day or two first, so that he may be a little less frisky when we take him out.'

> Once there was a goblin
> Living in a hole;
> Busy he was cobblin'
> A shoe without a sole.
>
> By came a birdie:
> 'Goblin, what do you do?'
> 'Cobble at a sturdie
> Upper leather shoe.'
>
> 'What's the good o' that, sir?'
> Said the little bird,
> 'Why it's very pat, sir—
> Plain without a word.
>
> Where 'tis all a hole, sir,
> Never can be holes:
> Why should their shoes have soles, sir,
> When *they*'ve got no souls?'

'What's that horrible noise?' cried the queen, shuddering from pot-metal head to granite shoes.

'I declare,' said the king with solemn indignation, 'it's the sun-creature in the hole!'

'Stop that disgusting noise!' cried the crown-prince valiantly, getting up and standing in front of the heap of stones, with his face towards Curdie's prison.—'Do now, or I'll break your head.'

'Break away,' shouted Curdie, and began singing again—

> 'Once there was a goblin,
> Living in a hole—'

'I really can*not* bear it,' said the queen. 'If I could only get at his horrid toes with my slippers again!'

'I think we had better go to bed,' said the king

'It's not time to go to bed,' said the queen.

'I would if I was you,' said Curdie.

'Impertinent wretch!' said the queen, with the utmost scorn in her voice.

'An impossible *if*,' said his majesty with dignity.

'Quite,' returned Curdie, and began singing again—

> 'Go to bed,
> Goblin, do.
> Help the queen
> Take off her shoe.
>
> If you do,
> It will disclose
> A horrid set
> Of sprouting toes.'

'What a lie!' roared the queen in a rage.

'By the way, that reminds me,' said the king, 'that, for as long as we have been married, I have never seen your feet, queen. I think you might take off your shoes when you go to bed! They positively hurt me sometimes.'

'I will do as I like,' retorted the queen sulkily.

'You ought to do as your own hubby wishes you,' said the kind.

'I will not,' said the queen.

'Then I insist upon it,' said the king.

Apparently his majesty approached the queen for the purpose of following the advice given by Curdie, for the latter heard a scuffle, and then a great roar from the king.

'Will you be quiet then?' said the queen wickedly.

'Yes, yes, queen. I only meant to coax you.'

'Hands off!' cried the queen triumphantly. 'I'm going to bed. You may come when you like. But as long as I am queen, I will sleep in my shoes. It is my royal privilege. Harelip, go to bed.'

'I'm going,' said Harelip sleepily.

'So am I,' said the king.

'Come along then,' said the queen; 'and mind you are good, or I'll—'

'Oh, no, no, no!' screamed the king, in the most supplicating of tones.

Curdie heard only a muttered reply in the distance; and then the cave was quite still.

They had left the fire burning, and the light came through brighter than before. Curdie thought it was time to try again if anything could be done. But he found he could not get even a finger through the chink between the slab and the rock. He gave a great rush with his shoulder against the slab, but it yielded no more than if it had been part of the rock. All he could do, was to sit down and think again.

By-and-by he came to the resolution to pretend to be dying, in the hope they might take him out before his strength was too much exhausted to let him have a chance. Then, for the creatures, if he could but find his axe again, he would have no fear of them; and if it were not for the queen's horrid shoes, he would have no fear at all.

Meantime, until they should come again at night, there was nothing for him to do but forge new rhymes, now his only weapons.* He had no intention of using them at present, of course; but it was well to have a stock, for he might live to want them, and the manufacture of them would help to while away the time.

XX

Irene's Clue

That same morning early, the princess woke in a terrible fright. There was a hideous noise in her room—of creatures snarling and hissing and racketing about as if they were fighting. The moment she came to herself, she remembered something she had never thought of again—what her grandmother told her to do when she was frightened. She immediately took off her ring and put it under her pillow. As she did so, she fancied she felt a finger and thumb take it gently from under her palm. 'It must be my grandmother!' she said to herself, and the thought gave her such courage that she stopped to put on her dainty little slippers before running from the room. While doing this, she caught sight of a long cloak of sky-blue, thrown over the back of a chair by her bedside. She had never seen it before, but it was evidently waiting for her. She put it on, and then, feeling with the forefinger of her right hand, soon found her grandmother's thread, which she proceeded at once to follow, expecting it would lead her straight up the old stair. When she reached the door, she found it went down and ran along the floor, so that she had almost to crawl in order to keep a hold of it. Then, to her surprise, and somewhat to her dismay, she found that instead of leading her towards the stair it turned in quite the opposite direction. It led her through certain narrow passages towards the kitchen, turning aside ere she reached it, and guiding her to a door which communicated with a small back yard. Some of the maids were already up, and this door was standing open. Across the yard the thread still ran along the ground, until it brought her to a door in the wall which opened upon the mountainside. When she had passed through, the thread rose to about half her height, and she could hold it with ease as she walked. It led her straight up the mountain.

The cause of her alarm was less frightful than she supposed. The cook's great black cat, pursued by the housekeeper's terrier, had bounced against her bedroom door, which had not been properly fastened, and the two had burst into the room together and commenced a battle royal. How the nurse came to sleep through it, was a mystery, but I suspect the old lady had something to do with it.

It was a clear warm morning. The wind blew deliciously over the mountainside. Here and there she saw a late prim-rose, but she did not stop to call upon them. The sky was mottled with small clouds. The sun was not yet up, but some of their fluffy edges had caught his light, and hung out orange and gold-coloured fringes upon the air. The dew lay in round drops upon the leaves, and hung like tiny diamond earrings from the blades of grass about her path.

'How lovely that bit of gossamer is!' thought the princess, looking at a long undulating line that shone at some distance from her up the hill. It was not the time for gossamers though; and Irene soon discovered it was her own thread she saw shining on before her in the light of the morning. It was leading her she knew not whither; but she had never in her life been out before sunrise, and everything was so fresh and cool and lively and full of something coming, that she felt too happy to be afraid of anything.

After leading her up a good distance, the thread turned to the left, and down the path upon which she and Lootie had met Curdie. But she never thought of that, for now in the morning light, with its far outlook over the country, no path could have been more open and airy and cheerful. She could see the road almost to the horizon, along which she had so often watched her king-papa and his troop come shining, with the bugle-blast cleaving the air before them; and it was like a companion to her. Down and down the path went, then up, and then down and then up again, getting rugged and more rugged as it went; and still along the path went the silvery thread, and still along the thread went Irene's little rosy-tipped forefinger. By and by she came to a little stream that jabbered and prattled down the hill, and up the side of the stream went both path and thread. And still the path grew rougher and steeper, and the mountain grew wilder, till Irene began to think she was going a very long way from home; and when she turned to look back, she saw that the level country had vanished and the rough bare mountain had closed in about her. But still on went the thread, and on went the princess. Everything around her was getting brighter and brighter as the sun came nearer; till at length his first rays all at once alighted on the top of a rock before her, like some golden creature fresh from the sky. Then she saw that the little stream ran out of a hole in that rock, that the path did not go past the rock, and that the thread was leading her straight up to it. A shudder ran through her from head to foot when she found that the thread was actually taking her into the hole out of which the stream ran. It ran out babbling joyously, but she had to go in.

She did not hesitate. Right into the hole she went, which was high enough to let her walk without stooping. For a little way there was a brown glimmer, but at the first turn it all but ceased, and before she had gone many paces she was in total darkness. Then she began to be frightened indeed. Every moment she kept feeling the thread backwards and forwards, and as she went farther and farther into the darkness of the great hollow mountain, she kept thinking more and more about her grandmother, and all that she had said to her, and how kind she had been, and how beautiful she was, and all about her lovely room, and the fire of roses, and the great lamp that sent its light through stone walls. And she became more and more sure that the thread could not have gone there of itself, and that her grandmother must have sent it. But it tried her dreadfully when the path went down very steep, and especially when she came to places where she had to go down rough stairs, and even sometimes a ladder. Through one narrow passage after another, over lumps of rock and sand and clay, the thread guided her, until she came to a small hole through which she had to creep. Finding no change on the other side—'Shall I ever get back?' she thought, over and over again, wondering at herself that she was not ten times more frightened, and often feeling as if she were only walking in the story of a dream. Sometimes she heard the noise of water, a dull gurgling inside the rock. By-and-by she heard the sounds of blows, which came nearer and nearer; but again they grew duller, and almost died away. In a hundred directions she turned, obedient* to the guiding thread.

At last she spied a dull red shine, and came up to the mica-window, and thence away and round about, and right into a cavern, where glowed the red embers of a fire. Here the thread began to rise. It rose as high as her head, and higher still. What *should* she do if she lost her hold? She was pulling it down! She might break it! She could see it far up, glowing as red as her fire-opal in the light of the embers.

But presently she came to a huge heap of stones, piled in a slope against the wall of the cavern. On these she climbed, and soon recovered the level of the thread—only however to find, the next moment, that it vanished through the heap of stones, and left her standing on it, with her face to the solid rock. For one terrible moment, she felt as if her grandmother had forsaken her. The thread which the spiders had spun far over the seas, which her grandmother had sat in the moonlight and spun again for her, which she had tempered in the rose-fire, and tied to her opal ring, had left her—had gone where she could no longer follow it—had brought her into a horrible cavern, and there left her! She was forsaken indeed!

'When *shall* I wake?' she said to herself in an agony, but the same moment knew that it was no dream. She threw herself upon the heap, and began to cry. It was well she did not know what creatures, one of them with stone shoes on her feet, were lying in the next cave. But neither did she know who was on the other side of the slab.

At length the thought struck her, that at least she could follow the thread backwards, and thus get out of the mountain, and home. She rose at once, and found the thread. But the instant she tried to feel it backwards, it vanished from her touch. Forwards, it led her hand up to the heap of stones—backwards it seemed nowhere. Neither could she see it as before in the light of the fire. She burst into a wailing cry, and again threw herself down on the stones.

XXI

The Escape

As the princess lay and sobbed, she kept feeling the thread mechanically, following it with her finger many times up to the stones in which it disappeared. By and by she began, still mechanically, to poke her finger in after it between the stones as far as she could. All at once it came into her head that she might remove some of the stones and see where the thread went next. Almost laughing at herself for never having thought of this before, she jumped to her feet. Her fear vanished; once more she was certain her grandmother's thread could not have brought her there just to leave her there; and she began to throw away the stones from the top as fast as she could, sometimes two or three at a handful, sometimes taking both hands to lift one. After clearing them away a little, she found that the thread turned and went straight downwards. Hence, as the heap sloped a good deal, growing of course wider towards its base, she had to throw away a multitude of stones to follow the thread. But this was not all, for she soon found that the thread, after going straight down for a little way, turned first sideways in one direction, then sideways in another, and then shot, at various angles, hither and thither inside the heap, so that she began to be afraid that to clear the thread, she must remove the whole huge gathering. She was dismayed at the very idea, but, losing no time, set to work with a will; and with aching back, and bleeding fingers and hands, she worked on, sustained by the pleasure of seeing the heap slowly diminish, and begin to show itself on the opposite side of the fire. Another thing which helped to keep up her courage was, that as often as she uncovered a turn of the thread, instead of lying loose upon the stones, it tightened up: this made her sure that her grandmother was at the end of it somewhere.

She had got about half-way down when she started, and nearly fell with fright. Close to her ear as it seemed, a voice broke out singing—

> 'Jabber, bother, smash!
> You'll have it all in a crash.
> Jabber, smash, bother!
> You'll have the worst of the pother*
> Smash, bother, jabber!—'

Here Curdie stopped, either because he could not find a rhyme to *jabber*, or because he remembered what he had forgotten when he woke up at the sound of Irene's labours, that his plan was to make the goblins think he was getting weak. But he had uttered enough to let Irene know who he was.

'It's Curdie!' she cried joyfully.

'Hush! hush!' came Curdie's voice again from somewhere. 'Speak softly.'

'Why, you were singing loud!' said Irene.

'Yes. But they know I am here, and they don't know you are. Who are you?'

'I'm Irene,' answered the princess. 'I know who you are quite well. You're Curdie.'

'Why, however did you come here, Irene?'

'My great-great-grandmother sent me; and I think I've found out why. You can't get out, I suppose?'

'No, I can't. What are you doing?'

'Clearing away a huge heap of stones.'

'There's a princess!' exclaimed Curdie, in a tone of delight, but still speaking in little more than a whisper. 'I can't think how you got here though.'

'My grandmother sent me after her thread.'

'I don't know what you mean,' said Curdie; 'but so you're there, it doesn't much matter.'

'Oh, yes it does!' returned Irene. 'I should never have been here but for her.'

'You can tell me all about it when we get out, then. There's no time to lose now, said Curdie.

And Irene went to work, as fresh as when she began.

'There's such a lot of stones!' she said. 'It will take me a long time to get them all away.'

'How far on have you got?' asked Curdie.

'I've got about the half away, but the other half is ever so much bigger.'

'I don't think you will have to move the lower half. Do you see a slab laid up against the wall?'

Irene looked, and felt about with her hands, and soon perceived the outlines of the slab.

'Yes,' she answered, 'I do.'

'Then, I think,' rejoined Curdie, 'when you have cleared the slab about half-way down, or a little more, I shall be able to push it over.'

'I must follow my thread,' returned Irene, 'whatever I do.'

'What *do* you mean?' exclaimed Curdie.

'You will see when you get out,' answered the princess, and went on harder than ever.

But she was soon satisfied that what Curdie wanted done, and what the thread wanted done, were one and the same thing. For she not only saw that by following the turns of the thread she had been clearing the face of the slab, but that, a little more than half-way down, the thread went through the chink between the slab and the wall into the place where Curdie was confined, so that she could not follow it any farther until the slab was out of her way. As soon as she found this, she said in a right joyous whisper—

'Now, Curdie! I think if you were to give a great push, the slab would tumble over.'

'Stand quite clear of it then,' said Curdie, 'and let me know when you are ready.'

Irene got off the heap, and stood on one side of it.

'Now, Curdie!' she cried.

Curdie gave a great rush with his shoulder against it. Out

tumbled the slab on the heap, and out crept Curdie over the top of it.

'You've saved my life, Irene!' he whispered.

'Oh, Curdie! I'm so glad! Let's get out of this horrid place as fast as we can.'

'That's easier said than done,' returned he.

'Oh, no! it's quite easy,' said Irene. 'We have only to follow my thread. I am sure that it's going to take us out now.'

She had already begun to follow it over the fallen slab into the hole, while Curdie was searching the floor of the cavern for his pickaxe.

'Here it is!' he cried. 'No, it is not!' he added, in a disappointed tone. 'What can it be then?—I declare it's a torch. That *is* jolly! It's better almost than my pickaxe. Much better if it weren't for those stone shoes!' he went on, as he lighted the torch by blowing the last embers of the expiring fire.

When he looked up, with the lighted torch casting a glare into the great darkness of the huge cavern, he caught sight of Irene disappearing in the hole out of which he had himself just come.

'Where are you going there?' he cried. 'That's not the way out. That's where I couldn't get out.'

'I know that,' whispered Irene. 'But this is the way my thread goes, and I must follow it.'

'What nonsense the child talks!' said Curdie to himself. 'I must follow her, though, and see that she comes to no harm. She will soon find she can't get out that way, and then she will come with me.'

So he crept over the slab once more into the hole with his torch in his hand. But when he looked about in it, he could see her nowhere. And now he discovered that although the hole was narrow, it was much longer than he had supposed; for in one direction the roof came down very low, and the hole went off in a narrow passage, of which he could not see the end. The princess must have crept in there. He got on his knees and one hand, holding the torch with the other, and crept after her. The hole twisted about, in some parts so low that he could hardly get through, in others so high that he could not see the roof, but everywhere it was narrow—far too narrow for a goblin to get through, and so I presume they never thought that Curdie might. He was beginning to feel very uncomfortable lest something should have befallen the princess, when he heard her voice almost close to his ear, whispering—

'Aren't you coming, Curdie?'

And when he turned the next corner, there she stood waiting for him.

'I knew you couldn't go wrong in that narrow hole, but now you must keep by me, for here is a great wide place,' she said.

'I can't understand it,' said Curdie, half to himself, half to Irene.

'Never mind,' she returned. 'Wait till we get out.'

Curdie, utterly astonished that she had already got so far, and by a path he had known nothing of, thought it better to let her do as she pleased.

'At all events,' he said again to himself, 'I know nothing about the way, miner as I am; and she seems to think she does know something about it, though how she should, passes my comprehension. So she's just as likely to find her way as I am, and as she insists on taking the lead, I must follow. We can't be much worse off than we are, anyhow.'

Reasoning thus, he followed her a few steps, and came out in another great cavern, across which Irene walked in a straight line, as confidently as if she knew every step of the way. Curdie went on after her, flashing his torch about, and trying to see something of what lay around them. Suddenly he started back a pace as the light fell upon something close by which Irene was passing. It was a platform of rock raised a few feet from the floor and covered with sheep skins, upon which lay two horrible figures asleep, at once recognized by Curdie as the king and queen of the goblins. He lowered his torch instantly lest the light should awake them. As he did so, it flashed upon his pickaxe, lying by the side of the queen, whose hand lay close by the handle of it.

'Stop one moment,' he whispered. 'Hold my torch, and don't let the light on their faces.'

Irene shuddered when she saw the frightful creatures, whom she had passed without observing them, but she did as he requested, and turning her back, held the torch low in front of her. Curdie drew his pickaxe carefully away, and as he did so, spied one of her feet, projecting from under the skins. The great clumsy granite shoe, exposed thus to his hand, was a temptation not to be resisted. He laid hold of it, and, with cautious efforts, drew it off. The moment he succeeded, he saw to his astonishment that what he had sung in ignorance, to annoy the queen, was actually true: she had six horrible toes. Overjoyed at his success, and seeing by the huge bump in the sheep skins where the other foot was, he proceeded to lift them gently, for, if he could only succeed in carrying away the other shoe as well, he would be no more afraid of the goblins than of so many flies. But as he pulled at the second shoe, the queen gave a growl and sat up in bed. The same instant the king awoke also, and sat up beside her.

'Run, Irene!' cried Curdie, for though he was not now in the least afraid for himself, he was for the princess.

Irene looked once round, saw the fearful creatures awake, and like the wise princess she was, dashed the torch on the ground and extinguished it, crying out—

'Here, Curdie, take my hand.'

He darted to her side, forgetting neither the queen's shoe nor his pickaxe, and caught hold of her hand, as she sped fearlessly where her thread guided her. They heard the queen give a great bellow; but they had a good start, for it would be some time before they could get torches lighted to pursue them. Just as they thought they saw a gleam behind them, the thread brought them to a very narrow opening, through which Irene crept easily, and Curdie with difficulty.

'Now,' said Curdie; 'I think we shall be safe.'

'Of course we shall,' returned Irene.

'Why do you think so? asked Curdie.

'Because my grandmother is taking care of us.'

'That's all nonsense,' said Curdie. 'I don't know what you mean.'

'Then if you don't know what I mean, what right have you to call it nonsense?' asked the princess, a little offended.

'I beg your pardon, Irene,' said Curdie; 'I did not mean to vex you.'

'Of course not,' returned the princess. 'But why do *you* think we shall be safe?'

'Because the king and queen are far too stout to get through that hole.'

'There might be ways round,' said the princess.

'To be sure there might: we are not out of it yet,' acknowledged Curdie.

'But what do you mean by the king and queen?' asked the princess. 'I should never call such creatures as those a king and a queen.'

'Their own people do, though,' answered Curdie.

The princess asked more questions, and Curdie, as they walked leisurely along, gave her a full account, not only of the character and habits of the goblins, so far as he knew them, but of his own adventures with them, beginning from the very night after that in which he had met her and Lootie upon the mountain. When he had finished, he begged Irene to tell him how it was that she had come to his rescue. So Irene too had to tell a long story, which she did in rather a roundabout manner, interrupted by many questions concerning things she had not explained. But her tale, as he did not believe more than half of it, left everything as unaccountable to him as before, and he was nearly as much perplexed as to what he must think of the princess. He could not believe that she was deliberately telling stories, and the only conclusion he could come to was that Lootie had been playing the child tricks, inventing no end of lies to frighten her for her own purposes.

'But how ever did Lootie come to let you go into the mountain alone?' he asked.

'Lootie knows nothing about it. I left her fast asleep—at least I think so. I hope my grandmother won't let her get into trouble, for it wasn't her fault at all, as my grandmother very well knows.'

'But how *did* you find your way to me?' persisted Curdie.

'I told you already,' answered Irene;—'by keeping my finger upon my grandmother's thread, as I am doing now.'

'You don't mean you've got the thread there?'

'Of course I do. I have told you so ten times already. I have hardly—except when I was removing the stones—taken my finger off it. There!' she added, guiding Curdie's hand to the thread; 'you feel it yourself—don't you?'

'I feel nothing at all,' replied Curdie,

'Then what *can* be the matter with your finger? *I* feel it perfectly. To be sure it is very thin, and in the sunlight looks just like the thread of a spider, though there are many of them twisted together to make it—but for all that I can't think why you shouldn't feel it as well as I do.'

Curdie was too polite to say he did not believe there was any thread there at all. What he did say was—

'Well, I can make nothing of it.'

'I can though, and you must be glad of that, for it will do for both of us.'

'We're not out yet,' said Curdie.

'We soon shall be,' returned Irene confidently.

And now the thread went downwards, and led Irene's hand to a hole in the floor of the cavern, whence came a sound of running water which they had been hearing for some time.

'It goes into ground now, Curdie,' she said, stopping.

He had been listening to another sound, which his prac-tised ear had caught long ago, and which also had been growing louder. It was the noise the goblin miners made at their work, and they seemed to be at no great distance now. Irene heard it the moment she stopped.

'What is that noise?' she asked. 'Do you know, Curdie?'

'Yes. It is the goblins digging and burrowing,' he answered.

'And you don't know what they do it for?'

'No; I haven't the least idea. Would you like to see them?' he asked, wishing to have another try after their secret.

'If my thread took me there, I shouldn't much mind; but I don't want too see them, and I can't leave my thread. It leads me down into the hole, and we had better go at once.'

'Very well. Shall I go in first?' said Curdie.

'No; better not. You can't feel the thread,' she answered, stepping down through a narrow break in the floor of the cavern. 'Oh!' she cried, 'I am in the water. It is running strong—but it is not deep, and there is just room to walk. Make haste, Curdie.'

He tried, but the hole was too small for him to get in.

'Go on a little bit,' he said, shouldering his pickaxe.

In a few moments he had cleared a larger opening and followed her. They went on, down and down with the running water, Curdie getting more and more afraid it was leading them to some terrible gulf in the heart of the mountain. In one or two places he had to break away the rock to make room before even Irene could get through—at least without hurting herself. But at length they spied a glimmer of light, and in a minute more, they were almost blinded by the full sunlight into which they emerged. It was some little time before the princess could see well enough to discover that they stood in her own garden, close by the seat on which she and her king-papa had sat that afternoon. They had come out by the channel of the little stream. She danced and clapped her hands with delight.

'Now, Curdie!' she cried, 'won't you believe what I told you about my grandmother and her thread?'

For she had felt all the time that Curdie was not believing what she told him.

'There!—don't you see it shining on before us?' she added.

'I don't see anything,' persisted Curdie.

'Then you must believe without seeing,'* said the princess; 'for you can't deny it has brought us out of the mountain.'

'I can't deny we *are* out of the mountain, and I should be very ungrateful indeed to deny that *you* had brought *me* out of it.'

'I couldn't have done it but for the thread,' persisted Irene.

'That's the part I don't understand.'

'Well, come along, and Lootie will get you something to eat. I am sure you must want it very much.'

'Indeed I do. But my father and mother will be so anxious about me, I must make haste—first up the mountain to tell my mother, and then down into the mine again to let my father know.'

'Very well, Curdie; but you can't get out without coming this way, and I will take you through the house, for that is nearest.'

They met no one by the way, for indeed, as before, the people were here and there and everywhere searching for the princess. When they got in, Irene found that the thread, as she had half expected, went up the old staircase, and a new thought struck her. She turned to Curdie and said—

'My grandmother wants me. Do come up with me, and see her. Then you will know that I have been telling you the truth. Do come—to please me, Curdie. I can't bear you should think I say what is not true.'

'I never doubted you believed what you said,' returned Curdie. 'I only thought you had some fancy in your head that was not correct.'

'But do come, dear Curdie.'

The little miner could not withstand this appeal, and though he felt shy in what seemed to him such a huge grand house, he yielded, and followed her up the stair.

XXII

The Old Lady and Curdie

Up the stair then they went, and the next and the next, and through the long rows of empty rooms, and up the little tower stair, Irene growing happier and happier as she ascended. There was no answer when she knocked at length at the door of the work-room, nor could she hear any sound of the spinning-wheel, and once more her heart sank within her—but only for one moment, as she turned and knocked at the other door.

'Come in,' answered the sweet voice of her grandmother, and Irene opened the door and entered, followed by Curdie.

'You darling!' cried the lady, who was seated by a fire of red roses mingled with white—'I've been waiting for you, and indeed getting a little anxious about you, and beginning to think whether I had not better go and fetch you myself.'

As she spoke she took the little princess in her arms and placed her upon her lap. She was dressed in white now, and looking if possible more lovely than ever.

'I've brought Curdie, grandmother. He wouldn't believe what I told him, and so I've brought him.'

'Yes—I see him. He is a good boy, Curdie, and a brave boy. Aren't you glad you've got him out?'

'Yes, grandmother. But it wasn't very good of him not to believe me when I was telling him the truth.'

'People must believe what they can, and those who believe more must not be hard upon those who believe less. I doubt if you would have believed it all yourself if you hadn't seen some of it.'

'Ah! yes, grandmother, I dare say. I'm sure you are right. But he'll believe now.'

'I don't know that,' replied her grandmother.

'Won't you, Curdie?' said Irene, looking round at him as she asked the question.

He was standing in the middle of the floor, staring, and looking strangely bewildered. This she thought came of his astonishment at the beauty of the lady.

'Make a bow to my grandmother, Curdie,' she said.

'I don't see any grandmother,' answered Curdie rather gruffly.

'Don't see my grandmother, when I'm sitting in her lap!' exclaimed the princess.

'No, I don't,' reiterated Curdie, in an offended tone.

'Don't you see the lovely fire of roses—white ones amongst them this time?' asked Irene, almost as bewildered as he.

'No, I don't,' answered Curdie, almost sulkily.

'Nor the blue bed? Nor the rose-coloured counterpane? Nor the beautiful light, like the moon, hanging from the roof?'

You're making game of me, your royal highness; and after what we have come through together this day, I don't think it is kind of you,' said Curdie, feeling very much hurt.

'Then what *do* you see?' asked Irene, who perceived at once that for her not to believe him was at least as bad as for him not to believe her.

'I see a big, bare, garret-room—like the one in mother's cottage, only big enough to take the cottage itself in, and leave a good margin all round,' answered Curdie.

'And what more do you see?'

'I see a tub, and a heap of musty straw, and a withered apple, and a ray of sunlight coming through a hole in the middle of the roof, and shining on your head, and making all the place look a curious dusky brown. I think you had better drop it, princess, and go down to the nursery, like a good girl.'

'But don't you hear my grandmother talking to me?' asked Irene, almost crying.

'No. I hear the cooing of a lot of pigeons. If you won't come down, I will go without you. I think that will be better anyhow, for I'm sure nobody who met us would believe a word we said to them. They would think we made it all up. I don't expect anybody but my own father and mother to believe me. They *know* I wouldn't tell a story.'

'And yet *you* won't believe *me*, Curdie?' expostulated the princess, now fairly crying with vexation, and sorrow at the gulf between her and Curdie.

'No. I *can't*, and I can't help it,' said Curdie, turning to leave the room.

'What *shall* I do, grandmother?' sobbed the princess, turning her face round upon the lady's bosom, and shaking with suppressed sobs.

'You must give him time,' said her grandmother; 'and you must be content not to be believed for a while. It is very hard to bear; but I have had to bear it, and shall have to bear it many a time yet. I will take care of what Curdie thinks of you in the end. You must let him go now.'

'You're not coming, are you?' asked Curdie.

'No, Curdie; my grandmother says I must let you go. Turn to the right when you get to the bottom of all the stairs, and that will take you to the hall where the great door is.'

'Oh! I don't doubt I can find my way—without you, princess, or your old grannie's thread either,' said Curdie quite rudely.

'Oh! Curdie! Curdie!'

'I wish I had gone home at once. I'm very much obliged to you, Irene, for getting me out of that hole, but I wish you hadn't made a fool of me afterwards.'

He said this as he opened the door, which he left open, and, without another word, went down the stair. Irene listened with dismay to his departing footsteps. Then turning again to the lady—

'What does it all mean, grandmother?' she sobbed, and burst into fresh tears.

'It means, my love, that I did not mean to show myself. Curdie is not yet able to believe some things. Seeing is not believing—it is only seeing. You remember I told you that if Lootie were to see me,* she would rub her eyes, forget the half she saw, and call the other half nonsense.'

'Yes; but I should have thought Curdie—'

'You are right. Curdie is much farther on than Lootie, and you will see what will come of it. But in the mean time, you must be content, I say, to be misunderstood for a while. We are all very anxious to be understood, and it is very hard not to be. But there is one thing much more necessary.'

'What is that, grandmother?'

'To understand other people.'

'Yes, grandmother. I must be fair—for if I'm not fair to other people, I'm not worth being understood myself. I see. So as Curdie can't help it, I will not be vexed with him, but just wait.'

'There's my own dear child,' said her grandmother, and pressed her close to her bosom.

'Why weren't you in your work-room, when we came up, grandmother?' asked Irene, after a few moments' silence.

'If I had been there,* Curdie would have seen me well enough. But why should I be there rather than in this beautiful room?'

'I thought you would be spinning.'

'I've nobody to spin for just at present. I never spin without knowing for whom I am spinning.'

'That reminds me—there is one thing that puzzles me,' said the princess: 'how are you to get the thread out of the mountain again? Surely you won't have to make another for *me*! That would be such a trouble!'

The lady set her down, and rose, and went to the fire. Putting in her hand, she drew it out again, and held up the shining ball between her finger and thumb.

'I've got it now, you see,' she said, coming back to the princess, 'all ready for you when you want it.'

Going to her cabinet, she laid it in the same drawer as before.

'And here is your ring,' she added, taking it from the little finger of her left hand, and putting it on the forefinger of Irene's right hand.

'Oh! thank you, grandmother. I feel so safe now!'

'You are very tired, my child,' the lady went on. 'Your hands are hurt with the stones, and I have counted nine bruises on you. Just look what you are like.'

And she held up to her a little mirror which she had brought from the cabinet. The princess burst into a merry laugh at the sight. She was so draggled with the stream, and dirty with creeping through narrow places, that if she had seen the reflection without knowing it was a reflection, she would have taken herself for some gypsy-child* whose face was washed and hair combed about once in a month. The lady laughed too, and lifting her again upon her knee, took off her cloak and night-gown. Then she carried her to the side of the room. Irene wondered what she was going to do with her, but asked no questions—only starting a little when she found that she was going to lay her in the large silver bath;* for as she looked into it, again she saw no bottom, but the stars shining miles away, as it seemed, in a great blue gulf. Her hands closed involuntarily on the beautiful arms that held her, and that was all.

The lady pressed her once more to her bosom, saying—

'Do not be afraid, my child.'

'No, grandmother,' answered the princess, with a little gasp; and the next instant she sank in the clear cool water.

When she opened her eyes, she saw nothing but a strange lovely blue over and beneath and all about her. The lady and the beautiful room had vanished from her sight, and she seemed utterly alone. But instead of being afraid, she felt more than happy—perfectly blissful. And from somewhere came the voice of the lady, singing a strange sweet song, of which she could distinguish every word; but of the sense she had only a feeling—no understanding.* Nor could she remember a single line after it was gone. It vanished, like the poetry in a dream, as fast as it came. In after years, however, she would sometimes fancy that snatches of melody suddenly rising in her brain, must be little phrases and fragments of the air of that song; and the very fancy would make her happier, and abler to do her duty.*

How long she lay in the water, she did not know. It seemed a long time—not from weariness, but from pleasure. But at last she felt the beautiful hands lay hold of her, and through the gurgling water she was lifted out into the lovely room. The lady carried her to the fire, and sat down with her in her lap, and dried her tenderly with the softest towel. It was so different from Lootie's drying! When the lady had done, she stooped to the fire, and drew from it her night-gown, as white as snow.

'How delicious!' exclaimed the princess. 'It smells of all the roses in the world, I think.'

When she stood up on the floor, she felt as if she had been made over again. Every bruise and all weariness were gone, and her hands were soft and whole as ever.

'Now I am going to put you to bed for a good sleep,' said her grandmother.

'But what will Lootie be thinking? And what am I to say to her when she asks me where I have been?'

'Don't trouble yourself about it. You will find it all come right,' said her grandmother, and laid her into the blue bed, under the rosy counterpane.*

'There is just one thing more,' said Irene. 'I am a little anxious about Curdie. As I brought him into the house, I ought to have seen him safe on his way home.'

'I took care of all that,' answered the lady. 'I told you to let him go, and therefore I was bound to look after him. Nobody saw him, and he is now eating a good dinner in his mother's cottage, far up the mountain.'

'Then I will go to sleep,' said Irene, and in a few minutes, she was fast asleep.

XXIII

Curdie and his Mother

Curdie went up the mountain neither whistling nor singing, for he was vexed with Irene for taking him in, as he called it; and he was vexed with himself for having spoken to her so angrily. His mother gave a cry of joy when she saw him, and at once set about getting him something to eat, asking him questions all the time, which he did not answer so cheerfully as usual. When his meal was ready, she left him to eat it, and hurried to the mine to let his father know he was safe. When she came back, she found him fast asleep upon her bed; nor did he wake until his father came home in the evening.

'Now, Curdie,' his mother said, as they sat at supper, 'tell us the whole story from beginning to end, just as it all happened.'

Curdie obeyed, and told everything to the point where they came out upon the lawn in the garden of the king's house.

'And what happened after that?' asked his mother. 'You haven't told us all. You ought to be very happy at having got away from those demons, and instead of that, I never saw you so gloomy. There must be something more. Besides, you do not speak of that lovely child as I should like to hear you. She saved your life at the risk of her own, and yet somehow you don't seem to think much of it.'

'She talked such nonsense!' answered Curdie, 'and told me a pack of things that weren't a bit true; and I can't get over it.'

'What were they?' asked his father. 'Your mother may be able to throw some light upon them.'

Then Curdie made a clean breast of it, and told them everything.

They all sat silent for some time, pondering the strange tale. At last Curdie's mother spoke.

'You confess, my boy,' she said, 'there is something about the whole affair you do not understand?'

'Yes, of course, mother,' he answered. 'I cannot understand how a child knowing nothing about the mountain, or even that I was shut up in it, should come all that way alone, straight to where I was; and then, after getting me out of the hole, lead me out of the mountain too, where I should not have known a step of the way if it had been as light as in the open air.'

'Then you have no right to say that what she told you was not true. She did take you out, and she must have had something to guide her: why not a thread as well as a rope, or anything else? There is something you cannot explain, and her explanation may be the right one.'

'It's no explanation at all, mother; and I can't believe it.'

'That may be only because you do not understand it. If you did, you would probably find it was an explanation, and believe it thoroughly. I don't blame you for not being able to believe it, but I do blame you for fancying such a child would try to deceive you. Why should she? Depend upon it, she told you all she knew. Until you had found a better way of accounting for it all, you might at least have been more sparing of your judgement.'

'That is what something inside me has been saying all the time,' said Curdie, hanging down his head. 'But what do you make of the grandmother? That is what I can't get over. To take me up to an old garret, and try to persuade me against the sight of my own eyes that it was a beautiful room, with blue walls and silver stars, and no end of things in it, when there was nothing there but an old tub and a withered apple and a heap of straw and a sunbeam! It was too bad! She *might* have had some old woman there at least to pass for her precious grandmother!'

'Didn't she speak as if she saw those other things herself, Curdie?'

'Yes. That's what bothers me. You would have thought she really meant and believed that she saw every one of the things she talked about. And not one of them there! It was too bad, I say.'

'Perhaps some people can see things other people can't see, Curdie,' said his mother very gravely. 'I think I will tell you something I saw myself once—only perhaps you won't believe me either!'

'Oh, mother, mother!' cried Curdie, bursting into tears; 'I don't deserve that, surely!'

'But what I am going to tell you is very strange,' persisted his mother; 'and if having heard it you were to say I must have been dreaming, I don't know that I should have any right to be vexed with you, though I know at least that I was not asleep.'

'Do tell me, mother. Perhaps it will help me to think better of the princess.'

'That's why I am tempted to tell you,' replied his mother. 'But first, I may as well mention, that according to old whispers, there is something more than common about the king's family; and the queen was of the same blood, for they were cousins of some degree. There were strange stories told concerning them—all good stories—but strange, very strange. What they were I cannot tell, for I only remember the faces of my grandmother and my mother as they talked together about them. There was wonder and awe—not fear, in their eyes, and they whispered, and never spoke aloud. But what I saw myself, was this: Your father was going to work in the mine, one night, and I had been down with his supper. It was soon after we were married, and not very long before you were born. He came with me to the mouth of the mine, and left me to go home alone, for I knew the way almost as well as the floor of our own cottage. It was pretty dark, and in some parts of the road where the rocks overhung, nearly quite dark. But I got along perfectly well, never thinking of being afraid, until I reached a spot you know well enough, Curdie, where the path has to make a sharp turn out of the way of a great rock on the left hand side. When I got there, I was suddenly surrounded by about half a dozen of the cobs, the first I had ever seen, although I had heard tell of them often enough. One of them blocked up the path, and they all began tormenting and teasing me in a way it makes me shudder to think of even now.'

'If I had only been with you!' cried father and son in a breath.

The mother gave a funny little smile, and went on.

'They had some of their horrible creatures with them too, and I must confess I was dreadfully frightened. They had torn my clothes very much,* and I was afraid they were going to tear myself to pieces, when suddenly a great white soft light shone upon me. I looked up. A broad ray, like a shining road, came down from a large globe of silvery light, not very high up, indeed not quite so high as the horizon—so it could not have been a new star or another moon or anything of that sort. The cobs dropped persecuting me, and looked dazed, and I thought they were going to run away, but presently they began again. The same moment, however, down the path from the globe of light came a bird, shining like silver in the sun. It gave a few rapid flaps first, and then, with its wings straight out, shot sliding down the slope of the light. It looked to me just like a white pigeon. But whatever it was, when the cobs caught sight of it coming straight down upon them, they took to their heels and scampered away across the mountain, leaving me safe, only much frightened. As soon as it had sent them off, the bird went gliding again up the light, and the moment it reached the globe, the light disappeared, just as if a shutter had been closed over a window, and I saw it no more. But I had no more trouble with the cobs that night, or ever after.'

'How strange!' exclaimed Curdie.

'Yes, it is strange; but I can't help believing it, whether you do or not,' said his mother.

'It's exactly as your mother told it to me the very next morning,' said his father.

'You don't think I'm doubting my own mother!' cried Curdie.

'There are other people in the world quite as well worth believing as your own mother,' said his mother. 'I don't know that she's so much the fitter to be believed that she happens to be *your* mother, Mr Curdie. There are mothers far more likely to tell lies than that little girl I saw talking to the primroses a few weeks ago. If she were to lie I should begin to doubt my own word.'

'But princesses *have* told lies as well as other people,' said Curdie.

'Yes, but not princesses like that child. She's a good girl, I am certain, and that's more than being a princess. Depend upon it you will have to be sorry for behaving so to her, Curdie. You ought at least to have held your tongue.'

'I am sorry now,' answered Curdie.

'You ought to go and tell her so, then.'

'I don't see how I could manage that. They wouldn't let a miner boy like me have a word with her alone; and I couldn't tell her before that nurse of hers. She'd be asking ever so many questions, and I don't know how many the little princess would like me to answer. She told me that Lootie didn't know anything about her coming to get me out of the mountain. I am certain she would have prevented her somehow if she had known of it. But I may have a chance before long, and mean time I must try to do something for her. I think, father, I have got on the track at last.'

'Have you, indeed, my boy?' said Peter. 'I am sure you deserve some success; you have worked very hard for it. What have you found out?'

'It's difficult you know, father, inside the mountain, especially in the dark, and not knowing what turns you have taken, to tell the lie of things outside.'

'Impossible, my boy, without a chart, or at least a compass,' returned his father.

'Well, I think I have nearly discovered in what direction the cobs are mining. If I am right, I know something else that I can put to it, and then one and one will make three.'

'They very often do, Curdie, as we miners ought to be well aware. Now tell us, my boy, what the two things are, and see whether we guess at the same third as you.'

'I don't see what that has to do with the princess,' interposed his mother.

'I will soon let you see that, mother. Perhaps you may think me foolish but until I am sure there is nothing in my present fancy, I am more determined than ever to go on with my observations. Just as we came to the channel by which we got out, I heard the miners at work somewhere near—I think down below us. Now since I began to watch them, they have mined a good half mile, in a straight line; and so far as I am aware, they are working in no other part of the mountain. But I never could tell in what direction they were going. When we came out in the king's garden, however, I thought at once whether it was possible they were working towards the king's house; and what I want to do tonight is to make sure whether they are or not. I will take a light with me——'

'Oh Curdie,' cried his mother, 'then they will see you.'

'I'm no more afraid of them now than I was before,' rejoined Curdie, '—now that I've got this precious shoe. They can't make another such in a hurry, and one bare foot will do for my purpose. Woman as she may be, I won't spare her next time. But I shall be careful with my light, for I don't want them to see me. I won't stick it in my hat.'

'Go on, then, and tell us what you mean to do.'

'I mean to take a bit of paper with me and a pencil, and go in at the mouth of the stream by which we came out. I shall mark on the paper as near as I can the angle of every turning I take until I find the cobs at work, and so get a good idea in what direction they are going. If it should prove to be nearly parallel with the stream, I shall know it is towards the king's house they are working.'

'And what if you should? How much wiser will you be then?'

'Wait a minute, mother, dear. I told you that when I came upon the royal family in the cave, they were talking of their prince—Harelip, they called him—marrying a sun-woman—that means one of us—one with toes to her feet. Now in the speech one of them made that night at their great gathering, of which I heard only a part, he said that peace would be secured for a generation at least by the pledge the prince would hold for the good behaviour of *her* relatives: that's what he said, and he must have meant the sun-woman the prince was to marry. I am quite sure the king is much too proud to wish his son to marry any but a princess, and much too knowing to fancy that his having a peasant woman for a wife would be of any great advantage to them.'

'I see what you are driving at now,' said his mother.

'But,' said his father, 'the king would dig the mountain to the plain before he would have his princess the wife of a cob, if he were ten times a prince.'

'Yes; but they think so much of themselves!' said his mother. 'Small creatures always do. The bantam is the proudest cock in my little yard.'

'And I fancy,' said Curdie, 'if they once got her, they would tell the king they would kill her except he consented to the marriage.'

'They might say so,' said his father, 'but they wouldn't kill her; they would keep her alive for the sake of the hold it gave them over our king. Whatever he did to them, they would threaten to do the same to the princess.'

'And they are bad enough to torment her just for their own amusement—I know that,' said his mother.

'Anyhow, I will keep a watch on them, and see what they are up to,' said Curdie. 'It's too horrible to think of. I daren't let myself do it. But they shan't have her—at least if I can help it. So, mother dear—my clue is all right—will you get me a bit of paper and a pencil and a lump of pease-pudding, and I will set out at once. I saw a place where I can climb over the wall of the garden quite easily.'

'You must mind and keep out of the way of the men on the watch,' said his mother.

'That I will. I don't want them to know anything about it. They would spoil it all. The cobs would only try some other plan—they are such obstinate creatures! I shall take good care, mother. They won't kill and eat me either, if they should come upon me. So you needn't mind them.'

His mother got him what he had asked for, and Curdie set out. Close beside the door by which the princess left the garden for the mountain, stood a great rock, and by climbing it Curdie got over the wall. He tied his clue to a stone just inside the channel of the stream, and took his pickaxe with him. He had not gone far before he encountered a horrid creature coming towards the mouth. The spot was too narrow for two of almost any size or shape, and besides Curdie had no wish to let the creature pass. Not being able to use his pickaxe, however, he had a severe struggle with him, and it was only after receiving many bites, some of them bad, that he succeeded in killing him with his pocket-knife. Having dragged him out, he made haste to get in again before another should stop up the way.

I need not follow him farther in this night's adventures. He returned to his breakfast, satisfied that the goblins were mining in the direction of the palace—on so low a level that their intention must, he thought, be to burrow under the walls of the king's house, and rise up inside it—in order, he fully believed, to lay hands on the little princess, and carry her off for a wife to their horrid Harelip.

XXIV

Irene Behaves Like a Princess

When the princess awoke from the sweetest of sleeps, she found her nurse bending above her, the housekeeper looking over the nurse's shoulder, and the laundry-maid looking over the housekeeper's. The room was full of women-servants; and the gentlemen-at-arms, with a long column of men-servants behind them, were peeping, or trying to peep in at the door of the nursery.

'Are those horrid creatures gone?' asked the princess, remembering first what had terrified her in the morning.

'You naughty, naughty little princess!' cried Lootie.

Her face was very pale, with red streaks in it, and she looked as if she were going to shake her; but Irene said nothing—only waited to hear what should come next.

'How *could* you get under the clothes like that, and make us all fancy you were lost! And keep it up all day too! You *are* the most obstinate child! It's anything but fun to us, I can tell you!'

It was the only way the nurse could account for her disappearance.

'I didn't do that, Lootie,' said Irene, very quietly.

'Don't tell stories!' cried her nurse quite rudely.

'I shall tell you nothing at all,' said Irene.

'That's just as bad,' said the nurse.

'Just as bad to say nothing at all as to tell stories!' exclaimed the princess. 'I will ask my papa about that. He won't say so. And I don't think he will like you to say so.'

'Tell me directly what you mean by it!' screamed the nurse, half-wild with anger at the princess, and fright at the possible consequences to herself.

'When I tell you the truth, Lootie,' said the princess, who somehow did not feel at all angry, 'you say to me *Don't tell stories*: it seems I must tell stories before you will believe me.'

'You are very rude, princess,' said the nurse.

'You are so rude, Lootie, that I will not speak to you again till you are sorry. Why should I, when I know you will not believe me?' returned the princess.

For she did know perfectly well that if she were to tell Lootie what she had been about, the more she went on to tell her, the less would she believe her.

'You are the most provoking child!' cried her nurse. 'You deserve to be well punished for your wicked behaviour.'

'Please, Mrs Housekeeper,' said the princess, 'will you take me to your room, and keep me till my king-papa comes? I will ask him to come as soon as he can.'

Every one stared at these words. Up to this moment, they had all regarded her as little more than a baby.

But the housekeeper was afraid of the nurse, and sought to patch matters up, saying—

'I am sure, princess, nursey did not mean to be rude to you.'

'I do not think my papa would wish me to have a nurse who spoke to me as Lootie does. If she thinks I tell lies, she had better either say so to my papa, or go away. Sir Walter, will you take charge of me?'

'With the greatest of pleasure, princess,' answered the captain of the gentlemen-at-arms, walking with his great stride into the room. The crowd of servants made eager way for him, and he bowed low before the little princess's bed. 'I shall send my servant at once, on the fastest horse in the stable, to tell your king-papa that your royal highness desires his presence. When you have chosen one of these under-servants to wait upon you, I shall order the room to be cleared.'

'Thank you very much, Sir Walter,' said the princess, and her eye glanced towards a rosy-cheeked girl who had lately come to the house as a scullery-maid.

But when Lootie saw the eyes of her dear princess going in search of another instead of her, she fell upon her knees by the bedside, and burst into a great cry of distress.

'I think, Sir Walter,' said the princess, 'I will keep Lootie. But I put myself under your care; and you need not trouble my king-papa until I speak to you again. Will you all please to go away. I am quite safe and well, and I did not hide myself for the sake either of amusing myself, or of troubling my people.—Lootie, will you please to dress me.'

XXV

Curdie Comes to Grief

Everything was for some time quiet above ground. The king
was still away in a distant part of his dominions. The men-at-
arms kept watching about the house. They had been considerably astonished by finding at the foot of the rock in the
garden, the hideous body of the goblin creature killed by
Curdie; but they came to the conclusion that it had been slain
in the mines, and had crept out there to die; and except an
occasional glimpse of a live one they saw nothing to cause
alarm. Curdie kept watching in the mountain, and the goblins
kept burrowing deeper into the earth. As long as they went
deeper, there was, Curdie judged, no immediate danger.

To Irene, the summer was as full of pleasure as ever,
and for a long time, although she often thought of her
grandmother during the day, and often dreamed about her
at night, she did not see her. The kids and the flowers were
as much her delight as ever, she made as much friendship
with the miners' children she met on the mountain as Lootie
would permit; but Lootie had very foolish notions concerning the dignity of a princess, not understanding that the
truest princess is just the one who loves all her brothers and
sisters best, and who is most able to do them good by being
humble towards them. At the same time she was considerably altered for the better in her behaviour to the princess.
She could not help seeing that she was no longer a mere
child, but wiser than her age would account for. She kept
foolishly whispering to the servants, however—sometimes
that the princess was not right in her mind,* sometimes that
she was too good to live, and other nonsense of the same sort.

All this time, Curdie had to be sorry, without a chance of
confessing, that he had behaved so unkindly to the princess.

This perhaps made him the more diligent in his endeavours to serve her. His mother and he often talked on the subject, and she comforted him, and told him she was sure he would some day have the opportunity he so much desired.

Here I should like to remark, for the sake of princes and princesses in general, that it is a low and contemptible thing to refuse to confess a fault, or even an error. If a true princess has done wrong, she is always uneasy until she has had an opportunity of throwing the wrongness away from her by saying, 'I did it; and I wish I had not; and I am sorry for having done it.' So you see there is some ground for supposing that Curdie was not a miner only, but a prince as well.* Many such instances have been known in the world's history.

At length, however, he began to see signs of a change in the proceedings of the goblin excavators: they were going no deeper, but had commenced running on a level; and he watched them, therefore, more closely than ever. All at once, one night, coming to a slope of very hard rock, they began to ascend along the inclined plane of its surface. Having reached its top, they went again on a level for a night or two, after which they began to ascend once more, and kept on, at a pretty steep angle. At length Curdie judged it time to transfer his observation to another quarter, and the next night, he did not go to the mine at all; but, leaving his pickaxe and clue at home, and taking only his usual lumps of bread and pease-pudding, went down the mountain to the king's house. He climbed over the wall, and remained in the garden the whole night, creeping on hands and knees from one spot to the other, and lying at full length with his ear to the ground, listening. But he heard nothing except the tread of the men-at-arms as they marched about, whose observation, as the night was cloudy and there was no moon, he had little difficulty in avoiding. For several following nights, he continued to haunt the garden and listen, but with no success.

At length, early one evening, whether it was that he had got careless of his own safety, or that the growing moon had become strong enough to expose him, his watching came to a sudden end. He was creeping from behind the rock where the stream ran out, for he had been listening all round it in the hope it might convey to his ear some indication of the whereabouts of the goblin miners, when just as he came into the moonlight on the lawn, a whizz in his ear and a blow upon his leg startled him. He instantly squatted in the hope of eluding further notice. But when he heard the sound of running feet, he jumped up to take the chance of escape by flight. He fell, however, with a keen shoot of pain, for the bolt of a crossbow had wounded his leg, and the blood was now streaming from it. He was instantly laid hold of by two or three of the men-at-arms. It was useless to struggle, and he submitted in silence.

'It's a boy!' cried several of them together, in a tone of amazement. 'I thought it was one of those demons.'

'What are you about here?'

'Going to have a little rough usage, apparently,' said Curdie laughing, as the men shook him.

'Impertinence will do you no good. You have no business here in the king's grounds, and if you don't give a true account of yourself, you shall fare as a thief.'

'Why, what else could he be?' said one.

'He might have been after a lost kid, you know,' suggested another.

'I see no good in trying to excuse him. He has no business here, anyhow.'

'Let me go away then, if you please,' said Curdie.

'But we don't please—not except you give a good account of yourself.'

'I don't feel quite sure whether I can trust you,' said Curdie.

'We are the king's own men-at-arms,' said the captain courteously, for he was taken with Curdie's appearance and courage.

'Well, I will tell you all about it—if you will promise to listen to me and not do anything rash.'

'I call that cool!' said one of the party laughing. 'He will tell us what mischief he was about, if we promise to do as pleases him.'

'I was about no mischief,' said Curdie.

But ere he could say more he turned faint, and fell senseless on the grass. Then first they discovered that the bolt they had shot, taking him for one of the goblin creatures, had wounded him.

They carried him into the house, and laid him down in the hall. The report spread that they had caught a robber, and the servants crowded in to see the villain. Amongst the rest came the nurse. The moment she saw him she exclaimed with indignation:

'I declare it's the same young rascal of a miner that was rude to me and the princess on the mountain. He actually wanted to kiss the princess. *I* took care of that—the wretch! And *he* was prowling about—was he? Just like his impudence!'

The princess being fast asleep, and Curdie in a faint, she could misrepresent at her pleasure.

When he heard this, the captain, although he had considerable doubt of its truth, resolved to keep Curdie a prisoner until they could search into the affair. So, after they had brought him round a little, and attended to his wound, which was rather a bad one, they laid him, still exhausted from the loss of blood, upon a mattress in a disused room—one of those already so often mentioned—and locked the door, and left him. He passed a troubled night, and in the morning they found him talking wildly. In the evening he came to himself, but felt very weak, and his leg was exceedingly painful. Wondering where he was, and seeing one of the men-at-arms in the room, he began to question him, and soon recalled the events of the preceding night. As he was himself unable to watch any more, he told the soldier all he knew about the goblins, and begged him to tell his companions, and stir them up to watch with tenfold vigilance; but whether it was that he did not talk quite coherently, or that the whole thing appeared incredible, certainly the man concluded that Curdie was only raving still, and tried to coax him into holding his tongue. This, of course, annoyed Curdie dreadfully, who now felt in his turn what it was not to be believed, and the consequence was that his fever returned, and by the time when, at his persistent entreaties, the captain was called, there could be no doubt that he was raving. They did for him what they could, and promised everything he wanted, but with no intention of fulfilment. At last he went to sleep, and when at length his sleep grew profound and peaceful, they left him, locked the door again, and withdrew, intending to revisit him early in the morning.

XXVI

The Goblin-Miners

That same night several of the servants were having a chat together before going to bed. 'What can that noise be?' said one of the housemaids, who had been listening for a moment or two.

'I've heard it the last two nights,' said the cook. 'If there were any about the place, I should have taken it for rats, but my Tom keeps them far enough.'

'I've heard though,' said the scullery-maid, 'that rats move about in great companies sometimes. There may be an army of them invading us. I've heard the noises yesterday and today too.'

'It'll be grand fun then for my Tom and Mrs. House-keeper's Bob,' said the cook. 'They'll be friends for once in their lives, and fight on the same side. I'll engage Tom and Bob together will put to flight any number of rats.'

'It seems to me,' said the nurse, 'that the noises are much too loud for that. I have heard them all day, and my princess has asked me several times what they could be. Sometimes they sound like distant thunder, and sometimes like the noises you hear in the mountain from those horrid miners underneath.'

'I shouldn't wonder,' said the cook, 'if it was the miners after all. They may have come on some hole in the mountain through which the noises reach to us. They are always boring and blasting and breaking, you know.'

As he spoke, there came a great rolling rumble beneath them, and the house quivered. They all started up in affright, and rushing to the hall found the gentlemen-at-arms in consternation also. They had sent to wake their captain, who said from their description that it must have been an earthquake, an occurrence which, although very rare in that country, had taken place almost within the century; and then went to bed again, strange to say, and fell fast asleep without once thinking of Curdie, or associating the noises they had heard with what he had told them. He had not believed Curdie. If he had, he would at once have thought of what he had said, and would have taken precautions. As they heard nothing more, they concluded that Sir Walter was right, and that the danger was over for perhaps another hundred years. The fact, as discovered afterwards, was that the goblins had, in working up a second sloping face of stone, arrived at a huge block which lay under the cellars of the house, within the line of the foundations. It was so round that when they succeeded, after hard work, in dislodging it without blasting, it rolled thundering down the slope with a bounding, jarring roll, which shook the foundations of the house. The goblins were themselves dismayed at the noise, for they knew, by careful spying and measuring, that they must now be very near, if not under, the king's house, and they feared giving an alarm. They, therefore remained quiet for a while, and when they began to work again, they no doubt thought themselves very fortunate in coming upon a vein of sand which filled a winding fissure in the rock on which the house was built. By scooping this away they soon came out in the king's wine-cellar.

No sooner did they find where they were, than they scurried back again, like rats into their holes, and running at full speed to the goblin palace, announced their success to the king and queen with shouts of triumph. In a moment the goblin royal family and the whole goblin people were on their way in hot haste to the king's house, each eager to have a share in the glory of carrying off that same night the Princess Irene.

The queen went stumping along in one shoe of stone and one of skin. This could not have been pleasant, and my readers may wonder that, with such skilful workmen about her, she had not yet replaced the shoe carried off by

Curdie. As the king however had more than one ground of objection to her stone shoes, he no doubt took advantage of the discovery of her toes, and threatened to expose her deformity if she had another made. I presume he insisted on her being content with skin-shoes, and allowed her to wear the remaining granite one on the present occasion only because she was going out to war.

They soon arrived in the king's wine-cellar, and regardless of its huge vessels, of which they did not know the use, proceeded at once, but as quietly as they could, to force the door that led upwards.

XXVII
The Goblins in the King's House

When Curdie fell asleep he began at once to dream. He thought he was ascending the mountainside from the mouth of the mine, whistling and singing '*Ring, dod, bang!*' when he came upon a woman and child who had lost their way; and from that point he went on dreaming everything that had happened to him since he thus met the princess and Lootie; how he had watched the goblins, how he had been taken by them, how he had been rescued by the princess; everything indeed, until he was wounded, captured, and imprisoned by the men-at-arms. And now he thought he was lying wide awake where they had laid him, when suddenly he heard a great thundering sound.

'The cobs are coming!' he said. 'They didn't believe a word I told them! The cobs 'll be carrying off the princess from under their stupid noses! But they shan't! that they shan't!'

He jumped up, as he thought, and began to dress, but to his dismay, found that he was still lying in bed.

'Now then I will!' he said. 'Here goes! I *am* up now!'

But yet again he found himself snug in bed. Twenty times he tried, and twenty times he failed; for in fact he was not awake, only dreaming that he was. At length in an agony of despair, fancying he heard the goblins all over the house, he gave a great cry. Then there came, as he thought, a hand upon the lock of his door. It opened, and, looking up, he saw a lady with white hair, carrying a silver box in her hand, enter the room. She came to his bed, he thought, stroked his head and face with cool, soft hands, took the dressing from his leg, rubbed it with something that smelt like roses, and then waved her hands over him three times. At the last wave of her hands everything vanished, he felt himself sinking into the profoundest slumber, and remembered nothing more until he woke in earnest.

The setting moon was throwing a feeble light through the casement, and the house was full of uproar. There was soft heavy multitudinous stamping, a clashing and clanging of weapons, the voices of men and the cries of women, mixed with a hideous bellowing, which sounded victorious. The cobs were in the house! He sprung from his bed, hurried on some of his clothes, not forgetting his shoes, which were armed with nails; then spying an old hunting-knife, or short sword, hanging on the wall, he caught it, and rushed down the stairs, guided by the sounds of strife, which grew louder and louder.

When he reached the ground floor he found the whole place swarming. All the goblins of the mountain seemed gathered there. He rushed amongst them, shouting—

> 'One, two,
> Hit and hew!
> Three, four,
> Blast and bore!'

and with every rhyme he came down a great stamp upon a foot, cutting at the same time at their faces—executing, indeed, a sword dance of the wildest description. Away scattered the goblins in every direction,—into closets, up stairs, into chimneys, up on rafters, and down to the cellars. Curdie went on stamping and slashing and singing, but saw nothing of the people of the house until he came to the great hall, in which, the moment he entered it, arose a great goblin shout. The last of the men-at-arms, the captain himself, was on the floor, buried beneath a wallowing crowd of goblins. For, while each knight was busy defending himself as well as he could, by stabs in the thick bodies of the goblins, for he had soon found their heads all but invulnerable, the queen had attacked his legs and feet with her horrible granite shoe, and he was soon down; but the captain had got his back to the wall and stood out longer. The goblins would have torn them all to pieces, but the king had given orders to carry them away alive, and over each of them, in twelve groups, was standing a knot of goblins, while as many as could find room were sitting upon their prostrate bodies.

Curdie burst in dancing and gyrating and stamping and singing like a small incarnate whirlwind.

> 'Where 'tis all a hole, sir,
>   Never can be holes:
> Why should their shoes have soles, sir,
>   When they've got no souls?
>
> But she upon her foot, sir,
>   Has a granite shoe:
> The strongest leather boot, sir,
>   Six would soon be through.'

The queen gave a howl of rage and dismay; and before she recovered her presence of mind, Curdie, having begun with the group nearest him, had eleven of the knights on their legs again.

'Stamp on their feet!' he cried as each man rose, and in a few minutes the hall was nearly empty, the goblins running from it as fast as they could, howling and shrieking and limping, and cowering every now and then as they ran to cuddle their wounded feet in their hard hands, or to protect them from the frightful stamp-stamp of the armed men.

And now Curdie approached the group which, trusting in the queen and her shoe, kept their guard over the prostrate captain. The king sat on the captain's head, but the queen stood in front, like an infuriated cat, with her perpendicular eyes gleaming green, and her hair standing half up from her horrid head. Her heart was quaking, however, and she kept moving about her skin-shod foot with nervous apprehension. When Curdie was within a few paces, she rushed at him, made one tremendous stamp at his opposing foot, which happily he withdrew in time, and caught him round the waist, to dash him on the marble floor. But

just as she caught him, he came down with all the weight
of his iron-shod shoe upon her skin-shod foot, and with
a hideous howl she dropped him, squatted on the floor
and took her foot in both her hands. Meanwhile the rest
rushed on the king and the bodyguard, sent them flying,
and lifted the prostrate captain, who was all but pressed to
death. It was some moments before he recovered breath and
consciousness.

'Where's the princess?' cried Curdie, again and again.

No one knew, and off they all rushed in search of her.

Through every room in the house they went, but nowhere
was she to be found. Neither was one of the servants to
be seen. But Curdie, who had kept to the lower part of
the house, which was now quiet enough, began to hear a
confused sound as of a distant hubbub, and set out to find
where it came from. The noise grew as his sharp ears guided
him to a stair and so to the wine cellar. It was full of goblins,
whom the butler was supplying with wine as fast as he could
draw it.

While the queen and her party had encountered the
men-at-arms, Harelip with another company had gone off
to search the house. They captured every one they met,
and when they could find no more, they hurried away to
carry them safe to the caverns below. But when the butler,
who was amongst them, found that their path lay through
the wine cellar, he bethought himself of persuading them to
taste the wine, and, as he had hoped, they no sooner tasted
than they wanted more. The routed goblins, on their way
below, joined them, and when Curdie entered, they were
all, with outstretched hands, in which were vessels of every
description from saucepan to silver cup, pressing around the
butler, who sat at the tap of a huge cask, filling and filling.
Curdie cast one glance around the place before commencing
his attack, and saw in the farthest corner a terrified group of
the domestics unwatched, but cowering without courage to
attempt their escape. Amongst them was the terror-stricken
face of Lootie; but nowhere could he see the princess. Seized

with the horrible conviction that Harelip had already carried her off, he rushed amongst them, unable for wrath to sing any more, but stamping and cutting with greater fury than ever.

'Stamp on their feet; stamp on their feet!' he shouted, and in a moment the goblins were disappearing through the hole in the floor like rats and mice.

They could not vanish so fast, however, but that many more goblin-feet had to go limping back over the underground ways of the mountain that morning.

Presently however they were reinforced from above by the king and his party, with the redoubtable queen at their head. Finding Curdie again busy amongst her unfortunate subjects, she rushed at him once more with the rage of despair, and this time gave him a bad bruise on the foot. Then a regular stamping fight got up between them, Curdie with the point of his hunting knife keeping her from clasping her mighty arms about him, as he watched his opportunity of getting once more a good stamp at her skin-shod foot. But the queen was more wary as well as more agile than hitherto.

The rest mean time, finding their adversary thus matched for the moment, paused in their headlong hurry, and turned to the shivering group of women in the corner. As if determined to emulate his father and have a sun-woman of some sort to share his future throne, Harelip rushed at them, caught up Lootie and sped with her to the hole. She gave a great shriek, and Curdie heard her, and saw the plight she was in. Gathering all his strength, he gave the queen a sudden cut across the face with his weapon, came down, as she started back, with all his weight on the proper foot, and sprung to Lootie's rescue. The prince had two defenceless feet, and on both of them Curdie stamped just as he reached the hole. He dropped his burden and rolled shrieking into the earth. Curdie made one stab at him as he disappeared, caught hold of the senseless Lootie, and having dragged her back to the corner, there mounted guard over her, preparing once more to encounter the queen. Her face streaming with blood, and her eyes flashing green lightning through it, she came on with her mouth open and her teeth grinning like a tiger's, followed by the king and her bodyguard of the thickest goblins. But the same moment in rushed the captain and his men, and ran at them stamping furiously. They dared not encounter such an onset. Away they scurried, the queen foremost. Of course the right thing would have been to take the king and queen prisoners, and hold them hostages for the princess, but they were so anxious to find her that no one thought of detaining them until it was too late.

Having thus rescued the servants, they set about searching the house once more. None of them could give the least information concerning the princess. Lootie was almost silly with terror, and although scarcely able to walk, would not leave Curdie's side for a single moment. Again he allowed the others to search the rest of the house—where, except a dismayed goblin lurking here and there, they found no one—while he requested Lootie to take him to the princess's room. She was as submissive and obedient as if he had been the king.

He found the bedclothes tossed about, and most of them on the floor, while the princess's garments were scattered all over the room, which was in the greatest confusion. It was only too evident that the goblins had been there, and Curdie had no longer any doubt that she had been carried off at the very first of the inroad. With a pang of despair he saw how wrong they had been in not securing the king and queen and prince; but he determined to find and rescue the princess as she had found and rescued him, or meet the worst fate to which the goblins could doom him.

XXVIII
Curdie's Guide

Just as the consolation of this resolve dawned upon his mind, and he was turning away for the cellar to follow the goblins into their hole, something touched his hand. It was the slightest touch, and when he looked he could see nothing. Feeling and peering about in the grey of the dawn, his fingers came upon a tight thread. He looked again, and narrowly, but still could see nothing. It flashed upon him that this must be the princess's thread. Without saying a word, for he knew no one would believe him any more than he had believed the princess, he followed the thread with his finger, contrived to give Lootie the slip, and was soon out of the house, and on the mountain side—surprised that, if the thread were indeed her grandmother's messenger, it should have led the princess, as he supposed it must, into the mountain, where she would be certain to meet the goblins rushing back enraged from their defeat. But he hurried on in the hope of overtaking her first. When he arrived however at the place where the path turned off for the mine, he found that the thread did not turn with it, but went straight up the mountain. Could it be that the thread was leading him home to his mother's cottage? Could the princess be there? He bounded up the mountain like one of its own goats, and before the sun was up, the thread had brought him indeed to his mother's door. There it vanished from his fingers, and he could not find it, search as he might.

The door was on the latch, and he entered. There sat his mother by the fire, and in her arms lay the princess fast asleep.

'Hush, Curdie!' said his mother. 'Do not wake her. I'm so glad you're come! I thought the cobs must have got you again!'

With a heart full of delight, Curdie sat down at a corner of the hearth, on a stool opposite his mother's chair, and gazed at the princess, who slept as peacefully as if she had been in her own bed. All at once she opened her eyes and fixed them on him.

'Oh, Curdie! you're come!' she said quietly. 'I thought you would!'

Curdie rose and stood before her with downcast eyes.

'Irene,' he said, 'I am very sorry I did not believe you.'

'Oh, never mind, Curdie!' answered the princess. 'You couldn't, you know. You do believe me now, don't you?'

'I can't help it now. I ought to have helped it before.'

'Why can't you help it now?'

'Because, just as I was going into the mountain to look for you, I got a hold of your thread, and it brought me here.'

'Then you've come from my house, have you?'

'Yes, I have.'

'I didn't know you were there.'

'I've been there two or three days, I believe.'

'And I never knew it!—Then perhaps you can tell me why my grandmother has brought me here? I can't think. Something woke me—I didn't know what, but I was frightened, and I felt for the thread, and there it was! I was more frightened still when it brought me out on the mountain, for I thought it was going to take me into it again, and I like the outside of it best. I supposed you were in trouble again, and I had to get you out. But it brought me here instead; and, oh Curdie! your mother has been so kind to me—just like my own grandmother!'

Here Curdie's mother gave the princess a hug, and the princess turned and gave her a sweet smile, and held up her mouth to kiss her.

'Then you didn't see the cobs?' asked Curdie.

'No; I haven't been into the mountain, I told you, Curdie.'

'But the cobs have been into your house—all over it—and into your bedroom, making such a row!'

'What did they want there? It was very rude of them.'

'They wanted you—to carry you off into the mountain with them, for a wife to their Prince Harelip.'

'Oh, how dreadful!'cried the princess shuddering.

'But you needn't be afraid, you know. Your grandmother takes care of you.'

'Ah! you do believe in my grandmother then? I'm so glad! She made me think you would some day.'

All at once Curdie remembered his dream, and was silent, thinking.

'But how did you come to be in my house, and me not know it?' asked the princess.

Then Curdie had to explain everything—how he had watched for her sake, how he had been wounded and shut up by the soldiers, how he heard the noises and could not rise, and how the beautiful old lady had come to him, and all that followed.

'Poor Curdie! to lie there hurt and ill, and me never to know it!' exclaimed the princess, stroking his rough hand. 'I would have come and nursed you, if they had told me.'

'I didn't see you were lame,' said his mother.

'Am I, mother? Oh—yes—I suppose I ought to be. I declare I've never thought of it since I got up to go down amongst the cobs!'

'Let me see the wound,' said his mother.

He pulled down his stocking—when behold, except a great scar, his leg was perfectly sound!

Curdie and his mother gazed in each other's eyes, full of wonder, but Irene called out—

'I thought so, Curdie! I was sure it wasn't a dream. I was sure my grandmother had been to see you.—Don't you smell the roses? It was my grandmother healed your leg, and sent you to help me.'

'No, Princess Irene,' said Curdie; 'I wasn't good enough to be allowed to help you: I didn't believe you. Your grandmother took care of you without me.'

'She sent you to help my people, anyhow. I wish my king-papa would come. I do want so to tell him how good you have been!'

'But,' said the mother, 'we are forgetting how frightened your people must be.—You must take the princess home at once, Curdie—or at least go and tell them where she is.'

'Yes, mother. Only I'm dreadfully hungry. Do let me have some breakfast first. They ought to have listened to me, and then they wouldn't have been taken by surprise as they were.'

'That is true, Curdie; but it is not for you to blame them much. You remember?'

'Yes, mother, I do. Only I must really have something to eat.'

'You shall, my boy—as fast as I can get it,' said his mother, rising and setting the princess on her chair.

But before his breakfast was ready, Curdie jumped up so suddenly as to startle both his companions.

'Mother, mother!' he cried, 'I was forgetting. You must take the princess home yourself. I must go and wake my father.'

Without a word of explanation, he rushed to the place where his father was sleeping. Having thoroughly roused him with what he told him, he darted out of the cottage.

XXIX

Mason-Work

He had all at once remembered the resolution of the goblins to carry out their second plan upon the failure of the first. No doubt they were already busy, and the mine was therefore in the greatest danger of being flooded and rendered useless—not to speak of the lives of the miners.

When he reached the mouth of the mine, after rousing all the miners within reach, he found his father and a good many more just entering. They all hurried to the gang by which he had found a way into the goblin country. There the foresight of Peter had already collected a great many blocks of stone, with cement, ready for building up the weak place—well enough known to the goblins. Although there was not room for more than two to be actually building at once, they managed, by setting all the rest to work in preparing the cement and passing the stones, to finish in the course of the day a huge buttress filling the whole gang, and supported everywhere by the live rock. Before the hour when they usually dropped work, they were satisfied the mine was secure.

They had heard goblin hammers and pickaxes busy all the time, and at length fancied they heard sounds of water they had never heard before. But that was otherwise accounted for when they left the mine; for they stepped out into a tremendous storm which was raging all over the mountain. The thunder was bellowing, and the lightning lancing out of a huge black cloud which lay above it, and hung down its edges of thick mist over its sides. The lightning was breaking out of the mountain, too, and flashing up into the cloud. From the state of the brooks, now swollen into raging torrents, it was evident that the storm had been storming all day.

The wind was blowing as if it would blow him off the mountain, but, anxious about his mother and the princess, Curdie darted up through the thick of the tempest. Even if they had not set out before the storm came on, he did not judge them safe, for, in such a storm even their poor little house was in danger. Indeed he soon found that but for a huge rock* against which it was built, and which protected it both from the blasts and the waters, it must have been swept if it was not blown away; for the two torrents into which this rock parted the rush of water behind it united again in front of the cottage—two roaring and dangerous streams, which his mother and the princess could not possibly have passed. It was with great difficulty that he forced his way through one of them, and up to the door.

The moment his hand fell on the latch, through all the uproar of winds and waters came the joyous cry of the princess:

'There's Curdie! Curdie! Curdie!'

She was sitting wrapped in blankets on the bed, his mother trying for the hundredth time to light the fire which had been drowned by the rain that came down the chimney. The clay floor was one mass of mud, and the whole place looked wretched. But the faces of the mother and the princess shone as if their troubles only made them the merrier. Curdie burst out laughing at the sight of them.

'I never *had* such fun!' said the princess, her eyes twinkling and her pretty teeth shining. 'How nice it must be to live in a cottage on the mountain!'

'It all depends on what kind your inside house is,' said the mother.

'I know what you mean,' said Irene. 'That's the kind of thing my grandmother says.'

By the time Peter returned, the storm was nearly over, but the streams were so fierce and so swollen, that it was not only out of the question for the princess to go down the mountain, but most dangerous for Peter even or Curdie to make the attempt in the gathering darkness.

'They will be dreadfully frightened about you,' said Peter to the princess, 'but we cannot help it. We must wait till the morning.'

With Curdie's help, the fire was lighted at last, and the mother set about making their supper; and after supper they all told the princess stories till she grew sleepy. Then Curdie's mother laid her in Curdie's bed, which was in a tiny little garret-room. As soon as she was in bed, through a little window low down in the roof she caught sight of her grandmother's lamp shining far away beneath, and she gazed at the beautiful silvery globe until she fell fast asleep.

XXX

The King and the Kiss

The next morning the sun rose so bright that Irene said the rain had washed his face and let the light out clean. The torrents were still roaring down the side of the mountain, but they were so much smaller as not to be dangerous in the daylight. After an early breakfast, Peter went to his work, and Curdie and his mother set out to take the princess home. They had difficulty in getting her dry across the streams, and Curdie had again and again to carry her, but at last they got safe on the broader part of the road, and walked gently down towards the king's house. And what should they see as they turned the last corner, but the last of the king's troop riding through the gate!

'Oh, Curdie!' cried Irene, clapping her hands right joyfully, 'my king-papa is come.'

The moment Curdie heard that, he caught her up in his arms, and set off at full speed, crying—

'Come on, mother dear! The king may break his heart before he knows that she is safe.'

Irene clung round his neck, and he ran with her like a deer. When he entered the gate into the court, there sat the king on his horse, with all the people of the house about him, weeping and hanging their heads. The king was not weeping, but his face was white as a dead man's, and he looked as if the life had gone out of him. The men-at-arms he had brought with him, sat with horror-stricken faces, but eyes flashing with rage, waiting only for the word of the king to do something—they did not know what, and nobody knew what.

The day before, the men-at-arms belonging to the house, as soon as they were satisfied the princess had been carried away, rushed after the goblins into the hole, but found that they had already so skilfully blockaded the narrowest part, not many feet below the cellar, that without miners and their tools they could do nothing. Not one of them knew where the mouth of the mine lay, and some of those who had set out to find it had been overtaken by the storm and had not even yet returned. Poor Sir Walter was especially filled with shame, and almost hoped the king would order his head to be cut off, for to think of that sweet little face down amongst the goblins was unendurable.

When Curdie ran in at the gate with the princess in his arms, they were all so absorbed in their own misery and awed by the king's presence and grief, that no one observed his arrival. He went straight up to the king, where he sat on his horse.

'Papa! papa!' the princess cried, stretching out her arms to him; 'here I am!'

The king started. The colour rushed to his face. He gave an inarticulate cry. Curdie held up the princess, and the king bent down and took her from his arms. As he clasped her to his bosom, the big tears went dropping down his cheeks and his beard. And such a shout arose from all the bystanders, that the startled horses pranced and capered, and the armour rang and clattered, and the rocks of the mountain echoed back the noises. The princess greeted them all as she nestled in her father's bosom, and the king did not set her down until she had told them all the story. But she had more to tell about Curdie than about herself, and what she did tell about herself none of them could understand except the king and Curdie, who stood by the king's knee stroking the neck of the great white horse. And still as she told what Curdie had done, Sir Walter and others added to what she told, even Lootie joining in the praises of his courage and energy.

Curdie held his peace, looking quietly up in the king's face. And his mother stood on the outskirts of the crowd listening with delight, for her son's deeds were pleasant in her ears, until the princess caught sight of her.

'And there is his mother, king-papa!' she said. 'See—
there. She is such a nice mother, and has been so kind
to me!'

They all parted asunder as the king made a sign to her to
come forward. She obeyed, and he gave her his hand, but
could not speak.

'And now, king-papa,' the princess went on, 'I must tell
you another thing. One night long ago Curdie drove the
goblins away and brought Lootie and me safe from the
mountain. And I promised him a kiss when we got home,
but Lootie wouldn't let me give it him. I don't want you to
scold Lootie, but I want you to tell her that a princess *must*
do as she promises.'

'Indeed she must, my child—except it be wrong,' said the
king. 'There, give Curdie a kiss.'

And as he spoke he held her towards him.

The princess reached down, threw her arms round Curdie's
neck, and kissed him on the mouth, saying—

'There, Curdie! There's the kiss I promised you!'

Then they all went into the house, and the cook rushed to
the kitchen, and the servants to their work. Lootie dressed
Irene in her shiningest clothes, and the king put off his
armour, and put on purple and gold; and a messenger was
sent for Peter and all the miners, and there was a great and a
grand feast, which continued long after the princess was put
to bed.

XXXI
The Subterranean Waters

The king's harper, who always formed a part of his escort, was chanting a ballad which he made as he went on playing on his instrument—about the princess and the goblins, and the prowess of Curdie, when all at once he ceased, with his eyes on one of the doors of the hall. Thereupon the eyes of the king and his guests turned thitherward also. The next moment, through the open doorway came the princess Irene. She went straight up to her father, with her right hand stretched out a little sideways, and her forefinger, as her father and Curdie understood, feeling its way along the invisible thread. The king took her on his knee, and she said in his ear—

'King-papa, do you hear that noise?'

'I hear nothing,' said the king.

'Listen,' she said, holding up her forefinger.

The king listened, and a great stillness fell upon the company. Each man, seeing that the king listened, listened also, and the harper sat with his harp between his arms, and his fingers silent upon the strings.

'I do hear a noise,' said the king at length—'a noise as of distant thunder. It is coming nearer and nearer. What can it be?'

They all heard it now, and each seemed ready to start to his feet as he listened. Yet all sat perfectly still. The noise came rapidly nearer.

'What *can* it be?' said the king again.

'I think it must be another storm coming over the mountain,' said Sir Walter.

Then Curdie, who at the first word of the king had slipped from his seat, and laid his ear to the ground, rose up quickly, and approaching the king said, speaking very fast—

'Please your majesty, I think I know what it is. I have no time to explain, for that might make it too late for some of us. Will your majesty give orders that everybody leave the house as quickly as possible, and get up the mountain.'

The king, who was the wisest man in the kingdom, knew well there was a time when things must be done, and questions left till afterwards. He had faith in Curdie, and rose instantly, with Irene in his arms.

'Every man and woman follow me,' he said, and strode out into the darkness.

Before he had reached the gate, the noise had grown to a great thundering roar, and the ground trembled, beneath their feet, and before the last of them had crossed the court, out after them from the great hall-door came a huge rush of turbid water, and almost swept them away. But they got safe out of the gate and up the mountain, while the torrent went roaring down the road into the valley beneath.

Curdie had left the king and the princess to look after his mother, whom he and his father, one on each side, caught up when the stream overtook them and carried safe and dry.

When the king had got out of the way of the water, a little up the mountain, he stood with the princess in his arms, looking back with amazement on the issuing torrent, which glimmered fierce and foamy through the night. There Curdie rejoined them.

'Now, Curdie,' said the king, 'what does it mean? Is this what you expected?'

'It is, your majesty,' said Curdie; and proceeded to tell him about the second scheme of the goblins, who, fancying the miners of more importance to the upper world than they were, had resolved, if they should fail in carrying off the king's daughter, to flood the mine and drown the miners. Then he explained what the miners had done to prevent it. The goblins had, in pursuance of their design, let loose all the underground reservoirs and streams, expecting the water to run down into the mine, which was lower than their part of the mountain, for they had, as they supposed, not knowing of the solid wall close behind, broken a passage through into it. But the readiest outlet the water could find had turned out to be the tunnel they had made to the king's house, the possibility of which catastrophe had not occurred to the young miner until he laid his ear to the floor of the hall.

What was then to be done? The house appeared in danger of falling, and every moment the torrent was increasing.

'We must set out at once,' said the king. 'But how to get at the horses!'

'Shall I see if we can manage that?' said Curdie.

'Do,' said the king.

Curdie gathered the men-at-arms, and took them over the garden wall, and so to the stables. They found their horses in terror; the water was rising fast around them, and it was quite time they were got out. But there was no way to get them out, except by riding them through the stream, which was now pouring from the lower windows as well as the door. As one horse was quite enough for any man to manage through such a torrent, Curdie got on the king's white charger, and leading the way, brought them all in safety to the rising ground.

'Look, look, Curdie!' cried Irene, the moment that, having dismounted, he led the horse up to the king.

Curdie did look, and saw, high in the air, somewhere about the top of the king's house, a great globe of light, shining like the purest silver.

'Oh!' he cried in some consternation, 'that is your grandmother's lamp! We *must* get her out. I will go and find her. The house may fall, you know.'

'My grandmother is in no danger,' said Irene, smiling.

'Here, Curdie, take the princess while I get on my horse,' said the king.

Curdie took the princess again, and both turned their eyes to the globe of light. The same moment there shot from it a white bird, which, descending with outstretched wings, made one circle round the king and Curdie and the princess, and then glided up again. The light and the pigeon vanished together.

'Now, Curdie,' said the princess, as he lifted her to her father's arms, 'you see my grandmother knows all about it, and isn't frightened. I believe she could walk through that water and it wouldn't wet her a bit.'

'But, my child,' said the king, 'you will be cold if you haven't something more on. Run, Curdie, my boy, and fetch anything you can lay your hands on, to keep the princess warm. We have a long ride before us.'

Curdie was gone in a moment, and soon returned with a great rich fur, and the news that dead goblins were tossing about in the current through the house. They had been caught in their own snare; instead of the mine they had flooded their own country, whence they were now swept up drowned. Irene shuddered, but the king held her close to his bosom. Then he turned to Sir Walter, and said—

'Bring Curdie's father and mother here.'

'I wish,' said the king, when they stood before him, 'to take your son with me. He shall enter my body-guard at once, and wait further promotion.'

Peter and his wife overcome, only murmured almost inaudible thanks. But Curdie spoke aloud.

'Please your majesty,' he said, I cannot leave my father and mother.'

'That's right, Curdie!' cried the princess. '*I* wouldn't if I was you.'

The king looked at the princess and then at Curdie with a glow of satisfaction on his countenance.

'I too think you are right, Curdie,' he said, 'and I will not ask you again. But I shall have a chance of doing something for you some time.'

'Your majesty has already allowed me to serve you,'* said Curdie.

'But, Curdie,' said his mother, 'why shouldn't you go with the king? We can get on very well without you.'

'But I can't get on very well without you,' said Curdie. 'The king is very kind, but I could not be half the use to him that I am to you. Please your majesty, if you wouldn't mind giving my mother a red petticoat! I should have got her one long ago, but for the goblins.'

'As soon as we get home,' said the king, 'Irene and I will search out the warmest one to be found, and send it by one of the gentlemen.'

'Yes, that we will, Curdie!' said the princess. 'And next summer we'll come back and see you wear it, Curdie's mother,' she added. 'Shan't we, king-papa?'

'Yes, my love; I hope so,' said the king.

Then turning to the miners, he said—

'Will you do the best you can for my servants tonight? I hope they will be able to return to the house tomorrow.'

The miners with one voice promised their hospitality.

Then the king commanded his servants to mind whatever Curdie should say to them, and after shaking hands with him and his father and mother, the king and the princess and all their company rode away down the side of the new stream which had already devoured half the road, into the starry night.

XXXII

The Last Chapter

All the rest went up the mountain, and separated in groups
to the homes of the miners. Curdie and his father and mother
took Lootie with them. And the whole way, a light, of which
all but Lootie understood the origin, shone upon their path.
But when they looked round they could see nothing of the
silvery globe.

For days and days the water continued to rush from the
doors and windows of the king's house, and a few goblin
bodies were swept out into the road.

Curdie saw that something must be done. He spoke to
his father and the rest of the miners, and they at once
proceeded to make another outlet for the waters. By setting
all hands to the work, tunnelling here and building there,
they soon succeeded; and having also made a little tunnel
to drain the water away from under the king's house, they
were soon able to get into the wine cellar, where they
found a multitude of dead goblins—among the rest the
queen, with the skin-shoe gone, and the stone one fast
to her ankle—for the water had swept away the barricade
which prevented the men-at-arms from following the goblins, and had greatly widened the passage. They built it
securely up, and then went back to their labours in the
mine.

A good many of the goblins with their creatures escaped
from the inundation out upon the mountain. But most
of them soon left that part of the country, and most
of those who remained grew milder in character, and
indeed became very much like the Scotch Brownies.*
There skulls became softer as well as their hearts, and
their feet grew harder, and by degrees they became friendly

with the inhabitants of the mountain and even with the miners. But the latter were merciless to any of the *cobs' creatures* that came in their way, until at length they all but disappeared.*

The rest of the history of *The Princess and Curdie* must be kept for another volume.

THE PRINCESS AND CURDIE

CONTENTS

I

The Mountain

Curdie was the son of Peter the miner. He lived with his father and mother in a cottage built on a mountain and he worked with his father inside the mountain. A mountain is a strange and awful thing. In old times, without knowing so much of their strangeness and awfulness as we do, people were yet more afraid of mountains.* But then somehow they had not come to see how beautiful they are as well as awful, and they hated them—and what people hate they must fear. Now that we have learned to look at them with admiration, perhaps we do not always feel quite awe enough of them. To me they are beautiful terrors.

I will try to tell you what they are. They are portions of the heart of the earth that have escaped from the dungeon down below, and rushed up and out.* For the heart of the earth is a great wallowing mass, not of blood, as in the hearts of men and animals, but of glowing hot melted metals and stones. And as our hearts keep us alive, so that great lump of heat keeps the earth alive: it is a huge power of buried sunlight—that is what it is. Now think: out of that cauldron, where all the bubbles would be as big as the Alps if it could get room for its boiling, certain bubbles have bubbled out and escaped—up and away, and there they stand in the cool, cold sky—mountains. Think of the change, and you will no more wonder that there should be something awful about the very look of a mountain: from the darkness—for where the light has nothing to shine upon, it is much the same as darkness—from the heat, from the endless tumult of boiling unrest—up, with a sudden heavenward shoot, into the wind, and the cold, and the starshine, and a cloak of snow that lies like ermine above the blue-green mail of the glaciers; and the great sun, their grandfather, up there in the sky; and their little old cold aunt, the moon, that comes wandering about the house at night; and everlasting stillness, except for the wind that turns the rocks and caverns into a roaring organ for the young archangels that are studying how to let out the pent-up praises of their hearts, and the molten music of the streams, rushing ever from the bosoms of the glaciers fresh-born. Think too of the change in their own substance—no longer molten and soft, heaving and glowing, but hard and shining and cold. Think of the creatures scampering over and burrowing in it, and the birds building their nests upon it, and the trees growing out of its sides, like hair to clothe it, and the lovely grass in the valleys, and the gracious flowers even at the very edge of its armour of ice, like the rich embroidery of the garment below, and the rivers galloping down the valleys in a tumult of white and green! And along with all these, think of the terrible precipices down which the traveller may fall and be lost, and the frightful gulfs of blue air cracked in the glaciers, and the dark profound lakes, covered like little arctic oceans with floating lumps of ice. All this outside the mountain! But the inside, who shall tell what lies there? Caverns of awfullest solitude, their walls miles thick, sparkling with ores of gold or silver, copper or iron, tin or mercury, studded perhaps with precious stones—perhaps a brook, with eyeless fish in it, running, running ceaseless, cold and babbling, through banks crusted with carbuncles and golden topazes, or over a gravel of which some of the stones are rubies and emeralds, perhaps diamonds and sapphires—who can tell?—and whoever can't tell is free to think—all waiting to flash, waiting for millions of ages*—ever since the earth flew off from the sun, a great blot of fire, and began to cool. Then there are caverns full of water, numbing cold, fiercely hot—hotter than any boiling water. From some of these the water cannot get out, and from others it runs in channels as the blood in the body: little veins bring it down* from the ice above into the great caverns of the mountain's heart, whence the arteries let it out again, gushing in pipes and clefts and ducts of all shapes and kinds, through and through its bulk, until it springs new-born to the light, and rushes down the mountainside in torrents, and down the valleys in rivers—down, down, rejoicing, to the mighty lungs of the world, that is the sea, where it is tossed in storms and cyclones, heaved up in billows, twisted in waterspouts, dashed to mist upon rocks, beaten by millions of tails, and breathed by millions of gills, whence at last, melted into vapour by the sun, it is lifted up pure into the air, and borne by the servant winds back to the mountain-tops and the snow, the solid ice, and the molten stream.

Well, when the heart of the earth has thus come rushing up among her children, bringing with it gifts of all that she possesses, then straightway into it rush her children to see what they can find there. With pickaxe and spade and crowbar, with boring chisel and blasting powder, they force their way back: is it to search for what toys they may have left in their long-forgotten nurseries? Hence the mountains that lift their heads into the clear air, and are dotted over with the dwellings of men, are tunnelled and bored in the darkness of their bosoms by the dwellers in the houses which they hold up to the sun and air.

Curdie and his father were of these: their business was to bring to light hidden things; they sought silver in the rock and found it, and carried it out. Of the many other precious things in their mountain they knew little or nothing. Silver ore was what they were sent to find, and in darkness and danger they found it. But oh, how sweet was the air on the mountain face when they came out at sunset to go home to wife and mother! They did breathe deep then!

The mines belonged to the king of the country, and the miners were his servants, working under his overseers and officers. He was a real king—that is one who ruled for the good of his people, and not to please himself, and he wanted the silver not to buy rich things for himself, but to help him to govern the country, and pay the armies that defended it from certain troublesome neighbours, and the judges whom he set to portion out righteousness amongst the people, that so they might learn it themselves, and come to do without judges at all. Nothing that could be got from the heart of the earth could have been put to better purposes than the silver the king's miners got for him. There were people in the country who, when it came into their hands, degraded it by locking it up in a chest, and then it grew diseased and was called *mammon*,* and bred all sorts of quarrels, but when first it left the king's hands it never made any but friends, and the air of the world kept it clean.

About a year before this story began, a series of very remarkable events had just ended. I will narrate as much of them as will serve to show the tops of the roots of my tree.

Upon the mountain, on one of its many claws, stood a grand old house, half farmhouse, half castle, belonging to the king; and there his only child, the Princess Irene, had been brought up till she was nearly nine years old, and would doubtless have continued much longer, but for the strange events to which I have referred.

At that time the hollow places of the mountain were inhabited by creatures called goblins, who for various reasons and in various ways made themselves troublesome to all, but to the little princess dangerous. Mainly by the watchful devotion and energy of Curdie, however, their designs had been utterly defeated, and made to recoil upon themselves to their own destruction, so that now there were very few of them left alive, and the miners did not believe there was a single goblin remaining in the whole inside of the mountain.

The king had been so pleased with the boy—then approaching thirteen years of age—that when he carried away his daughter he asked him to accompany them; but he was still better pleased with him when he found that he preferred staying with his father and mother. He was a right good king, and knew that the love of a boy who would not leave his father and mother to be made a great man, was worth ten thousand offers to die for his sake, and would prove so when the right time came. For his father and mother, they would have given him up without a grumble, for they were just as good as the king, and he and they perfectly understood each other; but in this matter, not seeing that he could do anything for the king which one of his numerous attendants could not do as well, Curdie felt that it was for him to decide. So the king took a kind farewell of them all and rode away, with his daughter on his horse before him.

A gloom fell upon the mountain and the miners when she was gone, and Curdie did not whistle for a whole week. As for his verses, there was no occasion to make any now. He had made them only to drive away the goblins, and they were all gone—a good riddance—only the princess was gone too! He would rather have had things as they were, except for the princess's sake. But whoever is diligent will soon be cheerful, and though the miners missed the household of the castle, they yet managed to get on without them.

Peter and his wife, however, were troubled with the fancy that they had stood in the way of their boy's good fortune. It would have been such a fine thing for him and them too, they thought, if he had ridden with the good king's train. How beautiful he looked, they said, when he rode the king's own horse through the river that the goblins had sent out of the hill! He might soon have been a captain, they did believe! The good, kind people did not reflect that the road to the next duty is the only straight one, or that, for their fancied good, we should never wish our children or friends to do what we would not do ourselves if we were in their position. We must accept righteous sacrifices as well as make them.

II

The White Pigeon

When in the winter they had had their supper and sat about the fire, or when in the summer they lay on the border of the rock-margined stream that ran through their little meadow, close by the door of their cottage, issuing from the far-up whiteness often folded in clouds, Curdie's mother would not seldom lead the conversation to one peculiar personage said and believed to have been much concerned in the late issue of events. That personage was the great-great-grandmother of the princess, of whom the princess had often talked, but whom neither Curdie nor his mother had ever seen. Curdie could indeed remember, although already it looked more like a dream than he could account for if it had really taken place, how the princess had once led him up many stairs to what she called a beautiful room in the top of the tower, where she went through all the—what should he call it?—the behaviour of presenting him to her grandmother, talking now to her and now to him, while all the time he saw nothing but a bare garret, a heap of musty straw, a sunbeam, and a withered apple. Lady, he would have declared before the king himself, young or old, there was none, except the princess herself, who was certainly vexed that he could not see what she at least believed she saw. And for his mother, she had once seen,* long before Curdie was born, a certain mysterious light of the same description with one Irene spoke of, calling it her grandmother's moon; and Curdie himself had seen this same light, shining from above the castle, just as the king and princess were taking their leave. Since that time neither had seen or heard anything that could be supposed connected with her. Strangely enough, however, nobody had seen her go away. If she was such an old lady, she could hardly be supposed to have set out alone and on foot when all the house was asleep. Still, away she must have gone, for of course, if she was so powerful, she would always be about the princess to take care of her.

But as Curdie grew older, he doubted more and more whether Irene had not been talking of some dream she had taken for reality: he had heard it said that children could not always distinguish betwixt dreams and actual events. At the same time there was his mother's testimony: what was he to do with that? His mother, through whom he had learned everything, could hardly be imagined by her own dutiful son to have mistaken a dream for a fact of the waking world. So he rather shrunk from thinking about it, and the less he thought about it, the less he was inclined to believe it when he did think about it, and therefore, of course, the less inclined to talk about it to his father and mother; for although his father was one of those men who for one word they say think twenty thoughts, Curdie was well assured that he would rather doubt his own eyes than his wife's testimony. There were no others to whom he could have talked about it. The miners were a mingled company—some good, some not so good, some rather bad—none of them so bad or so good as they might have been; Curdie liked most of them, and was a favourite with all; but they knew very little about the upper world, and what might or might not take place there. They knew silver from copper ore; they understood the underground ways of things, and they could look very wise with their lanterns in their hands searching after this or that sign of ore, or for some mark to guide their way in the hollows of the earth; but as to great-great-grandmothers, they would have mocked him all the rest of his life for the absurdity of not being absolutely certain that the solemn belief of his father and mother was nothing but ridiculous nonsense. Why, to them the very word 'great-great-grandmother' would have been a week's laughter! I am not sure that they were able quite to believe there were such persons as great-great-grandmothers; they had never seen one. They were not companions to give the best of help towards progress, and as Curdie grew, he grew at this time faster in body than in mind—with the usual consequence, that he was getting rather stupid—one of the chief signs of which was that he believed less and less of things he had never seen. At the same time I do not think he was ever so stupid as to imagine that this was a sign of superior faculty and strength of mind. Still, he was becoming more and more a miner, and less and less a man of the upper world where the wind blew. On his way to and from the mine he took less and less notice of bees and butterflies, moths, and dragon-flies, the flowers and the brooks and the clouds. He was gradually changing into a commonplace man. There is this difference between the growth of some human beings and that of others: in the one case it is a continuous dying, in the other a continuous resurrection. One of the latter sort comes at length to know at once whether a thing is true the moment it comes before him; one of the former class grows more and more afraid of being taken in, so afraid of it that he takes himself in altogether, and comes at length to believe in nothing but his dinner: to be sure of a thing with him is to have it between his teeth. Curdie was not in a very good way then at that time. His father and mother had, it is true, no fault to find with him—and yet—and yet—neither of them was ready to sing when the thought of him came up. There must be something wrong when a mother catches herself sighing over the time when her boy was in petticoats, or the father looks sad when he thinks how he used to carry him on his shoulder. The boy should enclose and keep, as his life, the old child at the heart of him, and never let it go. He must still, to be a right man, be his mother's darling, and more, his father's pride, and more. The child is not meant to die,* but to be for ever fresh-born.

Curdie had made himself a bow and some arrows, and was teaching himself to shoot with them. One evening in the early summer, as he was walking home from the mine with them in his hand, a light flashed across his eyes. He looked, and there was a snow-white pigeon settling on a rock in front of him, in the red light of the level sun. There it fell at once to work with one of its wings, in which a feather or two had got some sprays twisted, causing a certain roughness unpleasant to the fastidious creature of the air. It was indeed a lovely being, and Curdie thought how happy it must be flitting through the air with a flash—a live bolt of light. For a moment he became so one with the bird that he seemed to feel both its bill and its feathers, as the one adjusted the other to fly again, and his heart swelled with the pleasure of its involuntary sympathy. Another moment and it would have been aloft in the waves of rosy light—it was just bending its little legs to spring: that moment it fell on the path broken-winged and bleeding from Curdie's cruel arrow. With a gush of pride at his skill, and pleasure at its success, he ran to pick up his prey. I must say for him he picked it up gently—perhaps it was the beginning of his repentance. But when he had the white thing in his hands—its whiteness stained with another red than that of the sunset flood in which it had been revelling—ah God! who knows the joy of a bird, the ecstasy of a creature that has neither storehouse nor barn!—when he held it, I say, in his victorious hands, the winged thing looked up in his face—and with such eyes! asking what was the matter, and where the red sun had gone, and the clouds, and the wind of its flight. Then they closed, but to open again presently, with the same questions in them. And so they closed and opened several times, but always when they opened, their look was fixed on his. It did not once flutter or try to get away; it only throbbed and bled and looked at him. Curdie's heart began to grow very large in his bosom. What could it mean? It was nothing but a pigeon, and why should he not kill a pigeon? But the fact was, that not till this very moment had he ever known what a pigeon was. A good many discoveries of a similar kind have to be made by most of us. Once more it opened its eyes—then closed them again, and its throbbing ceased. Curdie gave a sob: its last look reminded him of the princess—he did not know why.

He remembered how hard he had laboured to set her beyond danger, and yet what dangers she had had to encounter for his sake: they had been saviours to each other—and what had he done now? He had stopped saving, and had begun killing! What had he been sent into the world for? Surely not to be a death to its joy and loveliness. He had done the thing that was contrary to gladness; he was a destroyer! He was not the Curdie he had been meant to be! Then the underground waters gushed from the boy's heart. And with the tears came the remembrance that a white pigeon, just before the princess went away with her father, came from somewhere—yes, from the grandmother's lamp, and flew round the king and Irene and himself, and then flew away: this might be that very pigeon! Horrible to think! And if it wasn't, yet it was a white pigeon, the same as it. And if she kept a great many pigeons—and white ones, as Irene had told him, then whose pigeon could he have killed but the grand old princess's? Suddenly everything round about him seemed against him. The red sunset stung him: the rocks frowned at him; the sweet wind that had been laving his face as he walked up the hill, dropped—as if he wasn't fit to be kissed any more. Was the whole world going to cast him out? Would he have to stand there for ever, not knowing what to do, with the dead pigeon in his hand? Things looked bad indeed. Was the whole world going to make a work about a pigeon—a white pigeon? The sun went down. Great clouds gathered over the west, and shortened the twilight. The wind gave a howl, and then lay down again. The clouds gathered thicker. Then came a rumbling. He thought it was thunder. It was a rock that fell inside the mountain. A goat ran past him down the hill, followed by a dog sent to fetch him home. He thought they were goblin creatures, and trembled. He used to despise them. And still he held the dead pigeon tenderly in his hand. It grew darker and darker. An evil something began to move in his heart. 'What a fool I am!' he said to himself. Then he grew angry, and was just going to throw the bird from him and whistle, when a brightness shone all round him. He lifted his eyes, and saw a great globe of light—like silver at the hottest heat: he had once seen silver run from the furnace. It shone from somewhere above the roofs of the castle: it must be the great old princess's moon! How could she be there? Of course she was not there! He had asked the whole household, and nobody knew anything about her or her globe either. It couldn't be! And yet what did that signify, when there was the white globe shining, and here was the dead white bird in his hand? That moment the pigeon gave a little flutter. '*It's not dead!*' cried Curdie, almost with a shriek. The same instant he was running full speed towards the castle, never letting his heels down, lest he should shake the poor wounded bird.

III

The Mistress of the Silver Moon

When Curdie reached the castle, and ran into the little garden in front of it, there stood the door wide open. This was as he had hoped, for what could he have said if he had had to knock at it? Those whose business it is to open doors, so often mistake and shut them! But the woman now in charge often puzzled herself greatly to account for the strange fact that however often she shut the door, which, like the rest, she took a great deal of unnecessary trouble to do, she was certain, the next time she went to it, to find it open. I speak now of the great front door, of course: the back door she as persistently kept wide: if people *could* only go in by that, she said, she would then know what sort they were, and what they wanted. But she would neither have known what sort Curdie was, nor what he wanted, and would assuredly have denied him admittance, for she knew nothing of who was in the tower. So the front door was left open for him, and in he walked.

But where to go next he could not tell. It was not quite dark: a dull, shineless twilight filled the place. All he knew was that he must go up, and that proved enough for the present, for there he saw the great staircase rising before him. When he reached the top of it, he knew there must be more stairs yet, for he could not be near the top of the tower. Indeed by the situation of the stair, he must be a good way from the tower itself. But those who work well in the depths more easily understand the heights, for indeed in their true nature they are one and the same: mines are in mountains; and Curdie from knowing the ways of the king's mines, and being able to calculate his whereabouts in them, was now able to find his way about the king's house. He knew its outside perfectly, and now his business was to get his notion of the inside right with the outside. So he shut his eyes and made a picture of the outside of it in his mind. Then he came in at the door of the picture, and yet kept the picture before him all the time—for you can do that kind of thing in your mind,—and took every turn of the stair over again, always watching to remember, every time he turned his face, how the tower lay, and then when he came to himself at the top where he stood, he knew exactly where it was, and walked at once in the right direction. On his way, however, he came to another stair, and up that he went of course, watching still at every turn how the tower must lie. At the top of this stair was yet another—they were the stairs up which the princess ran when first, without knowing it, she was on her way to find her great-great-grandmother. At the top of the second stair he could go no farther, and must therefore set out again to find the tower, which, as it rose far above the rest of the house, must have the last of its stairs inside itself. Having watched every turn to the very last, he still knew quite well in what direction he must go to find it, so he felt the stair and went down a passage that led, if not exactly towards it, yet nearer it. This passage was rather dark, for it was very long, with only one window at the end, and although there were doors on both sides of it, they were all shut. At the distant window glimmered the chill east, with a few feeble stars in it, and its light was dreary and old, growing brown, and looking as if it were thinking about the day that was just gone. Presently he turned into another passage, which also had a window at the end of it; and in at that window shone all that was left of the sunset, a few ashes, with here and there a little touch of warmth: it was nearly as sad as the east, only there was one difference—it was very plainly thinking of tomorrow. But at present* Curdie had nothing to do with today or tomorrow; his business was with the bird, and the tower where dwelt the grand old princess to whom it belonged. So he kept on his way, still eastward, and came to yet another passage, which brought him to a door. He was afraid to open it without first knocking. He knocked,* but heard no answer. He was answered nevertheless; for the door gently opened, and there was a narrow stair—and so steep that, big lad as he was, he too, like the Princess Irene before him, found his hands needful for the climbing. And it was a long climb, but he reached the top at last—a little landing, with a door in front and one on each side. Which should he knock at?

As he hesitated, he heard the noise of a spinning-wheel. He knew it at once, because his mother's spinning-wheel had been his governess long ago, and still taught him things. It was the spinning-wheel that first taught him to make verses, and to sing, and to think whether all was right inside him; or at least it had helped him in all these things. Hence it was no wonder he should know a spinning-wheel when he heard it sing—even although as the bird of paradise to other birds was the song of that wheel to the song of his mother's.

He stood listening so entranced that he forgot to knock, and the wheel went on and on, spinning in his brain songs and tales and rhymes, till he was almost asleep as well as dreaming, for sleep does not *always* come first. But suddenly came the thought of the poor bird, which had been lying motionless in his hand all the time, and that woke him up, and at once he knocked.

'Come in, Curdie,' said a voice.

Curdie shook. It was getting rather awful. The heart that had never much heeded an army of goblins, trembled at the soft word of invitation. But then there was the red-spotted white thing in his hand! He dared not hesitate, though. Gently he opened the door through which the sound came, and what did he see? Nothing at first—except indeed a great sloping shaft of moonlight, that came in at a high window, and rested on the floor. He stood and stared at it, forgetting to shut the door.

'Why don't you come in, Curdie?' said the voice. 'Did you never see moonlight before?'

'Never without a moon,' answered Curdie, in a trembling tone, but gathering courage.

'Certainly not,' returned the voice, which was thin and quavering: '*I* never saw moonlight without a moon.'

'But there's no moon outside,' said Curdie.

'Ah! but you're inside now,' said the voice.

The answer did not satisfy Curdie; but the voice went on.

'There are more moons than you know of, Curdie. Where there is one sun there are many moons—and of many sorts. Come in and look out of my window, and you will soon satisfy yourself that there is a moon looking in at it.'

The gentleness of the voice made Curdie remember his manners. He shut the door, and drew a step or two nearer to the moonlight.

All the time the sound of the spinning had been going on and on, and Curdie now caught sight of the wheel. Oh, it was such a thin, delicate thing—reminding him of a spider's web in a hedge! It stood in the middle of the moonlight, and it seemed as if the moonlight had nearly melted it away. A step nearer, he saw, with a start, two little hands at work with it. And then at last, in the shadow on the other side of the moonlight which came like a river between, he saw the form to which the hands belonged: a small, withered creature, so old that no age would have seemed too great to write under her picture, seated on a stool beyond the spinning-wheel, which looked very large beside her, but, as I said, very thin, like a long-legged spider holding up its own web, which was the round wheel itself. She sat crumpled together, a filmy thing that it seemed a puff would blow away, more like the body of a fly the big spider had sucked empty and left hanging in his web, than anything else I can think of.

When Curdie saw her, he stood still again, a good deal in wonder, a very little in reverence, a little in doubt, and, I must add, a little in amusement at the odd look of the old marvel. Her grey hair mixed with the moonlight so that he could not tell where the one began and the other ended. Her crooked back bent forward over her chest, her shoulders nearly swallowed up her head between them, and her two little hands were just like the grey claws of a hen, scratching at the thread, which to Curdie was of course invisible across the moonlight. Indeed, Curdie laughed within himself, just a little, at the sight; and when he thought of how the princess used to talk about her huge great old grandmother, he laughed more. But that moment the little lady leaned forward into the moonlight, and Curdie caught a glimpse of her eyes, and all the laugh went out of him.

'What do you come here for, Curdie?' she said, as gently as before.

Then Curdie remembered that he stood there as a culprit, and worst of all, as one who had his confession yet to make. There was no time to hesitate over it.

'Oh, ma'am! see here,' he said, and advanced a step or two, holding out the dead pigeon.

'What have you got there?' she asked.

Again Curdie advanced a few steps, and held out his hand with the pigeon, that she might see what it was, into the moonlight. The moment the rays fell upon it the pigeon gave a faint flutter. The old lady put out her old hands and took it, and held it to her bosom, and rocked it, murmuring over it as if it were a sick baby.

When Curdie saw how distressed she was he grew sorrier still, and said—

'I didn't mean to do any harm, ma'am. I didn't think of its being yours.'

'Ah, Curdie! if it weren't mine, what would become of it now?' she returned. 'You say you didn't mean any harm: did you mean any good, Curdie?'

'No,' answered Curdie.

'Remember, then, that whoever does not mean good is always in danger of harm. But I try to give everybody fair play; and those that are in the wrong are in far more need of it always than those who are in the right: they can afford to do without it. Therefore I say for you that when you shot that arrow you did not know what a pigeon is. Now that you do know, you are sorry. It is very dangerous to do things you don't know about.'

'But, please, ma'am—I don't mean to be rude or to contradict you,' said Curdie, 'but if a body was never to do anything but what he knew to be good, he would have to live half his time doing nothing.'

'There you are much mistaken,' said the old quavering voice. 'How little you must have thought! Why, you don't seem even to know the good of the things you are constantly doing. Now don't mistake me. I don't mean you are good for doing them. It is a good thing to eat your breakfast, but you don't fancy it's very good of you to do it. The thing is good—not you.'

Curdie laughed.

'There are a great many more good things than bad things to do. Now tell me what bad thing you have done today besides this sore hurt to my little white friend.'

While she talked Curdie had sunk into a sort of reverie, in which he hardly knew whether it was the old lady or his own heart that spoke. And when she asked him that question, he was at first much inclined to consider himself a very good fellow on the whole. 'I really don't think I did anything else that was very bad all day,' he said to himself. But at the same time he could not honestly feel that he was worth standing up for. All at once a light seemed to break in upon his mind, and he woke up, and there was the withered little atomy of the old lady on the other side of the moonlight, and there was the spinning-wheel singing on and on in the middle of it!

'I know now, ma'am; I understand now,' he said. 'Thank you, ma'am for spinning it into me with your wheel. I see now that I have been doing wrong the whole day, and such a many days besides! Indeed, I don't know when I ever did right, and yet it seems as if I had done right some time and had forgotten how. When I killed your bird I did not know I was doing wrong, just because I was always doing wrong, and the wrong had soaked all through me.'

'What wrong were you doing all day, Curdie? It is better to come to the point, you know,' said the old lady, and her voice was gentler even than before.

'I was doing the wrong of never wanting or trying to be better. And now I see that I have been letting things go as they would for a long time. Whatever came into my head I did, and whatever didn't come into my head I didn't do. I never sent anything away, and never looked out for anything to come. I haven't been attending to my mother—or my father either. And now I think of it, I know I have often seen them looking troubled, and I have never asked them what was the matter. And now I see too that I did not ask because I suspected it had something to do with me and my behaviour, and didn't want to hear the truth. And I know I have been grumbling at my work, and doing a hundred other things that are wrong.'

'You have got it, Curdie,' said the old lady, in a voice that sounded almost as if she had been crying. 'When people don't care to be better they must be doing everything wrong. I am so glad you shot my bird!'*

'Ma'am!' exclaimed Curdie. 'How *can* you be?'

'Because it has brought you to see what sort you were when you did it, and what sort you will grow to be again, only worse, if you don't mind. Now that you are sorry, my poor bird will be better. Look up, my dovey.'

The pigeon gave a flutter, and spread out one of its red-spotted wings across the old woman's bosom.

'I will mend the little angel,' she said, 'and in a week or two it will be flying again. So you may ease your heart about the pigeon.'

'Oh, thank you! thank you!' cried Curdie. 'I don't know how to thank you.'

'Then I will tell you. There is only one way I care for. Do better, and grow better, and be better. And never kill anything without a good reason for it.'

'Ma'am, I will go and fetch my bow and arrows, and you shall burn them yourself.'

'I have no fire that would burn your bow and arrows, Curdie.'

'Then I promise you to burn them all under my mother's porridge-pot tomorrow morning.'

'No, no, Curdie. Keep them, and practise with them every day, and grow a good shot. There are plenty of bad things that want killing, and a day will come when they will prove useful. But I must see first whether you will do as I tell you.'

'That I will!' said Curdie. 'What is it, ma'am?'

'Only something not to do,' answered the old lady; 'if you should hear any one speak about me, never to laugh or make fun of me.'

'Oh, ma'am!' exclaimed Curdie, shocked that she should think such a request needful.

'Stop, stop,' she went on. 'People hereabout sometimes tell very odd and in fact ridiculous stories of an old woman who watches what is going on, and occasionally interferes. They mean me, though what they say is often great nonsense. Now what I want of you is not to laugh, or side with them in any way; because they will take that to mean that you don't believe there is any such person a bit more than they do. Now that would not be the case—would it, Curdie?'

'No indeed, ma'am. I've seen you.'

The old woman smiled very oddly.

'Yes, you've seen me,' she said. 'But mind,' she continued, 'I don't want you to say anything—only to hold your tongue, and not seem to side with them.'

'That will be easy,' said Curdie, 'now that I've seen you with my very own eyes, ma'am.'

'Not so easy as you think, perhaps,' said the old lady, with another curious smile. 'I want to be your friend,' she added after a little pause, 'but I don't quite know yet whether you will let me.'

'Indeed I will, ma'am,' said Curdie.

'That is for me to find out,' she rejoined, with yet another strange smile. 'In the mean time all I can say is, come to me again when you find yourself in any trouble, and I will see what I can do for you—only the *canning** depends on yourself. I am greatly pleased with you for bringing me my pigeon, doing your best to set right what you had set wrong.'

As she spoke she held out her hand to him, and when he took it she made use of his to help herself up from her stool, and—when or how it came about, Curdie could not tell—the same instant she stood before him a tall, strong woman—plainly very old, but as grand as she was old, and only *rather* severe-looking. Every trace of the decrepitude and witheredness she showed as she hovered like a film about her wheel, had vanished. Her hair was very white, but it hung about her head in great plenty, and shone like silver in the moonlight. Straight as a pillar she stood before the astonished boy, and the wounded bird had now spread out both its wings across her bosom, like some great mystical ornament of frosted silver.

'Oh, now I can never forget you!' cried Curdie. 'I see now what you really are!'

'Did I not tell you the truth when I sat at my wheel?' said the old lady.

'Yes, ma'am,' answered Curdie.

'I can do no more than tell you the truth now,' she rejoined. 'It is a bad thing indeed to forget one who has told us the truth. Now go.'

Curdie obeyed, and took a few steps towards the door.

'Please, ma'am,'—'what am I to call you?' he was going to say; but when he turned to speak, he saw nobody. Whether she was there or not he could not tell, however, for the moonlight had vanished, and the room was utterly dark. A great fear, such as he had never before known, came upon him, and almost overwhelmed him. He groped his way to the door, and crawled down the stair—in doubt and anxiety as to how he should find his way out of the house in the dark. And the stair seemed ever so much longer than when he came up. Nor was that any wonder, for down and down he went, until at length his foot struck on a door, and when he rose and opened it he found himself under the starry, moonless sky at the foot of the tower. He soon discovered the way out of the garden, with which he had some acquaintance already, and in a few minutes was climbing the mountain with a solemn and cheerful heart. It was rather dark, but he knew the way well. As he passed the rock from which the poor pigeon fell wounded with his arrow, a great joy filled his heart at the thought that he was delivered from the blood of the little bird, and he ran the next hundred yards at full speed up the hill. Some dark shadows passed him: he did not even care to think what they were, but let them run. When he reached home, he found his father and mother waiting supper for him.

IV

Curdie's Father and Mother

The eyes of the fathers and mothers are quick to read their children's looks, and when Curdie entered the cottage, his parents saw at once that something unusual had taken place. When he said to his mother, 'I beg your pardon for being so late,' there was something in the tone beyond the politeness that went to her heart, for it seemed to come from the place where all lovely things were born before they began to grow in this world. When he set his father's chair to the table, an attention he had not shown him for a long time, Peter thanked him with more gratitude than the boy had ever yet felt in all his life. It was a small thing to do for the man who had been serving him since ever he was born, but I suspect there is nothing a man can be so grateful for as that to which he has the most right. There was a change upon Curdie, and father and mother felt there must be something to account for it, and therefore were pretty sure he had something to tell them. For when a child's heart is *all* right, it is not likely he will want to keep anything from his parents. But the story of the evening was too solemn for Curdie to come out with all at once. He must wait until they had had their porridge, and the affairs of this world were over for the day. But when they were seated on the grassy bank of the brook that went so sweetly blundering over the great stones of its rocky channel, for the whole meadow lay on the top of a huge rock, then he felt that the right hour had come for sharing with them the wonderful things that had come to him. It was perhaps the loveliest of all hours in the year. The summer was young and soft, and this was the warmest evening they had yet had—dusky, dark even below, while above the stars were bright and large and sharp in the blackest blue sky.

The night came close around them, clasping them in one universal arm of love, and although it neither spoke nor smiled, seemed all eye and ear, seemed to see and hear and know everything they said and did. It is a way the night has sometimes, and there is a reason for it. The only sound was that of the brook, for there was no wind, and no trees for it to make its music upon if there had been, for the cottage was high up on the mountain, on a great shoulder of stone where trees would not grow. There, to the accompaniment of the water, as it hurried down to the valley and the sea, talking busily of a thousand true things which it could not understand, Curdie told his tale, outside and in, to his father and mother. What a world had slipped in between the mouth of the mine and his mother's cottage! Neither of them said a word until he had ended.

'Now what am I to make of it, mother? It's so strange!' he said, and stopped.

'It's easy enough to see what Curdie has got to make of it—isn't it, Peter?' said the good woman, turning her face towards all she could see of her husband's.

'It seems so to me,' answered Peter, with a smile, which only the night saw, but his wife felt in the tone of his words. They were the happiest couple in that country, because they always understood each other, and that was because they always meant the same thing, and that was because they always loved what was fair and true and right better—not than anything else, but than everything else put together.

'Then will you tell Curdie?' said she.

'You can talk best, Joan,' said he. 'You tell him, and I will listen—and learn how to say what I think,' he added, laughing.

'*I*,' said Curdie, 'don't know what to think.'

'It does not matter so much,' said his mother. 'If only you know what to make of a thing, you'll know soon enough what to think of it. Now I needn't tell you, surely, Curdie, what you've got to do with this?'

'I suppose you mean, mother,' answered Curdie, 'that I must do as the old lady told me?'

'That is what I mean: what else could it be? Am I not right, Peter?'

'Quite right, Joan,' answered Peter, 'so far as my judgement goes. It is a very strange story, but you see the question is not about believing it, for Curdie knows what came to him.'

'And you remember, Curdie,' said his mother, 'that when the princess took you up that tower once before, and there talked to her great-great-grandmother, you came home quite angry with her, and said there was nothing in the place but an old tub, a heap of straw—oh, I remember your inventory quite well!—an old tub, a heap of straw, a withered apple, and a sunbeam. According to your eyes, that was all there was in the great old musty garret. But now you have had a glimpse of the old princess herself!'

'Yes, mother, I *did* see her—or if I didn't—' said Curdie very thoughtfully—then began again. 'The hardest thing to believe, though I saw it with my own eyes, was when the thin, filmy creature, that seemed almost to float about in the moonlight like a bit of the silver paper they put over pictures, or like a handkerchief made of spider-threads, took my hand, and rose up. She was taller and stronger than you, mother, ever so much!—at least, she looked so.'

'And most certainly was so, Curdie, if she looked so,' said Mrs Peterson.

'Well, I confess,' returned her son, 'that one thing, if there were no other, would make me doubt whether I was not dreaming after all, for as wide awake as I fancied myself to be.'

'Of course,' answered his mother, 'it is not for me to say whether you were dreaming or not if you are doubtful of it yourself; but it doesn't make me think I am dreaming when in the summer I hold in my hand the bunch of sweet-peas that make my heart glad with their colour and scent, and remember the dry, withered-looking little thing I dibbled into the hole in the same spot in the spring. I only think how wonderful and lovely it all is. It seems just as full of reason as it is of wonder. How it is done I can't tell, only there it is! And there is this in it too, Curdie—of which you would not be so ready to think—that when you come home to your father and mother, and they find you behaving more like a dear good son than you have behaved for a long time, they at least are not likely to think you were only dreaming.'

'Still,' said Curdie, looking a little ashamed, 'I might have dreamed my duty.'

'Then dream often, my son; for there must then be more truth in your dreams than in your waking thoughts. But however any of these things may be, this one point remains certain: there can be no harm in doing as she told you. And, indeed, until you are sure there is no such person, you are bound to do it, for you promised.'

'It seems to me,' said his father, 'that if a lady comes to you in a dream, Curdie, and tells you not to talk about her when you wake, the least you can do is to hold your tongue.'

'True, father!—Yes, mother, I'll do it,' said Curdie.

Then they went to bed, and sleep, which is the night of the soul, next took them in its arms and made them well.

V

The Miners

It much increased Curdie's feeling of the strangeness of the whole affair, that, the next morning, when they were at work in the mine, the party of which he and his father were two, just as if they had known what had happened to him the night before, began talking about all manner of wonderful tales that were abroad in the country, chiefly of course those connected with the mines, and the mountains in which they lay. Their wives and mothers and grandmothers* were their chief authorities. For when they sat by their firesides they heard their wives telling their children the selfsame tales, with little differences, and here and there one they had not heard before, which they had heard their mothers and grandmothers tell in one or other of the same cottages. At length they came to speak of a certain strange being they called Old Mother Wotherwop. Some said their wives had seen her. It appeared as they talked that not one had seen her more than once. Some of their mothers and grandmothers, however, had seen her also, and they all had told them tales about her when they were children. They said she could take any shape she liked, but that in reality she was a withered old woman, so old and so withered that she was as thin as a sieve with a lamp behind it; that she was never seen except at night, and when something terrible had taken place, or was going to take place—such as the falling in of the roof of a mine, or the breaking out of water in it. She had more than once been seen—it was always at night—beside some well, sitting on the brink of it, and leaning over and stirring it with her forefinger, which was six times as long as any of the rest. And whoever, for months after drank of that well was sure to be ill. To this one of them, however, added that he remembered his mother saying that whoever in bad health drank of the well was sure to get better. But the majority agreed that the former was the right version of the story—for was she not a witch, an old hating witch, whose delight was to do mischief? One said he had heard that she took the shape of a young woman sometimes, as beautiful as an angel, and then was most dangerous of all, for she struck every man who looked upon her stone-blind. Peter ventured the question whether she might not as likely be an angel that took the form of an old woman, as an old woman that took the form of an angel. But nobody except Curdie, who was holding his peace with all his might, saw any sense in the question. They said an old woman might be very glad to make herself look like a young one, but who ever heard of a young and beautiful one making herself look old and ugly? Peter asked why they were so much more ready to believe the bad that was said of her than the good. They answered because she was bad. He asked why they believed her to be bad, and they answered, because she did bad things. When he asked how they knew that, they said, because she was a bad creature. Even if they didn't know it, they said, a woman like that was so much more likely to be bad than good. Why did she go about at night? Why did she appear only now and then, and on such occasions? One went on to tell how one night when his grandfather had been having a jolly time of it with his friends in the market-town, she had served him so upon his way home that the poor man never drank* a drop of anything stronger than water after it to the day of his death. She dragged him into a bog, and tumbled him up and down in it till he was nearly dead.

'I suppose that was her way of teaching him what a good thing water was,' said Peter; but the man, who liked strong drink, did not see the joke.

'They do say,' said another, 'that she has lived in the old house over there ever since the little princess left it. They say too that the housekeeper knows all about it, and is hand and glove with the old witch. I don't doubt they have many a nice airing together on broomsticks. But I don't doubt either it's all nonsense, and there's no such person at all.'

'When our cow died,' said another, 'she was seen going round and round the cowhouse the same night. To be sure she left a fine calf behind her—I mean the cow did, not the witch. I wonder she didn't kill that too, for she'll be a far finer cow than ever her mother was.'

'My old woman came upon her one night, not long before the water broke out in the mine, sitting on a stone on the hillside with a whole congregation of cobs about her. When they saw my wife they all scampered off as far as they could run, and where the witch was sitting there was nothing to be seen but a withered bracken bush. I make no doubt myself she was putting them up to it.'

And so they went on with one foolish tale after another, while Peter put in a word now and then, and Curdie diligently held his peace. But his silence at last drew attention upon it, and one of them said—

'Come, young Curdie, what are you thinking of?'

'How do you know I'm thinking of anything?' asked Curdie.

'Because you're not saying anything.'

'Does it follow then that, as you are saying so much, you're not thinking at all?' said Curdie.

'I know what he's thinking,' said one who had not yet spoken; '—he's thinking what a set of fools you are to talk such rubbish; as if ever there was or could be such an old woman as you say! I'm sure Curdie knows better than all that comes to.'

'I think,' said Curdie, 'it would be better that he who says anything about her should be quite sure it is true, lest she should hear him, and not like to be slandered.'

'But would she like it any better if it were true?' said the same man. 'If she is what they say—I don't know—but I never knew a man that wouldn't go in a rage to be called the very thing he was.'

'If bad things were true of her, and I *knew* it,' said Curdie,

'I would not hesitate to say them, for I will never give in to being afraid of anything that's bad. I suspect that the things they tell, however, if we knew all about them, would turn out to have nothing but good in them;* and I won't say a word more for fear I should say something that mightn't be to her mind.'

They all burst into a loud laugh.

'Hear the parson!' they cried. 'He believes in the witch! Ha! Ha!'

'He's afraid of her!'

'And says all she does is good!'

'He wants to make friends with her, that she may help him to find the gangue.'*

'Give me my own eyes and a good divining-rod before all the witches in the world! and so I'd advise you too, Master Curdie; that is, when your eyes have grown to be worth anything, and you have learned to cut the hazel fork.'*

Thus they all mocked and jeered at him, but he did his best to keep his temper and go quietly on with his work. He got as close to his father as he could, however, for that helped him to bear it. As soon as they were tired of laughing and mocking, Curdie was friendly with them, and long before their midday meal all between them was as it had been.

But when the evening came, Peter and Curdie felt that they would rather walk home together without other company, and therefore lingered behind when the rest of the men left the mine.

VI

The Emerald*

Father and son had seated themselves on a projecting piece
of the rock at a corner where three galleries met—the one
they had come along from their work, one to the right leading out of the mountain, and the other to the left leading far
into a portion of it which had been long disused. Since the
inundation caused by the goblins, it had indeed been rendered impassable by the settlement of a quantity of the water, forming a small but very deep lake, in a part where was
a considerable descent. They had just risen and were turning
to the right, when a gleam caught their eyes, and made them
look along the whole gangue. Far up they saw a pale green
light, whence issuing they could not tell, about half-way
between floor and roof of the passage. They saw nothing
but the light, which was like a large star, with a point of
darker colour yet brighter radiance in the heart of it, whence
the rest of the light shot out in rays that faded towards the
ends until they vanished. It shed hardly any light around
it, although in itself it was so bright as to sting the eyes
that beheld it. Wonderful stories had from ages gone been
current in the mines about certain magic gems which gave
out light of themselves, and this light looked just like what
might be supposed to shoot from the heart of such a gem.
They went up the old gallery to find out what it could be.

To their surprise they found, however, that, after going
some distance, they were no nearer to it, so far as they could
judge, than when they started. It did not seem to move, and
yet they moving did not approach it. Still they persevered,
for it was far too wonderful a thing to lose sight of so long
as they could keep it. At length they drew near the hollow
where the water lay, and still were no nearer the light. Where

they expected to be stopped by the water, however, water was none: something had taken place in some part of the mine that had drained it off, and the gallery lay open as in former times. And now, to their surprise, the light, instead of being in front of them, was shining at the same distance to the right, where they did not know there was any passage at all. Then they discovered, by the light of the lanterns they carried, that there the water had broken through, and made an adit* to a part of the mountain of which Peter knew nothing. But they were hardly well into it, still following the light, before Curdie thought he recognized some of the passages he had so often gone through when he was watching the goblins. After they had advanced a long way, with many turnings, now to the right, now to the left, all at once their eyes seemed to come suddenly to themselves, and they became aware that the light which they had taken to be a great way from them was in reality almost within reach of their hands. The same instant it began to grow larger and thinner, the point of light grew dim as it spread, the greenness melted away, and in a moment or two, instead of the star, a dark, dark and yet luminous face was looking at them with living eyes. And Curdie felt a great awe swell up in his heart, for he thought he had seen those eyes before.

'I see you know me, Curdie,' said a voice.

'If your eyes are you, ma'am, then I know you,' said Curdie. 'But I never saw your face before.'

'Yes, you have seen it, Curdie,' said the voice.

And with that the darkness of its complexion melted away, and down from the face dawned out the form that belonged to it, until at last Curdie and his father beheld a lady, 'beautiful exceedingly,'* dressed in something pale green, like velvet, over which her hair fell in cataracts of a rich golden colour. It looked as if it were pouring down from her head, and, like the water of the Dust-brook, vanishing in a golden vapour ere it reached the floor. It came flowing from under the edge of a coronet of gold, set with alternated pearls and emeralds. In front of the crown was a great emerald, which looked somehow as if out of it had come the light they had followed. There was no ornament else about her, except on her slippers, which were one mass of gleaming emeralds, of various shades of green, all mingling lovelily like the waving of grass in the wind and sun. She looked about five-and-twenty years old. And for all the difference, Curdie knew somehow or other, he could not have told how, that the face before him was that of the old princess, Irene's great-great-grandmother.

By this time all around them had grown light, and now first they could see where they were. They stood in a great splendid cavern, which Curdie recognized as that in which the goblins held their state assemblies.* But, strange to tell, the light by which they saw came streaming, sparkling, and shooting from stones of many colours in the sides and roof and floor of the cavern—stones of all the colours of the rainbow, and many more. It was a glorious sight—the whole rugged place flashing with colours—in one spot a great light of deep carbuncular red, in another of sapphirine blue, in another of topaz-yellow; while here and there were groups of stones of all hues and sizes, and again nebulous spaces of thousands of tiniest spots of brilliancy of every conceivable shade. Sometimes the colours ran together, and made a little river or lake of lambent interfusing and changing tints, which, by their variegation, seemed to imitate the flowing of water, or waves made by the wind. Curdie would have gazed entranced, but that all the beauty of the cavern, yes, of all he knew of the whole creation, seemed gathered in one centre of harmony and loveliness in the person of the ancient lady who stood before him in the very summer of beauty and strength. Turning from the first glance at the circumfulgent* splendour, it dwindled into nothing as he looked again at the lady. Nothing flashed or glowed or shone about her, and yet it was with a prevision of the truth that he said—

'I was here once before, ma'am.'

'I know that, Curdie,' she replied.

'The place was full of torches, and the walls gleamed, but nothing as they do now, and there is no light in the place.'

'You want to know where the light comes from?' she said, smiling.

'Yes, ma'am.'

'Then see: I will go out of the cavern. Do not be afraid, but watch.'

She went slowly out. The moment she turned her back to go, the light began to pale and fade; the moment she was out of their sight the place was black as night, save that now the smoky yellow-red of their lamps, which they thought had gone out long ago, cast a dusky glimmer around them.

VII

What *is* in a Name?*

For a time that seemed to them long, the two men stood waiting, while still the Mother of Light* did not return. So long was she absent that they began to grow anxious: how were they to find their way from the natural hollows of the mountain crossed by goblin paths, if their lamps should go out? To spend the night there would mean to sit and wait until an earthquake rent the mountain, or the earth herself fell back into the smelting furnace of the sun whence she had issued—for it was all night and no faintest dawn in the bosom of the world. So long did they wait unrevisited, that, had there not been two of them, either would at length have concluded the vision a home-born product of his own seething brain. And their lamps *were* going out, for they grew redder and smokier! But they did not lose courage, for there is a kind of capillary attraction in the facing of two souls, that lifts faith quite beyond the level to which either could raise it alone: they knew that they had seen the lady of emeralds, and it was to give them their own desire that she had gone from them, and neither would yield for a moment to the half-doubts and half-dreads that awoke in his heart. And still she who with her absence darkened their air did not return. They grew weary, and sat down on the rocky floor, for wait they would—indeed, wait they must. Each set his lamp by his knee, and watched it die. Slowly it sank, dulled, looked lazy and stupid. But ever as it sank and dulled, the image in his mind of the Lady of Light grew stronger and clearer. Together the two lamps panted and shuddered. First one, then the other went out, leaving for a moment a great red, evil-smelling snuff. Then all was the blackness of darkness up to their very hearts and everywhere around them. Was it? No. Far away—it looked miles away—shone one minute faint point of green light—where, who could tell? They only knew that it shone. It grew larger, and seemed to draw nearer, until at last, as they watched with speechless delight and expectation, it seemed once more within reach of an outstretched hand. Then it spread and melted away as before, and there were eyes—and a face—and a lovely form—and lo! the whole cavern blazing with lights innumerable, and gorgeous, yet soft and interfused—so blended, indeed, that the eye had to search and see in order to separate distinct spots of special colour.

The moment they saw the speck in the vast distance they had risen and stood on their feet. When it came nearer they bowed their heads. Yet now they looked with fearless eyes, for the woman that was old and yet young was a joy to see, and filled their hearts with reverent delight. She turned first to Peter.

'I have known you long,' she said, 'I have met you going to and from the mine, and seen you working in it for the last forty years.'

'How should it be, madam, that a grand lady like you should take notice of a poor man like me?' said Peter, humbly, but more foolishly than he could then have understood.

'I am poor as well as rich,' said she. 'I too work for my bread, and I show myself no favour when I pay myself my own wages. Last night when you sat by the brook, and Curdie told you about my pigeon, and my spinning, and wondered whether he could believe that he had actually seen me, I heard all you said to each other. I am always about, as the miners said the other night when they talked of me as Old Mother Wotherwop.'

The lovely lady laughed, and her laugh was a lightning of delight in their souls.

'Yes,' she went on, 'you have got to thank me that you are so poor, Peter. I have seen to that, and it has done well for both you and me, my friend. Things come to the poor that can't get in at the door of the rich. Their money somehow blocks it up. It is a great privilege to be poor, Peter—one that no man ever coveted, and but a very few have sought to retain, but one that yet many have learned to prize. You must not mistake, however, and imagine it a virtue; it is but a privilege, and one also that, like other privileges, may be terribly misused. Hadst thou been rich, my Peter, thou wouldst not have been so good as some rich men I know. And now I am going to tell you what no one knows but myself: you, Peter, and your wife have both the blood of the royal family in your veins. I have been trying to cultivate your family tree, every branch of which is known to me, and I expect Curdie to turn out a blossom on it. Therefore I have been training him for a work that must soon be done. I was near losing him, and had to send my pigeon. Had he not shot it, that would have been better; but he repented, and that shall be as good in the end.'

She turned to Curdie and smiled.

'Ma'am,' said Curdie, 'may I ask questions?'

'Why not, Curdie?'

'Because I have been told, ma'am, that nobody must ask the king questions.'

'The king never made that law,' she answered, with some displeasure. 'You may ask me as many as you please—that is, so long as they are sensible. Only I may take a few thousand years to answer some of them. But that's nothing. Of all things time is the cheapest.'

'Then would you mind telling me now, ma'am, for I feel very confused about it—are you the Lady of the Silver Moon?'

'Yes, Curdie; you may call me that if you like. What it means is true.'

'And now I see you dark, and clothed in green, and the mother of all the light that dwells in the stones of the earth! And up there they call you Old Mother Wotherwop!

And the Princess Irene told me you were her great-great-grandmother! And you spin the spider-threads, and take care of a whole people of pigeons; and you are worn to a pale shadow with old age; and are as young as anybody can be, not to be too young; and as strong, I do believe, as I am.'

The lady stooped towards a large green stone bedded in the rock of the floor, and looking like a well of grassy light in it. She laid hold of it with her fingers, broke it out, and gave it to Peter.

'There!' cried Curdie, 'I told you so. Twenty men could not have done that. And your fingers are white and smooth as any lady's in the land. I don't know what to make of it.'

'I could give you twenty names more to call me, Curdie, and not one of them would be a false one. What does it matter how many names if the person is one?'

'Ah! but it is not names only, ma'am. Look at what you were like last night, and what I see you now!'

'Shapes are only dresses, Curdie, and dresses are only names. That which is inside is the same all the time.'

'But then how can all the shapes speak the truth?'

'It would want thousands more to speak the truth, Curdie; and then they could not. But there is a point I must not let you mistake about. It is one thing the shape I choose to put on, and quite another the shape that foolish talk and nursery tale may please to put upon me. Also, it is one thing what you or your father may think about me, and quite another what a foolish or bad man may see in me. For instance, if a thief were to come in here just now, he would think he saw the demon of the mine, all in green flames, come to protect her treasure, and would run like a hunted wild goat. I should be all the same, but his evil eyes would see me as I was not.'

'I think I understand,' said Curdie.

'Peter,' said the lady, turning then to him, 'you will have to give up Curdie for a little while.'

'So long as he loves us, ma'am, that will not matter—much.'

'Ah! you are right there, my friend,' said the beautiful princess.

And as she said it she put out her hand, and took the hard, horny hand of the miner in it, and held it for a moment lovingly.

'I need say no more,' she added, 'for we understand each other—you and I, Peter.'

The tears came into Peter's eyes. He bowed his head in thankfulness, and his heart was much too full to speak.

Then the great old young beautiful princess turned to Curdie.

'Now, Curdie, are you ready?' she said.

'Yes, ma'am,' answered Curdie.

'You do not know what for.'

'You do, ma'am. That is enough.'

'You could not have given me a better answer, or done more to prepare yourself, Curdie,' she returned, with one of her radiant smiles. 'Do you think you will know me again?'

'I think so. But how can I tell what you may look like next?'

'Ah, that indeed! How can you tell? Or how could I expect you should? But those who know me *well*, know me whatever new dress or shape or name I may be in; and by-and-by you will have learned to do so too.'

'But if you want me to know you again, ma'am, for certain sure,' said Curdie, 'could you not give me some sign, or tell me something about you that never changes—or some other way to know you, or thing to know you by?'

'No, Curdie; that would be to keep you from knowing me. You must know me in quite another way from that. It would not be the least use to you or me either if I were to make you know me in that way. It would be but to know the sign of me—not to know me myself. It would be no better than if I were to take this emerald out of my crown and give it you to take home with

you, and you were to call it me, and talk to it as if it
heard and saw and loved you. Much good that would do
you, Curdie! No; you must do what you can to know
me, and if you do, you will. You shall see me again—in
very different circumstances from these, and, I will tell
you so much, it *may* be in a very different shape. But
come now, I will lead you out of this cavern; my good
Joan will be getting too anxious about you. One word
more: you will allow that the men knew little what they
were talking about this morning, when they told all those
tales of Old Mother Wotherwop; but did it occur to you
to think how it was they fell to talking about me at all?—It
was because I came to them; I was beside them all the time
they were talking about me, though they were far enough
from knowing it, and had very little besides foolishness to
say.'

As she spoke she turned and led the way from the cavern,
which, as if a door had been closed, sunk into absolute
blackness behind them. And now they saw nothing more
of the lady except the green star, which again seemed a
good distance in front of them, and to which they came
no nearer, although following it at a quick pace through
the mountain. Such was their confidence in her guidance,
however, and so fearless were they in consequence, that they
felt their way neither with hand nor foot, but walked straight
on through the pitch dark galleries. When at length the night
of the upper world looked in at the mouth of the mine, the
green light seemed to lose its way amongst the stars, and they
saw it no more.

Out they came into the cool, blessed night. It was very
late, and only starlight. To their surprise, three paces away
they saw, seated upon a stone, an old countrywoman, in a
cloak which they took for black. When they came close up
to it, they saw it was red.

'Good evening!' said Peter.

'Good evening!' returned the old woman, in a voice as old
as herself.

But Curdie took off his cap and said—

'I am your servant, Princess.'

The old woman replied—

'Come to me in the dove-tower tomorrow night, Curdie—alone.'

'I will, ma'am,' said Curdie.

So they parted, and father and son went home to wife and mother—two persons in one rich, happy woman.

VIII
Curdie's Mission

The next night Curdie went home from the mine a little earlier than usual, to make himself tidy before going to the dove-tower. The princess had not appointed an exact time for him to be there; he would go as near the time he had gone first as he could. On his way to the bottom of the hill, he met his father coming up. The sun was then down, and the warm first of the twilight filled the evening. He came rather wearily up the hill: the road, he thought, must have grown steeper in parts since he was Curdie's age. His back was to the light of the sunset, which closed him all round in a beautiful setting, and Curdie thought what a grand-looking man his father was, even when he was tired. It is greed and laziness and selfishness, not hunger or weariness or cold, that take the dignity out of a man, and make him look mean.

'Ah, Curdie! there you are!' he said, seeing his son come bounding along as if it were morning with him and not evening.

'You look tired, father,' said Curdie.

'Yes, my boy. I'm not so young as you.'

'Nor so old as the princess,' said Curdie.

'Tell me this,' said Peter: "why do people talk about going down hill when they begin to get old? It seems to me that then first they begin to go up hill.'

'You looked to me, father, when I caught sight of you, as if you had been climbing the hill all your life, and were soon to get the top.'

'Nobody can tell when that will be,' returned Peter. 'We're so ready to think we're just at the top when it lies miles away. But I must not keep you, my boy, for you are wanted; and we shall be anxious to know what the princess says to you—that is, if she will allow you to tell us.'

'I think she will, for she knows there is nobody more to be trusted than my father and mother,' said Curdie, with pride.

And away he shot, and ran, and jumped, and seemed almost to fly down the long, winding, steep path, until he came to the gate of the king's house.

There he met an unexpected obstruction: in the open door stood the housekeeper, and she seemed to broaden herself out until she almost filled the doorway.

'So!' she said; 'it's you, is it, young man? You are the person that comes in and goes out when he pleases, and keeps running up and down my stairs, without ever saying by your leave, or even wiping his shoes, and always leaves the door open! Don't you know that this is my house?'

'No, I do not,' returned Curdie, respectfully. 'You forget, ma'am, that it is the king's house.'

'That is all the same. The king left it to me to take care of, and that you shall know!'

'Is the king dead, ma'am, that he has left it to you?' asked Curdie, half in doubt from the self-assertion of the woman.

'Insolent fellow!' exclaimed the housekeeper. 'Don't you see by my dress that I am in the king's service?'

'And am I not one of his miners?'

'Ah! that goes for nothing. I am one of his household. You are an out-of-doors labourer. You are a nobody. You carry a pickaxe. I carry the keys at my girdle. See!'

'But you must not call me a nobody to whom the king has spoken,' said Curdie.

'Go along with you!' cried the housekeeper, and would have shut the door in his face, had she not been afraid that when she stepped back he would step in ere she could get it in motion, for it was very heavy, and always seemed unwilling to shut. Curdie came a pace nearer. She lifted the great house key from her side, and threatened to strike him down with it, calling aloud on Mar and Whelk and Plout, the menservants under her, to come and help her. Ere one of them could answer, however, she gave a great shriek and turned and fled, leaving the door wide open.

Curdie looked behind him, and saw an animal whose gruesome oddity even he, who knew so many of the strange creatures, two of which were never the same, that used to live inside the mountain with their masters the goblins, had never seen equalled. Its eyes were flaming with anger, but it seemed to be at the housekeeper, for it came cowering and creeping up, and laid its head on the ground at Curdie's feet. Curdie hardly waited to look at it, however, but ran into the house, eager to get up the stairs before any of the men should come to annoy—he had no fear of their preventing him. Without halt or hindrance, though the passages were nearly dark, he reached the door of the princess's work-room, and knocked.

'Come in,' said the voice of the princess.

Curdie opened the door—but, to his astonishment, saw no room there. Could he have opened a wrong door? There was the great sky, and the stars, and beneath he could see nothing—only darkness! But what was that in the sky, straight in front of him? A great wheel of fire, turning and turning, and flashing out blue lights!

'Come in, Curdie,' said the voice again.

'I would at once, ma'am,' said Curdie, 'if I were sure I was standing at your door.'

'Why should you doubt it, Curdie?'

'Because I see neither walls nor floor, only darkness and the great sky.'

'That is all right, Curdie. Come in.'

Curdie stepped forward at once. He was indeed, for the very crumb of a moment, tempted to feel before him with his foot; but he saw that would be to distrust the princess, and a greater rudeness he could not offer her. So he stepped straight in—I will not say without a little tremble at the thought of finding no floor beneath his foot. But that which had need of the floor found it, and his foot was satisfied.

No sooner was he in than he saw that the great revolving wheel in the sky was the princess's spinning-wheel, near the other end of the room, turning very fast. He could see no sky or stars any more, but the wheel was flashing out blue—oh such lovely sky-blue light!—and behind it of course sat the princess, but whether an old woman as thin as a skeleton leaf, or a glorious lady as young as perfection, he could not tell for the turning and flashing of the wheel.

'Listen to the wheel,' said the voice which had already grown dear to Curdie: its very tone was precious like a jewel, not *as* a jewel, for no jewel could compare with it in preciousness.

And Curdie listened and listened.

'What is it saying?' asked the voice.

'It is singing,' answered Curdie.

'What is it singing?'

Curdie tried to make out, but thought he could not; for no sooner had he got a hold of something than it vanished again. Yet he listened, and listened, entranced with delight.

'Thank you, Curdie,' said the voice.

'Ma'am,' said Curdie, 'I did try hard for a while, but I could not make anything of it.'

'Oh, yes, you did, and you have been telling it to me! Shall I tell you again what I told my wheel, and my wheel told you, and you have just told me without knowing it?'

'Please, ma'am.'

Then the lady began to sing and her wheel spun an accompaniment to her song, and the music of the wheel was like the music of an Aeolian harp* blown upon by the wind that bloweth where it listeth. Oh! the sweet sounds of that spinning-wheel! Now they were gold, now silver, now grass, now palm-trees, now ancient cities, now rubies, now mountain-brooks, now peacock's feathers, now clouds, now snow-drops, and now mid-sea islands. But for the voice that sang through it all, about that I have no words to tell. It would make you weep if I were able to tell you what that was like

like, it was so beautiful and true and lovely. But this is something like the words of its song:

The stars are spinning their threads,
  And the clouds are the dust that flies,
And the suns are weaving them up
  For the time when the sleepers shall rise.

The ocean in music rolls,
  And gems are turning to eyes,
And the trees are gathering souls
  For the time when the sleepers shall rise.

The weepers are learning to smile,
  And laughter to glean the sighs;
Burn and bury the care and guile,
  For the day when the sleepers shall rise.

Oh, the dews and the moths and the daisy-red,
  The larks and the glimmers and flows!
The lilies and sparrows and daily bread,
  And the something that nobody knows!

The princess stopped, her wheel stopped, and she laughed. And her laugh was sweeter than song and wheel; sweeter than running brook and silver bell; sweeter than joy itself, for the heart of the laugh was love.

'Come now, Curdie, to this side of my wheel, and you will find me,' she said; and her laugh seemed sounding on still in the words, as if they were made of breath that had laughed.

Curdie obeyed, and passed the wheel, and there she stood to receive him!—fairer than when he saw her last, a little younger still, and dressed not in green and emeralds, but in pale blue, with a coronet of silver set with pearls, and slippers covered with opals, that gleamed every colour of the rainbow. It was some time before Curdie could take his eyes from the marvel of her loveliness. Fearing at last that he was rude, he turned them away; and, behold, he was in a room that was for beauty marvellous! The lofty ceiling was all a golden vine, whose great clusters of carbuncles, rubies, and chrysoberyls, hung down like the bosses of groined arches, and in its centre hung the most glorious lamp that human eyes ever saw—the Silver Moon itself, a globe of silver, as it seemed, with a heart of light so wondrous potent that it rendered the mass translucent, and altogether radiant.

The room was so large that, looking back, he could scarcely see the end at which he entered; but the other was only a few yards from him—and there he saw another wonder: on a huge hearth a great fire was burning, and the fire was a huge heap of roses, and yet it was fire. The smell of the roses filled the air, and the heat of the flames of them glowed upon his face. He turned an inquiring look upon the lady, and saw that she was now seated in an ancient chair, the legs of which were crusted with gems, but the upper part like a nest of daisies and moss and green grass.

'Curdie,' she said in answer to his eyes, 'you have stood more than one trial already, and have stood them well: now I am going to put you to a harder. Do you think you are prepared for it?'

'How can I tell, ma'am?' he returned, 'seeing I do not know what it is, or what preparation it needs? Judge me yourself, ma'am.'

'It needs only trust and obedience,' answered the lady.

'I dare not say anything, ma'am. If you think me fit, command me.'

'It will hurt you terribly, Curdie, but that will be all; no real hurt, but much real good will come to you from it.'

Curdie made no answer, but stood gazing with parted lips in the lady's face.

'Go and thrust both your hands into that fire,' she said quickly, almost hurriedly.

Curdie dared not stop to think. It was much too terrible to think about. He rushed to the fire, and thrust both his hands right into the middle of the heap of flaming roses, and his arms halfway up to the elbows. And it *did* hurt! But he did not draw them back. He held the pain as if it were a thing that would kill him if he let it go—as indeed it would have done. He was in terrible fear lest it should conquer him. But when it had risen to the pitch that he thought he *could* bear it no longer, it began to fall again, and went on growing less and less until by contrast with its former severity it had become rather pleasant. At last it ceased altogether, and Curdie thought his hands must be burnt to cinders if not ashes, for he did not feel them at all. The princess told him to take them out and look at them. He did so, and found that all that was gone of them was the rough hard skin; they were white and smooth like the princess's.

'Come to me,' she said.

He obeyed, and saw, to his surprise, that her face looked as if she had been weeping.

'Oh, princess! what *is* the matter?' he cried. 'Did I make a noise and vex you?'

'No, Curdie,' she answered; 'but it was very bad.'

'Did you feel it too then?'

'Of course I did. But now it is over, and all is well.—Would you like to know why I made you put your hands in the fire?'

Curdie looked at them again—then said,—

'To take the marks of the work off them, and make them fit for the king's court, I suppose.'

'No, Curdie,' answered the princess, shaking her head, for she was not pleased with the answer. 'It would be a poor way of making your hands fit for the king's court to take off them all signs of his service. There is a far greater difference on them than that. Do you feel none?'

'No, ma'am.'

'You will, though, by and by, when the time comes. But perhaps even then you might not know what had been given you, therefore I will tell you.—Have you ever heard what some philosophers say*—that men were all animals once?'

'No ma'am.'

'It is of no consequence. But there is another thing that is of the greatest consequence—this: that all men, if they do not take care, go down the hill to the animals' country; that many men are actually, all their lives, going to be beasts. People knew it once, but it is long since they forgot it.'

'I am not surprised to hear it, ma'am, when I think of some of our miners.'

'Ah! but you must beware, Curdie, how you say of this man or that man that he is travelling beastward. There are not nearly so many going that way as at first sight you might think. When you met your father on the hill tonight, you stood and spoke together on the same spot; and although one of you was going up and the other coming down, at a little distance no one could have told which was bound in the one direction and which in the other. Just so two people may be at the same spot in manners and behaviour, and yet one may be getting better and the other worse, which is just the greatest of all differences that could possibly exist between them.'

'But, ma'am,' said Curdie, 'where is the good of knowing that there is such a difference, if you can never know where it is?'

'Now, Curdie, you must mind exactly what words I use, because although the right words cannot do exactly what I want them to do, the wrong words will certainly do what I do not want them to do. I did not say *you can never know*. When there is a necessity for your knowing, when you have to do important business with this or that man, there is always a way of knowing enough to keep you from any great blunder. And as you will have important business to do by and by, and that with people of whom you yet know nothing, it will be necessary that you should have some better means than usual of learning the nature of them. Now listen. Since it is always what they *do*, whether in their minds or their bodies, that makes men go down to be less than men, that is, beasts, the change always comes first in their hands—and first of all in the inside hands, to which the outside ones are but as the gloves. They do not know it of course; for a beast does not know that he is a beast, and the nearer a man gets to being a beast the less he knows it. Neither can their best friends, or their worst enemies indeed, *see* any difference in their hands, for they see only the living gloves of them. But there are not a few who feel a vague something repulsive in the hand of a man who is growing a beast. Now here is what the rose-fire has done for you: it has made your hands so knowing and wise, it has brought your real hands so near the outside of your flesh-gloves, that you will henceforth be able to know at once the hand of a man who is growing into a beast; nay, more—you will at once feel the foot of the beast he is growing, just as if there were no glove made like a man's hand between you and it. Hence of course it follows that you will be able often, and with further education in zoology, will be able always to tell, not only when a man is growing a beast, but what beast he is growing to, for you will know the foot—what it is and what beast's it is. According then to your knowledge of that beast, will be your knowledge of the man you have to do with. Only there is one beautiful and awful thing about it, that if any one gifted with this perception once uses it for his own ends, it is taken from him, and then, not knowing that it is gone, he is in a far worse condition than before, for he trusts to what he has not got.'

'How dreadful!' said Curdie. 'I must mind what I am about.'

'Yes, indeed, Curdie.'

'But may not one sometimes make a mistake without being able to help it?'

'Yes. But so long as he is not after his own ends, he will never make a serious mistake.'

'I suppose you want me, ma'am, to warn every one whose hand tells me that he is growing a beast—because, as you say, he does not know it himself.'

The princess smiled.

'Much good that would do, Curdie! I don't say there are no cases in which it would be of use, but they are very rare and peculiar cases, and if such come you will know them. To such a person there is in general no insult like the truth.

He cannot endure it, not because he is growing a beast, but because he is ceasing to be a man. It is the dying man in him that it makes uncomfortable, and he trots, or creeps, or swims, or flutters out of its way—calls it a foolish feeling, a whim, an old wives' fable, a bit of priests' humbug, an effete superstition, and so on.'

'And is there no hope for him? Can nothing be done? It's so awful to think of going down, down, down like that!'

'Even when it is with his own will?'

'That's what seems to me to make it worst of all,' said Curdie.

'You are right,' answered the princess, nodding her head; 'but there is this amount of excuse to make for all such, remember—that they do not know what or how horrid their coming fate is. Many a lady, so delicate and nice that she can bear nothing coarser than the finest linen to touch her body, if she had a mirror that could show her the animal she is growing to, as it lies waiting within the fair skin and the fine linen and the silk and the jewels, would receive a shock that might possibly wake her up.'

'Why then, ma'am, shouldn't she have it?'

The princess held her peace.

'Come here, Lina,' she said after a long pause.

From somewhere behind Curdie, crept forward the same hideous animal which had fawned at his feet at the door, and which, without his knowing it, had followed him every step up the dove-tower. She ran to the princess, and lay down at her feet, looking up at her with an expression so pitiful that in Curdie's heart it overcame all the ludicrousness of her horrible mass of incongruities. She had a very short body, and very long legs made like an elephant's, so that in lying down she kneeled with both pairs. Her tail, which dragged on the floor behind her, was twice as long and quite as thick as her body. Her head was something between that of a polar bear and a snake. Her eyes were dark green, with a yellow light in them. Her under teeth came up like a fringe of icicles, only very white, outside of her upper lip. Her throat looked as if the hair had been plucked off. It showed a skin white and smooth.

'Give Curdie a paw, Lina,' said the princess.

The creature rose, and, lifting a long fore leg, held up a great dog-like paw to Curdie. He took it gently. But what a shudder, as of terrified delight, ran through him, when, instead of the paw of a dog, such as it seemed to his eyes, he clasped in his great mining fist the soft, neat little hand of a child! He took it in both of his, and held it as if he could not let it go. The green eyes stared at him with their yellow light, and the mouth was turned up towards him with its constant half-grin; but here *was* the child's hand! If he could but pull the child out of the beast! His eyes sought the princess. She was watching him with evident satisfaction.

'Ma'am, here is a child's hand!' said Curdie.

'Your gift does more for you than it promised. It is yet better to perceive a hidden good than a hidden evil.'

'But,' began Curdie.

'I am not going to answer any more questions this evening,' interrupted the princess. 'You have not half got to the bottom of the answers I have already given you. That paw in your hand now might almost teach you the whole science of natural history—the heavenly sort, I mean.'

'I will think,' said Curdie. 'But oh! please! one word more: may I tell my father and mother all about it?'

'Certainly—though perhaps now it may be their turn to find it a little difficult to believe that things went just as you must tell them.'

'They shall see that I believe it all this time,' said Curdie.

'Tell them that tomorrow morning you must set out for the court—not like a great man, but just as poor as you are. They had better not speak about it. Tell them also that it will be a long time before they hear of you again, but they must not lose heart. And tell your father to lay that stone I gave him last night in a safe place—not because of the greatness of its price, although it is such an emerald as no prince has in his crown, but because it will be a news-bearer between you and him. As often as he gets at all anxious about you, he must take it and lay it in the fire, and leave it there when he goes to bed. In the morning he must find it in the ashes, and if it be as green as ever, then all goes well with you; if it have lost colour, things go ill with you; but if it be very pale indeed, then you are in great danger, and he must come to me.'

'Yes, ma'am,' said Curdie. 'Please, am I to go now?'

'Yes,' answered the princess, and held out her hand to him.

Curdie took it, trembling with joy. It was a very beautiful hand—not small, very smooth, but not very soft—and just the same to his fire-taught touch that it was to his eyes. He would have stood there all night holding it if she had not gently withdrawn it.

'I will provide you a servant,' she said, 'for your journey, and to wait upon you afterwards.'

'But where am I to go, ma'am, and what am I to do? You have given me no message to carry, neither have you said what I am wanted for. I go without a notion whether I am to walk this way or that, or what I am to do when I get I don't know where.'

'Curdie!' said the princess, and there was a tone of reminder in his own name as she spoke it, 'did I not tell you to tell your father and mother that you were to set out for the court? and you *know* that lies to the north. You must learn to use far less direct directions than that. You must not be like a dull servant that needs to be told again and again before he will understand. You have orders enough to start with, and you will find, as you go on, and as you need to know, what you have to do. But I warn you that perhaps it will not look the least like what you may have been fancying I should require of you. I have one idea of you and your work, and you have another. I do not blame you for that—you cannot help it yet; but you must be ready to let my idea, which sets you working, set your idea right. Be true and honest and fearless, and all shall go well with you and your work, and all with whom your work lies, and so with your parents—and me too, Curdie,' she added after a little pause.

The young miner bowed his head low, patted the strange head that lay at the princess's feet, and turned away.

As soon as he passed the spinning-wheel, which looked, in the midst of the glorious room, just like any wheel you might find in a country cottage—old and worn and dingy and dusty—the splendour of the place vanished, and he saw but the big bare room he seemed at first to have entered, with the moon—the princess's moon no doubt—shining in at one of the windows upon the spinning-wheel.

IX

Hands

Curdie went home, pondering much, and told everything to his father and mother. As the old princess had said, it was now their turn to find what they heard hard to believe. If they had not been able to trust Curdie himself, they would have refused to believe more than the half of what he reported, then they would have refused that half too, and at last would most likely for a time have disbelieved in the very existence of the princess, what evidence their own senses had given them notwithstanding. For he had nothing conclusive to show in proof of what he told them. When he held out his hands to them, his mother said they looked as if he had been washing them with soft soap, only they did smell of something nicer than that, and she must allow it was more like roses than anything else she knew. His father could not see any difference upon his hands, but then it was night, he said, and their poor little lamp was not enough for his old eyes. As to the feel of them, each of his own hands, he said, was hard and horny enough for two, and it must be the fault of the dulness of his own thick skin that he felt no change on Curdie's palms.

'Here, Curdie,' said his mother, 'try my hand, and see what beast's paw lies inside it.'

'No, mother,' answered Curdie, half-beseeching, half-indignant, 'I will not insult my new gift by making pretence to try it. That would be mockery. There is no hand within yours but the hand of a true woman, my mother.'

'I should like you just to take hold of my hand, though,' said his mother. 'You are my son, and may know all the bad there is in me.'

Then at once Curdie took her hand in his. And when he had it, he kept it, stroking it gently with his other hand.

'Mother,' he said at length, 'your hand feels just like that of the princess.'

'What! my horny, cracked, rheumatic old hand, with its big joints, and its short nails all worn down to the quick with hard work—like the hand of the beautiful princess! Why, my child, you will make me fancy your fingers have grown very dull indeed, instead of sharp and delicate, if you talk such nonsense. Mine is such an ugly hand I should be ashamed to show it to any but one that loved me. But love makes all safe—doesn't it, Curdie?'

'Well, mother, all I can say is that I don't feel a roughness, or a crack, or a big joint, or a short nail. Your hand feels just and exactly, as near as I can recollect, and it's not now more than two hours since I had it in mine—well, I will say, very like indeed to that of the old princess.'

'Go away, you flatterer,' said his mother, with a smile that showed how she prized the love that lay beneath what she took for its hyperbole. The praise even which one cannot accept is sweet from a true mouth. 'If that is all your new gift can do, it won't make a warlock* of you,' she added.

'Mother, it tells me nothing but the truth,' insisted Curdie, 'however unlike the truth it may seem. It wants no gift to tell what anybody's outside hands are like. But by it I *know* your inside hands are like the princess's.'

'And I am sure the boy speaks true,' said Peter. 'He only says about your hand what I have known ever so long about yourself, Joan. Curdie, your mother's foot is as pretty a foot as any lady's in the land, and where her hand is not so pretty it comes of killing its beauty for you and me, my boy. And I can tell you more, Curdie. I don't know much about ladies and gentlemen, but I am sure your inside mother must be a lady, as her hand tells you, and I will try to say how I know it. This is how: when I forget myself looking at her as she goes about her work—and that happens oftener as I grow older—I fancy for a moment or two that I am a gentleman; and when I wake up from my little dream, it is only to feel the more strongly that I must do everything as a gentleman should. I will try to tell you what I mean, Curdie. If a gentleman—I mean a real gentleman, not a pretended one, of which sort they say there are a many above ground—if a real gentleman were to lose all his money and come down to work in the mines to get bread for his family—do you think, Curdie, he would work like the lazy ones? Would he try to do as little as he could for his wages? I know the sort of the true gentleman—pretty near as well as he does himself. And my wife, that's your mother, Curdie, she's a true lady, you may take my word for it, for it's she that makes me want to be a true gentleman. Wife, the boy is in the right about your hand.'

'Now, father, let me feel yours,' said Curdie, daring a little more.

'No, no, my boy,' answered Peter. 'I don't want to hear anything about my hand or my head or my heart. I am what I am, and I hope growing better, and that's enough. No, you shan't feel my hand. You must go to bed, for you must start with the sun.'

It was not as if Curdie had been leaving them to go to prison, or to make a fortune, and although they were sorry enough to lose him, they were not in the least heartbroken or even troubled at his going.

As the princess had said he was to go like the poor man he was, Curdie came down in the morning from his little loft dressed in his working clothes. His mother, who was busy getting his breakfast for him, while his father sat reading to her out of an old book, would have had him put on his holiday garments, which, she said, would look poor enough amongst the fine ladies and gentlemen he was going to. But Curdie said he did not know that he was going amongst ladies and gentlemen, and that as work was better than play, his workday clothes must on the whole be better than his playday clothes; and as his father accepted the argument, his mother gave in.

When he had eaten his breakfast, she took a pouch made of goatskin, with the long hair on it, filled it with bread and cheese, and hung it over his shoulder. Then his father gave him a stick he had cut for him in the wood, and he bade them goodbye rather hurriedly, for he was afraid of breaking down. As he went out, he caught up his mattock and took it with him. It had on the one side a pointed curve of strong steel, for loosening the earth and the ore, and on the other a steel hammer for breaking the stones and rocks. Just as he crossed the threshold the sun showed the first segment of his disc above the horizon.

X

The Heath

He had to go to the bottom of the hill to get into a country he could cross, for the mountains to the north were full of precipices, and it would have been losing time to go that way. Not until he had reached the king's house was it any use to turn northwards. Many a look did he raise, as he passed it, to the dove-tower, and as long as it was in sight, but he saw nothing of the lady of the pigeons.

On and on he fared, and came in a few hours to a country where there were no mountains more—only hills with great stretches of desolate heath. Here and there was a village, but that brought him little pleasure, for the people were rougher and worse-mannered than those in the mountains, and as he passed through, the children came behind and mocked him.

'There's a monkey running away from the mines!' they cried.

Sometimes their parents came out and encouraged them.

'He don't want to find gold for the king any longer—the lazybones!' they would say. 'He'll be well taxed down here though, and he won't like that either.'

But it was little to Curdie that men who did not know what he was about should not approve of his proceedings. He gave them a merry answer now and then, and held diligently on his way. When they got so rude as nearly to make him angry, he would treat them as he used to treat the goblins, and sing his own songs to keep out their foolish noises. Once a child fell as he turned to run away after throwing a stone at him. He picked him up, kissed him, and carried him to his mother. The woman had run out in terror when she saw the strange miner about, as she thought, to take vengeance on her boy. When he put him in her arms, she blessed him, and Curdie went on his way rejoicing.

And so the day went on, and the evening came, and in the middle of a great desolate heath he began to feel tired, and sat down under an ancient hawthorn, through which every now and then a lone wind that seemed to come from nowhere and to go nowhither sighed and hissed. It was very old and distorted. There was not another tree for miles all around. It seemed to have lived so long, and to have been so torn and tossed by the tempests on that moor, that it had at last gathered a wind of its own, which got up now and then, tumbled itself about, and lay down again.

Curdie had been so eager to get on that he had eaten nothing since his breakfast. But he had had plenty of water, for many little streams had crossed his path. He now opened the wallet his mother had given him, and began to eat his supper. Then sun was setting. A few clouds had gathered about the west, but there was not a single cloud anywhere else to be seen.

Now Curdie did not know that this was a part of the country very hard to get through. Nobody lived there, though many had tried to build in it. Some died very soon. Some rushed out of it. Those who stayed longest went raving mad, and died a terrible death. Such as walked straight on, and did not spend a night there, got through well, and were nothing the worse. But those who slept even a single night in it were sure to meet with something they could never forget, and which often left a mark everybody could read. And that old hawthorn might have been enough for a warning—it looked so like a human being dried up and distorted with age and suffering, with cares instead of loves, and things instead of thoughts. Both it and the heath around it, which stretched on all sides as far as he could see, were so withered that it was impossible to say whether they were alive or not.

And while Curdie ate there came a change. Clouds had gathered over his head, and seemed drifting about in every direction, as if not 'shepherded by the slow, unwilling wind,'* but hunted in all directions by wolfish flaws across the plains of the sky. The sun was going down in a storm of lurid crimson, and out of the west came a wind that felt red and hot the one moment, and cold and pale the other. And very strangely it sung in the dreary old hawthorn tree, and very cheerily it blew about Curdie, now making him creep close up to the tree for shelter from its shivery cold, now fan himself with his cap, it was so sultry and stifling. It seemed to come from the deathbed of the sun, dying in fever and ague.

And as he gazed at the sun, now on the verge of the horizon, very large and very red and very dull—for though the clouds had broken away a dusty fog was spread all over him—Curdie saw something strange appear against him, moving about like a fly over his burning face. It looked as if it were coming out of his hot furnace-heart, and was a living creature of some kind surely; but its shape was very uncertain, because the dazzle of the light all around it melted its outlines. It was growing larger, it must be approaching! It grew so rapidly that by the time the sun was half down its head reached the top of his arch, and presently nothing but its legs were to be seen, crossing and recrossing the face of the vanishing disc. When the sun was down he could see nothing of it more, but in a moment he heard its feet galloping over the dry crackling heather, and seeming to come straight for him. He stood up, lifted his pickaxe, and threw the hammer end over his shoulder: he was going to have a fight for his life! And now it appeared again, vague, yet very awful, in the dim twilight the sun had left behind him. But just before it reached him, down from its four long legs it dropped flat on the ground, and came crawling towards him, wagging a huge tail as it came.

XI
Lina

It was Lina. All at once Curdie recognized her—the frightful creature he had seen at the princess's. He dropped his pick-axe, and held out his hand. She crept nearer and nearer, and laid her chin in his palm, and he patted her ugly head. Then she crept away behind the tree, and lay down, panting hard. Curdie did not much like the idea of her being behind him. Horrible as she was to look at, she seemed to his mind more horrible when he was not looking at her. But he remembered the child's hand, and never thought of driving her away. Now and then he gave a glance behind him, and there she lay flat, with her eyes closed and her terrible teeth gleaming between her two huge fore-paws.

After his supper and his long day's journey it was no wonder Curdie should now be sleepy. Since the sun set the air had been warm and pleasant. He lay down under the tree, closed his eyes, and thought to sleep. He found himself mistaken however. But although he could not sleep, he was yet aware of resting delightfully. Presently he heard a sweet sound of singing somewhere, such as he had never heard before—a singing as of curious birds far off, which drew nearer and nearer. At length he heard their wings, and, opening his eyes, saw a number of very large birds, as it seemed, alighting around him, still singing. It was strange to hear song from the throats of such big birds. And still singing, with large and round but not the less bird-like voices, they began to weave a strange dance about him, moving their wings in time with their legs. But the dance seemed somehow to be troubled and broken, and to return upon itself in an eddy, in place of sweeping smoothly on. And he soon learned, in the low short growls behind him, the cause of the imperfection: they wanted to dance all round the tree, but Lina would not permit them to come on her side.

Now Curdie liked the birds, and did not altogether *like* Lina. But neither, nor both together, made a *reason* for driving away the princess's creature. Doubtless she *had been* a goblins' creature, but the last time he saw her was in the king's house and the dove-tower, and at the old princess's feet. So he left her to do as she would, and the dance of the birds continued only a semicircle, troubled at the edges, and returning upon itself. But their song and their motions, nevertheless, and the waving of their wings, began at length to make him very sleepy. All the time he had kept doubting every now and then whether they could really be birds, and the sleepier he got, the more he imagined them something else, but he suspected no harm. Suddenly, just as he was sinking beneath the waves of slumber, he awoke in fierce pain. The birds were upon him—all over him—and had begun to tear him with beaks and claws. He had but time, however, to feel that he could not move under their weight, when they set up a hideous screaming, and scattered like a cloud. Lina was amongst them, snapping and striking with her paws, while her tail knocked them over and over. But they flew up, gathered, and descended on her in a swarm, perching upon every part of her body, so that he could see only a huge misshapen mass, which seemed to go rolling away into the darkness. He got up and tried to follow, but could see nothing, and after wandering about hither and thither for some time, found himself again beside the hawthorn. He feared greatly that the birds had been too much for Lina, and had torn her to pieces. In a little while, however, she came limping back, and lay down in her old place. Curdie also lay down, but, from the pain of his wounds, there was no sleep for him. When the light came he found his clothes a good deal torn and his skin as well, but gladly wondered why the wicked birds had not at once attacked his eyes. Then he turned looking for Lina. She rose and crept to him. But she was in far worse plight than he—plucked and gashed and torn with the beaks and claws of the birds, especially about the bare part of her neck, so that she was pitiful to see. And those worst wounds she could not reach to lick.

'Poor Lina!' said Curdie; 'you got all those helping me.'

She wagged her tail, and made it clear she understood him. Then it flashed upon Curdie's mind that perhaps this was the companion the princess had promised him. For the princess did so many things differently from what anybody looked for! Lina was no beauty certainly, but already, the first night, she had saved his life.

'Come along, Lina,' he said; 'we want water.'

She put her nose to the earth, and after snuffing for a moment, darted off in a straight line. Curdie followed. The ground was so uneven, that after losing sight of her many times, at last he seemed to have lost her altogether. In a few minutes, however, he came upon her waiting for him. Instantly she darted off again. After he had lost and found her again many times, he found her the last time lying beside a great stone. As soon as he came up she began scratching at it with her paws. When he had raised it an inch or two, she shoved in first her nose and then her teeth, and lifted with all the might of her strong neck.

When at length between them they got it up, there was a beautiful little well. He filled his cap with the clearest and sweetest water, and drank. Then he gave to Lina, and she drank plentifully. Next he washed her wound's very carefully. And as he did so, he noted how much the bareness of her neck added to the strange repulsiveness of her appearance. Then he bethought him of the goatskin wallet his mother had given him, and taking it from his shoulders, tried whether it would do to make a collar of for the poor animal. He found there was just enough, and the hair so similar in colour to Lina's, that no one could suspect it of having grown somewhere else. He took his knife, ripped up the seams of the wallet, and began trying the skin to her neck. It was plain she understood perfectly what he wished, for she endeavoured to hold her neck conveniently, turning it this way and that while he contrived, with his rather scanty material, to make the collar fit. As his mother had taken care to provide him with needles and thread, he soon had a nice gorget* ready for her. He laced it on with one of his boot-laces, which its long hair covered.

Poor Lina looked much better in it. Nor could any one have called it a piece of finery. If ever green eyes with a yellow light in them looked grateful, hers did.

As they had no longer any bag to carry them in, Curdie and Lina now ate what was left of the provisions. Then they set out again upon their journey. For seven days it lasted. They met with various adventures, and in all of them Lina proved so helpful, and so ready to risk her life for the sake of her companion, that Curdie grew not merely very fond but very trustful of her, and her ugliness, which at first only moved his pity, now actually increased his affection for her. One day, looking at her stretched on the grass before him, he said—

'Oh, Lina! if the princess would but burn you in her fire of roses!'

She looked up at him, gave a mournful whine like a dog, and laid her head on his feet. What or how much he could not tell, but clearly she had gathered something from his words.

XII

More Creatures

One day from morning till night they had been passing
through a forest. As soon as the sun was down Curdie began
to be aware that there were more in it than themselves. First
he saw only the swift rush of a figure across the trees at some
distance. Then he saw another and then another at shorter
intervals. Then he saw others both further off and nearer.
At last, missing Lina and looking about after her, he saw
an appearance almost as marvellous as herself steal up to
her, and begin conversing with her after some beast fashion
which evidently she understood.

Presently what seemed a quarrel arose between them, and
stranger noises followed, mingled with growling. At length it
came to a fight, which had not lasted long, however, before
the creature of the wood threw itself upon its back, and
held up its paws to Lina. She instantly walked on, and the
creature got up and followed her. They had not gone far
before another strange animal appeared, approaching Lina,
when precisely the same thing was repeated, the vanquished
animal rising and following with the former. Again, and yet
again and again, a fresh animal came up, seemed to be
reasoned and certainly was fought with and overcome by
Lina, until at last, before they were out of the wood, she
was followed by forty-nine of the most grotesquely ugly, the
most extravagantly abnormal animals imagination can con-
ceive. To describe them were a hopeless task. I knew a boy
who used to make animals out of heather roots. Wherever
he could find four legs, he was pretty sure to find a head
and a tail. His beasts were a most comic menagerie, and
right fruitful of laughter. But they were not so grotesque
and extravagant as Lina and her followers. One of them,

for instance, was like a boa constrictor walking on four little stumpy legs near its tail. About the same distance from his head were two little wings, which it was for ever fluttering as if trying to fly with them. Curdie thought it fancied it did fly with them, when it was merely plodding on busily with its four little stumps. How it managed to keep up he could not think, till once when he missed it from the group: the same moment he caught sight of something at a distance plunging at an awful serpentine rate through the trees, and presently, from behind a huge ash, this same creature fell again into the group, quietly waddling along on its four stumps. Watching it after this, he saw that, when it was not able to keep up any longer, and they had all got a little space ahead, it shot into the wood away from the route, and made a great round, serpenting along in huge billows of motion, devouring the ground, undulating awfully, galloping as if it were all legs together, and its four stumps nowhere. In this mad fashion it shot ahead, and, a few minutes after, toddled in again amongst the rest, walking peacefully and somewhat painfully on its few fours.

From the time it takes to describe one of them it will be readily seen that it would hardly do to attempt a description of each of the forty-nine. They were not a goodly company,* but well worth contemplating nevertheless; and Curdie had been too long used to the goblins' creatures in the mines and on mountain, to feel the least uncomfortable at being followed by such a herd. On the contrary the marvellous vagaries of shape they manifested amused him greatly, and shortened the journey much. Before they were all gathered, however, it had got so dark that he could see some of them only a part at a time, and every now and then, as the company wandered on, he would be startled by some extraordinary limb or feature, undreamed of by him before, thrusting itself out of the darkness into the range of his ken. Probably there were some of his old acquaintances among them, although such had been the conditions of semi-darkness in which alone he had ever seen any of them, that it was not likely he would be able to identify any of them.

On they marched solemnly, almost in silence, for either with feet or voice the creatures seldom made any noise. By the time they reached the outside of the wood it was morning twilight. Into the open trooped the strange torrent of deformity, each one following Lina. Suddenly she stopped, turned towards them, and said something which they understood, although to Curdie's ear the sounds she made seemed to have no articulation. Instantly they all turned, and vanished in the forest, and Lina alone came trotting lithely and clumsily after her master.

XIII

The Baker's Wife

They were now passing through a lovely country of hill and dale and rushing stream. The hills were abrupt, with broken chasms for water-courses, and deep little valleys full of trees. But now and then they came to a larger valley, with a fine river, whose level banks and the adjacent meadows were dotted all over with red and white kine, while on the fields above, that sloped a little to the foot of the hills, grew oats and barley and wheat, and on the sides of the hills themselves vines hung and chestnuts rose. They came at last to a broad, beautiful river, up which they must go to arrive at the city of Gwyntystorm, where the king had his court. As they went the valley narrowed, and then the river, but still it was wide enough for large boats. After this, while the river kept its size, the banks narrowed, until there was only room for a road between the river and the great cliffs that overhung it. At last river and road took a sudden turn, and lo! a great rock in the river, which dividing flowed around it, and on the top of the rock the city, with lofty walls and towers and battlements, and above the city the palace of the king, built like a strong castle. But the fortifications had long been neglected, for the whole country was now under one king, and all men said there was no more need for weapons or walls. No man pretended to love his neighbour, but every one said he knew that peace and quiet behaviour was the best thing for himself, and that, he said, was quite as useful, and a great deal more reasonable. The city was prosperous and rich, and if anybody was not comfortable, everybody else said he ought to be.

When Curdie got up opposite the mighty rock, which sparkled all over with crystals, he found a narrow bridge, defended by gates and portcullis and towers with loopholes. But the gates stood wide open, and were dropping from their great hinges; the portcullis was eaten away with rust, and clung to the grooves evidently immovable; while the loopholed towers had neither floor nor roof, and their tops were fast filling up their interiors. Curdie thought it a pity, if only for their old story, that they should be thus neglected. But everybody in the city regarded these signs of decay as the best proof of the prosperity of the place. Commerce and self-interest, they said, had got the better of violence, and the troubles of the past were whelmed in the riches that flowed in at their open gates. Indeed there was one sect of philosophers* in it which taught that it would be better to forget all the past history of the city, were it not that its former imperfections taught its present inhabitants how superior they and their times were, and enabled them to glory over their ancestors. There were even certain quacks in the city who advertised pills for enabling people to think well of themselves, and some few bought of them, but most laughed, and said, with evident truth, that they did not require them. Indeed, the general theme of discourse when they met was, how much wiser they were than their fathers.

Curdie crossed the river, and began to ascend the winding road that led up to the city. They met a good many idlers, and all stared at them. It was no wonder they should stare, but there was an unfriendliness in their looks which Curdie did not like. No one, however, offered them any molestation: Lina did not invite liberties. After a long ascent, they reached the principal gate of the city and entered.

The street was very steep, ascending towards the palace, which rose in great strength above all the houses. Just as they entered, a baker, whose shop was a few doors inside the gate, came out in his white apron, and ran to the shop of his friend the barber on the opposite side of the way. But as he ran he stumbled and fell heavily. Curdie hastened to help him up, and found he had bruised his forehead badly. He swore grievously at the stone for tripping him up, declaring it was the third time he had fallen over it within the last month; and saying what was the king about that he allowed such a stone to stick up for ever on the main street of his royal residence of Gwyntystorm! What was a king for if he would not take care of his people's heads! And he stroked his forehead tenderly.

'Was it your head or your feet that ought to bear the blame of your fall?' asked Curdie.

'Why, you booby of a miner! my feet, of course,' answered the baker.

'Nay, then,' said Curdie, 'the king can't be to blame.'

'Oh, I see!' said the baker. 'You're laying a trap for me. Of course, if you come to that, it was my head that ought to have looked after my feet. But it is the king's part to look after us all, and have his streets smooth.'

'Well, I don't see,' said Curdie, 'why the king should take care of the baker, when the baker's head won't take care of the baker's feet.'

'Who are you to make game of the king's baker?' cried the man in a rage.

But, instead of answering, Curdie went up to the bump on the street which had repeated itself on the baker's head, and turning the hammer end of his mattock, struck it such a blow that it flew wide in pieces. Blow after blow he struck, until he had levelled it with the street.

But out flew the barber upon him in a rage.

'What do you break my window for, you rascal, with your pickaxe?'

'I am very sorry,' said Curdie. 'It must have been a bit of stone that flew from my mattock. I couldn't help it, you know,'

'Couldn't help it! A fine story! What do you go breaking the rock for—the very rock upon which the city stands?'

'Look at your friend's forehead,' said Curdie. 'See what a lump he has got on it with falling over that same stone.'

'What's that to my window?' cried the barber. 'His forehead can mend itself; my poor window can't.'

'But he's the king's baker,' said Curdie, more and more surprised at the man's anger.

'What's that to me? This is a free city. Every man here takes care of himself, and the king takes care of us all. I'll have the price of my window out of you, or the exchequer* shall pay for it.'

Something caught Curdie's eye. He stooped, picked up a piece of the stone he had just broken, and put it in his pocket.

'I suppose you are going to break another of my windows with that stone!' said the barber.

'Oh no,' said Curdie. 'I didn't mean to break your window, and I certainly won't break another.'

'Give me that stone,' said the barber.

Curdie gave it him, and the barber threw it over the city wall.

'I thought you wanted the stone,' said Curdie.

'No, you fool!' answered the barber. 'What should I want with a stone?' Curdie stooped and picked up another.

'Give me that stone,' said the barber.

'No,' answered Curdie. 'You have just told me you don't want a stone, and I do.'

The barber took Curdie by the collar.

'Come, now! you pay me for that window.'

'How much?' asked Curdie.

The barber said, 'A crown.'* But the baker, annoyed at the heartlessness of the barber, in thinking more of his broken window than the bump on his friend's forehead, interfered.

'No, no,' he said to Curdie; 'don't you pay any such sum. A little pane like that cost only a quarter.'

'Well, to be certain,' said Curdie, 'I'll give him a half.' For he doubted the baker as well as the barber. 'Perhaps one day, if he find he has asked too much, he will bring me the difference.'

'Ha! ha!' laughed the barber. 'A fool and his money are soon parted.'

But as he took the coin from Curdie's hand he grasped it in affected reconciliation and real satisfaction. In Curdie's, his was the cold smooth leathery palm of a monkey. He looked up, almost expecting to see him pop the money in his cheek;

but he had not yet got so far as that, though he was well on the road to it: then he would have no other pocket.

'I'm glad that stone is gone, anyhow,' said the baker. 'It was the bane of my life. I had no idea how easy it was to remove it. Give me your pickaxe, young miner, and I will show you how a baker can make the stones fly.'

He caught the tool out of Curdie's hand, and flew at one of the foundation stones of the gateway. But he jarred his arm terribly, scarcely chipped the stone, dropped the mattock with a cry of pain, and ran into his shop. Curdie picked up his implement, and looking after the baker, saw bread in the window, and followed him. But the baker, ashamed of himself, and thinking he was coming to laugh at him, popped out of the back door, and when Curdie entered, the baker's wife came from the bakehouse to serve him. Curdie requested to know the price of a certain good-sized loaf.

Now the baker's wife had been watching what had passed since first her husband ran out of the shop, and she liked the look of Curdie. Also she was more honest than her husband. Casting a glance to the back door, she replied—

'That is not the best bread. I will sell you a loaf of what we bake for ourselves.' And when she had spoken she laid a finger on her lips. 'Take care of yourself in this place, my son,' she added. 'They do not love strangers. I was once a stranger here, and I know what I say.' Then fancying she heard her husband—'That is a strange animal you have,' she said in a louder voice.

'Yes,' answered Curdie. 'She is no beauty, but she is very good, and we love each other. Don't we, Lina?'

Lina looked up and whined. Curdie threw her the half of his loaf, which she ate while her master and the baker's wife talked a little. Then the baker's wife gave them some water, and Curdie having paid for his loaf, he and Lina went up the street together.

XIV

The Dogs of Gwyntystorm

The steep street led them straight up to a large market-place, with butchers' shops, about which were many dogs. The moment they caught sight of Lina, one and all they came rushing down upon her, giving her no chance of explaining herself. When Curdie saw the dogs coming he heaved up his mattock over his shoulder, and was ready, if they would have it so. Seeing him thus prepared to defend his follower, a great ugly bulldog flew at him. With the first blow Curdie struck him through the brain, and the brute fell dead at his feet. But he could not at once recover his weapon, which stuck in the skull of his foe, and a huge mastiff, seeing him thus hampered, flew at him next. Now Lina, who had shown herself so brave upon the road thither, had grown shy upon entering the city, and kept always at Curdie's heel. But it was her turn now. The moment she saw her master in danger she seemed to go mad with rage. As the mastiff jumped at Curdie's throat, Lina flew at his, seized him with her tremendous jaws, gave one roaring grind, and he lay beside the bulldog with his neck broken. They were the best dogs in the market, after the judgement of the butchers of Gwyntystorm. Down came their masters, knife in hand.

Curdie drew himself up fearlessly, mattock on shoulder, and awaited their coming, while at his heel his awful attendant showed not only her outside fringe of icicleteeth, but a double row of right serviceable fangs she wore inside her mouth, and her green eyes flashed yellow as gold. The butchers not liking the look either of them or of the dogs at their feet, drew back, and began to remonstrate in the manner of outraged men.

'Stranger,' said the first, 'that bulldog is mine.'

'Take him, then,' said Curdie, indignant.

'You've killed him!'

'Yes—else he would have killed me.'

'That's no business of mine.'

'No?'

'No.'

'That makes it the more mine, then.'

'This sort of thing won't do, you know,' said the other butcher.

'That's true,' said Curdie.

'That's my mastiff,' said the butcher.

'And as he ought to be,' said Curdie.

'Your brute shall be burnt alive for it,' said the butcher.

'Not yet,' answered Curdie. 'We have done no wrong. We were walking quietly up your street, when your dogs flew at us. If you don't teach your dogs how to treat strangers, you must take the consequences.'

'They treat them quite properly,' said the butcher. 'What right has any one to bring an abomination like that into our city? The horror is enough to make an idiot of every child in the place.'

'We are both subjects of the king, and my poor animal can't help her looks. How would you like to be served like that because you were ugly? She's not a bit fonder of her looks than you are—only what can she do to change them?'

'I'll do to change them,' said the fellow.

Thereupon the butchers brandished their long knives and advanced, keeping their eyes upon Lina.

'Don't be afraid, Lina,' cried Curdie. 'I'll kill one—you kill the other.'

Lina gave a howl that might have terrified an army, and crouched ready to spring. The butchers turned and ran.

By this time a great crowd had gathered behind the butchers, and in it a number of boys returning from school, who began to stone the strangers. It was a way they had with man or beast they did not expect to make anything by. One of the stones struck Lina; she caught it in her teeth and crunched it that it fell in gravel from her mouth. Some of the foremost of the crowd saw this, and it terrified them. They drew back; the rest took fright from their retreat; the panic spread; and at last the crowd scattered in all directions. They ran, and cried out, and said the devil and his dam were come to Gwyntystorm. So Curdie and Lina were left standing unmolested in the market-place. But the terror of them spread throughout the city, and everybody began to shut and lock his door, so that by the time the setting sun shone down the street, there was not a shop left open, for fear of the devil and his horrible dam. But all the upper windows within sight of them were crowded with heads watching them where they stood lonely in the deserted market-place.

Curdie looked carefully all round, but could not see one open door. He caught sight of the sign of an inn however, and laying down his mattock, and telling Lina to take care of it, walked up to the door of it and knocked. But the people in the house, instead of opening the door, threw things at him from the windows. They would not listen to a word he said, but sent him back to Lina with the blood running down his face. When Lina saw that, she leaped up in a fury and was rushing at the house, into which she would certainly have broken; but Curdie called her, and made her lie down beside him while he bethought him what next he should do.

'Lina,' he said, 'the people keep their gates open, but their houses and their hearts shut.'

As if she knew it was her presence that had brought this trouble upon him, she rose, and went round and round him, purring like a tigress, and rubbing herself against his legs.

Now there was one little thatched house that stood squeezed in between two tall gables, and the sides of the two great houses shot out projecting windows that nearly met across the roof of the little one, so that it lay in the street like a doll's house. In this house lived a poor old woman, with a grandchild. And because she never gossiped or quarrelled, or chaffered in the market, but went without what she could not afford, the people called her a witch, and would have done her many an ill turn if they had not been afraid of her. Now while Curdie was looking in another direction the door opened, and out came a little dark-haired, black-eyed, gypsy-looking child, and toddled across the market-place towards the outcasts. The moment they saw her coming, Lina lay down flat on the road, and with her two huge forepaws covered her mouth, while Curdie went to meet her, holding out his arms. The little one came straight to him, and held up her mouth to be kissed. Then she took him by the hand, and drew him towards the house, and Curdie yielded to the silent invitation. But when Lina rose to follow, the child shrunk from her, frightened a little. Curdie took her up, and holding her on one arm, patted Lina with the other hand. Then the child wanted also to pat doggy, as she called her by a right bountiful stretch of courtesy, and having once patted her, nothing would serve but Curdie must let her have a ride on doggy. So he set her on Lina's back, holding her hand, and she rode home in merry triumph, all unconscious of the hundreds of eyes staring at her foolhardiness from the windows about the market-place, or the murmur of deep disapproval that rose from as many lips. At the door stood the grandmother to receive them. She caught the child to her bosom with delight at her courage, welcomed Curdie, and showed no dread of Lina. Many were the significant nods exchanged, and many a one said to another that the devil and the witch were old friends. But the woman was only a wise woman, who having seen how Curdie and and Lina behaved to each other, judged from that what sort they were, and so made them welcome to her house. She was not like her fellow-townspeople, for that they were strangers recommended them to her.

The moment her door was shut, the other doors began to open, and soon there appeared little groups about here and there a threshold, while a few of the more courageous ventured out upon the square—all ready to make for their houses again, however, upon the least sign of movement in the little thatched one.

The baker and the barber had joined one of these groups, and were busily wagging their tongues against Curdie and his horrible beast.

'He can't be honest,' said the barber; 'for he paid me double the worth of the pane he broke in my window.'

And then he told them how Curdie broke his window by breaking a stone in the street with his hammer. There the baker struck in.

'Now that was the stone,' said he, 'over which I had fallen three times within the last month: could it be by fair means he broke that to pieces at the first blow? Just to make up my mind on that point I tried his own hammer against a stone in the gate; it nearly broke both my arms, and loosened half the teeth in my head!'

XV

Derba and Barbara

Meantime the wanderers were hospitably entertained by the old woman and her grandchild, and they were all very comfortable and happy together. Little Barbara sat upon Curdie's knee, and he told her stories about the mines and his adventures in them. But he never mentioned the king or the princess, for all that story was hard to believe. And he told her about his mother and his father, and how good they were. And Derba sat and listened. At last little Barbara fell asleep in Curdie's arms, and her grandmother carried her to bed.

It was a poor little house, and Derba gave up her own room to Curdie, because he was honest and talked wisely. Curdie saw how it was, and begged her to allow him to lie on the floor, but she would not hear of it.

In the night he was waked by Lina pulling at him. As soon as he spoke to her she ceased, and Curdie, listening, thought he heard some one trying to get in. He rose, took his mattock, and went about the house, listening and watching; but although he heard noises now at one place, now at another, he could not think what they meant, for no one appeared. Certainly, considering how she had frightened them all in the day, it was not likely any one would attack Lina at night. By-and-by the noises ceased, and Curdie went back to his bed, and slept undisturbed.

In the morning, however, Derba came to him in great agitation, and said they had fastened up the door, so that she could not get out. Curdie rose immediately and went with her: they found that not only the door, but every window in the house was so secured on the outside that it was impossible to open one of them without using great force. Poor Derba looked anxiously in Curdie's face. He broke out laughing.

'They are much mistaken,' he said, 'if they fancy they could keep Lina and a miner in any house in Gwyntystorm—even if they built up doors and windows.'

With that he shouldered his mattock. But Derba begged him not to make a hole in her house just yet. She had plenty for breakfast, she said, and before it was time for dinner they would know what the people meant by it.

And indeed they did. For within an hour appeared one of the chief magistrates of the city, accompanied by a score of soldiers with drawn swords, and followed by a great multitude of the people, requiring the miner and his brute to yield themselves, the one that he might be tried for the disturbance he had occasioned and the injury he had committed, the other that she might be roasted above for her part in killing two valuable and harmless animals belonging to worthy citizens. The summons was preceded and followed by flourish of trumpet, and was read with every formality by the city marshal himself.

The moment he ended, Lina ran into the little passage, and stood opposite the door.

'I surrender,' cried Curdie.

'Then tie up your brute, and give her here.'

'No, no,' cried Curdie through the door. 'I surrender; but I'm not going to do your hangman's work. If you want my dog, you must take her.'

'Then we shall set the house on fire, and burn witch and all.'

'It will go hard with us but we shall kill a few dozen of you first,' cried Curdie. 'We're not the least afraid of you.'

With that Curdie turned to Derba, and said:

'Don't be frightened. I have a strong feeling that all will be well. Surely no trouble will come to you for being good to strangers.'

'But the poor dog!' said Derba.

Now Curdie and Lina understood each other more than a little by this time, and not only had he seen that she understood the proclamation, but when she looked up at him after it was read, it was with such a grin, and such a yellow flash, that he saw also she was determined to take care of herself.

'The dog will probably give you reason to think a little more of her ere long,' he answered. 'But now,' he went on, 'I fear I must hurt your house a little. I have great confidence, however, that I shall be able to make up to you for it one day.'

'Never mind the house, if only you can get safe off,' she answered. 'I don't think they will hurt this precious lamb,' she added, clasping little Barbara to her bosom. 'For myself, it is all one; I am ready for anything.'

'It is but a little hole for Lina I want to make,' said Curdie. 'She can creep through a much smaller one than you would think.'

Again he took his mattock, and went to the back wall.

'They won't burn the house,' he said to himself. 'There is too good a one on each side of it.'

The tumult had kept increasing every moment, and the city marshal had been shouting, but Curdie had not listened to him. When now they heard the blows of his mattock, there went up a great cry, and the people taunted the soldiers that they were afraid of a dog and his miner. The soldiers therefore made a rush at the door, and cut its fastenings.

The moment they opened it, out leaped Lina, with a roar so unnaturally horrible that the sword-arms of the soldiers dropped by their sides, paralysed with the terror of that cry; the crowd fled in every direction, shrieking and yelling with mortal dismay; and without even knocking down with her tail, not to say biting a man of them with her pulverizing jaws, Lina vanished—no one knew whither, for not one of the crowd had had courage to look upon her.

The moment she was gone, Curdie advanced and gave himself up. The soldiers were so filled with fear, shame, and chagrin, that they were ready to kill him on the spot. But he stood quietly facing them, with his mattock on his shoulder; and the magistrate wishing to examine him, and the people to see him made an example of, the soldiers had to content themselves with taking him. Partly for derision, partly to hurt him, they laid his mattock against his back, and tied his arms to it.

They led him up a very steep street, and up another still, all the crowd following. The king's palace-castle rose towering above them; but they stopped before they reached it, at a low-browed door in a great, dull, heavy-looking building.

The city marshal opened it with a key which hung at his girdle, and ordered Curdie to enter. The place within was dark as night, and while he was feeling his way with his feet, the marshal gave him a rough push. He fell, and rolled once or twice over, unable to help himself because his hands were tied behind him.

It was the hour of the magistrate's second and more important breakfast, and until that was over he never found himself capable of attending to a case with concentration sufficient to the distinguishing of the side upon which his own advantage lay; and hence was this respite for Curdie, with time to collect his thoughts. But indeed he had very few to collect, for all he had to do, so far as he could see, was to wait for what would come next. Neither had he much power to collect them, for he was a good deal shaken.

In a few minutes he discovered, to his great relief, that, from the projection of the pick-end of his mattock beyond his body, the fall had loosened the ropes tied round it. He got one hand disengaged, and then the other; and presently stood free, with his good mattock once more in right serviceable relation to his arms and legs.

XVI

The Mattock

While the magistrate reinvigorated his selfishness with a greedy breakfast, Curdie found doing nothing in the dark rather wearisome work. It was useless attempting to think what he should do next, seeing the circumstances in which he was presently to find himself were altogether unknown to him. So he began to think about his father and mother in their little cottage home, high in the clear air of the open mountainside, and the thought, instead of making his dungeon gloomier by the contrast, made a light in his soul that destroyed the power of darkness and captivity. But he was at length startled from his waking dream by a swell in the noise outside. All the time there had been a few of the more ideal of the inhabitants about the door, but they had been rather quiet. Now, however, the sounds of feet and voices began to grow, and grew so rapidly that it was plain a multitude was gathering. For the people of Gwyntystorm always gave themselves an hour of pleasure after their second breakfast, and what greater pleasure could they have than to see a stranger abused by the officers of justice? The noise grew till it was like the roaring of the sea, and that roaring went on a long time, for the magistrate, being a great man, liked to know that he was waited for: it added to the enjoyment of his breakfast, and, indeed, enabled him to eat a little more after he had thought his powers exhausted. But at length, in the waves of the human noises rose a bigger wave, and by the running and shouting and outcry, Curdie learned that the magistrate was approaching.

Presently came the sound of the great rusty key in the lock, which yielded with groaning reluctance; the door was thrown back, the light rushed in, and with it came the voice of the city marshal, calling upon Curdie, by many legal epithets opprobrious, to come forth and be tried for his life, inasmuch as he had raised a tumult in his majesty's city of Gwyntystorm, troubled the hearts of the king's baker and barber, and slain the faithful dogs of his majesty's well-beloved butchers.

He was still reading, and Curdie was still seated in the brown twilight of the vault, not listening, but pondering with himself how this king the city marshal talked of could be the same with the majesty he had seen ride away on his grand white horse, with the Princess Irene on a cushion before him, when a scream of agonized terror arose on the farthest skirt of the crowd, and, swifter than flood or flame, the horror spread shrieking. In a moment the air was filled with hideous howling, cries of unspeakable dismay, and the multitudinous noise of running feet. The next moment, in at the door of the vault bounded Lina, her two green eyes flaming yellow as sunflowers, and seeming to light up the dungeon. With one spring she threw herself at Curdie's feet, and laid her head upon them panting. Then came a rush of two or three soldiers darkening the doorway, but it was only to lay hold of the key, pull the door to, and lock it; so that once more Curdie and Lina were prisoners together.

For a few moments Lina lay panting hard: it is breathless work leaping and roaring both at once, and that in a way to scatter thousands of people. Then she jumped up, and began snuffing about all over the place; and Curdie saw what he had never seen before—two faint spots of light cast from her eyes upon the ground, one on each side of her snuffing nose. He got out his tinder-box—a miner is never without one—and lighted a precious bit of candle he carried in a division of it—just for a moment, for he must not waste it.

The light revealed a vault without any window or other opening than the door. It was very old and much neglected. The mortar had vanished from between the stones, and it was half filled with a heap of all sorts of rubbish, beaten down in the middle, but looser at the sides; it sloped from the door to the foot of the opposite wall: evidently for a long time the vault had been left open, and every sort of refuse thrown into it. A single minute served for the survey, so little was there to note.

Meantime, down in the angle between the back wall and the base of the heap Lina was scratching furiously with all the eighteen great strong claws of her mighty feet.

'Ah, ha!' said Curdie to himself, catching sight of her, 'if only they will leave us long enough to ourselves!'

With that he ran to the door, to see if there was any fastening on the inside. There was none: in all its long history it never had had one. But a few blows of the right sort, now from the one, now from the other end of his mattock, were as good as any bolt, for they so ruined the lock that no key could ever turn in it again. Those who heard them fancied he was trying to get out and laughed spitefully. As soon as he had done, he extinguished his candle, and went down to Lina.

She had reached the hard rock which formed the floor of the dungeon, and was now clearing away the earth a little wider. Presently she looked up in his face and whined, as much as to say, 'My paws are not hard enough to get any further.'

'Then get out of my way, Lina,' said Curdie, 'and mind you keep your eyes shining, for fear I should hit you.'

So saying, he heaved his mattock, and assailed with the hammer end of it the spot she had cleared.

The rock was very hard, but when it did break it broke in good-sized pieces. Now with hammer, now with pick, he worked till he was weary, then rested, and then set to again. He could not tell how the day went, as he had no light but the lamping of Lina's eyes. The darkness hampered him greatly, for he would not let Lina come close enough to give him all the light she could, lest he should strike her. So he had, every now and then, to feel with his hands to know how he was getting on, and to discover in what direction to strike: the exact spot was a mere imagination.

He was getting very tired and hungry, and beginning to

lose heart a little, when out of the ground, as if he had struck a spring of it, burst a dull, gleamy, lead-coloured light, and the next moment he heard a hollow splash and echo. A piece of rock had fallen out of the floor, and dropped into water beneath. Already Lina, who had been lying a few yards off all the time he had worked, was on her feet and peering through the hole. Curdie got down on his hands and knees, and looked. They were over what seemed a natural cave in the rock, to which apparently the river had access, for, at a great distance below, a faint light was gleaming upon water. If they could but reach it, they might get out; but even if it was deep enough, the height was very dangerous. The first thing, whatever might follow, was to make the hole larger. It was comparatively easy to break away the sides of it, and in the course of another hour he had it large enough to get through.

And now he must reconnoitre. He took the rope they had tied him with—for Curdie's hindrances were always his furtherance—and fastened one end of it by a slip-knot round the handle of his pickaxe, then dropped the other end through, and laid the pickaxe so that, when he was through himself, and hanging on to the edge, he could place it across the hole to support him on the rope. This done, he took the rope in his hands, and, beginning to descend, found himself in a narrow cleft widening into a cave. His rope was not very long, and would not do much to lessen the force of his fall—he thought with himself—if he should have to drop into the water; but he was not more than a couple of yards below the dungeon when he spied an opening on the opposite side of the cleft: it might be but a shallow hole, or it might lead them out. He dropped himself a little below its level, gave the rope a swing by pushing his feet against the side of the cleft, and so penduled himself into it. Then he laid a stone on the end of the rope that it should not forsake him, called to Lina, whose yellow eyes were gleaming over the mattock-grating above, to watch there till he returned, and went cautiously in.

It proved a passage, level for some distance, then sloping

gently up. He advanced carefully, feeling his way as he went. At length he was stopped by a door—a small door, studded with iron. But the wood was in places so much decayed that some of the bolts had dropped out, and he felt sure of being able to open it. He returned, therefore, to fetch Lina and his mattock. Arrived at the cleft, his strong miner arms bore him swiftly up along the rope and through the hole into the dungeon. There he undid the rope from his mattock, and making Lina take the end of it in her teeth, and get through the hole, he lowered her—it was all he could do, she was so heavy. When she came opposite the passage, with a slight push of her tail she shot herself into it, and let go the rope, which Curdie drew up. Then he lighted his candle and searching in the rubbish found a bit of iron to take the place of his pickaxe across the hole. Then he searched again in the rubbish, and found half an old shutter. This he propped up leaning a little over the hole, with a bit of stick, and heaped against the back of it a quantity of the loosened earth. Next he tied his mattock to the end of the rope, dropped it, and let it hang. Last, he got through the hole himself, and pulled away the propping stick, so that the shutter fell over the hole with a quantity of earth on the top of it. A few motions of hand over hand, and he swung himself and his mattock into the passage beside Lina. There he secured the end of the rope, and they went on together to the door.

XVII

The Wine-Cellar

He lighted his candle and examined it. Decayed and broken as it was, it was strongly secured in its place by hinges on the one side, and either lock or bolt, he could not tell which, on the other. A brief use of his pocket-knife was enough to make room for his hand and arm to get through, and then he found a great iron bolt—but so rusty that he could not move it. Lina whimpered. He took his knife again, made the hole bigger, and stood back. In she shot her small head and long neck, seized the bolt with her teeth, and dragged it grating and complaining back. A push then opened the door. It was at the foot of a short flight of steps. They ascended, and at the top Curdie found himself in a space which, from the echo to his stamp, appeared of some size, though of what sort he could not at first tell, for his hands, feeling about, came upon nothing. Presently, however, they fell on a great thing: it was a wine-cask. He was just setting out to explore the place by a thorough palpation,* when he heard steps coming down a stair. He stood still, not knowing whether the door would open an inch from his nose or twenty yards behind his back. It did neither. He heard the key turn in the lock, and a stream of light shot in, ruining the darkness, about fifteen yards away on his right.

A man carrying a candle in one hand and a large silver flagon in the other, entered, and came towards him. The light revealed a row of huge wine-casks, that stretched away into the darkness of the other end of the long vault. Curdie retreated into the recess of the stair, and peeping round the corner of it, watched him, thinking what he could do to prevent him from locking them in. He came on and on, until Curdie feared he would pass the recess and see them.

He was just preparing to rush out, and master him before he should give alarm, not in the least knowing what he should do next, when, to his relief, the man stopped at the third cask from where he stood. He set down his light on the top of it, removed what seemed a large vent-peg, and poured into the cask a quantity of something from the flagon. Then he turned to the next cask, drew some wine, rinsed the flagon, threw the wine away, drew and rinsed and threw away again, then drew and drank, draining to the bottom. Last of all, he filled the flagon from the cask he had first visited, replaced then the vent-peg, took up his candle, and turned towards the door.

'There is something wrong here!' thought Curdie.

'Speak to him, Lina,' he whispered.

The sudden howl she gave made Curdie himself start and tremble for a moment. As to the man, he answered Lina's with another horrible howl, forced from him by the convulsive shudder of every muscle of his body, then reeled gasping to and fro, and dropped his candle. But just as Curdie expected to see him fall dead he recovered himself, and flew to the door, through which he darted, leaving it open behind him. The moment he ran, Curdie stepped out, picked up the candle still alight, sped after him to the door, drew out the key, and then returned to the stair and waited. In a few minutes he heard the sound of many feet and voices. Instantly he turned the tap of the cask from which the man had been drinking, set the candle beside it on the floor, went down the steps and out of the little door, followed by Lina, and closed it behind them.

Through the hole in it he could see a little, and hear all. He could see how the light of many candles filled the place, and could hear how some two dozen feet ran hither and thither through the echoing cellar; he could hear the clash of iron, probably spits and pokers, now and then; and at last heard how, finding nothing remarkable except the best wine running to waste, they all turned on the butler, and accused him of having fooled them with a drunken dream. He did his best to defend himself, appealing to the evidence of their own senses that he was as sober as they were. They replied that a fright was no less a fright that the cause was imaginary, and a dream no less a dream that the fright had waked him from it. When he discovered, and triumphantly adduced as corroboration, that the key was gone from the door, they said it merely showed how drunk he had been—either that or how frightened, for he had certainly dropped it. In vain he protested that he had never taken it out of the lock—that he never did when he went in, and certainly had not this time stopped to do so when he came out; they asked him why he had to go to the cellar at such a time of the day, and said it was because the had already drunk all the wine that was left from dinner. He said if he had dropped the key, the key was to be found, and they must help him to find it. They told him they wouldn't move a peg for him. He declared, with much language, he would have them all turned out of the king's service. They said they would swear he was drunk. And so positive were they about it, that at last the butler himself began to think whether it was possible they could be in the right. For he knew that sometimes when he had been drunk he fancied things had taken place which he found afterwards could not have happened. Certain of his fellow-servants, however, had all the time a doubt whether the cellar goblin had not appeared to him, or at least roared at him, to protect the wine. In any case nobody wanted to find the key for him; nothing could please them better than the door of the wine-cellar should never more be locked. By degrees the hubbub died away, and they departed, not even pulling to the door, for there was neither handle nor latch to it.

As soon as they were gone, Curdie returned, knowing now that they were in the wine-cellar of the palace, as, indeed, he had suspected. Finding a pool of wine in a hollow of the floor, Lina lapped it up eagerly: she had had no breakfast, and was now very thirsty as well as hungry. Her master was in a similar plight, for he had but just begun to eat when the magistrate arrived with the soldiers. If only they were all in bed, he thought, that he might find his way to the larder! For he said to himself that, as he was sent there by the young princess's great-great-grandmother to serve her or her father in some way, surely he must have a right to his food in the palace, without which he could do nothing. He would go at once and reconnoitre.

So he crept up the stair that led from the cellar. At the top was a door, opening on a long passage, dimly lighted by a lamp. He told Lina to lie down upon the stair while he went on. At the end of the passage he found a door ajar, and, peeping through, saw right into a great stone hall, where a huge fire was blazing, and through which men in the king's livery were constantly coming and going. Some also in the same livery were lounging about the fire. He noted that their colours were the same with those he himself, as king's miner, wore; but from what he had seen and heard of the habits of the place, he could not hope they would treat him the better for that.

The one interesting thing at the moment, however, was the plentiful supper with which the table was spread. It was something at least to stand in sight of food, and he was unwilling to turn his back on the prospect so long as a share in it was not absolutely hopeless. Peeping thus, he soon made up his mind that if at any moment the hall should be empty, he would at that moment rush in and attempt to carry off a dish. That he might lose no time by indecision he selected a large pie upon which to pounce instantaneously. But after he had watched for some minutes, it did not seem at all likely the chance would arrive before supper-time, and he was just about to turn away and rejoin Lina, when he saw that there was not a person in the place. Curdie never made up his mind and then hesitated. He darted in, seized the pie, and bore it, swiftly and noiselessly, to the cellar stair.

XVIII

The King's Kitchen

Back to the cellar Curdie and Lina sped with their booty, where, seated on the steps, Curdie lighted his bit of candle for a moment. A very little bit it was now, but they did not waste much of it in examination of the pie; that they effected by a more summary process. Curdie thought it the nicest food he had ever tasted, and between them they soon ate it up. Then Curdie would have thrown the dish along with the bones into the water, that there might be no traces of them; but he thought of his mother, and hid it instead; and the very next minute they wanted it to draw some wine into. He was careful it should be from the cask of which he had seen the butler drink. Then they sat down again upon the steps, and waited until the house should be quiet. For he was there to do something, and if it did not come to him in the cellar, he must go to meet it in other places. Therefore, lest he should fall asleep, he set the end of the helve of his mattock on the ground, and seated himself on the cross part, leaning against the wall, so that as long as he kept awake he should rest, but the moment he began to fall asleep he must fall awake instead. He quite expected some of the servants would visit the cellar again the night, but whether it was that they were afraid of each other, or believed more of the butler's story than they had chosen to allow, not one of them appeared.

When at length he thought he might venture, he shouldered his mattock and crept up the stair. The lamp was out in the passage, but he could not miss his way to the servants' hall. Trusting to Lina's quickness in concealing herself, he took her with him.

When they reached the hall they found it quiet and nearly dark. The last of the great fire was glowing red, but giving little light. Curdie stood and warmed himself for a few moments: miner as he was, he had found the cellar cold to sit in doing nothing; and standing thus he thought of looking if there were any bits of candle about. There were many candlesticks on the supper-table, but to his disappointment and indignation their candles seemed to have been all left to burn out,* and some of them, indeed, he found still hot in the neck.

Presently, one after another, he came upon seven men fast asleep, most of them upon tables, one in a chair, and one on the floor. They seemed from their shape and colour, to have eaten and drunk so much that they might be burned alive without waking. He grasped the hand of each in succession, and found two ox-hoofs, three pig-hoofs, one concerning which he could not be sure whether it was the hoof of a donkey or a pony, and one dog's paw. 'A nice set of people to be about a king!' thought Curdie to himself, and turned again to his candle-hunt. He did at last find two or three little pieces, and stowed them away in his pockets.

They now left the hall by another door, and entered a short passage, which led them to the huge kitchen, vaulted, and black with smoke. There too the fire was still burning, so that he was able to see a little of the state of things in this quarter also. The place was dirty and disorderly. In a recess, on a heap of brushwood, lay a kitchenmaid, with a table-cover around her, and a skillet in her hand: evidently she too had been drinking. In another corner lay a page, and Curdie noted how like his dress was to his own. In the cinders before the hearth were huddled three dogs and five cats, all fast asleep, while the rats were running about the floor. Curdie's heart ached to think of the lovely child-princess living over such a sty. The mine was a paradise to a palace with such servants in it.

Leaving the kitchen, he got into the region of the sculleries.* There horrible smells were wandering about, like evil spirits that come forth with the darkness. He lighted a candle —but only to see ugly sights. Everywhere was filth and disorder. Mangy turn-spit dogs* were lying about, and grey rats were gnawing at refuse in the sinks. It was like a hideous dream. He felt as if he should never get out of it, and longed for one glimpse of his mother's poor little kitchen, so clean and bright and airy. Turning from it at last in miserable disgust, he almost ran back through the kitchen, re-entered the hall, and crossed it to another door.

It opened upon a wider passage, leading to an arch in a stately corridor, all its length lighted by lamps in niches. At the end of it was a large and beautiful hall, with great pillars. There sat three men in the royal livery, fast asleep, each in a great armchair, with his feet on a huge footstool. They looked like fools dreaming themselves kings; and Lina looked as if she longed to throttle them. At one side of the hall was the grand staircase, and they went up.

Everything that now met Curdie's eyes was rich—not glorious like the splendours of the mountain cavern, but rich and soft—except where, now and then, some rough old rib of the ancient fortress came through, hard and discoloured. Now some dark bare arch of stone, now some rugged and blackened pillar, now some huge beam, brown with the smoke and dust of centuries, looked like a thistle in the midst of daisies, or a rock in a smooth lawn.

They wandered about a good while, again and again finding themselves where they had been before. Gradually, however, Curdie was gaining some idea of the place. By and by Lina began to look frightened, and as they went on Curdie saw that she looked more and more frightened. Now, by this time he had come to understand that what made her look frightened was always the fear of frightening, and he therefore concluded they must be drawing nigh to somebody. At last, in a gorgeously painted gallery, he saw a curtain of crimson, and on the curtain a royal crown wrought in silks and stones. He felt sure this must be the king's chamber, and it was here he was wanted; or, if it was not the place he was bound for, something would meet him and turn him aside; for he had come to think that so long as a man wants to do right he may go where he can: when he can go no further, then it is not the way. 'Only,' said his father, in assenting to the theory, 'he must really want to do right, and not merely fancy he does. He must want it with his heart and will, and not with his rag of a tongue.'

So he gently lifted the corner of the curtain, and there behind it was a half-open door. He entered, and the moment he was in, Lina stretched herself along the threshold between the curtain and the door.

XIX

The King's Chamber

He found himself in a large room, dimly lighted by a silver lamp that hung from the ceiling. Far at the other end was a great bed, surrounded with dark heavy curtains. He went softly towards it, his heart beating fast. It was a dreadful thing to be alone in the king's chamber at the dead of night. To gain courage he had to remind himself of the beautiful princess who had sent him. But when he was about half-way to the bed, a figure appeared from the farther side of it, and came towards him, with a hand raised warningly. He stood still. The light was dim, and he could distinguish little more than the outline of a young girl. But though the form he saw was much taller than the princess he remembered, he never doubted it was she. For one thing, he knew that most girls would have been frightened to see him there in the dead of the night, but like a true princess, and the princess he used to know, she walked straight on to meet him. As she came she lowered the hand she had lifted, and laid the forefinger of it upon her lips. Nearer and nearer, quite near, close up to him she came, then stopped, and stood a moment looking at him.

'You are Curdie,' she said.

'And you are the Princess Irene,' he returned.

'Then we know each other still,' she said, with a sad smile of pleasure. 'You will help me.'

'That I will,' answered Curdie. He did not say, 'If I can;' for he knew that what he was sent to do, that he could do. 'May I kiss your hand, little princess?'

She was only between nine and ten, though indeed she looked several years older, and her eyes almost those of a grown woman, for she had had terrible trouble of late.

She held out her hand.

'I am not the *little* princess any more. I have grown up since I saw you last, Mr Miner.'

The smile which accompanied the words had in it a strange mixture of playfulness and sadness.

'So I see, Miss Princess,' returned Curdie; 'and therefore, being more of a princess, you are the more my princess. Here I am, sent by your great-great-grandmother, to be your servant.—May I ask why you are up so late, princess?'

'Because my father wakes *so* frightened, and I don't know what he *would* do if he didn't find me by his bedside. There! he's waking now.'

She darted off to the side of the bed she had come from. Curdie stood where he was.

A voice altogether unlike what he remembered of the mighty, noble king on his white horse came from the bed, thin, feeble, hollow, and husky, and in tone like that of a petulant child:

'I will not, I will not. I am a king, and I *will* be a king. I hate you and despise you, and you shall not torture me!'

'Never mind them, father dear,' said the princess. 'I am here, and they shan't touch you. They dare not, you know, so long as you defy them.'

'They want my crown, darling; and I can't give them my crown, can I? for what is a king without his crown?'

'They shall never have your crown, my king,' said Irene. 'Here it is—all safe, you see. I am watching it for you.'

Curdie drew near the bed on the other side. There lay the grand old king—he looked grand still, and twenty years older. His body was pillowed high; his beard descended long and white over the crimson coverlid; and his crown, its diamonds and emeralds gleaming in the twilight of the curtains, lay in front of him, his long, thin old hands folded round the rigol,* and the ends of his beard straying among the lovely stones. His face was like that of a man who had died fighting nobly; but one thing made it dreadful: his eyes, while they moved about as if searching in this direction and in that, looked more dead than his face. He saw neither his daughter nor his crown: it was the voice of the one and the touch of the other that comforted him. He kept murmuring what seemed words, but was unintelligible to Curdie, although, to judge from the look of Irene's face, she learned and concluded from it.

By degrees his voice sank away and the murmuring ceased, although still his lips moved. Thus lay the old king on his bed, slumbering with his crown between his hands; on one side of him stood a lovely little maiden, with blue eyes, and brown hair going a little back from her temples, as if blown by a wind that no one felt but herself; and on the other a stalwart young miner, with his mattock over his shoulder. Stranger sight still was Lina lying along the threshold—only nobody saw her just then.

A moment more and the king's lips ceased to move. His breathing had grown regular and quiet. The princess gave a sigh of relief, and came round to Curdie.

'We can talk a little now,' she said, leading him towards the middle of the room. 'My father will sleep now till the doctor wakes him to give him his medicine. It is not really medicine, though, but wine. Nothing but that, the doctor says, could have kept him so long alive. He always comes in the middle of the night to give it him with his own hands. But it makes me cry to see him waked up when so nicely asleep.'

'What sort of man is your doctor?' asked Curdie.

'Oh, such a dear, good, kind gentleman!' replied the princess. 'He speaks so softly, and is so sorry for his dear king! He will be here presently, and you shall see for yourself. You will like him very much.'

'Has your king-father been long ill?' asked Curdie.

'A whole year now,' she replied. 'Did you not know? That's how your mother never got the red petticoat my father promised her. The lord chancellor told me that not only Gwyntystorm but the whole land was mourning over the illness of the good man.'

Now Curdie himself had not heard a word of his majesty's illness, and had no ground for believing that a single soul in any place he had visited on his journey had heard of it.

Moreover, although mention had been made of his majesty again and again in his hearing since he came to Gwyntystorm, never once had he heard an allusion to the state of his health. And now it dawned upon him also that he had never heard the least expression of love to him. But just for the time he thought it better to say nothing on either point.

'Does the king wander like this every night?' he asked.

'Every night,' answered Irene, shaking her head mournfully. 'That is why I never go to bed at night. He is better during the day—a little, and then I sleep—in the dressing-room there, to be with him in a moment if he should call me. It is *so* sad he should have only me and not my mamma! A princess is nothing to a queen!'

'I wish he would like me,' said Curdie, 'for then I might watch by him at night, and let you go to bed, princess.'

'Don't you know then?' returned Irene, in wonder. 'How was it you came? —Ah! you said my grandmother sent you. But I thought you knew that he wanted you.'

And again she opened wide her blue stars.

'Not I,' said Curdie, also bewildered, but very glad.

'He used to be constantly saying—he was not so ill then as he is now—that he wished he had you about him.'

'And I never to know it!' said Curdie, with displeasure.

'The master of the horse told papa's own secretary that he had written to the miner-general to find you and send you up; but the miner-general wrote back to the master of the horse, and he told the secretary, and the secretary told my father, that they had searched every mine in the kingdom and could hear nothing of you. My father gave a great sigh, and said he feared the goblins had got you after all, and your father and mother were dead of grief. And he has never mentioned you since, except when wandering. I cried very much. But one of my grandmother's pigeons with its white wing flashed a message to me through the window one day, and then I knew that my Curdie wasn't eaten by the goblins, for my grandmother wouldn't have taken care of him one time to let him be eaten the next. Where were you, Curdie, that they couldn't find you?'

'We will talk about that another time, when we are not expecting the doctor,' said Curdie.

As he spoke, his eyes fell upon something shining on the table under the lamp. His heart gave a great throb, and he went nearer—Yes, there could be no doubt;—it was the same flagon that the butler had filled in the wine-cellar.

'It looks worse and worse!' he said to himself, and went back to Irene, where she stood half dreaming.

'When will the doctor be here?' he asked once more—this time hurriedly.

The question was answered—not by the princess, but by something which that instant tumbled heavily into the room. Curdie flew towards it in vague terror about Lina.

On the floor lay a little round man, puffing and blowing, and uttering incoherent language. Curdie thought of his mattock, and ran and laid it aside.

'Oh, dear Dr Kelman!' cried the princess, running up and taking hold of his arm; 'I am *so* sorry!' She pulled and pulled, but might almost as well have tried to set up a cannon-ball. 'I hope you have not hurt yourself?'

'Not at all, not at all,' said the doctor, trying to smile and to rise both at once, but finding it impossible to do either.

'If he slept on the floor he would be late for breakfast,' said Curdie to himself, and held out his hand to help him.

But when he took hold of it, Curdie very nearly let him fall again, for what he held was not even a foot: it was the belly of a creeping thing. He managed, however, to hold both his peace and his grasp, and pulled the doctor roughly on his legs—such as they were.

'Your royal highness has rather a thick mat at the door,' said the doctor, patting his palms together. 'I hope my awkwardness may not have startled his majesty.'

While he talked Curdie went to the door: Lina was not there.

The doctor approached the bed.

'And how has my beloved king slept tonight?' he asked.

'No better,' answered Irene, with a mournful shake of her head.

'Ah, that is very well!' returned the doctor, his fall seeming to have muddled either his words or his meaning. 'We must give him his wine, and then he will be better still.'

Curdie darted at the flagon, and lifted it high, as if he had expected to find it full, but had found it empty.

'That stupid butler! I heard them say he was drunk!' he cried in a loud whisper, and was gliding from the room.

'Come here with that flagon, you! page!' cried the doctor.

Curdie came a few steps towards him with the flagon dangling from his hand, heedless of the gushes that fell noiseless on the thick carpet.

'Are you aware, young man,' said the doctor, 'that it is not every wine can do his majesty the benefit I intend he should derive from my prescription?'

'Quite aware, sir,' answered Curdie. 'The wine for his majesty's use is in the third cask from the corner.'

'Fly, then,' said the doctor, looking satisfied.

Curdie stopped outside the curtain and blew an audible breath—no more: up came Lina noiseless as a shadow. He showed her the flagon.

'The cellar, Lina: go,' he said.

She galloped away on her soft feet, and Curdie had indeed to fly to keep up with her. Not once did she make even a dubious turn. From the king's gorgeous chamber to the cold cellar they shot. Curdie dashed the wine down the back stair, rinsed the flagon out as he had seen the butler do, filled it from the cask of which he had seen the butler drink, and hastened with it up again to the king's room.

The little doctor took it, poured out a full glass, smelt, but did not taste it, and set it down. Then he leaned over the bed, shouted in the king's ear, blew upon his eyes, and pinched his arm: Curdie thought he saw him run something bright into it. At last the king half woke. The doctor seized the glass, raised his head, poured the wine down his throat, and let his head fall back on the pillow again. Tenderly wiping his beard, and bidding the princess goodnight in paternal tones, he then took his leave. Curdie would gladly have driven his pick into his head, but that was not in his commission, and he let him go.

The little round man looked very carefully to his feet as he crossed the threshold.

'That attentive fellow of a page had removed the mat,' he said to himself, as he walked along the corridor. 'I must remember him.'

XX

Counter-Plotting

Curdie was already sufficiently enlightened as to how things were going, to see that he must have the princess of one mind with him, and they must work together. It was clear that amongst those about the king there was a plot against him: for one thing, they had agreed in a lie concerning himself; and it was plain also that the doctor was working out a design against the health and reason of his majesty, rendering the question of his life a matter of little moment. It was in itself sufficient to justify the worst fears, that the people outside the palace were ignorant of his majesty's condition: he believed those inside it also—the butler excepted—were ignorant of it as well. Doubtless his majesty's councillors desired to alienate the hearts of his subjects from their sovereign. Curdie's idea was that they intended to kill the king, marry the princess to one of themselves, and found a new dynasty; but whatever their purpose, there was treason in the palace of the worst sort: they were making and keeping the king incapable, in order to effect that purpose. The first thing to be seen to therefore was, that his majesty should neither eat morsel nor drink drop of anything prepared for him in the palace. Could this have been managed without the princess, Curdie would have preferred leaving her in ignorance of the horrors from which he sought to deliver her. He feared also the danger of her knowledge betraying itself to the evil eyes about her; but it must be risked—and she had always been a wise child.

Another thing was clear to him—that with such traitors no terms of honour were either binding or possible, and that, short of lying, he might use any means to foil them. And he could not doubt that the old princess had sent him expressly to frustrate their plans.

While he stood thinking thus with himself, the princess was earnestly watching the king, with looks of childish love and womanly tenderness that went to Curdie's heart. Now and then with a great fan of peacock feathers she would fan him very softly; now and then, seeing a cloud begin to gather upon the sky of his sleeping face, she would climb upon the bed, and bending to his ear whisper into it, then draw back and watch again—generally to see the cloud disperse. In his deepest slumber, the soul of the king lay open to the voice of his child, and that voice had power either to change the aspect of his visions, or, which was better still, to breathe hope into his heart, and courage to endure them.

Curdie came near, and softly called her.

'I can't leave papa just yet,' she returned, in a low voice.

'I will wait,' said Curdie: 'but I want very much to say something.'

In a few minutes she came to him where he stood under the lamp.

'Well, Curdie, what is it?' she said.

'Princess,' he replied, 'I want to tell you that I have found why your grandmother sent me.'

'Come this way, then,' she answered, 'where I can see the face of my king.'

Curdie placed a chair for her in the spot she chose, where she would be near enough to mark any slightest change on her father's countenance, yet where their low-voiced talk would not disturb him. There he sat down beside her and told her all the story—how her grandmother had sent her good pigeon for him, and how she had instructed him, and sent him there without telling him what he had to do. Then he told her what he had discovered of the state of things generally in Gwyntystorm, and specially what he had heard and seen in the palace that night.

'Things are in a bad state enough,' he said in conclusion; —'lying and selfishness and inhospitality and dishonesty everywhere; and to crown all, they speak with disrespect of the good king, and not a man of them knows he is ill.'

'You frighten me dreadfully,' said Irene, trembling.

'You must be brave for your king's sake,' said Curdie.

'Indeed I will,' she replied, and turned a long loving look upon the beautiful face of her father. 'But what *is* to be done? And how *am* I to believe such horrible things of Dr Kelman?'

'My dear princess,' replied Curdie, 'you know nothing of him but his face and his tongue, and they are both false. Either you must beware of him, or you must doubt your grandmother and me; for I tell you, by the gift she gave me of testing hands, that this man is a snake. That round body he shows is but the case of a serpent. Perhaps the creature lies there, as in its nest, coiled round and round inside.'

'Horrible!' said Irene.

'Horrible indeed; but we must not try to get rid of horrible things by refusing to look at them, and saying they are not there. Is not your beautiful father sleeping better since he had the wine?'

'Yes.'

'Does he always sleep better after having it?'

She reflected an instant.

'No; always worse—till tonight,' she answered.

'Then remember that was the wine I got him—not what the butler drew. Nothing that passes through any hand in the house except yours or mine must henceforth, till he is well, reach his majesty's lips.'

'But how, dear Curdie?' said the princess, almost crying.

'That we must contrive,' answered Curdie. 'I know how to take care of the wine; but for his food—now we must think.'

'He takes hardly any,' said the princess, with a pathetic shake of her little head which Curdie had almost learned to look for.

'The more need,' he replied, 'there should be no poison in it.' Irene shuddered. 'As soon as he has honest food he will begin to grow better. And you must be just as careful with yourself, princess,' Curdie went on, 'for you don't know when they may begin to poison you too.'

'There's no fear of me; don't talk about me,' said Irene. 'The good food!—how are we to get it, Curdie? That is the whole question.'

'I am thinking hard,' answered Curdie. 'The good food? Let me see—let me see!—Such servants as I saw below are sure to have the best of everything for themselves: I will go and see what I can find on their supper-table.'

'The chancellor sleeps in the house, and he and the master of the king's horse always have their supper together in a room off the great hall, to the right as you go down the stair,' said Irene. 'I would go with you, but I dare not leave my father. Alas! he scarcely ever takes more than a mouthful. I can't think how he lives! And the very thing he would like, and often asks for—a bit of bread—I can hardly ever get for him: Dr Kelman has forbidden it, and says it is nothing less than poison to him.'

'Bread at least he *shall* have,' said Curdie; 'and that, with the honest wine,* will do as well as anything, I do believe. I will go at once and look for some. But I want you to see Lina first, and know her, lest, coming upon her by accident at any time, you should be frightened.'

'I should like much to see her,' said the princess.

Warning her not to be startled by her ugliness, he went to the door and called her.

She entered, creeping with downcast head, and dragging her tail over the floor behind her. Curdie watched the princess as the frightful creature came nearer and nearer. One shudder went from head to foot of her, and next instant she stepped to meet her. Lina dropped flat on the floor, and covered her face with her two big paws. It went to the heart of the princess: in a moment she was on her knees beside her, stroking her ugly head, and patting her all over.

'Good dog! Dear ugly dog!' she said.

Lina whimpered.

'I believe,' said Curdie, 'from what your grandmother told

me, that Lina is a woman, and that she was naughty, but is now growing good.'

Lina had lifted her head while Irene was caressing her; now she dropped it again between her paws; but the princess took it in her hands, and kissed the forehead betwixt the gold-green eyes.

'Shall I take her with me or leave her?' asked Curdie.

'Leave her, poor dear,' said Irene, and Curdie, knowing the way now, went without her.

He took his way first to the room the princess had spoken of, and there also were the remains of supper; but neither there nor in the kitchen could he find a scrap of plain wholesome-looking bread. So he returned and told her that as soon as it was light he would go into the city for some, and asked her for a handkerchief to tie it in. If he could not bring it himself, he would send it by Lina, who would keep out of sight better than he, and as soon as all was quiet at night he would come to her again. He also asked her to tell the king that he was in the house.

His hope lay in the fact that bakers everywhere go to work early. But it was yet much too early. So he persuaded the princess to lie down, promising to call her if the king should stir.

XXI

The Loaf

His majesty slept very quietly. The dawn had grown almost day, and still Curdie lingered, unwilling to disturb the princess.

At last, however, he called her, and she was in the room in a moment. She had slept, she said, and felt quite fresh. Delighted to find her father still asleep, and so peacefully, she pushed her chair close to the bed, and sat down with her hands in her lap.

Curdie got his mattock from where he had hidden it behind a great mirror, and went to the cellar, followed by Lina. They took some breakfast with them as they passed through the hall, and as soon as they had eaten it went out the back way.

At the mouth of the passage Curdie seized the rope, drew himself up, pushed away the shutter, and entered the dungeon. Then he swung the end of the rope to Lina, and she caught it in her teeth. When her master said, 'Now Lina!' she gave a great spring, and he ran away with the end of the rope as fast as ever he could. And such a spring had she made, that by the time he had to bear her weight she was within a few feet of the hole. The instant she got a paw through, she was all through.

Apparently their enemies were waiting till hunger should have cowed them, for there was no sign of any attempt having been made to open the door. A blow or two of Curdie's mattock drove the shattered lock clean from it, and telling Lina to wait there till he came back, and let no one in, he walked out into the silent street, and drew the door to behind him. He could hardly believe it was not yet a whole day since he had been thrown in there with his hands tied at his back.

Down the town he went, walking in the middle of the street, that, if any one saw him, he might see he was not afraid, and hesitate to rouse an attack on him. As to the dogs, ever since the death of their two companions, a shadow that looked like a mattock was enough to make them scamper. As soon as he reached the archway of the city gate he turned to reconnoitre the baker's shop, and perceiving no sign of movement, waited there watching for the first.

After about an hour, the door opened, and the baker's man appeared with a pail in his hand. He went to a pump that stood in the street, and having filled his pail returned with it into the shop. Curdie stole after him, found the door on the latch, opened it very gently, peeped in, saw nobody, and entered. Remembering perfectly from what shelf the baker's wife had taken the loaf she said was the best, and seeing just one upon it, he seized it, laid the price of it on the counter, and sped softly out, and up the street. Once more in the dungeon beside Lina, his first thought was to fasten up the door again, which would have been easy, so many iron fragments of all sorts and sizes lay about; but he bethought himself that if he left it as it was, and they came to find him, they would conclude at once that they had made their escape by it, and would look no father so as to discover the hole. He therefore merely pushed the door close and left it. Then once more carefully arranging the earth behind the shutter, so that it should again fall with it, he returned to the cellar.

And now he had to convey the loaf to the princess. If he could venture to take it himself, well; if not, he would send Lina. He crept to the door of the servants' hall, and found the sleepers beginning to stir. One said it was time to go to bed; another, that he would go to the cellar instead, and have a mug of wine to waken him up; while a third challenged a fourth to give him his revenge at some game or other.

'Oh, hang your losses!' answered his companion; 'you'll soon pick up twice as much about the house, if you but keep your eyes open.'

Perceiving there would be risk in attempting to pass through, and reflecting that the porters in the great hall would probably be awake also, Curdie went back to the cellar, took Irene's handkerchief with the loaf in it, tied it round Lina's neck, and told her to take it to the princess.

Using every shadow and every shelter, Lina slid through the servants like a shapeless terror through a guilty mind, and so, by corridor and great hall, up the stair to the king's chamber.

Irene trembled a little when she saw her glide soundless in across the silent dusk of the morning, that filtered through the heavy drapery of the windows, but she recovered herself at once when she saw the bundle about her neck, for it both assured her of Curdie's safety, and gave her hope of her father's. She untied it with joy, and Lina stole away, silent as she had come. Her joy was the greater that the king had woke up a little while before, and expressed a desire for food—not that he felt exactly hungry, he said, and yet he wanted something. If only he might have a piece of nice fresh bread! Irene had no knife, but with eager hands she broke a great piece from the loaf, and poured out a full glass of wine. The king ate and drank, enjoyed the bread and the wine much, and instantly fell asleep again.

It was hours before the lazy people brought their breakfast. When it came, Irene crumbled a little about, threw some into the fireplace, and managed to make the tray look just as usual.

In the mean time, down below in the cellar, Curdie was lying in the hollow between the upper sides of two of the great casks, the warmest place he could find. Lina was watching. She lay at his feet, across the two casks, and did her best so to arrange her huge tail that it should be a warm coverlid for her master.

By and by Dr Kelman called to see his patient; and now that Irene's eyes were opened, she saw clearly enough that he was both annoyed and puzzled at finding his majesty rather better. He pretended however to congratulate him, saying

he believed he was quite fit to see the lord chamberlain: he
wanted his signature to something important; only he must
not strain his mind to understand it, whatever it might be:
if his majesty did, he would not be answerable for the consequences. The king said he would see the lord chamberlain,
and the doctor went. Then Irene gave him more bread and
wine, and the king ate and drank, and smiled a feeble smile,
the first real one she had seen for many a day. He said he felt
much better, and would soon be able to take matters into
his own hands again. He had a strange miserable feeling,
he said, that things were going terribly wrong, although he
could not tell how. Then the princess told him that Curdie
was come, and that at night, when all was quiet, for nobody
in the palace must know, he would pay his majesty a visit.
Her great-great-grandmother had sent him, she said. The
king looked strangely upon her, but, the strange look passed
into a smile clearer than the first, and Irene's heart throbbed
with delight.

XXII

The Lord Chamberlain

At noon the lord chamberlain appeared. With a long, low bow, and paper in hand, he stepped softly into the room. Greeting his majesty with every appearance of the profoundest respect, and congratulating him on the evident progress he had made, he declared himself sorry to trouble him, but there were certain papers, he said, which required his signature—and therewith drew nearer to the king, who lay looking at him doubtfully. He was a lean, long, yellow man, with a small head, bald over the top, and tufted at the back and about the ears. He had a very thin, prominent, hooked nose, and a quantity of loose skin under his chin and about the throat, which came craning up out of his neckcloth. His eyes were very small, sharp, and glittering, and looked black as jet. He had hardly enough of a mouth to make a smile with. His left hand held the paper, and the long, skinny fingers of his right a pen just dipped in ink.

But the king, who for weeks had scarcely known what he did, was today so much himself as to be aware that he was not quite himself; and the moment he saw the paper, he resolved that he would not sign without understanding and approving of it. He requested the lord chamberlain therefore to read it. His lordship commenced at once but the difficulties he seemed to encounter, and the fits of stammering that seized him, roused the king's suspicion tenfold. He called the princess.

'I trouble his lordship too much,' he said to her: 'you can read print well, my child—let me hear how you can read writing. Take that paper from his lordship's hand, and read it to me from beginning to end, while my lord drinks a glass of my favourite wine, and watches for your blunders.'

'Pardon me, your majesty,' said the lord chamberlain, with

as much of a smile as he was able to extemporize, 'but it were a thousand pities to put the attainments of her royal highness to a test altogether too severe. Your majesty can scarcely with justice expect the very organs of her speech to prove capable of compassing words so long, and to her so unintelligible.'

'I think much of my little princess and her capabilities,' returned the king, more and more aroused. 'Pray, my lord, permit her to try.'

'Consider, your majesty: the thing would be altogether without precedent. It would be to make sport of statecraft,' said the lord chamberlain.

'Perhaps you are right, my lord,' answered the king with more meaning than he intended should be manifest while to his growing joy he felt new life and power throbbing in heart and brain. 'So this morning we shall read no farther. I am indeed ill able for business of such weight.'

'Will your majesty please sign your royal name here?' said the lord chamberlain, preferring the request as a matter of course, and approaching with the feather end of the pen pointed to a spot where was a great red seal.

'Not today, my lord,' replied the king.

'It is of the greatest importance, your majesty,' softly insisted the other.

'I descried no such importance in it,' said the king.

'Your majesty heard but a part.'

'And I can hear no more today.'

'I trust your majesty has ground enough, in a case of necessity like the present, to sign upon the representation of his loyal subject and chamberlain?—Or shall I call the lord chancellor?' he added, rising.

'There is no need. I have the very highest opinion of your judgement, my lord,' answered the king; '—that is, with respect to means: we *might* differ as to ends.'

The lord chamberlain made yet further attempts at persuasion; but they grew feebler and feebler, and he was at last compelled to retire without having gained his object. And well might his annoyance be keen! For that paper was the king's will, drawn up by the attorney-general; nor until they had the king's signature to it was there much use in venturing farther. But his worst sense of discomfiture arose from finding the king with so much capacity left, for the doctor had pledged himself so to weaken his brain that he should be as a child in their hands, incapable of refusing anything requested of him: his lordship began to doubt the doctor's fidelity to the conspiracy.

The princess was in high delight. She had not for weeks heard so many words, not to say words of such strength and reason, from her father's lips: day by day he had been growing weaker and more lethargic. He was so much exhausted however after this effort, that he asked for another piece of bread and more wine, and fell fast asleep the moment he had taken them.

The lord chamberlain sent in a rage for Dr Kelman. He came, and while professing himself unable to understand the symptoms described by his lordship, yet pledged himself again that on the morrow the king should do whatever was required of him.

The day went on. When his majesty was awake, the princess read to him—one story-book after another; and whatever she read, the king listened as if he had never heard anything so good before, making out in it the wisest meanings. Every now and then he asked for a piece of bread and a little wine, and every time he ate and drank he slept, and every time he woke he seemed better than the last time. The princess bearing her part, the loaf was eaten up and the flagon emptied before night. The butler took the flagon away, and brought it back filled to the brim, but both were thirsty as well as hungry when Curdie came again.

Meantime he and Lina, watching and waking alternately, had plenty of sleep. In the afternoon, peeping from the recess, they saw several of the servants enter hurriedly, one after the other, draw wine, drink it, and steal out; but their business was to take care of the king, not of his cellar, and they let them drink. Also, when the butler came to fill the flagon, they restrained themselves, for the villain's fate was not yet ready for him. He looked terribly frightened, and had brought with him a large candle and a small terrier—which latter indeed threatened to be troublesome, for he went roving and sniffing about until he came to the recess where they were. But as soon as he showed himself, Lina opened her jaws so wide, and glared at him so horribly, that, without even uttering a whimper, he tucked his tail between his legs and ran to his master. He was drawing the wicked wine at the moment, and did not see him, else he would doubtless have run too.

When supper-time approached, Curdie took his place at the door into the servants' hall; but after a long hour's vain watch, he began to fear he should get nothing: there was so much idling about, as well as coming and going. It was hard to bear—chiefly from the attractions of a splendid loaf, just fresh out of the oven, which he longed to secure for the king and princess. At length his chance did arrive: he pounced upon the loaf and carried it away, and soon after got hold of a pie.

This time, however, both loaf and pie were missed. The cook was called. He declared he had provided both. One of themselves, he said, must have carried them away for some friend outside the palace. Then a housemaid, who had not long been one of them, said she had seen some one like a page running in the direction of the cellar with something in his hands. Instantly all turned upon the pages, accusing them, one after another. All denied, but nobody believed one of them: where there is no truth there can be no faith.

To the cellar they all set out to look for the missing pie and loaf. Lina heard them coming, as well she might, for they were talking and quarrelling loud, and gave her master warning. They snatched up everything, and got all signs of their presence out at the back door before the servants entered. When they found nothing, they all turned on the chambermaid, and accused her, not only of lying against the pages, but of having taken the things herself. Their language and behaviour so disgusted Curdie, who could hear a great part of what passed, and he saw the danger of discovery now so much increased, that he began to devise how best at once to rid the palace of the whole pack of them. That, however, would be small gain so long as the treacherous officers of state continued in it. They must be first dealt with. A thought came to him, and the longer he looked at it the better he liked it.

As soon as the servants were gone, quarrelling and accusing all the way, they returned and finished their supper. Then Curdie, who had long been satisfied that Lina understood almost every word he said, communicated his plan to her, and knew by the wagging of her tail and the flashing of her eyes that she comprehended it. Until they had the king safe through the worst part of the night, however, nothing could be done.

They had now merely to go on waiting where they were till the household should be asleep. This waiting and waiting was much the hardest thing Curdie had to do in the whole affair. He took his mattock, and going again into the long passage, lighted a candle-end, and proceeded to examine the rock on all sides. But this was not merely to pass the time: he had a reason for it. When he broke the stone in the street, over which the baker fell, its appearance led him to pocket a fragment for further examination; and since then he had satisfied himself that it was the kind of stone in which gold is found, and that the yellow particles in it were pure metal. If such stone existed here in any plenty, he could soon make the king rich, and independent of his ill-conditioned subjects. He was therefore now bent on an examination of the rock; nor had he been at it long before he was persuaded that there were large quantities of gold in the half-crystalline white stone, with its veins of opaque white and of green, of which the rock, so far as he had been able to inspect it, seemed almost entirely to consist. Every piece he broke was spotted with particles and little lumps of a lovely greenish yellow—and that was gold. Hitherto he had worked only in silver, but he had read, and heard talk, and knew therefore about gold. As soon as he had got the king free of rogues and villains, he would have all the best and most honest miners, with his father at the head of them, to work for the king.

It was a great delight to him to use his mattock once more. The time went quickly, and when he left the passage to go to the king's chamber, he had already a good heap of fragments behind the broken door.

XXIII

Dr Kelman

As soon as he had reason to hope the way was clear, Curdie ventured softly into the hall, with Lina behind him. There was no one asleep on the bench or floor, but by the fading fire sat a girl weeping. It was the same who had seen him carrying off the food, and had been so hardly used for saying so. She opened her eyes when he appeared, but did not seem frightened at him.

'I know why you weep,' said Curdie; 'and I am sorry for you.'

'It *is* hard not to be believed just *because* one speaks the truth,' said the girl, 'but that seems reason enough with some people. My mother taught me to speak the truth, and took such pains with me that I should find it hard to tell a lie, though I could invent many a story these servants would believe at once; for the truth is a strange thing here, and they don't know it when they see it. Show it them, and they'll all stare as if it were a wicked lie, and that with the lie yet warm that has just left their own mouths!—You are a stranger,' she said, and burst out weeping afresh, 'but the stranger you are to such a place and such people the better!'

'I am the person,' said Curdie, 'whom you saw carrying the things from the supper-table.' He showed her the loaf. 'If you can trust, as well as speak the truth, I will trust you.—Can you trust me?'

She looked at him steadily for a moment.

'I can,' she answered.

'One thing more,' said Curdie: 'have you courage as well as faith?'

'I think so.'

'Look my dog in the face and don't cry out.—Come here, Lina.'

Lina obeyed. The girl looked at her, and laid her hand on her head.

'Now I know you are a true woman,' said Curdie. '—I am come to set things right in this house.* Not one of the servants knows I am here. Will you tell them tomorrow morning, that, if they do not alter their ways, and give over drinking, and lying, and stealing, and unkindness, they shall every one of them be driven from the palace?'

'They will not believe me.'

'Most likely; but will you give them the chance?'

'I will.'

'Then I will be your friend. Wait here till I come again.'

She looked him once more in the face, and sat down.

When he reached the royal chamber, he found his majesty awake, and very anxiously expecting him. He received him with the utmost kindness, and at once as it were put himself in his hands by telling him all he knew concerning the state he was in. His voice was feeble, but his eye was clear, and although now and then his words and thoughts seemed to wander, Curdie could not be certain that the cause of their not being intelligible to him did not lie in himself. The king told him that for some years, ever since his queen's death, he had been losing heart over the wickedness of his people. He had tried hard to make them good, but they got worse and worse. Evil teachers, unknown to him, had crept into the schools; there was a general decay of truth and right principle at least in the city; and as that set the example to the nation, it must spread. The main cause of his illness was the despondency with which the degeneration of his people affected him. He could not sleep, and had terrible dreams; while, to his unspeakable shame and distress, he doubted almost everybody. He had striven against his suspicion, but in vain, and his heart was sore, for his courtiers and councillors were really kind; only he could not think why none of their ladies came near his princess. The whole country was discontented, he heard, and there were signs of gathering storm outside as well as inside his borders. The master of the horse gave him sad news of the insubordination of the army; and his great white horse was dead, they told him; and his sword had lost its temper: it bent double the last time he tried it!—only perhaps that was in a dream; and they could not find his shield; and one of his spurs had lost the rowel. Thus the poor king went wandering in a maze of sorrows, some of which were purely imaginary, while others were truer than he understood. He told how thieves came at night and tried to take his crown, so that he never dared let it out of his hands even when he slept; and how, every night, an evil demon in the shape of his physician came and poured poison down his throat. He knew it to be poison, he said, somehow, although it tasted like wine.

Here he stopped, faint with the unusual exertion of talking. Curdie seized the flagon, and ran to the wine-cellar.

In the servants' hall the girl still sat by the fire, waiting for him. As he returned he told her to follow him, and left her at the chamber door till he should rejoin her. When the king had had a little wine, he informed him that he had already discovered certain of his majesty's enemies, and one of the worst of them was the doctor, for it was no other demon than the doctor himself who had been coming every night, and giving him a slow poison.

'So!' said the king. 'Then I have not been suspicious enough, for I thought it was but a dream! Is it possible Kelman can be such a wretch? Who then am I to trust?'

'Not one in the house, except the princess and myself,' said Curdie.

'I will not go to sleep,' said the king.

'That would be as bad as taking the poison,' said Curdie. 'No, no, sire; you must show your confidence by leaving all the watching to me, and doing all the sleeping your majesty can.'

The king smiled a contented smile, turned on his side, and was presently fast asleep. Then Curdie persuaded the

princess also to go to sleep, and telling Lina to watch, went
to the housemaid. He asked her if she could inform him
which of the council slept in the palace, and show him their
rooms. She knew every one of them, she said, and took him
the round of all their doors, telling him which slept in each
room. He then dismissed her, and returning to the king's
chamber, seated himself behind a curtain at the head of the
bed, on the side farthest from the king. He told Lina to get
under the bed, and make no noise.

About one o'clock the doctor came stealing in. He looked
round for the princess, and seeing no one, smiled with
satisfaction as he approached the wine where it stood under
the lamp. Having partly filled a glass, he took from his
pocket a small phial, and filled up the glass from it. The
light fell upon his face from above, and Curdie saw the
snake in it plainly visible. He had never beheld such an
evil countenance: the man hated the king, and delighted in
doing him wrong.

With the glass in his hand, he drew near the bed, set it
down, and began his usual rude rousing of his majesty. Not
at once succeeding, he took a lancet from his pocket, and was
parting its cover with an involuntary hiss of hate between his
closed teeth, when Curdie stooped and whispered to Lina,
'Take him by the leg, Lina.' She darted noiselessly upon
him. With a face of horrible consternation, he gave his leg
one tug to free it; the next instant Curdie heard the one
scrunch with which she crushed the bone like a stick of
celery. He tumbled on the floor with a yell.

'Drag him out, Lina,' said Curdie.

Lina took him by the collar, and dragged him out. Her
master followed to direct her, and they left him lying across
the lord chamberlain's door, where he gave another horrible
yell, and fainted.

The king had waked at his first cry, and by the time
Curdie re-entered he had got at his sword where it hung
from the centre of the tester,* had drawn it, and was trying
to get out of bed. But when Curdie told him all was well, he

lay down again as quietly as a child comforted by his mother from a troubled dream. Curdie went to the door to watch.

The doctor's yells had roused many, but not one had yet ventured to appear. Bells were rung violently, but none were answered; and in a minute or two Curdie had what he was watching for. The door of the lord chamberlain's room opened, and, pale with hideous terror, his lordship peeped out. Seeing no one, he advanced to step into the corridor, and tumbled over the doctor. Curdie ran up, and held out his hand. He received in it the claw of a bird of prey—vulture or eagle, he could not tell which.

His lordship, as soon as he was on his legs, taking him for one of the pages, abused him heartily for not coming sooner, and threatened him with dismissal from the king's service of cowardice and neglect. He began indeed what bade fair to be a sermon on the duties of a page, but catching sight of the man who lay at his door, and seeing it was the doctor, he fell out upon Curdie afresh for standing there doing nothing, and ordered him to fetch immediate assistance. Curdie left him, but slipped into the king's chamber, closed and locked the door, and left the rascals to look after each other. Ere long he heard hurrying footsteps, and for a few minutes there was a great muffled tumult of scuffling feet, low voices, and deep groanings; then all was still again.

Irene slept through the whole—so confidently did she rest, knowing Curdie was in her father's room watching over him.

XXIV

The Prophecy

Curdie sat and watched every motion of the sleeping king. All the night, to his ear, the palace lay as quiet as a nursery of healthful children. At sunrise he called the princess.

'How has his Majesty slept?' were her first words as she entered the room.

'Quite quietly,' answered Curdie; 'that is, since the doctor was got rid of.'

'How did you manage that?' inquired Irene; and Curdie had to tell all about it.

'How terrible!' she said. 'Did it not startle the king dreadfully?'

'It did rather. I found him getting out of bed, sword in hand.'

'The brave old man!' cried the princess.

'Not so old!' said Curdie, '—as you will soon see. He went off again in a minute or so; but for a little while he was restless, and once when he lifted his hand it came down on the spikes of his crown, and he half waked.'

'But where *is* the crown?' cried Irene, in sudden terror.

'I stroked his hands,' answered Curdie, 'and took the crown from them; and ever since he has slept quietly, and again and again smiled in his sleep.'

'I have never seen him do that,' said the princess. 'But what have you done with the crown, Curdie?'

'Look,' said Curdie, moving away from the bedside.

Irene followed him—and there, in the middle of the floor, she saw a strange sight. Lina lay at full length, fast asleep, her tail stretched out straight behind her and her forelegs before her: between the two paws meeting in front of it, her nose just touching it behind, glowed and flashed the crown, like a nest for the humming-birds of heaven.

Irene gazed, and looked up with a smile.

'But what if the thief were to come, and she not to wake?' she said. 'Shall I try her?' And as she spoke she stooped towards the crown.

'No, no, no!' cried Curdie, terrified. 'She would frighten you out of your wits. I would do it to show you, but she would wake your father. You have no conception with what a roar she would spring at my throat. But you shall see how lightly she wakes the moment I speak to her.—Lina!'

She was on her feet the same instant, with her great tail sticking out straight behind her, just as it had been lying.

'Good dog!' said the princess, and patted her head. Lina wagged her tail solemnly, like the boom of an anchored sloop.* Irene took the crown, and laid it where the king would see it when he woke.

'Now, princess,' said Curdie, 'I must leave you for a few minutes. You must bolt the door, please, and not open it to any one.'

Away to the cellar he went with Lina, taking care, as they passed through the servants' hall, to get her a good breakfast. In about one minute she had eaten what he gave her, and looked up in his face: it was not more she wanted, but work. So out of the cellar they went through the passage, and Curdie into the dungeon, where he pulled up Lina, opened the door, let her out, and shut it again behind her. As he reached the door of the king's chamber, Lina was flying out of the gate of Gwyntystorm as fast as her mighty legs could carry her.

'What's come to the wench?' growled the men-servants one to another, when the chambermaid appeared among them the next morning. There was something in her face which they could not understand, and did not like.

'Are we all dirt?' they said. 'What are you thinking about? Have you seen yourself in the glass this morning, miss?'

She made no answer.

'Do you want to be treated as you deserve, or will you speak, you hussy?' said the first woman-cook. 'I would fain know what right *you* have to put on a face like that!'

'You won't believe me,' said the girl.

'Of course not. What is it?'

'I must tell you, whether you believe me or not,' she said.

'Of course you must.'

'It is this, then: if you do not repent of your bad ways, you are all going to be punished—all turned out of the palace together.'

'A mighty punishment!' said the butler. 'A good riddance, say I, of the trouble of keeping minxes like you in order! And why, pray, should we be turned out? What have I to repent of now, your holiness?'

'That you know best yourself,' said the girl.

'A pretty piece of insolence! How should *I* know, forsooth, what a menial like you has got against me! There *are* people in this house—oh! I'm not blind to their ways! but every one for himself, say I!—Pray, Miss Judgement, who gave you such an impertinent message to his majesty's household?'

'One who is come* to set things right in the king's house.'

'Right, indeed!' cried the butler; but that moment the thought came back to him of the roar he had heard in the cellar, and he turned pale and was silent.

The steward took it up next.

'And pray, pretty prophetess,' he said, attempting to chuck her under the chin, 'what have *I* got to repent of?'

'That you know best yourself,' said the girl. 'You have but to look into your books or your heart.'

'Can you tell *me*, then, what I have to repent of?' said the groom of the chambers.

'That you know best yourself,' said the girl once more. 'The person who told me to tell you said the servants of this house had to repent of thieving, and lying, and unkindness, and drinking; and they will be made to repent of them one way, if they don't do it of themselves another.'

Then arose a great hubbub; for by this time all the servants in the house were gathered about her, and all talked together, in towering indignation.

'Thieving, indeed!' cried one. 'A pretty word in a house where everything is left lying about in a shameless way, tempting poor innocent girls!—a house where nobody cares for anything, or has the least respect to the value of property!'

'I suppose you envy me this brooch of mine,' said another. 'There was just a half-sheet of notepaper about it, not a scrap more, in a drawer that's always open in the writing-table in the study! What sort of a place is that for a jewel? Can you call it stealing to take a thing from such a place as that? Nobody cared a straw about it. It might as well have been in the dust-hole! If it had been locked up—then, to be sure!'

'Drinking!' said the chief porter, with a husky laugh. 'And who wouldn't drink when he had a chance? Or who would repent it, except that the drink was gone? Tell me that, Miss Innocence.'

'Lying!' said a great, coarse footman. 'I suppose you mean when I told you yesterday you were a pretty girl when you didn't pout? Lying, indeed! Tell us something worth repenting of! Lying is the way of Gwyntystorm. You should have heard Jabez lying to the cook last night! He wanted a sweetbread for his pup, and pretended it was for the princess! Ha! ha! ha!'

'Unkindness! I wonder who's unkind! Going and listening to any stranger against her fellow-servants, and then bringing back his wicked words to trouble them!' said the oldest and worst of the housemaids. '—One of ourselves, too!—Come, you hypocrite! this is all an invention of yours and your young man's, to take your revenge of us because we found you out in a lie last night. Tell true now: wasn't it the same that stole the loaf and the pie that sent you with the impudent message?'

As she said this, she stepped up to the housemaid and gave her, instead of time to answer, a box on the ear that almost threw her down; and whoever could get at her began to push and hustle and pinch and punch her.

'You invite your fate,' she said quietly.

They fell furiously upon her, drove her from the hall with kicks and blows, hustled her along the passage, and threw her down the stair to the wine-cellar, then locked the door at the top of it, and went back to their breakfast.

In the mean time the king and the princess had had their bread and wine, and the princess, with Curdie's help, had made the room as tidy as she could—they were terribly neglected by the servants. And now Curdie set himself to interest and amuse the king, and prevent him from thinking too much, in order that he might the sooner think the better. Presently, at his majesty's request, he began from the beginning, and told everything he could recall of his life, about his father and mother and their cottage on the mountain, of the inside of the mountain and the work there, about the goblins and his adventures with them. When he came to finding the princess and her nurse overtaken by the twilight on the mountain, Irene took up her share of the tale, and told all about herself to that point, and then Curdie took it up again; and so they went on, each fitting in the part that the other did not know, thus keeping the hoop of the story running straight; and the king listened with wondering and delighted ears, astonished to find what he could so ill comprehend, yet fitting so well together from the lips of two narrators. At last, with the mission given him by the wonderful princess and his consequent adventures, Curdie brought up the whole tale to the present moment. Then a silence fell, and Irene and Curdie thought the king was asleep. But he was far from it; he was thinking about many things. After a long pause he said:

'Now at last, my children, I am compelled to believe many things I could not and do not yet understand—things I used to hear, and sometimes see, as often as I visited my mother's home. Once, for instance, I heard my mother say to her father—speaking of me—"He is a good, honest boy, but he will be an old man before he understands;" and my grandfather answered, "Keep up your heart, child: my mother will look after him." I thought often of their words, and the many strange things besides I both heard and saw in that house; but by degrees, because I could not understand them, I gave up thinking of them. And indeed I had almost forgotten them, when you, my child, talking that day about the Queen Irene and her pigeons, and what you had seen in her garret, brought them all back to my mind in a vague mass. But now they keep coming back to me, one by one, every one for itself; and I shall just hold my peace, and lie here quite still, and think about them all till I get well again.'

What he meant they could not quite understand, but they saw plainly that already he was better.

'Put away my crown,' he said. 'I am tired of seeing it, and have no more any fear of its safety.'

They put it away together, withdrew from the bedside, and left him in peace.

XXV

The Avengers

There was nothing now to be dreaded from Dr Kelman, but it made Curdie anxious, as the evening drew near, to think that not a soul belonging to the court had been to visit the king, or ask how he did, that day. He feared, in some shape or other, a more determined assault. He had provided himself a place in the room, to which he might retreat upon approach, and whence he could watch; but not once had he had to betake himself to it.

Towards night the king fell asleep. Curdie thought more and more uneasily of the moment when he must again leave them for a little while. Deeper and deeper fell the shadows. No one came to light the lamp. The princess drew her chair close to Curdie: she would rather it were not so dark, she said. She was afraid of something—she could not tell what; nor could she give any reason for her fear but that all was so dreadfully still. When it had been dark about an hour, Curdie thought Lina might be returned; and reflected that the sooner he went the less danger was there of any assault while he was away. There was more risk of his own presence being discovered, no doubt, but things were now drawing to a crisis, and it must be run. So, telling the princess to lock all the doors of the bedchamber, and let no one in, he took his mattock, and with here a run, and there a halt under cover, gained the door at the head of the cellar-stair in safety. To his surprise he found it locked, and the key was gone. There was no time for deliberation. He felt where the lock was, and dealt it a tremendous blow with his mattock. It needed but a second to dash the door open. Some one laid a hand on his arm.

'Who is it?' said Curdie.

'I told you they wouldn't believe me, sir,' said the house-maid. 'I have been here all day.'

He took her hand, and said, 'You are a good, brave girl. Now come with me, lest your enemies imprison you again.'

He took her to the cellar, locked the door, lighted a bit of candle, gave her a little wine, told her to wait there till he came, and went out the back way.

Swiftly he swung himself up into the dungeon. Lina had done her part. The place was swarming with creatures—animal forms wilder and more grotesque than ever ramped* in nightmare dream. Close by the hole, waiting his coming, her green eyes piercing the gulf below, Lina had but just laid herself down when he appeared. All about the vault and up the slope of the rubbish-heap lay and stood and squatted the forty-nine whose friendship Lina had conquered in the wood. They all came crowding about Curdie.

He must get them into the cellar as quickly as ever he could. But when he looked at the size of some of them, he feared it would be a long business to enlarge the hole sufficiently to let them through. At it he rushed, hitting vigorously at its edge with his mattock. At the very first blow came a splash from the water beneath, but ere he could heave a third, a creature like a tapir, only that the grasping point of its proboscis was hard as the steel of Curdie's hammer, pushed him gently aside, making room for another creature, with a head like a great club, which it began banging upon the floor with terrible force and noise. After about a minute of this battery, the tapir came up again, shoved Clubhead aside, and putting its own head into the hole began gnawing at the sides of it with the finger of its nose, in such a fashion that the fragments fell in a continuous gravelly shower into the water. In a few minutes the opening was large enough for the biggest creature amongst them to get through it.

Next came the difficulty of letting them down: some were quite light, but the half of them were too heavy for the rope, not to say for his arms. The creatures themselves seemed to be puzzling where or how they were to go. One after another of them came up, looked down through the hole, and drew back. Curdie thought if he let Lina down, perhaps that would suggest something; possibly they did not see the opening on the other side. He did so, and Lina stood lighting up the entrance of the passage with her gleaming eyes. One by one the creatures looked down again, and one by one they drew back, each standing aside to glance at the next, as if to say, *Now you have a look*. At last it came to the turn of the serpent with the long body, the four short legs behind, and the little wings before. No sooner had he poked his head through than he poked it farther through—and farther, and farther yet, until there was little more than his legs left in the dungeon. By that time he had got his head and neck well into the passage beside Lina. Then his legs gave a great waddle and spring, and he tumbled himself, far as there was betwixt them, heels over head into the passage.

'That is all very well for you, Mr Legserpent!' thought Curdie to himself; 'but what is to be done with the rest?'

He had hardly time to think it, however, before the creature's head appeared again through the floor. He caught hold of the bar of iron to which Curdie's rope was tied, and settling it securely across the narrowest part of the irregular opening, held fast to it with his teeth. It was plain to Curdie, from the universal hardness amongst them, that they must all, at one time or another, have been creatures of the mines.

He saw at once what this one was after. He had planted his feet firmly upon the floor of the passage, and stretched his long body up and across the chasm to serve as a bridge for the rest. He mounted instantly upon his neck, threw his arms round him as far as they would go, and slid down in ease and safety, the bridge just bending a little as his weight glided over it. But he thought some of the creatures would try his teeth.

One by one the oddities followed, and slid down in safety. When they seemed to be all landed, he counted them: there were but forty-eight. Up the rope again he went, and found one which had been afraid to trust himself to the bridge, and no wonder! for he had neither legs nor head nor arms nor tail:

he was just a round thing, about a foot in diameter, with a nose and mouth and eyes on one side of the ball. He had made his journey by rolling as swiftly as the fleetest of them could run. The back of the legserpent not being flat, he could not quite trust himself to roll straight and not drop into the gulf. Curdie took him in his arms, and the moment he looked down through the hole, the bridge made itself again, and he slid into the passage in safety, with Ballbody in his bosom.

He ran first to the cellar, to warn the girl not to be frightened at the avengers of wickedness. Then he called to Lina to bring in her friends.

One after another they came trooping in, till the cellar seemed full of them. The housemaid regarded them without fear.

'Sir,' she said, 'there is one of the pages I don't take to be a bad fellow.'

'Then keep him near you,' said Curdie. 'And now can you show me a way to the king's chamber not through the servants' hall?'

'There is a way through the chamber of the colonel of the guard,' she answered, 'but he is ill, and in bed.'

'Take me that way,' said Curdie.

By many ups and downs and windings and turnings she brought him to a dimly lighted room, where lay an elderly man asleep. His arm was outside the coverlid, and Curdie gave his hand a hurried grasp as he went by. His heart beat for joy, for he had found a good, honest human hand.

'I suppose that is why he is ill,' he said to himself.

It was now close upon supper-time, and when the girl stopped at the door of the king's chamber, he told her to go and give the servants one warning more.

'Say the messenger sent you,' he said. 'I will be with you very soon.'

The king was still asleep. Curdie talked to the princess for a few minutes, told her not to be frightened whatever noises she heard, only to keep her door locked till he came, and left her.

XXVI

The Vengeance

By the time the girl reached the servants' hall they were seated
at supper. A loud, confused exclamation arose when she entered. No one made room for her; all stared with unfriendly
eyes. A page, who entered the next minute by another door,
came to her side.

'Where do *you* come from, hussy?' shouted the butler, and
knocked his fist on the table with a loud clang.

He had gone to fetch wine, had found the stair door broken
open and the cellar door locked, and had turned and fled.
Amongst his fellows, however, he had now regained what
courage could be called his.

'From the cellar,' she replied. 'The messenger broke open
the door, and sent me to you again.'

'The messenger! Pooh! What messenger?'

'The same who sent me before to tell you to repent.'

'What! will you go fooling it still? Haven't you had enough
of it?' cried the butler in a rage, and starting to his feet, drew
near threateningly.

'I must do as I am told,' said the girl.

'Then why *don't* you do as *I* tell you, and hold your tongue?'
said the butler. 'Who wants your preachments? If anybody
here has anything to repent of, isn't that enough—and more
than enough for him—but you must come bothering about,
and stirring up, till not a drop of quiet will settle inside him?
You come along with me, young woman; we'll see if we can't
find a lock somewhere in the house that'll hold you in!'

'Hands off, Mr Butler!' said the page, and stepped between.

'Oh, oh!' cried the butler, and pointed his fat finger at him.
'That's you, is it, my fine fellow? So it's you that's up to her
tricks, is it?'

The youth did not answer, only stood with flashing eyes fixed on him, until, growing angrier and angrier, but not daring a step nearer, he burst out with rude but quavering authority,—

'Leave the house, both of you! Be off, or I'll have Mr Steward to talk to you. Threaten your masters, indeed! Out of the house with you, and show us the way you tell us of!'

Two or three of the footmen got up and ranged themselves behind the butler.

'Don't say *I* threaten you, Mr Butler,' expostulated the girl from behind the page. 'The messenger said I was to tell you again, and give you one chance more.'

'Did the *messenger* mention me in particular?' asked the butler, looking the page unsteadily in the face.

'No, sir,' answered the girl.

'I thought not! I should like to hear him!'

'Then hear him now,' said Curdie, who that moment entered at the opposite corner of the hall. 'I speak of the butler in particular when I say that I know more evil of him than of any of the rest. He will not let either his own conscience or my messenger speak to him: I therefore now speak myself. I proclaim him a villain, and a traitor to his majesty the king.—But what better is any one of you who cares only for himself, eats, drinks, takes good money, and gives vile service in return, stealing, and wasting the king's property, and making of the palace, which ought to be an example of order and sobriety, a disgrace to the country?'

For a moment all stood astonished into silence by this bold speech from a stranger. True, they saw by his mattock over his shoulder that he was nothing but a miner-boy, yet for a moment the truth told notwithstanding. Then a great roaring laugh burst from the biggest of the footmen as he came shouldering his way through the crowd towards Curdie.

'Yes, I'm right,' he cried; 'I thought as much! This *messenger*, forsooth, is nothing but a gallows-bird—a fellow the city marshal was going to hang, but unfortunately put it off till he should be starved enough to save rope and be throttled with a pack-thread. He broke prison, and here he is preaching!'

As he spoke, he stretched out his great hand to lay hold of him. Curdie caught it in his left hand, and heaved his mattock with the other. Finding, however, nothing worse than an ox-hoof, he restrained himself, stepped back a pace or two, shifted his mattock to his left hand, and struck him a little smart blow on the shoulder. His arm dropped by his side, he gave a roar, and drew back.

His fellows came crowding upon Curdie. Some called to the dogs; others swore; the women screamed; the footmen and pages got round him in a half-circle, which he kept from closing by swinging his mattock, and here and there threatening a blow.

'Whoever confesses to having done anything wrong in this house, however small, however great, and means to do better, let him come to this corner of the room,' he cried.

None moved but the page, who went towards him skirting the wall. When they caught sight of him, the crowd broke into a hiss of derision.

'There! see! Look at the sinner! He confesses! actually confesses! Come, what is it you stole? The barefaced hypocrite! There's your sort to set up for reproving other people! Where's the other now?'

But the maid had left the room, and they let the page pass, for he looked dangerous to stop. Curdie had just put him betwixt him and the wall, behind the door, when in rushed the butler with the huge kitchen poker, the point of which he had blown red-hot in the fire, followed by the cook with his longest spit. Through the crowd, which scattered right and left before them, they came down upon Curdie. Uttering a shrill whistle, he caught the poker a blow with his mattock, knocking the point to the ground, while the page behind him started forward, and seizing the point of the spit, held on to it with both hands, the cook kicking him furiously.

Ere the butler could raise the poker again, or the cook recover the spit, with a roar to terrify the dead, Lina dashed into the room, her eyes flaming like candles. She went straight at the butler. He was down in a moment, and she on the top of him, wagging her tail over him like a lioness.

'Don't kill him, Lina,' said Curdie.

'Oh, Mr Miner!' cried the butler.

'Put your foot on his mouth, Lina,' said Curdie. 'The truth Fear tells is not much better than her lies.'

The rest of the creatures now came stalking, rolling, leaping, gliding, hobbling into the room, and each as he came took the next place along the wall, until, solemn and grotesque, all stood ranged, awaiting orders.

And now some of the culprits were stealing to the doors nearest them. Curdie whispered the two creatures next him. Off went Ballbody, rolling and bounding through the crowd like a spent cannon shot, and when the foremost reached the door to the corridor, there he lay at the foot of it grinning; to the other door scuttled a scorpion, as big as a huge crab. The rest stood so still that some began to think they were only boys dressed up to look awful; they persuaded themselves they were only another part of the housemaid and page's vengeful contrivance, and their evil spirits began to rise again. Meantime Curdie had, with a second sharp blow from the hammer of his mattock, disabled the cook, so that he yielded the spit with a groan. He now turned to the avengers.

'Go at them,' he said.

The whole nine-and-forty obeyed at once, each for himself, and after his own fashion. A scene of confusion and terror followed.* The crowd scattered like a dance or flies. The creatures had been instructed not to hurt much, but to hunt incessantly, until every one had rushed from the house. The women shrieked, and ran hither and thither through the hall, pursued each by her own horror, and snapped at by every other in passing. If one threw herself down in hysterical despair, she was instantly poked or clawed or nibbled up again. Though they were quite as frightened at first, the men did not run so fast; and by and by some of them, finding they were only glared at, and followed, and pushed, began to summon up courage once more, and with courage came impudence. The tapir had the big footman in charge: the fellow stood stock-still, and let the beast come up to him, then put out his finger and playfully patted his nose. The tapir gave the nose a little twist, and the finger lay on the floor. Then indeed the footman ran, and did more than run, but nobody heeded his cries. Gradually the avengers grew more severe, and the terrors of the imagination were fast yielding to those of sensuous experience, when a page, perceiving one of the doors no longer guarded, sprang at it, and ran out. Another and another followed. Not a beast went after, until, one by one, they were every one gone from the hall, and the whole menie* in the kitchen. There they were beginning to congratulate themselves that all was over, when in came the creatures trooping after them, and the second act of their terror and pain began. They were flung about in all directions; their clothes were torn from them; they were pinched and scratched any and everywhere; Ballbody kept rolling up them and over them, confining his attentions to no one in particular; the scorpion kept grabbing at their legs with his huge pincers; a three-foot centipede kept screwing up their bodies nipping as he went; varied as numerous were their woes. Nor was it long before the last of them had fled from the kitchen to the sculleries. But thither also they were followed, and there again they were hunted about. They were bespattered with the dirt of their own neglect; they were soused in the stinking water that had boiled greens; they were smeared with rancid dripping; their faces were rubbed in maggots: I dare not tell all that was done to them. At last they got the door into a back-yard open, and rushed out. Then first they knew that the wind was howling and the rain falling in sheets. But there was no rest for them even there. Thither also were they followed by the inexorable avengers, and the only door here was a door out of the palace: out every soul of them was driven, and left, some standing, some lying, some crawling, to the farther buffeting of the waterspouts and whirlwinds ranging every street of the city. The door was flung to behind them, and they heard it locked and bolted and barred against them.

XXVII

More Vengeance

As soon as they were gone, Curdie brought the creatures back to the servants' hall, and told them to eat up everything on the table. It *was* a sight to see them all standing round it—except such as had to get upon it—eating and drinking, each after its fashion, without a smile, or a word, or a glance of fellowship in the act. A very few moments served to make everything eatable vanish, and then Curdie requested them to clean the house, and the page who stood by to assist them.

Every one set about it except Ballbody: he could do nothing at cleaning, for the more he rolled, the more he spread the dirt. Curdie was curious to know what he had been, and how he had come to be such as he was; but he could only conjecture that he was a gluttonous alderman whom nature had treated homoeopathically.*

And now there was such a cleaning* and clearing out of neglected places, such a burying and burning of refuse, such a rinsing of jugs, such a swilling of sinks, and such a flushing of drains, as would have delighted the eyes of all true housekeepers and lovers of cleanliness generally.

Curdie meantime was with the king, telling him all he had done. They had heard a little noise, but not much, for he had told the avengers to repress outcry as much as possible; and they had seen to it that the more any one cried out the more he had to cry out upon, while the patient ones they scarcely hurt at all.*

Having promised his majesty and her royal highness a good breakfast, Curdie now went to finish the business. The courtiers must be dealt with. A few who were the worst, and the leaders of the rest, must be made examples of; the others should be driven from their beds to the street.

He found the chiefs of the conspiracy holding a final consultation in the smaller room off the hall. These were the lord chamberlain, the attorney-general, the master of the horse, and the king's private secretary: the lord chancellor and the rest, as foolish as faithless, were but the tools of these.

The housemaid had shown him a little closet, opening from a passage behind, where he could overhear all that passed in that room; and now Curdie heard enough to understand that they had determined, in the dead of that night, rather in the deepest dark before the morning, to bring a certain company of soldiers into the palace, make away with the king, secure the princess, announce the sudden death of his majesty, read as his the will they had drawn up, and proceed to govern the country at their ease, and with results: they would at once levy severer taxes, and pick a quarrel with the most powerful of their neighbours. Everything settled, they agreed to retire, and have a few hours' quiet sleep first—all but the secretary, who was to sit up and call them at the proper moment. Curdie stole away, allowed them half an hour to get to bed, and then set about completing his purgation of the palace.

First he called Lina, and opened the door of the room where the secretary sat. She crept in, and laid herself down against it. When the secretary, rising to stretch his legs, caught sight of her eyes, he stood frozen with terror. She made neither motion nor sound. Gathering courage, and taking the thing for a spectral illusion, he made a step forward. She showed her other teeth, with a growl neither more than audible nor less than horrible. The secretary sank fainting into a chair. He was not a brave man, and besides, his conscience had gone over to the enemy, and was sitting against the door by Lina.

To the lord chamberlain's door next, Curdie conducted the legserpent, and let him in.

Now his lordship had had a bedstead made for himself, sweetly fashioned of rods of silver gilt: upon it the legserpent found him asleep, and under it he crept. But out he came on the other side, and crept over it next, and again under it, and so over it, under it, over it, five or six times, every time leaving a coil of himself behind him, until he had softly folded all his length about the lord chamberlain and his bed. This done, he set up his head, looking down with curved neck right over his lordship's, and began to hiss in his face. He woke in terror unspeakable, and would have started up; but the moment he moved, the legserpent drew his coils closer, and closer still, and drew and drew until the quaking traitor heard the joints of his beadstead grinding and gnarring.* Presently he persuaded himself that it was only a horrid nightmare, and began to struggle with all his strength to throw it off. Thereupon the legserpent gave his hooked nose such a bite, that his teeth met through it—but it was hardly thicker than the bowl of a spoon; and then the vulture knew that he was in the grasp of his enemy the snake, and yielded. As soon as he was quiet the legserpent began to untwist and retwist, to uncoil and recoil himself, swinging and swaying, knotting and relaxing himself with strangest curves and convolutions, always, however, leaving at least one coil around his victim. At last he undid himself entirely, and crept from the bed. Then first the lord chamberlain discovered that his tormentor had bent and twisted the bedstead, legs and canopy and all, so about him, that he was shut in a silver cage out of which it was impossible for him to find a way. Once more, thinking his enemy was gone, he began to shout for help. But the instant he opened his mouth his keeper darted at him and bit him, and after three or four such essays, with like result, he lay still.

The master of the horse Curdie gave in charge to the tapir. When the soldier saw him enter—for he was not yet asleep—he sprang from his bed, and flew at him with his sword. But the creature's hide was invulnerable to his blows, and he pecked at his legs with his proboscis until he jumped into bed again, groaning, and covered himself up; after which the tapir contented himself with now and then paying a visit to his toes.

For the attorney-general, Curdie led to his door a huge spider, about two feet long in the body, which, having made an excellent supper, was full of webbing. The attorney-general had not gone to bed, but sat in a chair asleep before a great mirror. He had been trying the effect of a diamond star which he had that morning taken from the jewel-room. When he woke he fancied himself paralysed; every limb, every finger even, was motionless: coils and coils of broad spider-ribbon bandaged his members to his body, and all to the chair. In the glass he saw himself wound about, under and over and around, with slavery infinite. On a footstool a yard off sat the spider glaring at him.

Clubhead had mounted guard over the butler, where he lay tied hand and foot under the third cask. From that cask he had seen the wine run into a great bath, and therein he expected to be drowned. The doctor, with his crushed leg, needed no one to guard him.

And now Curdie proceeded to the expulsion of the rest. Great men or underlings, he treated them all alike. From room to room over the house he went, and sleeping or waking took the man by the hand. Such was the state to which a year of wicked rule had reduced the moral condition of the court, that in it all he found but three with human hands. The possessors of these he allowed to dress themselves and depart in peace. When they perceived his mission, and how he was backed, they yielded without dispute.

Then commenced a general hunt, to clear the house of the vermin. Out of the beds in their night-clothing, out of their rooms, gorgeous chambers or garret nooks, the creatures hunted them. Not one was allowed to escape. Tumult and noise there was little, for the fear was too deadly for outcry. Ferreting them out everywhere, following them upstairs and downstairs, yielding no instant of repose except upon the way out, the avengers persecuted the miscreants, until the last of them was shivering outside the palace gates, with hardly sense enough left to know where to turn.

When they set out to look for shelter, they found every inn full of the servants expelled before them, and not one would yield his place to a superior suddenly levelled with himself. Most houses refused to admit them on the ground of the wickedness that must have drawn on them such a punishment; and not a few would have been left in the streets all night, had not Derba, roused by the vain entreaties at the doors on each side of her cottage, opened hers, and given up everything to them. The lord chancellor was only too glad to share a mattress with a stable-boy, and steal his bare feet under his jacket.

In the morning Curdie appeared, and the outcasts were in terror, thinking he had come after them again. But he took no notice of them: his object was to request Derba to go to the palace: the king required her services. She needed take no trouble about her cottage, he said; the palace was henceforward her home: she was the king's chatelaine* over men and maidens of his household. And this very morning she must cook his majesty a nice breakfast.

XXVIII

The Preacher

Various reports went undulating through the city as to the nature of what had taken place in the palace. The people gathered, and stared at the house, eyeing it as if it had sprung up in the night. But it looked sedate enough, remaining closed and silent, like a house that was dead. They saw no one come out or go in. Smoke rose from a chimney or two; there was hardly another sign of life. It was not for some little time generally understood that the highest officers of the crown as well as the lowest menials of the palace had been dismissed in disgrace: for who was to recognize a lord chancellor in his night-shirt? and what lord chancellor would, so attired in the street, proclaim his rank and office aloud? Before it was day most of the courtiers crept down to the river, hired boats, and betook themselves to their homes or their friends in the country.

It was assumed in the city that the domestics had been discharged upon a sudden discovery of general and unpardonable peculation;* for, almost everybody being guilty of it himself, petty dishonesty was the crime most easily credited and least easily passed over in Gwyntystorm.

Now that same day was Religion day, and not a few of the clergy, always glad to seize on any passing event to give interest to the dull and monotonic grind of their intellectual machines, made this remarkable one the ground of discourse to their congregations. More especially than the rest, the first priest of the great temple where was the royal pew, judged himself, from his relation to the palace, called upon to 'improve the occasion'—for they talked ever about improvement at Gwyntystorm, all the time they were going downhill with a rush.

The book which had, of late years, come to be considered the most sacred, was called The Book of Nations,* and consisted of proverbs, and history traced through custom: from it the first priest chose his text; and his text was, *Honesty is the best Policy*. He was considered a very eloquent man, but I can offer only a few of the larger bones of his sermon. The main proof of the verity of their religion, he said, was, that things always went well with those who professed it; and its first fundamental principle, grounded in inborn invariable instinct, was, that every One should take care of that One. This was the first duty of Man. If every one would but obey this law, number one, then would every one be perfectly cared for—one being always equal to one. But the faculty or care was in excess of need, and all that overflowed, and would otherwise run to waste, ought to be gently turned in the direction of one's neighbour, seeing that this also wrought for the fulfilling of the law, inasmuch as the reaction of excess so directed was upon the director of the same, to the comfort, that is, and well-being of the original self. To be just and friendly was to build the warmest and safest of all nests, and to be kind and loving was to line it with the softest of all furs and feathers, for the one precious, comfort-loving self there to lie, revelling in downiest bliss. One of the laws therefore most binding upon men because of its relation to the first and greatest of all duties, was embodied in the Proverb he had just read; and what stronger proof of its wisdom and truth could they desire than the sudden and complete vengeance which had fallen upon those worse than ordinary sinners who had offended against the king's majesty by forgetting that *Honesty is the best Policy*?

At this point of the discourse the head of the legserpent rose from the floor of the temple, towering above the pulpit, above the priest, then curving downwards, with open mouth slowly descended upon him. Horror froze the sermon-pump. He stared upwards aghast. The great teeth of the animal closed upon a mouthful of the sacred vestments, and slowly he lifted the preacher from the pulpit, like a handful of linen from a wash-tub, and, on his four solemn stumps, bore him out of the temple, dangling aloft from his jaws. At the back of it he dropped him into the dust-hole amongst the remnants of a library whose age had destroyed its value in the eyes of the chapter. They found him burrowing in it, a lunatic henceforth—whose madness presented the peculiar feature, that in its paroxysms he jabbered sense.

Bone-freezing horror pervaded Gwyntystorm. If their best and wisest were treated with such contempt, what might not the rest of them look for? Alas for their city! their grandly respectable city! their loftily reasonable city! Where it was all to end, the Convenient alone could tell!

But something must be done. Hastily assembling, the priests chose a new first priest, and in full conclave unanimously declared and accepted, that the king in his retirement had, through the practice of the blackest magic, turned the palace into a nest of demons in the midst of them. A grand exorcism was therefore indispensable.

In the mean time the fact came out that the greater part of the courtiers had been dismissed as well as the servants, and this fact swelled the hope of the Party of Decency, as they called themselves. Upon it they proceeded to act, and strengthened themselves on all sides.

The action of the king's bodyguard remained for a time uncertain. But when at length its officers were satisfied that both the master of the horse and their colonel were missing, they placed themselves under the orders of the first priest.

Everyone dated the culmination of the evil from the visit of the miner and his mongrel; and the butchers vowed, if they could but get hold of them again, they would roast both of them alive. At once they formed themselves into a regiment, and put their dogs in training for attack.

Incessant was the talk, innumerable were the suggestions, and great was the deliberation. The general consent, however, was that as soon as the priests should have expelled the demons, they would depose the king, and, attired in all his regal insignia, shut him in a cage for public show; then choose governors, with the lord chancellor at their head, whose first duty should be to remit every possible tax; and the magistrates, by the mouth of the city marshal, required all able-bodied citizens, in order to do their part towards the carrying out of these and a multitude of other reforms, to be ready to take arms at the first summons.

Things needful were prepared as speedily as possible, and a mighty ceremony, in the temple, in the market-place, and in front of the palace, was performed for the expulsion of the demons. This over, the leaders retired to arrange an attack upon the palace.

But that night events occurred which, proving the failure of their first, induced the abandonment of their second intent. Certain of the prowling order of the community, whose numbers had of late been steadily on the increase, reported frightful things. Demons of indescribable ugliness had been espied careering through the midnight streets and courts. A citizen—some said in the very act of housebreaking, but no one cared to look into trifles at such a crisis—had been seized from behind, he could not see by what, and soused in the river. A well-known receiver of stolen goods had had his shop broken open, and when he came down in the morning had found everything in ruin on the pavement. The wooden image of justice over the door of the city marshal had had the arm that held the sword *bitten* off. The gluttonous magistrate had been pulled from his bed in the dark, by beings of which he could see nothing but the flaming eyes, and treated to a bath of the turtle soup that had been left simmering by the side of the kitchen fire. Having poured it over him, they put him again into his bed, where he soon learned how a mummy must feel in its cerements.* Worst of all, in the market-place was fixed up a paper, with the king's own signature, to the effect that whoever henceforth should show inhospitality to strangers, and should be convicted of the same, should be instantly expelled the city; while a second, in the butchers' quarter, ordained that any dog which henceforward should attack a stranger should be immediately destroyed. It was plain, said the butchers, that the clergy were of no use; *they* could not exorcise demons! That afternoon, catching sight of a poor old fellow in rags and tatters, quietly walking up the street, they hounded their dogs upon him, and had it not been that the door of Derba's cottage was standing open, and was near enough for him to dart in and shut it ere they reached him, he would have been torn in pieces.

And thus things went on for some days.

XXIX
Barbara

In the mean time, with Derba to minister to his wants, with Curdie to protect him, and Irene to nurse him, the king was getting rapidly stronger. Good food was what he most wanted, and of that, at least of certain kinds of it, there was plentiful store in the palace. Everywhere since the cleansing of the lower regions of it, the air was clean and sweet, and under the honest hands of the one housemaid the king's chamber became a pleasure to his eyes. With such changes it was no wonder if his heart grew lighter as well as his brain clearer.

But still evil dreams came and troubled him, the lingering results of the wicked medicines the doctor had given him. Every night, sometimes twice or thrice, he would wake up in terror, and it would be minutes ere he could come to himself. The consequence was that he was always worse in the morning, and had loss to make up during the day. This retarded his recovery greatly. While he slept, Irene or Curdie, one or the other, must still be always by his side.

One night, when it was Curdie's turn with the king, he heard a cry somewhere in the house, and as there was no other child, concluded, notwithstanding the distance of her grandmother's room, that it must be Barbara. Fearing something might be wrong, and noting the king's sleep more quiet than usual, he ran to see. He found the child in the middle of the floor, weeping bitterly, and Derba slumbering peacefully in bed. The instant she saw him the night-lost thing ceased her crying, smiled, and stretched out her arms to him. Unwilling to wake the old woman, who had been working hard all day, he took the child, and carried her with him. She clung to him so, pressing her tear-wet radiant face against his, that her little arms threatened to choke him. When he re-entered the chamber, he found the king sitting up in bed, fighting the phantoms of some hideous dream. Generally upon such occasions, although he saw his watcher, he could not dissociate him from the dream, and went raving on. But the moment his eyes fell upon little Barbara, whom he had never seen before, his soul came into them with a rush, and a smile like the dawn of an eternal day overspread his countenance: the dream was nowhere, and the child was in his heart. He stretched out his arms to her, the child stretched out hers to him, and in five minutes they were both asleep, each in the other's embrace. From that night Barbara had a crib in the king's chamber, and as often as he woke, Irene or Curdie, whichever was watching, took the sleeping child and laid her in his arms, upon which, invariably and instantly, the dream would vanish. A great part of the day too she would be playing on or about the king's bed; and it was a delight to the heart of the princess to see her amusing herself with the crown, now sitting upon it, now rolling it hither and thither about the room like a hoop. Her grandmother entering once while she was pretending to make porridge in it, held up her hands in horror-struck amazement; but the king would not allow her to interfere, for the king was now Barbara's playmate, and his crown their plaything.

The colonel of the guard also was growing better. Curdie went often to see him. They were soon friends, for the best people understand each other the easiest, and the grim old warrior loved the miner-boy as if he were at once his son and his angel. He was very anxious about his regiment. He said the officers were mostly honest men, he believed, but how they might be doing without him, or what they might resolve, in ignorance of the real state of affairs, and exposed to every misrepresentation, who could tell? Curdie proposed that he should send for the major, offering to be the messenger. The colonel agreed, and Curdie went—not without his mattock, because of the dogs.

But the officers had been told by the master of the horse

that their colonel was dead, and although they were amazed he should be buried without the attendance of his regiment, they never doubted the information. The handwriting itself of their colonel was insufficient, counteracted by the fresh reports daily current, to destroy the lie. The major regarded the letter as a trap for the next officer in command, and sent his orderly to arrest the messenger. But Curdie had had the wisdom not to wait for an answer.

The king's enemies said that he had first poisoned the good colonel of the guard, and then murdered the master of the horse, and other faithful councillors; and that his oldest and most attached domestics had but escaped from the palace with their lives—nor all of them, for the butler was missing. Mad or wicked, he was not only unfit to rule any longer, but worse than unfit to have in his power and under his influence the young princess, only hope of Gwyntystorm and the kingdom.

The moment the lord chancellor reached his house in the country and had got himself clothed, he began to devise how yet to destroy his master; and the very next morning set out for the neighbouring kingdom of Borsagrass, to invite invasion, and offer a compact with its monarch.

XXX

Peter

At the cottage on the mountain everything for a time went on just as before. It was indeed dull without Curdie, but as often as they looked at the emerald it was gloriously green, and with nothing to fear or regret, and everything to hope, they required little comforting. One morning, however, at last, Peter, who had been consulting the gem, rather now from habit than anxiety, as a farmer his barometer in undoubtful weather, turned suddenly to his wife, the stone in his hand, and held it up with a look of ghastly dismay.

'Why, that's never the emerald!' said Joan.

'It is,' answered Peter; 'but it were small blame to any one that took it for a bit of bottle glass!'

For, all save one spot right in the centre, of intensest and most brilliant green, it looked as if the colour had been burnt out of it.

'Run, run, Peter!' cried his wife. 'Run and tell the old princess. It may not be too late. The boy must be lying at death's door.'

Without a word Peter caught up his mattock, darted from the cottage, and was at the bottom of the hill in less time than he usually took to get half way.

The door of the king's house stood open; he rushed in and up the stair. But after wandering about in vain for an hour, opening door after door, and finding no way further up, the heart of the old man had well-nigh failed him. Empty rooms, empty rooms!—desertion and desolation everywhere.

At last he did come upon the door to the tower-stair. Up he darted. Arrived at the top, he found three doors, and, one after the other, knocked at them all. But there was neither voice nor hearing. Urged by his faith and his dread, slowly, hesitatingly, he opened one. It revealed a bare garret-room, nothing in it but one chair and one spinning-wheel. He closed it, and opened the next—to start back in terror, for he saw nothing but a great gulf, a moonless night, full of stars, and, for all the stars, dark, dark!—a fathomless abyss. He opened the third door, and a rush like the tide of a living sea invaded his ears. Multitudinous wings flapped and flashed in the sun, and, like the ascending column from a volcano, white birds innumerable shot into the air, darkening the day with the shadow of their cloud, and then, with a sharp sweep, as if bent sideways by a sudden wind, flew northward, swiftly away, and vanished. The place felt like a tomb. There seemed no breath of life left in it. Despair laid hold upon him; he rushed down thundering with heavy feet. Out upon him darted the housekeeper like an ogress-spider, and after her came her men; but Peter rushed past them, heedless and careless—for had not the princess mocked him?—and sped along the road to Gwyntystorm. What help lay in a miner's mattock, a man's arm, a father's heart, he would bear to his boy.

Joan sat up all night waiting his return, hoping and hoping. The mountain was very still, and the sky was clear; but all night long the miner sped northwards, and the heart of his wife was troubled.

XXXI

The Sacrifice

Things in the palace were in a strange condition: the king playing with a child and dreaming wise dreams, waited upon by a little princess with the heart of a queen, and a youth from the mines, who went nowhere, not even into the king's chamber, without his mattock on his shoulder and a horrible animal at his heels; in a room nearby the colonel of his guard, also in bed, without a soldier to obey him; in six other rooms, far apart, six miscreants, each watched by a beast-gaoler; ministers to them all, an old woman, a young woman, and a page; and in the wine-cellar, forty-three animals, creatures more grotesque than ever brain of man invented. None dared approach its gates, and seldom one issued from them.

All the dwellers in the city were united in enmity to the palace. It swarmed with evil spirits, they said; whereas the evil spirits were in the city, unsuspected. One consequence of their presence was that, when the rumour came that a great army was on the march against Gwyntystorm, instead of rushing to their defences, to make new gates, free portcullises and drawbridges, and bar the river, each and all flew first to their treasures, burying them in their cellars and gardens, and hiding them behind stones in their chimneys; and, next to rebellion, signing an invitation to his majesty of Borsagrass to enter at their open gates, destroy their king, and annex their country to his own.

The straits of isolation were soon found in the palace: its invalids were requiring stronger food, and what was to be done? for if the butchers sent meat to the palace, was it not likely enough to be poisoned? Curdie said to Derba he would think of some plan before morning.

But that same night, as soon as it was dark, Lina came to her master, and let him understand she wanted to go out. He unlocked a little private postern* for her, left it so that she could push it open when she returned, and told the crocodile to stretch himself across it inside. Before midnight she came back with a young deer.

Early the next morning the legserpent crept out of the wine-cellar, through the broken door behind, shot into the river, and soon appeared in the kitchen with a splendid sturgeon. Every night Lina went out hunting, and every morning Legserpent went out fishing, and both invalids and household had plenty to eat. As to news, the page, in plain clothes, would now and then venture out into the market-place, and gather some.

One night he came back with the report that the army of the king of Borsagrass had crossed the border. Two days after, he brought the news that the enemy was now but twenty miles from Gwyntystorm.

The colonel of the guard rose, and began furbishing his armour—but gave it over to the page, and staggered across to the barracks, which were in the next street. The sentry took him for a ghost or worse, ran into the guard-room, bolted the door, and stopped his ears. The poor colonel, who was yet hardly able to stand, crawled back despairing.

For Curdie, he had already, as soon as the first rumour reached him, resolved, if no other instructions came, and the king continued unable to give orders, to call Lina and the creatures, and march to meet the enemy. If he died, he died for the right, and there was a right end of it. He had no preparations to make, except a good sleep.

He asked the king to let the housemaid take his place by his majesty that night, and went and lay down on the floor of the corridor, no farther off than a whisper would reach from the door of the chamber. There, with an old mantle of the king's thrown over him, he was soon fast asleep.

Somewhere about the middle of the night, he woke suddenly, started to his feet, and rubbed his eyes. He could not tell what had waked him. But could he be awake, or was he not dreaming? The curtain of the king's door, a dull red ever before, was glowing a gorgeous, a radiant purple; and the crown wrought upon it in silks and gems was flashing as if it burned! What could it mean? Was the king's chamber on fire? He darted to the door and lifted the curtain. Glorious terrible sight!

A long and broad marble table, that stood at one end of the room, had been drawn into the middle of it, and thereon burned a great fire, of a sort that Curdie knew—a fire of glowing, flaming roses,* red and white. In the midst of the roses lay the king, moaning, but motionless. Every rose that fell from the table to the floor, someone, whom Curdie could not plainly see for the brightness, lifted and laid burning upon the king's face, until at length his face too was covered with the live roses, and he lay all within the fire, moaning still, with now and then a shuddering sob. And the shape that Curdie saw and could not see, wept over the king as he lay in the fire, and often she hid her face in handfuls of her shadowy hair, and from her hair the water of her weeping dropped like sunset rain in the light of the roses. At last she lifted a great armful of her hair, and shook it over the fire, and the drops fell from it in showers, and they did not hiss in the flames, but there arose instead as it were the sound of running brooks. And the glow of the red fire died away, and the glow of the white fire grew grey, and the light was gone, and on the table all was black—except the face of the king, which shone from under the burnt roses like a diamond in the ashes of a furnace.

Then Curdie, no longer dazzled, saw and knew the old princess. The room was lighted with the splendour of her face, of her blue eyes, of her sapphire crown. Her golden hair went streaming out from her through the air till it went off in mist and light. She was large and strong as a Titaness. She stooped over the table-altar, put her mighty arms under the living sacrifice, lifted the king, as if he were but a little child, to her bosom, walked with him up the floor, and laid him in his bed. Then darkness fell.

The miner-boy turned silent away, and laid himself down again in the corridor. An absolute joy filled his heart, his bosom, his head, his whole body. All was safe; all was well. With the helve of his mattock tight in his grasp, he sank into a dreamless sleep.

XXXII

The King's Army

He woke like a giant refreshed with wine.

When he went into the king's chamber, the housemaid sat where he had left her, and everything in the room was as it had been the night before, save that a heavenly odour of roses filled the air of it. He went up to the bed. The king opened his eyes, and the soul of perfect health shone out of them. Nor was Curdie amazed in his delight.

'Is it not time to rise, Curdie?' said the king.

'It is, your majesty. Today we must be doing,' answered Curdie.

'What must we be doing today, Curdie?'

'Fighting, sire.'

'Then fetch me my armour—that of plated steel, in the chest there. You will find the underclothing with it.'

As he spoke, he reached out his hand for his sword, which hung in the bed before him, drew it, and examined the blade.

'A little rusty!' he said, 'but the edge is there. We shall polish it ourselves today—not on the wheel. Curdie, my son, I wake from a troubled dream. A glorious torture has ended it, and I live. I know not well how things are, but thou shalt explain them to me as I get on my armour.—No, I need no bath. I am clean.—Call the colonel of the guard.'

In complete steel the old man stepped into the chamber. He knew it not, but the old princess had passed through his room in the night.

'Why, Sir Bronzebeard!' said the king, 'you are dressed before me! Thou needest no valet, old man, when there is battle in the wind!'

'Battle, sire!' returned the colonel. '—Where then are our soldiers?'

'Why, there, and here,' answered the king, pointing to the colonel first, and then to himself. 'Where else, man?—The enemy will be upon us ere sunset, if we be not upon him ere noon. What other thing was in thy brave brain when thou didst don thine armour, friend?'

'Your majesty's orders, sire,' answered Sir Bronzebeard.

The king smiled and turned to Curdie.

'And what was in thine, Curdie—for thy first word was of battle?'

'See, your majesty,' answered Curdie; 'I have polished my mattock. If your majesty had not taken the command, I would have met the enemy at the head of my beasts, and died in comfort, or done better.'

'Brave boy!' said the king. 'He who takes his life in his hand is the only soldier. Thou shalt head thy beasts today.—Sir Bronzebeard, wilt thou die with me if need be?'

'Seven times, my king,' said the colonel.

'Then shall we win this battle!' said the king.

'—Curdie, go and bind securely the six, that we lose not their guards.—Canst thou find us a horse, think'st thou, Sir Bronzebeard? Alas! they told us our white charger was dead.'

'I will go and fright the varletry with my presence, and secure, I trust, a horse for your majesty, and one for myself.'

'And look you, brother!' said the king; 'bring one for my miner-boy too, and a sober old charger for the princess, for she too must go to the battle, and conquer with us.'

'Pardon me, sire,' said Curdie; 'a miner can fight best on foot. I might smite my horse dead under me with a missed blow. And besides, I must be near my beasts.'

'As you will,' said the king. '—Three horses then, Sir Bronzebeard.'

The colonel departed, doubting sorely in his heart how to accoutre and lead from the barrack stables three horses, in the teeth of his revolted regiment.

In the hall he met the housemaid.

'Can you lead a horse?' he asked.

'Yes, sir.'

'Are you willing to die for the king?'

'Yes, Sir.'

'Can you do as you are bid?'

'I can keep on trying, sir.'

'Come, then. Were I not a man I would be a woman such as thou.'

When they entered the barrack-yard, the soldiers scattered like autumn leaves before a blast of winter. They went into the stable unchallenged—and lo! in a stall, before the colonel's eyes, stood the king's white charger, with the royal saddle and bridle hung high beside him!

'Traitorous thieves!' muttered the old man in his beard, and went along the stalls, looking for his own black charger. Having found him, he returned to saddle first the king's. But the maid had already the saddle upon him, and so girt that the colonel could thrust no fingertip between girth and skin. He left her to finish what she had so well begun, and went and graithed* his own. He then chose for the princess a great red horse, twenty years old, which he knew to possess every equine virtue. This and his own he led to the palace, and the maid led the king's.

The king and Curdie stood in the court, the king in full armour of silvered steel, with a circlet of rubies and diamonds round his helmet. He almost leaped for joy when he saw his great white charger come in, gentle as a child to the hand of the housemaid. But when the horse saw his master in his armour, he reared and bounded in jubilation, yet did not break from the hand that held him. Then out came the princess attired and ready, with a hunting-knife her father had given her by her side. They brought her mother's saddle, splendent with gems and gold, set it on the great red horse, and lifted her to it. But the saddle was so big, and the horse so tall, that the child found no comfort in them.

'Please, king-papa,' she said, 'can I not have my white pony?'

'I did not think of him, little one,' said the king. 'Where is he?'

'In the stable,' answered the maid. 'I found him half-starved, the only horse within the gates, the day after the servants were driven out. He has been well fed since.'

'Go and fetch him,' said the king.

As the maid appeared with the pony, from a side door came Lina and the forty-nine, following Curdie.

'I will go with Curdie and the Uglies,' cried the princess; and as soon as she was mounted she got into the middle of the pack.

So out they set,* the strangest force that ever went against an enemy. The king in silver armour sat stately on his white steed, with the stones flashing on his helmet; beside him the grim old colonel, armed in steel, rode his black charger; behind the king, a little to the right, Curdie walked afoot, his mattock shining in the sun; Lina followed at his heel; behind her came the wonderful company of Uglies; in the midst of them rode the gracious little Irene, dressed in blue, and mounted on the prettiest of white ponies; behind the colonel, a little to the left, walked the page, armed in a breastplate, headpiece, and trooper's sword he had found in the palace, all much too big for him, and carrying a huge brass trumpet which he did his best to blow; and the king smiled and seemed pleased with his music, although it was but the grunt of a brazen unrest. Alongside of the beasts walked Derba carrying Barbara—their refuge the mountains, should the cause of the king be lost; as soon as they were over the river they turned aside to ascend the cliff, and there awaited the forging of the day's history. Then first Curdie saw that the housemaid, whom they had all forgotten, was following, mounted on the great red horse, and seated in the royal saddle.

Many were the eyes unfriendly of women that had stared at them from door and window as they passed through the city; and low laughter and mockery and evil words from the lips of children had rippled about their ears; but the men were all gone to welcome the enemy, the butchers the first, the king's guard the last. And now on the heels of the king's army rushed out the women and children also, to gather flowers and branches, wherewith to welcome their conquerors.

About a mile down the river, Curdie, happening to look behind him, saw the maid, whom he had supposed gone with Derba, still following on the great red horse. The same moment the king, a few paces in front of him, caught sight of the enemy's tents, pitched where, the cliffs receding, the bank of the river widened to a little plain.

XXXIII
The Battle

He commanded the page to blow his trumpet; and, in strength of the moment, the youth uttered a right warlike defiance.

But the butchers and the guard, who had gone over armed to the enemy, thinking that the king had come to make his peace also, and that it might thereafter go hard with them, rushed at once to make short work with him, and both secure and commend themselves. The butchers came on first—for the guards had slackened their saddle-girths—brandishing their knives, and talking to their dogs. Curdie and the page, with Lina and her pack, bounded to meet them. Curdie struck down the foremost with his mattock. The page, finding his sword too much for him, threw it away and seized the butcher's knife, which as he rose he plunged into the foremost dog. Lina rushed raging and gnashing amongst them. She would not look at a dog so long as there was a butcher on his legs, and she never stopped to kill a butcher, only with one grind of her jaws crushed a leg of him. When they were all down, then indeed she flashed amongst the dogs.

Meantime the king and the colonel had spurred towards the advancing guard. The king clove the major through skull and collar-bone, and the colonel stabbed the captain in the throat. Then a fierce combat commenced—two against many. But the butchers and their dogs quickly disposed of, up came Curdie and his beasts. The horses of the guard, struck with terror, turned in spite of the spur, and fled in confusion.

Thereupon the forces of Borsagrass, which could see little of the affair, but correctly imagined a small determined body in front of them, hastened to the attack. No sooner did their first advancing wave appear through the foam of the retreating one, than the king and the colonel and the page, Curdie and the beasts, went charging upon them. Their attack, especially the rush of the Uglies, threw the first line into great confusion, but the second came up quickly; the beasts could not be everywhere, there were thousands to one against them, and the king and his three companions were in the greatest possible danger.

A dense cloud came over the sun, and sank rapidly towards the earth. The cloud moved 'all together',* and yet the thousands of white flakes of which it was made up moved each for itself in ceaseless and rapid motion: those flakes were the wings of pigeons. Down swooped the birds upon the invaders; right in the face of man and horse they flew with swift-beating wings, blinding eyes and confounding brain. Horses reared and plunged and wheeled. All was at once in confusion. The men made frantic efforts to seize their tormentors, but not one could they touch; and they outdoubled them in numbers. Between every wild clutch came a peck of beak and a buffet of pinion in the face. Generally the bird would, with sharp-clapping wings, dart its whole body, with the swiftness of an arrow, against its singled mark, yet so as to glance aloft the same instant, and descend skimming; much as the thin stone, shot with horizontal cast of arm, having touched and torn the surface of the lake, ascends to skim, touch, and tear again. So mingled the feathered multitude in the grim game of war. It was a storm in which the wind was birds, and the sea men. And ever as each bird arrived at the rear of the enemy, it turned, ascended, and sped to the front to charge again.

The moment the battle began, the princess's pony took fright, and turned and fled. But the maid wheeled her horse across the road and stopped him; and they waited together the result of the battle.

As they waited, it seemed to the princess right strange that the pigeons, every one as it came to the rear, and fetched a compass to gather force for the re-attack, should make the head of her attendant on the red horse the goal around which it turned; so that about them was an unintermittent flapping and flashing of wings, and a curving, sweeping torrent of the side-poised wheeling bodies of birds. Strange also it seemed that the maid should be constantly waving her arm towards the battle. And the time of the motion of her arm so fitted with the rushes of birds, that it looked as if the birds obeyed her gesture, and she were casting living javelins by the thousand against the enemy. The moment a pigeon had rounded her head, it went off straight as bolt from bow, and with trebled velocity.

But of these strange things, others besides the princess had taken note. From a rising ground whence they watched the battle in growing dismay, the leaders of the enemy saw the maid and her motions, and, concluding her an enchantress, whose were the airy legions humiliating them, set spurs to their horses, made a circuit, outflanked the king, and came down upon her. But suddenly by her side stood a stalwart old man in the garb of a miner, who, as the general rode at her, sword in hand, heaved his swift mattock, and brought it down with such force on the forehead of his charger, that he fell to the ground like a log. His rider shot over his head and lay stunned. Had not the great red horse reared and wheeled, he would have fallen beneath that of the general.

With lifted sabre, one of his attendant officers rode at the miner. But a mass of pigeons darted in the faces of him and his horse, and the next moment he lay beside his commander. The rest of them turned and fled, pursued by the birds.

'Ah, friend Peter!' said the maid; 'thou hast come as I told thee! Welcome and thanks!'

By this time the battle was over. The rout was general. The enemy stormed back upon their own camp, with the beasts roaring in the midst of them, and the king and his army, now reinforced by one, pursuing.

But presently the king drew rein.

'Call off your hounds, Curdie, and let the pigeons do the rest,' he shouted, and turned to see what had become of the princess.

In full panic fled the invaders, sweeping down their tents, stumbling over their baggage, trampling on their dead and wounded, ceaselessly pursued and buffeted by the white-winged army of heaven. Homeward they rushed the road they had come, straight for the borders, many dropping from pure fatigue, and lying where they fell. And still the pigeons were in their necks as they ran. At length to the eyes of the king and his army nothing was visible save a dust-cloud below, and a bird-cloud above.

Before night the bird-cloud came back, flying high over Gwyntystorm. Sinking swiftly, it disappeared among the ancient roofs of the palace.

XXXIV
Judgement

The King and his army returned, bringing with them one prisoner only, the lord chancellor. Curdie had dragged him from under a fallen tent, not by the hand of a man, but by the foot of a mule.

When they entered the city, it was still as the grave. The citizens had fled home. 'We must submit,' they cried 'or the king and his demons will destroy us.' The king rode through the streets in silence, ill-pleased with his people. But he stopped his horse in the midst of the market-place, and called, in a voice loud and clear as the cry of a silver trumpet,* 'Go and find your own. Bury your dead,* and bring home your wounded.' Then he turned him gloomily to the palace.

Just as they reached the gates, Peter, who, as they went, had been telling his tale to Curdie, ended it with the words—

'And so there I was, in the nick of time to save the two princesses!'

'The *two* princesses, father! The one on the great red horse was the housemaid,' said Curdie, and ran to open the gates for the king.

They found Derba returned before them, and already busy preparing them food. The king put up his charger with his own hands, rubbed him down, and fed him.

When they had washed, and eaten and drunk, he called the colonel, and told Curdie and the page to bring out the traitors and the beasts, and attend him to the market-place.

By this time the people were crowding back into the city, bearing their dead and wounded. And there was lamentation in Gwyntystorm, for no one could comfort himself, and no one had any to comfort him. The nation was victorious, but the people were conquered.

The king stood in the centre of the market-place, upon the steps of the ancient cross. He had laid aside his helmet and put on his crown, but he stood all armed beside, with his sword in his hand. He called the people to him, and, for all the terror of the beasts, they dared not disobey him. Those even, who were carrying their wounded laid them down, and drew near trembling.

Then the king said to Curdie and the page,—

'Set the evil men before me.'

He looked upon them for a moment in mingled anger and pity, then turned to the people and said—

'Behold your trust! Ye slaves, behold your leaders! I would have freed you, but ye would not be free. Now shall ye be ruled with a rod of iron, that ye may learn what freedom is, and love it and seek it. These wretches I will send where they shall mislead you no longer.'

He made a sign to Curdie, who immediately brought up the legserpent. To the body of the animal they bound the lord chamberlain, speechless with horror. The butler began to shriek and pray, but they bound him on the back of Clubhead. One after another, upon the largest of the creatures they bound the whole seven, each through the unveiling terror looking the villain he was. Then said the king,—

'I thank you, my good beasts; and I hope to visit you ere long. Take these evil men with you, and go to your place.'

Like a whirlwind they were in the crowd, scattering it like dust. Like hounds they rushed from the city, their burdens howling and raving.

What became of them I have never heard.

Then the king turned once more to the people and said, 'Go to your houses:' nor vouchsafed them another word. They crept home like chidden hounds.

The king returned to the palace. He made the colonel a duke, and the page a knight, and Peter he appointed general of all his mines. But to Curdie he said,—

'You are my own boy, Curdie. My child cannot choose but love you, and when you are both grown up—if you both will—you shall marry each other, and be king and queen when I am gone. Till then be the king's Curdie.'

Irene held out her arms to Curdie. He raised her in his, and she kissed him.

'And my Curdie too!' she said.

Thereafter the people called him Prince Conrad; but the king always called him either just *Curdie*, or *My miner-boy*.

They sat down to supper, and Derba and the knight and the housemaid waited, and Barbara sat on the king's left hand. The housemaid poured out the wine; and as she poured out for Curdie red wine that foamed in the cup, as if glad to see the light whence it had been banished so long, she looked him in the eyes. And Curdie started, and sprang from his seat, and dropped on his knees, and burst into tears. And the maid said with a smile, such as none but one could smile,—

'Did I not tell you, Curdie, that it might be you would not know me when next you saw me?'

Then she went from the room, and in a moment returned in royal purple, with a crown of diamonds and rubies, from under which her hair went flowing to the floor, all about her ruby-slippered feet. Her face was radiant with joy, the joy overshadowed by a faint mist as of unfulfilment. The king rose and kneeled on one knee before her. All kneeled in like homage. Then the king would have yielded her his royal chair. But she made them all sit down, and with her own hands placed at the table seats for Derba and the page. Then in ruby crown and royal purple she served them all.

XXXV

The End

The king sent Curdie out into his dominions to search for men and women that had human hands. And many such he found, honest and true, and brought them to his master. So a new and upright government, a new and upright court, was formed, and strength returned to the nation.

But the exchequer was almost empty, for the evil men had squandered everything, and the king hated taxes unwillingly paid. Then came Curdie and said to the king that the city stood upon gold. And the king sent for men wise in the ways of the earth, and they built smelting furnaces, and Peter brought miners, and they mined the gold, and smelted it, and the king coined it into money, and therewith established things well in the land.

The same day on which he found his boy, Peter set out to go home. When he told the good news to Joan his wife, she rose from her chair and said, 'Let us go.' And they left the cottage, and repaired to Gwyntystorm. And on a mountain above the city they built themselves a warm house for their old age, high in the clear air.

As Peter mined one day by himself, at the back of the king's wine-cellar, he broke into a cavern all crusted with gems, and much wealth flowed therefrom, and the king used it wisely.

Queen Irene—that was the right name of the old princess—was thereafter seldom long absent from the palace. Once or twice when she was missing, Barbara, who seemed to know of her sometimes when nobody else had a notion whither she had gone, said she was with the dear old Uglies in the wood. Curdie thought that perhaps her business might be with others there as well. All the uppermost rooms in the palace were left to her use, and when any one was in need of her help, up thither he must go. But even when she was there, he did not always succeed in finding her. She, however, always knew that such a one had been looking for her.

Curdie went to find her one day. As he ascended the last stair, to meet him came the well-known scent of her roses; and when he opened her door, lo! there was the same gorgeous room in which his touch had been glorified by her fire! And there burned the fire—a huge heap of red and white roses. Before the hearth stood the princess, an old grey-haired woman, with Lina a little behind her, slowly wagging her tail, and looking like a beast of prey that can hardly so long restrain itself from springing as to be sure of its victim. The queen was casting roses, more and more roses, upon the fire. At last she turned and said, 'Now, Lina!'—and Lina dashed burrowing into the fire. There went up a black smoke and a dust, and Lina was never more seen in the palace.

Irene and Curdie were married. The old king died, and they were king and queen. As long as they lived Gwyntystorm was a better city, and good people grew in it. But they had no children, and when they died the people chose a king. And the new king went mining and mining in the rock under the city, and grew more and more eager after the gold, and paid less and less heed to his people. Rapidly they sunk towards their old wickedness. But still the king went on mining, and coining gold by the pailful, until the people were worse even than in the old time. And so greedy was the king after gold, that when at last the ore began to fail, he caused the miners to reduce the pillars which Peter and they that followed him had left standing to bear the city. And from the girth of an oak of a thousand years, they chipped them down to that of a fir tree of fifty.

One day at noon, when life was at its highest, the whole city fell with a roaring crash. The cries of men and the shrieks of women went up with its dust and then there was a great silence.

Where the mighty rock once towered, crowded with homes and crowned with a palace, now rushes and raves a stone-obstructed rapid of the river. All around spreads a wilderness of wild deer, and the very name of Gwyntystorm has ceased from the lips of men.

EXPLANATORY NOTES

THE PRINCESS AND THE GOBLIN

Abbreviations

ABNW	George MacDonald, *At the Back of the North Wind* (New York, Airmont, 1966).
DG	George MacDonald, *Donal Grant* (New York, Routledge & Sons, 1883).
DO	George MacDonald, *A Dish of Orts* (London: Sampson Low, Marston, 1895).
US 1	George MacDonald, *Unspoken Sermons. First Series* (London, Alexander Strahan, 1867).
US 2	George MacDonald, *Unspoken Sermons. Second Series* (London, Longmans, Green & Co., 1886).
GMHW	Greville MacDonald, *George MacDonald and His Wife* (London, George Allen & Unwin, 1924).
GM	William Raeper, *George MacDonald* (Icknield Way, Tring, Lion, 1987).
GK	Robert Lee Wolff, *The Golden Key: A Study of the Fiction of George MacDonald* (New Haven, Cn., Yale University Press, 1961).
OED	Oxford English Dictionary (1st edn.).
VFM	Walter Houghton, *The Victorian Frame of Mind* (New Haven, Cn., Yale University Press, 1970).

5 *a little princess whose*: at this point in the magazine version of the story, MacDonald interrupts his narrative with the following exchange between the 'Editor' and his reader:

'But, Mr. Editor, why do you always write about princesses?'

'Because every little girl is a princess.'

'You will make them vain if you tell them that.'

'Not if they understand what I mean.'

'Then what do you mean?'

'What do you mean by a princess?'

'The daughter of a king.'

'Very well; then every little girl is a princess, and there

would be no need to say anything about it except that she is always in danger of forgetting her rank, and behaving as if she had grown out of the mud. I have seen little princesses behave like the children of thieves and lying beggars, and that is why they need to be told they are princesses. And that is why, when I tell a story of this kind, I like to tell it about a princess. Then I can say better what I mean, because I can then give her every beautiful thing I want her to have.'

'Please go on.'

The story then begins again and proceeds as in the published version. This frame, however, makes appearances in Chapter 3 and in Chapter 32, the final chapter.

Irene: MacDonald's fifth child, his daughter Irene, was born on 31 August 1857. The name Irene derives from the Greek word for 'peace'. Lesley Willis also points out that Irene is an anagram of the French 'reine' or queen. See '"Born Again": The Metamorphosis of Irene in George MacDonald's *The Princess and the Goblin*', *Scottish Literary Journal*, 12 (1985), 24.

The ceiling of her nursery was blue, with stars in it: in 1867 the MacDonald family moved to a large house in Hammersmith; this house they named 'The Retreat'. MacDonald's study was decorated by an artist friend named Cottier; the study had 'crimson-flock wall-paper with black fleur-de-lis stencilled over, a dark blue ceiling with scattered stars in silver and gold, and a silver crescent moon . . .' (*GMHW*, 386).

hollow places underneath: MacDonald is likely to have found his source for the underground caverns and mines of the two 'Princess' books in his reading of the German Romantic writers. E. T. A. Hoffmann's 'The Mines of Falun', Ludwig Tieck's 'The Runenberg', and Novalis's *Heinrich von Ofterdingen* all employ mines as symbolic settings. Wordsworth's *Peter Bell* (1819) also makes mention of mines and miners. For a description of MacDonald's German sources see *GK*, 87–91.

6 *gnomes . . . kobolds . . . goblins*: both Thomas Keightley (*The Fairy Mythology* (1828) and Jacob Grimm (*Teutonic Mythology*, 2nd edn. (1844)) categorize kobolds and goblins as 'Home sprites', akin to the Scottish Brownie who inhabits a home and does chores for the family while remaining unseen.

Grimm calls the kobold 'the tiny tricky home-sprite' (Dover edn., vol. ii (1966), 502). Also of interest, in light of the clownish behaviour of Glump and his goblin family in *The Princess and the Goblin*, is the connection between both kobold and goblin and the court-fool (Grimm, ii. 503). *OED* gives this for kobold: 'an underground spirit haunting mines or caves, a goblin or gnome.' As for the gnome, Pope says in the Dedication to *The Rape of the Lock* (1714): 'The Gnomes, or Daemons of earth, delight in mischief.'

had greatly altered in the course of generations: the goblins represent MacDonald's concept of devolution, his revisionary reading of Darwin whereby creatures may evolve positively or negatively depending on their spiritual states. 'Evolution, for MacDonald, was clearly not only a physical, but a moral question' (*GM*, 248). Wolff remarks on MacDonald's indebtedness to Novalis and other German Romantics for his 'elaborate theory of evolution' (*GK*, 38). The strange creatures in *The Princess and Curdie* are also examples of MacDonald's notion of an evolution which can move in either a positive or negative direction.

7 *who had caused their expulsion*: the echo here is to the expulsion of Satan and his followers from Heaven. In Milton's *Paradise Regained* (1671) Book 2, Satan tells his followers, 'such an Enemy | Is ris'n to invade us, who no less 'such an Enemy | Is ris'n to invade us, who no less | Threat'ns than our expulsion down to Hell' (lll 126–8).

8 *And this is how it begins*: MacDonald's sensitivity to convention is apparent, as it is in other works such as *The Light Princess* (1864). By delaying for one whole chapter the beginning of his story, MacDonald draws attention to the whole notion of beginnings. Just as endings are impossible to envisage, so too are beginnings, and this story begins after it has begun.

you can't get tired of a thing before you have it: the idea of a thing is more important than its material form, and the idea is approached through man's imagination. MacDonald writes: 'it is not the things we see the most clearly that influence us the most powerfully; undefined, yet vivid visions of something beyond, something which eye has not seen or ear heard have far more influence than any logical sequences whereby the same things may be demonstrated to the intellect' (*DO*, 27–8). And in *US 2* he writes: 'It is imperative on us to get rid of the tyranny of *things*' (37).

If the artist . . . with the toys: the artist who illustrated MacDonald's story is Arthur Hughes (1830–1915) who is associated with the Pre-Raphaelite movement. Hughes apparently took MacDonald's advice since his illustration of this scene contains no toys. Hughes took MacDonald himself as his model for the king in this story. Other works of MacDonald's illustrated by Hughes include *Dealings with the Fairies* (1867), *At the Back of the North Wind* (1871), and *Phantastes* (1905).

The next moment . . . her nurse goes out of the room: Hughes's illustration shows Irene wearily holding her head while sitting in a chair and her nurse, Lootie, bending over her.

9 *old stair of worm-eaten oak*: oak cabinets appear in *Phantastes* (1858) and *Wilfrid Cumbermede* (1872). Traditionally, the oak is associated with hospitality, strength, virtue, and endurance. Grimm discusses the Holy Oak in *Teutonic Mythology*, 72–4.

It doesn't follow that she was lost . . . though: MacDonald echoes Christ's words in Matt. 10: 39: 'He that findeth his life shall lose it: and he that loseth his life for my sake shall find it.'

like a true princess: MacDonald makes plain here and elsewhere (pp. 12 and 137) that 'princess' is a metaphor for any girl who behaves properly and obediently. On p. 137 MacDonald writes: 'the truest princess is just the one who loves all her brothers and sisters best.' His friend, John Ruskin, employs a similar metaphor, that of the 'queen', in *Sesame and Lilies* (1865).

10 *It was very narrow*: 'Because strait is the gate, and narrow is the way, which leadeth unto life, and few there be that find it' (Matt. 7: 14). Also of interest here are MacDonald's two sermons, 'The Way' and 'The Hardness of the Way', in *US 2*.

11 *her curiosity*: compare Irene here with that most curious child, Alice, in Lewis Carroll's *Alice's Adventures in Wonderland* (1865). For the friendship between MacDonald and Carroll see *GMHW*, 342–6, and R. B. Shaberman's 'Lewis Carroll and George MacDonald', *Jabberwocky* (1976), 67–87.

A very old lady who sat spinning: at this point in the magazine version the following paragraph appears:

> 'Oh, Mr. Editor! I know the story you are going to tell: it's The Sleeping Beauty; only you're spinning too, and making it longer.'
> 'No, indeed, it is not that story. Why should I tell one that every properly educated child knows already? More old ladies than one have sat spinning in a garret. Besides, the old lady in that story was only spinning with a spindle, and this one was spinning with a spinning-wheel, else how could the princess have heard the sweet noise through the door? Do you know the difference? Did you ever see a spindle or a spinning-wheel? I dare say you never did. Well, ask your mamma to explain to you the difference. Between ourselves, however, I shouldn't wonder if she didn't know much better than you. Another thing is, that this is not a fairy story; but a goblin story. And one thing more, this old lady spinning was not an old nurse—but—you shall see what. I think I have now made it quite plain that this is not that lovely story of The Sleeping Beauty. It is quite a new one, I assure you, and I will try to tell it as prettily as I can.'

Here MacDonald acknowledges the famous story, 'Sleeping Beauty', as a source for his story. He is probably thinking of the version by the brothers Grimm, first published in *Kinder-und Hausmarchen* (1812). He parodies the story in *The Light Princess* (1864) and *Little Daylight* (1871). His use of the spinning woman, however, draws on other sources from German folklore and literature. For example, Fable in Novalis's 'Klingsohr's Marchen' is a spinner. The spinners spin variously life, music, art.

the old lady . . . skin was smooth and white: this ancient lady who is eternally young appears in many of MacDonald's fantasies: *Phantastes* (1858), *The Golden Key* (1867), *At the Back of the North Wind* (1871), 'The Carasoyn' (1871), *The Wise Woman* or *The Lost Princess* (1875).

12 *vulgar*: common.

she washed and wiped the bright little face: for a discussion of the Victorian insistence on cleanliness and its relevance to this book see Tony Tanner, 'Mountains and Depths—An

Approach to Nineteenth Century Dualism', *Review of English Literature*, 3 (1962), 51–61.

13 *her hair shone like silver*: throughout *The Princess and the Goblin* MacDonald associates the female with the moon and silver, and the male with the sun and gold.

I'm your great-great-grandmother: an echo of E. T. A. Hoffmann's *The Golden Pot* in which the hero Lindhorst has a 'great-great-great-great grandmother'.

18 *'No, I didn't dream it'*: MacDonald often plays with the possibility that experiences such as Irene's (or Diamond's in *At the Back of the North Wind* or Vane's in *Lilith*) are dreams. Dream and reality shift their relationship in MacDonald who was fond of quoting Novalis's epigram: 'our life is no dream, but it should and will perhaps become one.'

20 *'Nurse, that's very rude'*: quoting a passage from *Annals of a Quiet Neighbourhood* (1867) in which the narrator comments upon the permanence of a childhood experience, Greville MacDonald remarks that the 'clue to my father's thoughts and imagery' is the phrase, 'the child is father of the man' (*GMHW*, 155). The phrase is of course Wordsworth's. MacDonald's preternaturally wise children, such as Irene, are like Wordsworth's little girl in 'We Are Seven' or Edward in 'Anecdote for Fathers'; they have something to teach adults.

21 *an enormous little breakfast*: oxymoron and paradox are typical of MacDonald's style.

23 *fancy*: MacDonald often refers to the distinction between fancy and imagination made famous by Coleridge. The products of the fancy are, MacDonald says, 'mere inventions'. In a rather cryptic passage, MacDonald defines imagination as 'the tailor that cuts the garments, for truth and fancy as the journeyman who 'embroiders the button-holes' (*DO*, 314, 315). Irene's experiences with her great-great-grandmother are imaginative ideas; they speak of higher things.

25 *Suddenly the shadow of a great mountain peak . . . in front of them*: compare with the boating scene from Book 2 of Wordsworth's *The Prelude* quoted *DO*, 248: 'a huge peak, black and huge,| As if with voluntary power instinct, | Upreared its head'.

27 *Something like what he sang*: MacDonald is fond of comparing poetry (and the fairy-tale) to music which does not so much 'convey a meaning' as 'wake a meaning'. See MacDonald's well-known essay, 'The Fantastic Imagination' (*DO*, 313–22). His narrators often claim only to capture 'something' of what a character sings; see for example Chapter 16 of *At the Back of the North Wind*.

whispered shriek: oxymoron. Compare n. to p. 21 above.

28 *eyes as dark as the mines*: compare the simile here with the one MacDonald uses to describe Irene's eyes in Chapter 1.

I'm Peter's Son: Curdie's father is a miner whose house is built on a rock. MacDonald alludes here to Peter, one of the twelve apostles and founder of the first Church, whose name means rock or stone (*petros* is Greek for stone). In *The Princess and Curdie*, Curdie's father is Peter Peterson; this suggests that not only is Curdie a son of the true Church, but so is his father. Their house, built on a rock, is emblematic of the true Church. For MacDonald's concept of sonship see his sermon 'Abba, Father!' (*US 2*, 115–37).

mind: pun on mind which here means (1) 'take heed of or obey', and (2) 'to care or object'.

29 *misses a word, or says a wrong one*: a contradiction? Elsewhere in the book, MacDonald says (p. 37) that a 'New rhyme' is the most effectual rhyme to rout the goblins.

30 *Curdie*: a pastoral name of MacDonald's invention. Here, as elsewhere in the book and throughout his writing, MacDonald is aware of the symbolic nature of naming. On names see MacDonald's sermon, 'The New Name' (*US 1*, 100–17).

32 *cobs*: one of its several meanings is a roundish mass or lump, as of coal. MacDonald may also be playing on the word 'kobold'.

36 *the miners' night was the goblins' day*: goblin society parodies human society; they have a political system which includes a monarchy, with an aggressively authoritarian Queen, and a 'parliament' with a Chancellor, and the semblance of democratic participation from the goblin-people.

40 *Why they come so soft*: the softness of the goblins' feet refers to their lack of soles/souls. Their hard heads reflect their lack of imagination, their intellectual or rational bent.

40 *silly*: used in the sense of 'foolish'. In Scotland, however, the word may mean moronic. And MacDonald also uses the word in its archaic sense meaning close to God. See Chapter 35 of *At the Back of the North Wind*. All senses of the word apply here.

outlandish: a pun meaning (1) 'freakish', and (2) 'from another place', in this instance above ground, outside the earth.

43 *who had had more schooling than the rest*: MacDonald makes fun of modern education and evolutionary theory. Novels that deal directly with education are MacDonald's *David Elginbrod* (1863) and *Gutta Percha Willie* (1873). See also F. W. Lewis. 'The Pedagogics of George MacDonald', *Education*, 19 (1899), 357–67.

49 *Hence it appears . . . behaviour*: MacDonald here satirizes the language of politics.

50 *excogitated*: to think out carefully. The goblins are thinkers, not imaginers. The word here indicates the pompous and inflated language of the goblins (and of politics).

52 *choke-damp . . . firedamp*: choke-damp is also known as black damp: carbon dioxide mixed with nitrogen, produced by mine fires and the explosion of firedamp. Firedamp is a combustible gas, chiefly methane, that enters mines from coal seams. It explodes when mixed with air.

63 *the rock*: *OED* gives: (1) 'a distaff', and (2) 'a distaff together with the wool or flax attached to it; the quantity of wool or flax placed on a distaff for spinning'.

64 *The walls were also blue*: compare n. to p. 5 above.

gossamer-like cambric: cambric is a fine white linen; gossamer is strands of spider's silk. A connection exists between the spider's thread the great-great-grandmother spins for Irene and this fine cotton of her handkerchief.

washed her feet: here and elsewhere the great-great-grandmother reminds us of Christ. On p. 86 she implies she is nearly two thousand years old; Jesus remarks: 'Before Abraham was, I am' (John 8: 58). Like Christ, the great-great-grandmother comforts, cleanses, heals, forgives, and saves. See Lesley Willis, '"Born Again"', n. 2 to p. 5.

65 *nobody could find the room except I pleased*: compare: 'No man

can come to me, except the Father which hath sent me draw him' (John 6: 44).

67 *She made . . . hillside*: the centre of Victorian life, as Walter Houghton notes, is the family, and at the centre of the family is the wife, the angel in the house, as Coventry Patmore has it. See Patmore's *The Angel in the House* (1854). 'Man for the field and woman for the hearth', Tennyson writes in *The Princess* (1847). See Houghton, *VFM*, 341–93.

Hop-o'-my-Thumb: Iona and Peter Opie write: 'The story of "Le petit Poucet", which in English has become the story of "Hop o' my Thumb", was the last of the tales Perrault included in *Histoires ou contes du temps passe*, 1697' (*The Classic Fairy Tales*, (London, Oxford University Press, 1974), 128). Hop-o'-my-Thumb uses pebbles and later pieces of bread, just as Hans does in 'Hansel and Grethel', in order to leave a trail by which he and his brothers can find their way home from the woods after their father and mother leave them there.

68 *sappers*: *OED* defines 'sap' as a noun: 'some kind of spade or mattock', and as a verb: 'the process of undermining a wall or defensive work.' For 'sapper' *OED* gives: 'one who saps', and 'a soldier employed in working at saps, the building and repairing of fortifications, the execution of field-works and the like.'

71 *The original stocks*: MacDonald believed that animals, as well as humans, would be saved. Consequently, they too could move up or down the evolutionary scale. See *GK*, 273–74.

75 *that is the way fear serves us*: MacDonald has much to say concerning fear in his sermons; like all else, it serves a positive purpose. See *US 1*, 27–49, and *US 2*, 157–71.

76 *her terror was lost in astonishment*: 'Endless must be our terror, until we come heart to heart with the fire-core of the universe' (*US 2*, 166). For MacDonald, God is a consuming fire, a God of light.

79 *a fire . . . of the loveliest and reddest roses*: compare Novalis: 'I need flowers . . . that have been raised in fire' (*Heinrich von Ofterdingen* (1800), trans. Palmer Hilty (New York, Frederick Ungar, 1964 edn.), 141).

79 *two cherubs of shining silver*: compare Ezek. 10: 2: 'And he spake unto the man clothed with linen, and said, Go in between the wheels, even unto the cherub, and fill thine hand with coals of fire from between the cherubims, and scatter them over the city.' See also Ezek. 41: 18. For cherubims of gold see Exod. 25: 18 and 37: 7.

81 *everybody will have it*: MacDonald is a Universalist, that is, he believes that everyone will be saved, even the Devil. Compare, 1 Tim. 2: 3–4: 'For this is good and acceptable in the sight of God our Saviour, who will have all men to be saved, and to come unto the knowledge of the truth.' See also Phil. 2: 10–11.

83 *her right hand*: both the Old and New Testaments give special significance to the right hand. To be placed on the right is to be given the place of dignity and honour. See 1 Kgs. 2: 19 and Ps. 45: 9.

   a fire-opal: a variety of opal having translucent orange yellow to red colours suggesting flames.

85 *this is my home*: 'Home is ever so far away in the palm of your hand . . . Everybody who is not at home, has to go home' (*Lilith*, chap. 9). 'Home', for MacDonald, is akin to individuation; the self is in harmony with the non-self, subject and object are reconciled. 'Yea, no home at last will do, but the home of God's heart' (quoted *GM*, 255).

89 *looking grave*: possibly a pun on 'grave' since the king's words suggest that Irene's mother is dead.

92 *Curdie's Clue*: *OED* gives: (1) 'A ball of yarn or thread', and (2) 'A ball of thread, employed to guide anyone in "threading" his way into or out of a labyrinth . . . or maze.'

93 *mica, or Muscovy glass, called sheep-silver in Scotland*: mica is any of a class of hydrous silicates of widely varying composition, cleaving into tough, thin, often transparent and flexible laminae; muscovite is a light colourless mica.

98 *sabots*: a wooden shoe.

101 *either salt or fresh*: before the invention of the refrigerator, people preserved meat with salt. The goblins intend to give Curdie no meat, either meat cured with salt or meat freshly killed.

104 *new rhymes, now his only weapons*: the tradition of words as weapons is old and has biblical resonance. In Rev., the Son of Man appears with a 'sharp two-edged sword' coming from his mouth (1: 16). In Eph. 6: 17, 'the sword of the Spirit . . . is the word of God' (see also Heb. 4: 12). In Bunyan's *Pilgrim's Progress*, which the MacDonald family produced many times as a public stage play, Christian triumphs over Apollyon as much with words as with a sword.

108 *obedient*: the notion of obedience to one's duty, to one's parents or one's superiors is common in the nineteenth century and MacDonald's work often returns to this theme. 'Obedience is the joining of the links of the eternal round. Obedience is but the one side of the creative will. Will is God's will, obedience is man's will; the two make one' (*US 2*, 154). 'Obedience is the one condition of progress' (*DO*, 289). 'Obedience is the grandest thing in the world to begin with' (*DO*, 307).

111 *pother*: fuss, worry, bother.

119 *Then you must believe without seeing*: compare p. 123 below, where the grandmother says: 'Seeing is not believing—it is only seeing.' To come to 'see', as Curdie will in *The Princess and Curdie*, is to see into things: 'The true soul sees, or will come to see, that his [God's] words, his figures always represent more than they are able to present' (*US 2*, 225). To see the more that God's words and figures represent, that nature represents, one must use one's 'deeper eyes' (*US 2*, 99).

123 *if Lootie were to see me*: compare the sermon, 'The Last Farthing', in which MacDonald speaks of those who cannot see. They 'are punished by having the way closed before them' (*US 2*, 101).

If I had been there: Curdie has, as Willis says, 'no supernatural faith' ('"Born Again"', 31). MacDonald associates Curdie with the practical world of work, just as he does the king. The bedroom represents a deeper realm of the spiritual than the workroom does.

124 *gypsy-child*: unwashed and often parentless child. The urban version of this child is the 'street arab', about whom MacDonald writes in *Sir Gibbie* (1879).

124 *large silver bath*: compare, the description that follows with Heinrich's dream of the basin and the blue flower in Novalis's *Heinrich von Ofterdingen* (16–17).

   of the sense she had only a feeling—no understanding: this accords with MacDonald's idea of the effect a fairy-tale should have. See his essay, 'The Fantastic Imagination' (*DO*, 313–22). The passage from Novalis which MacDonald uses as epigraph to *Phantastes* closely resembles the thought here. Part of it reads: 'poems that are indeed good to hear and full of beautiful words, but also without any meaning and coherence, with at the most single stanzas comprehensible, like fragments of the most varied sort of things.' ('Gedichte, die bloss wohlklingend und voll schöner Worte sind, aber auch ohne allen Sinn und Zusammenhang, höchstens einzelne Strophen verständlich, wie Bruchstücke aus den verschiedenartigsten Dingen.')

125 *duty*: Goerge Eliot comments that three words inspired 'trumpet-calls of men,—the words *God, Immortality, Duty*' (quoted *VFM*, 238). To do one's duty was to act and to set aside doubts and anxiety. MacDonald's work is filled with calls to duty. In a letter of his father's quoted by Greville MacDonald, MacDonald writes: 'In every heart there is a consciousness of some duty or other required of it: that is the will of God. He who would be saved must get up and do that will' (*GMDW*, 374). In *Donal Grant*, MacDonald writes: 'faith, in its simplest, truest, mightiest form, is—to do his will in the one thing revealing itself at the moment as duty' (18).

   counterpane: a coverlet or quilt for a bed.

129 *They had torn my clothes very much*: compare with the description of the goblins' attack on Lizzie in Christina Rossetti's *Goblin Market* (1862).

137 *was not right in her mind*: the preternatural child is akin to the wise fool. Compare Diamond in *At the Back of the North Wind* whom Nanny and Jim describe as having a 'tile loose' (264).

138 *but a prince as well*: MacDonald speaks metaphorically, but as we learn in *The Princess and Curdie*, Curdie becomes Prince Conrad. Wolff suggests that 'Curdie and his family must also be given royal blood to make him eligible for the princess' (*GK*, 178).

156 *but for a huge rock*: Compare n. 2 to p. 28 above. Also relevant here is the parable of the houses built on rock and sand. See Matt. 7: 24–7.

164 *allowed me to serve you*: see MacDonald's sermon, 'The True Christian Ministering' (*DO*, 298–312).

166 *Scotch Brownies*: 'The spirit called Brownie appeared like a rough man, and haunted divers houses without doing any evill, but doing, as it were, necessarie turns up and down the house' (King James, quoted in Keightley, *The World Guide to Gnomes, Fairies, Elves and Other Little People*, 357). MacDonald has his character Sir Gibbie Galbraith serve as Brownie to some country people in *Sir Gibbie*.

167 *all but disappeared*: at this point in the magazine version the following passage appears:

> 'But, Mr. Editor, we would rather hear more about the Princess and Curdie. We don't care about the goblins and their nasty creatures. They frighten us—rather.'
>
> 'But you know if you once get rid of the goblins there is no fear of the princess or of Curdie.'
>
> 'But we want to know more about them.'
>
> 'Some day, perhaps, I may tell you the further history of both of them; how Curdie came to visit Irene's grandmother, and what she did for him; and how the princess and he met again after they were older—and how—But there! I don't mean to go any farther at present.'
>
> 'Then you're leaving the story unfinished Mr. Editor!'
>
> 'Not more unfinished than a story ought to be, I hope. If you ever knew a story finished, all I can say is, I *never* did. Somehow stories won't finish. I think I know why, but I won't say that either now.'

MacDonald often alludes to the endless story and deferred endings. The last chapter of *Lilith* is 'The Endless Ending', and the narrator of *The Lost Princess* remarks in the last paragraph of that story: 'If you think it [the story] is not finished—I never knew a story that was.' Cosmo, in *Castle Warlock* (1882), writes works that do not end: 'to him the end of things never came; nothing that has an end was worth employing his art upon' (327).

THE PRINCESS AND CURDIE

173 *people were yet more afraid of mountains*: MacDonald echoes John Ruskin's 'Mountain Gloom' and 'Mountain Glory', the titles of Chapters 19 and 20 of *Modern Painters*, Book V (1856). It is true that up to the seventeenth century mountains were generally considered warts and wens on the earth's surface, and they inspired fear in their observers. MacDonald takes his sense of mountains as 'beautiful terrors' from the Romantic tradition of the sublime. Wordsworth, Colerdige, and Shelley all write of the visionary splendour of mountains. Like both Wordsworth and Shelley, MacDonald experienced first hand the glories of the Alps which he visited in 1865 and which he wrote about in *Wilfrid Cumbermede* (1872). For the changing perception of mountains in the seventeenth and eighteenth centuries see Margery Nicholson, *Mountain Gloom and Mountain Glory* (Ithaca, NY, Cornell University Press, 1959).

rushed up and out: the so-called catastrophic school of geologists had argued that the earth takes its shape from cataclysms such as floods, earthquakes, and volcanoes.

174 *waiting for millions of ages*: MacDonald here and throughout these pages draws upon the work of the nineteenth-century geologist Sir Charles Lyell who was one of the century's scientists to show that the earth was millions of years old and not the six thousand years of theological speculation. See *Principles of Geology* (1830–3). Another popular work MacDonald may have known is Robert Chambers's *Vestiges of the Natural History of Creation* (1844). At King's College, Aberdeen, MacDonald studied, among other things, Chemistry and Natural Philosophy (Physics). He was from an early age interested in science, and he thought of becoming a physician.

little veins bring it down: that MacDonald knew the work of William Blake is certain (see *GMHW*, 554–5), and this passage with its mention of veins, arteries, lungs, and heart echoes Blake's visionary descriptions of nature as the one man (the giant Albion) in *Jerusalem*. The Adam Kadmon of Cabbalistic lore also comes to mind. Blake is a continual presence in *The Princess and Curdie*.

176 mammon: an Aramaic word meaning riches. In *Sir Gibbie*, MacDonald writes that 'the most degrading superstition of all' is 'the worship of Mammon' (187). 'Ye cannot serve God and mammon' (Matt. 6: 24).

178 *his mother, she had once seen*: see Chapter 23 of *The Princess and the Goblin*.

180 *The child is not meant to die*: 'Childhood belongs to the divine nature' (see the sermon 'The Child in the Midst,' (*US 1*, 1–26)).

185 *But at present*: in the previous passage Curdie comes to a crossroads, a point between east and west and between past and future. He experiences an 'eternal *now*' (see *Sir Gibbie*, 7); in other words he has a visionary experience. In what follows he proceeds in an easterly direction, the same direction Anodos takes in *Phantastes*, the direction to new mornings, new birth.

He knocked: 'to him that knocketh it shall be opened' (Matt. 7: 8).

190 *I am so glad you shot my bird*: Curdie's fall has been fortunate. He follows the pattern of what MacDonald envisages, in his story 'The Broken Swords' (1854), as the archetypal Christian tragedy, a beginning in harmony with the world, followed by a fall from innocence, a dark night of the soul, and then a new beginning with renewed hope. The echo here is to Coleridge's *The Rime of the Ancient Mariner* (1797).

192 *canning*: the doing, of course, but MacDonald is aware of the word's association with cunning and knowing. See the Old English *cunnan*: to know. To do is to know: 'Do the truth you know, and you shall learn the truth you need to know' (*DO*, 76).

198 *Their wives and mothers and grandmothers*: MacDonald here draws on the tradition of the female story-teller, the Mother Goose, who spins her winter's tales by the fireside, a tradition perpetuated by the Brothers Grimm with their so-called 'fairy-tale grandmother', Dorothea Viehmann.

199 *the poor man never drank*: compare Burns's *Tam o'Shanter*.

201 *Would turn out to have nothing but good in them*: 'What we call

evil, is the only and best shape, which, for the person and his condition at the time, could be assumed by the best good' (*Phantastes*, 182).

gangue: in mining the non-metalliferous or worthless minerals found in a vein of ore.

to cut the hazel fork: a forked twig or branch of hazel or willow was used as a divining-rod to find underground water or metals. The miners, despite their derisive attitude towards Old Mother Wotherwop, have their own superstitions.

202 *The Emerald*: the second row of stones in the high priest's breastplate consists of 'an emerald, a sapphire, and a diamond' (Exod. 28: 18). Emeralds also form part of the New Jerusalem (Rev. 21: 19).

203 *an adit*: a nearly horizontal entrance to a mine.

beautiful exceedingly: the quotation is from Coleridge's *Christabel* (1816) (Part 1, l.68), where it applies to Geraldine, the *femme fatale* of the poem.

204 *in which the goblins held their state assemblies*: see Chapter 9 of *The Princess and the Goblin*.

circumfulgent: from the Latin *circumfulgere*: to shine around.

206 *What is in a Name?*: see MacDonald's sermon 'The New Name' (*US 1*, 100–17).

the Mother of Light: several writers have noted that MacDonald's God is distinctly feminine, but it is true that he refers throughout his writings to God as the Father of Light. William Raeper is surely right to note that MacDonald's God is both Father and Mother: 'The great-great-grandmother in *The Princess and the Goblin* and *The Princess and Curdie* . . . is a face of God, welcoming, loving and motherly' (*GM*, 262). Raeper then quotes MacDonald's novel *Adela Cathcart* (1864): 'Him who is Father and Mother both in one' (quoted *GM*, 262).

216 *an Aeolian harp*: a stringed instrument so constructed as to produce musical sounds when exposed to air currents. The Romantic poets were fond of using it as an analogy for the mind in its creative activity or for the work of art itself. As part of the epigaph to *Phantastes*, MacDonald quotes Novalis who says that the fairy-tale is a 'musical phantasy, the harmonic

sequences of an Aeolian harp' ('eine Musikalische Phantasie, die harmonischen Folgen einer Aeolsharfe').

219 *what some philosophers say*: among others, Darwin, whose *On the Origin of Species* appeared in 1859, is undoubtedly implied here.

227 *a warlock*: a wizard, sorcerer, often associated with the Devil. Old English *wærloga*: traitor, foe, devil.

231 *shepherded by the slow, unwilling wind*: the quotation is from Shelley's *Prometheus Unbound*, II. 1. 147. MacDonald contributed an essay on Shelley to the 8th edn. of *Encyclopaedia Britannica* (1860). The essay is reprinted *DO*, 264–81.

236 *gorget*: armour which protects the throat or a piece of clothing which covers the neck and breast. A wimple.

238 *a goodly company*: the allusion is to Coleridge's *The Rime of the Ancient Mariner*, Part 7, l.604.

241 *one sect of philosophers*: the most influential of the mid-Victorian optimists is T. B. Macauley, whom Arnold called 'the great apostle of the Philistines' (quoted *VFM*, 123). MacDonald may also refer here to the followers of Jeremy Bentham who espoused the doctrines of Utilitarianism, at least in its devotion to material interests and aims.

243 *exchequer*: the treasury of a state or nation.

   A crown: worth five shillings (twenty-five new pence).

259 *palpation*: the process of examining or exploring by means of touch.

264 *their candles seemed to have been all left to burn out*: compare, Job 18: 5–6: 'Yea, the light of the wicked shall be put out . . . and his candle shall be put out with him.' The rest of this chapter is relevant to the situation in *The Princess and Curdie*.

   sculleries: a back kitchen where utensils are kept. Old French *escuelerie*: care of dishes.

   Mangy turn-spit dogs: a dog is a device for holding logs, but MacDonald puns on the word 'dog' here and elsewhere in the book. The people of Gwyntystorm are a mangy lot.

268 *the rigol*: a ring or groove at the top.

277 *Bread . . . with the honest wine*: the eucharistic meal.

290 *I am come to set things right in this house*: compare 2 Kgs. 20: 1:

'In those days was Hezekiah sick unto death. And the prophet Isaiah the son of Amoz came to him, and said unto him, Thus saith the Lord, Set thine house in order; for thou shalt die and not live.' See also Isa. 38: 1.

292 *the tester*: a flat canopy over a tomb, pulpit, or bed.

295 *like the boom of an anchored sloop*: the boom is a long pole used to hold or extend certain sails, and a sloop is a single-masted sailing-ship.

296 *One who is come*: see n. to p. 290. The servant girl, Jabez, plays the role of John the Baptist who prophesies the coming of the Redeemer.

301 *ramped*: to ramp is to rear up on the hind legs and stretch out the forelegs in the manner of a quadruped. In heraldry to ramp is to be in a rampant or threatening position. To storm or rampage.

307 *A scene of confusion and terror followed*: the paragraph following this sentence echoes Odysseus's cleansing of his palace in Ithaca in Homer's *The Odyssey*, Book 22.

308 *menie*: *OED* gives: 'obsolete form of Many, Meinie.' I suspect MacDonald wanted the suggestion of 'menagerie' and perhaps 'menial'.

309 *homoeopathically*: a means of treating illness by inducing the symptoms of the particular disease being treated. Nature has begun to cure the gluttonous alderman by rendering him nothing but a round belly.

And now there was such a cleaning: compare *The Odyssey*, Book 22, where after the completion of the battle with the suitors, Odysseus orders that the palace be cleaned and sponged with water, then fumigated with fire.

311 *gnarring*: to gnar is to snarl or growl.

313 *chatelaine*: the mistress of a chateau, castle, or any fashionable household.

314 *peculation*: embezzlement.

The Book of Nations: Perhaps an allusion to Adam Smith's *An Enquiry into the Nature and Causes of the Wealth of Nations* (1776) or to George R. Porter's *The Progress of the Nation* (1851). Jeremy Bentham and Benthamism (Utilitarianism) are also the targets here. For Bentham, the 'only valid sanction [for morality] was self-interest, properly trained and enlightened' (*VFM*, 267–8). Enlightened selfishness is central to Benthamism as it is to the people of Gwnytystorm (see the following para.).

317 *cerements*: winding-sheet; cloth treated with wax used for wrapping the dead.

325 *postern*: a small back gate or door, especially in a fortification or castle.

326 *a fire of glowing, flaming roses*: in Matt., John the Baptist remarks: 'I indeed baptize you with water unto repentence; but he that cometh after me is mightier than I . . . He shall baptize you with the Holy Ghost and with fire' (3: 11; see also Luke 3: 16).

330 *graithed*: OED gives 'to make ready, prepare, put in order, repair. Also to fit out or array.'

331 *So out they set*: in this para. the coloured horses and trumpet recall Book of Revelation 6.

334 *all together*: compare Wordsworth's 'Resolution and Independence': 'And moveth all together, if it [a cloud] move at all' (l.77).

337 *in a voice loud and clear as the cry of a silver trumpet*: compare Rev. 4: 1: 'and the first voice which I heard was as it were of a trumpet talking with me.'

Go and find your own. Bury your dead: compare Matt. 8: 22 where Jesus says to a disciple, 'Follow me; and let the dead bury their dead.' See also Luke 9: 59.

are also the targets here. For Pentheus, the 'only wild
smock' (for *morality*) was self-interest, properly named
and enlightened' (VPM, 267–8). Enlightened selfishness is
singular libertarianism as it is to the people of Greyhaven:
[see the following parts].

317 **cerecloth**: winding-sheet; cloth treated with wax, used for
wrapping the dead.

325 **postern**: a small back gate or door, especially in a fortification
or castle.

326 **a day of gracing**: *Naming*, taken in Matt. John the Baptist
remarks: 'I indeed baptize you with water unto repentance
but he that cometh after me is mightier than I . . . He shall
baptize you with the Holy Ghost and with fire' (3: 11; see also
Luke 3: 16).

329 **marshal**: OED gives 'to make ready, prepare, put in order,
regulate. Also to set out or array'.

331 **So outlasted it**: in this part, the coloured horses and trumpet
recall Book of Revelation 6.

333 **half to their compass**: unit with a *Revolution* and Independence. 'And moved all together, if it [a cloud] move at all'
(I. 75).

337 **as a sane loud and clear as the cry of a stick**: trumpet continues
Rev. 4: 1, 'and the first voice which I heard was as it were of
a trumpet talking with me'.

'Go that I'led view you': they were dead, compare Matt. 8: 22
where Jesus says to a disciple: 'Follow me; and let the dead
bury their dead'. See also Luke 9: 59.

The Two Drovers and Other Stories
Edited by Graham Tulloch
Introduction by Lord David Cecil

SIR PHILIP SIDNEY:
The Countess of Pembroke's Arcadia (The Old Arcadia)
Edited by Katherine Duncan-Jones

TOBIAS SMOLLETT: The Expedition of Humphry Clinker
Edited by Lewis M. Knapp
Revised by Paul-Gabriel Boucé

ROBERT LOUIS STEVENSON: Treasure Island
Edited by Emma Letley

ANTHONY TROLLOPE: The American Senator
Edited by John Halperin

A complete list of Oxford Paperbacks, including The World's Classics, OPUS, Past Masters, Oxford Authors, Oxford Shakespeare, and Oxford Paperback Reference, is available in the UK from the Arts and Reference Publicity Department (RS), Oxford University Press, Walton Street, Oxford OX2 6DP.

In the USA, complete lists are available from the Paperbacks Marketing Manager, Oxford University Press, 200 Madison Avenue, New York, NY 10016.

Oxford Paperbacks are available from all good bookshops. In case of difficulty, customers in the UK can order direct from Oxford University Press Bookshop, Freepost, 116 High Street, Oxford, OX1 4BR, enclosing full payment. Please add 10 per cent of published price for postage and packing.